THE BLUE PEARL

(THE REPAIRMAN SERIES)

L.J. MARTIN

The Blue Pearl
(The Repairman Series)

Paperback Edition

Wolfpack Publishing
6032 Wheat Penny Avenue
Las Vegas, NV 89122

wolfpackpublishing.com

This book is a work of fiction. Any references to historical events, real people or real places are used fictitiously. Other names, characters, places and events are products of the author's imagination, and any resemblance to actual events, places or persons, living or dead, is entirely coincidental.

Paperback ISBN 978-1-64119-956-8
eBook ISBN 978-1-64119-755-7

THE BLUE PEARL

Bible: Samuel 13:19-20

Now there was no blacksmith to be found throughout all the land of Israel, for the Philistines said, "Lest the Hebrews make themselves swords or spears." But every one of the Israelites went down to the Philistines to sharpen his plowshare, his mattock, his axe, or his sickle.

Quran 3:56

As to those who reject faith, I will punish them with terrible agony in this world and in the Hereafter, nor will they have anyone to help.

1

Being a recovery expert is a little like being a cop, a soldier, or a mercenary. You spend a lot of time waiting and watching, like I'm doing now. Then at times, it's assholes and elbows and you do your damnedest to keep from losing your head...and I mean literally. And the guys I'm coming up against at the moment are famous for delivering that severed appendage back to friends and family.

It does discourage retribution.

"What the hell are you doing?" Pax asks. It's loud and clear in my earbud. "You've been in there a half hour."

"What do you think I'm doing, dip shit?" I respond. "I'm in the friggin' rafters covered with spider webs, flying the drone, dodging black widows, trying to spot Fenderson's Maybach. I'll get it. There are a hundred or more Mercedes below, but it looks like ninety percent are C Class and a few E's, an equal number of Audis, and a couple of dozen Infinitis. These guys are picking the low hanging fruit, stuff easy to deal off."

Pax is stationed atop a massive water cooler tower at the Quesadilla Potato Chip plant across a two-lane surface street from the warehouse I've broken into. He's watching my back, making sure I'm not busted by the Fu Chong Snake Tong, some very bad boys who've stolen these luxury rides for export to China. A stack of shipping containers is mounded at the rear of the warehouse, stacked three high by ten wide and a half dozen deep—one hundred eighty of the giant steel boxes by my count. Enough containers for three hundred sixty cars. They'll average fifty grand apiece in Macau and Hong Kong. That's an eighteen-million-dollar haul, so you can see why this L.A. tong is in the biz.

Our drone, which is now two hundred feet or more from my perch in the rafters—I broke in through a roof-mounted vent—is a tiny devil, the size of my palm, with an excellent high res camera that transmits in real time to the app on my iPhone. Al Fenderson's Mercedes is top of the line, a twelve-cylinder Mercedes-Maybach which he claims set him back a quarter million. It's distinctive, but still the drone must dip close in this low light to make out make and model.

We saw a pattern in Beverly Hills and Hollywood stolen luxury cars. Most were boosted from five-star restaurants or shortly after they'd left same—a dozen of them by blatant car-jacking. I guess they figured it was easier if the driver's nerves were calmed by a few glasses of pinot grigio.

Not having sworn to protect and serve, and not being constrained by legalities, we acquired fifty trackers the size of your thumbnail. We placed the little magnetic gizmos in the fender wells of Beverly Hills Mercedes-Benzes—paying parking attendants at four different five-star restaurants ten bucks for each placement—then sat back in my partner's Las Vegas office and waited until a couple of them showed up as being in the same location. After three false alarms, voila, we zeroed in on a Long Beach warehouse near the harbor where not two, but three, showed up in close proximity. And here I am. The cops can't take such liberties without warrants.

Eight hundred thousand cars are boosted in the USA every year, so our odds weren't bad when we learned Beverly Hills and Hollywood were providing more than their share to the thieves.

"I got it," I say, spotting Fenderson's custom maroon and gray paint job and press the home button, the * sign, on my phone so the drone will return automatically to the exact place from which it was launched.

"Trouble!" he shouts into the handheld Motorolas we use. "Two cars, no three cars, full of bogies, turning in."

"I'm backing out toward the vent."

"Move it, they're hustling like they don't want to be late to the party. One car is heading to the back."

"We're dicked," I say, with a moan, "the damn drone ran into a cross member and went down like a duck that took a load of buckshot and is not responding."

"Screw the drone. Get the hell out of there."

Easy for him to say. It was my two-grand laid out for the toy. I can see the big double sliding doors at the front of the warehouse, and one's sliding open, flooding the area in the front with sunlight.

As I back to the exhaust-air vent I've pried open, I see two big black Mercedes-Benzes cruise in and slide to a stop. Eight guys, all Asian I imagine, pile out and spread out. And they are expecting trouble as each have palmed a weapon—more than one carry AR's.

Looks to me like the caca is about to hit the fan and the odds aren't good. Eight inside, another car at the rear, probably with four more. I checked for an alarm system before prying off the vent cover but saw nothing outside. And I set off nothing audible when I dropped in on the huge truss, but these are the kind of dudes who'd have silent alarms as they'd like to catch you in the act, not scare you off. If they catch you, they can convince you to never come again, probably with concrete boots and a trip to the bottom of Long Beach Harbor. That ensures never again.

And me with only my Springfield .45 and two spare magazines. However, my partner, Pax, is in position a hundred yards from the front of the warehouse, has the high ground and is a Marine Recon trained sniper. He's hell on wheels with the .338 Lapua he has in hand.

I don't think I've been made, manage to back out and reseat the vent and am on the roof, but thirty feet above the paved driveway. Whatever the plant was used for prior to becoming a repository for stolen luxury vehicles required a huge tank, twenty feet in diameter and four stories high. The steel ladder up the tank, which is nestled against the building, serves both it and roof access. I can get down, but where the hell are the guys in the outside vehicle? I'll be like the flop-down metal rabbit in the shooting gallery if I'm spotted half-way down.

I get to the edge of the nearly flat roof, with the ladder only feet from my position, but don't want to be spotted, so I go to my other pair of eyes.

I radio Pax. "Hey, dingus, I'm at the ladder. Where are the guys in the last car?"

"They parked at the rear. I saw them exit, but they're out of sight now. Let's hope they went inside a rear door."

"I don't want to get back-shot while I'm descending the ladder," I say.

"And I don't want to have to console that new girlfriend of yours. We'll hold hands as we cry and scatter your ashes."

"Chuck you, Farley," I snap at him. He's not funny at the moment. "I'm starting down."

Since we're private operators, we really don't want to spill blood as it would be a long-drawn-out courtroom affair if we did. Even if the blood was that of bad guys caught red-handed with over two hundred luxury vehicles they've boosted—this is California after all. As we discovered, this is the third warehouse full they've packed in ocean containers for shipment to China. Of course, the containers are marked agricultural equipment. I guess you could plow with a Mercedes?

Pax goes to serious mode. "I got you, move it."

I don't do the ladder a rung at a time, rather plant my insoles hard against the outside railings and slide. I have on driving gloves, otherwise I'd bark my hands with the rapid sliding descent.

My .45 is holstered at the small of my back, and I'm only two thirds of the way down when a goombah boy, built like a barrel, rounds the back corner no more than one hundred feet from me. He looks a little like a charging hippopotamus.

The bad news is, when I make the pavement, I'll be out of Pax's view, hidden by the tank.

The Asian guy with a face as round and flat as a salad plate is ambling my way and has a revolver in hand that would shame Dirty Harry's .44 mag.

And he's grinning like it's Chinese New Year and he just won a ten-grand street-numbers lottery. Another of the enterprises of this Asian gang—numbers.

I jump the last six feet, but he's only twenty feet away and closing, and has his .454 or whatever it is, laid down on me.

As quickly as I can move, I put both hands on top my head, in apparent surrender, as reaching for my Springfield would leave me at least three seconds late.

2

A Lapua .338 mag makes a hell of a noise if not suppressed, and the big slug creasing the pavement just behind plate-face and slamming into the metal building, makes him spin and drop to one knee. I'm sure he felt the shock of the passing slug.

I charge, pulling the .45 as I go, and catch him turning back my way. He's a very big guy and I'm sure ox-strong, but agile is not on his resume. He stumbles trying to spin on the knee he dropped to. I'm not interested in blowing his gray matter all over the pavement, so take the next best tact and slam the heavy semiauto into the side of his head.

Did I say ox-strong? Ox-hard-headed is more like it. His eyes are spinning, but he's not down and is trying to raise the .454. I deflect it with a kick and slam him again, then again, and finally he flops to his back on the pavement. I kick his revolver as hard as I can, and it slides in front of me toward the hole I've cut in the cyclone fence.

As I'm slipping through, trying to negotiate the fence cut without cutting my nuts off or even ripping my jeans, I realize the

.454 would make a nice souvenir. I reach back through the fence and snake it up.

Foolish, as a slug ricochets off the pavement. Had I been a half second later, it would likely have taken my arm off at the elbow.

I scramble to get in between the cars in the parking lot of the adjacent warehouse when I hear the Lapua roar another one by me and look back to see a second Asian who's rounded the back corner. He's kicking up gravel behind as he retraces his steps and looks for cover.

I'm picking them up and putting 'em down as I haul ass away from the dozen bad guys, round the smaller warehouse next door and see my white knight. Pax is already crossing the parking lot of the potato chip plant and heading for our van.

In less than three minutes, he's pulled up beside me and we're heading for the Long Beach Freeway.

"You whole?" he asks.

"Far as I know. You threw a little lead around and got no blood. You losing your eye old man?"

"As I recall, we agreed the rules of engagement were leave 'em whole unless we fear getting holes in us."

"That was it. Just making sure you meant to miss."

"One hundred eighty yards? I could have notched his ears if I'd wanted no. Yes, I meant to miss. Call Uncle Al and tell the pompous prick we've found his wheels but the LA County Sheriff will have to gather them up, and we still expect to be paid."

I do, and Mercedes dealer Albert Fenderson answers his cell on the first ring.

"Reardon," he recognizes the incoming number, "you get my little darling?"

"Didn't get it, per se, but know where it is, in fact had eyes on it."

"Then why don't you have it?"

"A little matter of eight hostiles with automatic weapons. We're calling in the local law and you'll have it back."

"That wasn't the deal," he says.

"Your deal was finding the car. My deal was finding the car and don't get killed."

"The deal was recovering the car. Isn't that what it says on your card; recoveries?"

"It does. Okay, forget it. We quit."

"Where's the car."

"In a warehouse in L A County."

"There're million warehouses in L A County."

"No shit, Sherlock," I say. "Good luck." And I disconnect and wink at Pax.

I hardly get the phone down, when it rings again.

"Reardon, recoveries of all kinds," I answer, knowing it's him calling back.

"Forty thousand was the deal, right?" he says.

"That was the deal. But now it's forty-two thou. I lost a drone."

"Good for the goose, good for the gander. Forty if the cops recover your drone, another two if not."

"Deal."

"I'm at the Wilshire dealership. Come on over and we'll settle up, conditionally, of course."

"Of course. It'll be most of an hour to get there."

"I'll hang," he says, "besides, I got other business to talk to you two numb-nuts about," and rings off.

I dial the private number of a buddy of mine, a dick with the L.A. County Sheriff. "Morganstein, do I have a deal for you," I say, when he answers.

"Reardon, the last deal you had for me got me shot in the ass. I still pucker up every time I climb up on a bar stool."

"Which is way too often. I heard the brain has no nerves or pain receptors, so it shouldn't hurt when you sit on yours?"

"Ho, ho. Lay it out."

And I do. And all those fine cars are now a problem for my old buddy Morganstein and the L.A. Sheriff. I tell him the charge for the tip is getting Fenderson's car to him quickly, and he agrees.

Pax is admiring the revolver in my lap. "That's a Ruger .454 Casull?"

"Sounds right."

"Since I saved your ass, I presume you're giving that to me?"

"I love you like a brother and would never risk you being the receiver of stolen property. So, I'm keeping it, but thanks for asking."

"You friggin' cheapskate."

"It was my ass waiting to get busted by it, so, yes, I'm keeping it. It will always bring back fond memories of me remaining alive. Be a good boy and I'll put it in your stocking come Christmas time."

Pax glances over. "It'll be six by the time we get there. Can we at least stick Fenderson for a fat steak at The Palm or Ruth's Chris?"

"I doubt it," I say.

"I'll talk him into it."

I have to laugh. Pax is always hungry. "Save your breath, dingus, you got to blow up your date when you get home."

He gives me the finger, but I'm happy to say puts the hand right back on the wheel. You need both hands in L.A. traffic.

This is not a high paying gig; forty grand tops. In fact, we may barely break even. But things have been slow since we ducked in and out of North Korea, and Pax and I bore easily. So, we took the job, mostly because the cat whose car was stolen is the uncle of one of Weatherwax Internet Services' favorite employees, Sol, who's back in the fold after a long spell in rehab. It seems what was done to him, and what he did as retribution, screwed with his very big brain. So, it's kind of a family thing, even if his Uncle Albert is a bit of a dickhead.

WIS is Pax's company, founded with dough he got when he separated from the Marine Corps—separated with one leg three quarters of an inch shorter than the other, thanks to taking a whack from an AK47 while trying to drag me out of harm's way. All I got was a boot in the butt and a general discharge—not dishonorable but not honorable either—and maybe a scrambled brain if you listen to Pax. The Corps took umbrage at me sending an Iraqi general to his seventy-two virgins. As much as I love the Corps, I'd do it again as he was among those stoning to death a couple of young Iraqi lasses. One of those freak things the Quran endorses is so-called honor killing. You can kill, stone to death with impunity, one of your own children if they've offended you. And if your wife is accused of infidelity, stone that woman even if you have your buddy accuse her—or if you're merely tired of her. Cheaper than divorce, I guess. If that flew in the U.S., half the younger generation would likely be dodging boulders or concrete blocks, and women would never get married.

That said, both the Quran and the Bible have instructions modern religious devotees would as soon see excluded. Times do change and we cling to what our personality and mores are attracted to. And some personalities are attracted to violence.

Pax and I now team up for the occasional gig doing recoveries or whatever else raises its head—occasional bounty hunting and fewer improbable tasks the U.S. government wants done but doesn't want to appear to have anything to do with. Plausible deniability they call it. I call it federal fucking around where they normally shouldn't. But it pays well. Gigs that are legal or at least reasonably so.

USA legal at least.

Semi-legal at least.

3

Pax didn't save his breath and I'm happy he didn't as we're perched in a booth at Ruth's Chris, on Beverly Drive in posh Beverly Hills, awaiting a medium rare New York, *pommes frites*, and sautéed spinach while gnawing warm hard bread and sipping a Jack rocks. My partner, Paxton Weatherwax, is at my left with Uncle Al across the table, swirling a single malt and still negotiating.

I prefer the wait staff at Hooters, but Frederick, our waiter, is a sly old dog and puts up with Uncle Al's condescending bull crap like a pro. I'm enjoying Frederick far more than Al, except for the fact Al's buying and the tab would likely cause me indigestion.

"Look, Reardon, it's a commission-driven world. If I get you this job, you should knock at least ten grand off finding my Maybach."

"Uncle Al, you're Sol's uncle, not mine, as much as we love and respect your nephew. And a gig that pays twenty grand a month for two months, maybe less, is suddenly only thirty grand not forty, if I give up ten on this one. Al, we've made four trips over from Vegas to run down your car for you and paid out a chunk of dough for gear. Fact is, we're losing money already."

"Oy vey, you're the first cousin to a raghead rug merchant. But think of the prestige," he says, smiling with only half his mouth, which comes across more as smirk than smile. "Besides, you'll have the gear for the next job."

I roll my eyes and shake my head. "Prestige buys no ammo. No question, it's prestigious to bodyguard a twenty-five-year-old blonde dipshit with twenty grand of Beverly Hill's surgical work who got her music published and pushed by an old man who's one of the biggest producers in Hollywierd. As God is my witness, I don't see the connection to prestige, and when did prestige ever make a couple of country boys a buck? Besides, I've got a new lady friend and don't want to be gone while I'm seeing where this will lead."

He smiles, only this time with the other half of his mouth, again a smirk. "You're way off, numb-nuts, it's probably a hundred grand in plastic surgeon's work. It's obvious you've never had an eye lift or boob job at Beverly Hills rates." We both laugh at that. "Look," he says, changing his tone, now speaking slowly like he's talking to a ten-year-old, "it's prestigious to work with Simone and you'll be next to her while the paparazzi is snapping pics all over the Med. It'll bring you lots of celebrity work."

I laugh. "Actually, I've avoided having my picture taken. There are times when it's unhealthy to be easily recognized. And celebs? I prefer to work with folks who pay twenty-nine ninety-five for their jeans and got the holes in the knees from honest labor, and with guys who have five days' beard because they don't have time to shave or are downrange ducking lead. Not with assholes trying to prove their masculinity with perfectly trimmed stubble."

"Look," he again says, "I'll talk Mort into paying your lady's way as well. You'll have a great cabin with a huge window looking at Spanish sunsets. Your toughest duty will be deflecting Simone's fans who'd like to steal her hairbrush for a souvenir. Look at it like a vacation. Cruising from England to France to Portugal to Spain can't be all bad. Then over to the film festival in Cannes. Hell, you should pay him."

"It's a month, right?"

"A month, maybe six weeks," he repeats.

"I'll do it for a hundred grand, providing it's no longer than six weeks and I can convince my new darling to go along."

"You're fucking nuts," he says.

"Yeah, and nuts is what you occasionally need in a good bodyguard."

"I'll convey your offer to Mort, but don't hold your breath."

"Provisional offer. I have to check with Connie."

Pax has been strangely silent, cutting his eyes back and forth from Al to me like he's watching a tennis match, while he, too, sips a Jack rocks, so I turn to him. "What's with you? When did you stop putting in your two cents worth?"

"Anything that'll get you out of my hair for a month is good news to me." He gives me a phony grin.

I return the phony smile. "That alone will encourage me to take this gig. Getting away from you."

Al laughs, then asks, "How long have you two been working together?"

Both of us say in unison, "Too fucking long."

Near the East London Mosque, situated in the London Borough of Tower Hamlets between Whitechapel and Aldgate is a teahouse. It serves Great Britain's largest Muslim community. As there are over six hundred thousand Muslims in London, a safe meeting place is easy to find.

Three bearded men, a Kenyan, an American, and a Somali, none of whom have met before, enter the Swahili Tea Room, not far from the banks of the Thames River, at two-thirty in the afternoon with the place near empty.

The largest and darkest of them, Mumin Amir, the Somali, is already seated and rises as the others approach.

"*As' Salam alaikum,*" he says as greeting. "May peace be upon you and God's blessings."

"*Waa alaikum as'salam,*" the others both reply.

"Know that paradise…" Mumin Amir, their leader, begins. He sits, then awaits a reply.

"Is under the shades of swords," Abdul, the Kenyan, says, as he takes a seat.

The American—half-Irish, half-Nigerian—adds the balance of their coded greeting. "*Sahih Bukhari,* fifty-two seventy-three," the location of the quote in the Quran.

"You will take tea?" Mumin offers, and waves to a Yemini waiter. As he approaches, Mumin cautions the others. "We will converse only using our assigned names. I, of course, am Mumin, and you are Abdul and Mohamid, as you have been instructed. Understand? Our contact at the union has filed papers with the purser using those names."

Both men nod as the waiter pauses, and Mumin turns to him. "Three dark teas, sugar please."

The waiter leaves for the kitchen and Mumin continues.

"Mohamid, as you are the most conversant in English, of course, you will report to the purser as Mohamid Ahmed who will work as a steward in the upper suite floors until we near Cadiz. An

American Marine General and his wife are among those who will be in one of those suites. He's a prime target." Then he turns to Abdul, "And Abdul, as you have kitchen and restaurant experience you are assigned to stores. You'll be receiving meat, vegetables, and canned and boxed goods and will stow them per the instruction of a cook's helper, a man we will know as Gama, also a Sudanese. As you know, as you've had experience on a cruise ship, all dry and canned stores and frozen meat arrive at designated ports in containers. Crimson Cruise Line has a facility near Rome, and we have two compatriots at work there. Our special packages are already packed at that location."

"And your job on board?"

"I will be a passenger."

They speak for an hour until the place begins to fill up for four o'clock tea and pastries. Then Mumin rises. Abdul has one more question, "How will we remain devout? Won't it be obvious— "

Mumin stops him with another quote, "If you are so devout you should know this quote: ...and when you travel in the land, there is no sin on you if you shorten your Salat, your prayers, if you fear that the disbelievers may attack you, verily, the disbelievers are ever unto you open enemies." He speaks harshly as he adds, "Shave your face clean, pray only when alone, ignore all that will point out to infidels that you are devout. You may even drink alcohol and eat pork, if necessary."

Mohamid, the American, adds with a smile, "...unbelievers are to be killed and wounded, if necessary. Survivors are to be held captive for ransom. The only reason Allah doesn't do the dirty work himself is to test the faithfulness of Muslims. Those who kill pass the test. Do not let so-called humanity cloud your judgement. Remember the millions Americans and Christians have killed of our people."

Mumin smiles tightly for the first time. "It is good you know the most important quotes from the Quran. At least the intent of those important sections if not verbatim. Allah be with you," he said, then hands them each a cell phone. "These are pay-as-you-go phones. Use them only to call me and, only then, if something happens that will keep you from our objective. My number is the only number encoded in the phone's memory. Do not, I repeat, do not use the pay-as-you-go for any other reason, even if you lose your own or the battery dies." And he leaves.

4

We're home, each twenty grand, less costs, richer. The cops raided the warehouse while we were enjoying those medium rare New York strips and Uncle Al is scheduled to get his Maybach back in less than a week. I knew his car was insured so I wondered why he was willing to cough up to get it returned. At supper, he told me how far out the orders are for the top of the line Mercedes and he'd be a year or more without one, even being a dealer. It seems all those Arab sheiks have orders in for fleets of the things and Mercedes is more than a year behind. The Arabs like the fold down trays like they have on their jets—guess they like to eat on the go. Or maybe, they just like the peons to see them in quarter-million-dollar rides. So, I shrug it off. I learned early on, it's not always wise to worry about a client's motives.

I'm by the pool at Pax's condo with my new squeeze, Constance Nordstrom, who has only recently separated from fifteen years with the CIA. A blonde beauty with hair to the center of her back and other superior attributes—that said, I love her for her brain. She's quick with a quip and has no problem keeping up with Pax and me in the smart-ass department. She has an ass that's far more than merely smart. Pax has accused me of getting serious, and made me wonder if I actually am.

I haven't mentioned the possibility of going on an all-expense-paid cruise as I thought it very unlikely to happen, when my cell sings with an unknown caller tone.

He wastes no time. "Mort Meyer here. Fenderson told you I'd call?"

Mort Meyer is the typical snotty Hollywood producer, but I can put up with an arrogant prick for a hundred grand and a month or six-week vacation. He's just asked me if Al Fenderson, whose Maybach we recovered, had given me a heads up that he would call.

"He said you might."

"I'm calling from the jet. Meet me at Signature in a half hour."

"Signature?" I ask, then realize he means the private terminal.

"Yeah, you don't know from Signature?"

"Sure. My jet's there," I say, and roll my eyes at Connie.

"Right. A half hour."

"Can't make a half hour. I'm at the pool and it's a twenty-minute drive."

"I thought you were a man of action. Did I hear wrong?"

"Actually, I'm getting a little action at the moment," and I give Connie a wink, "but for you, Mort, I'll break off. Have a cup of coffee and I'll see you in forty-five."

"If that's the best you can do."

I ring off and turn to the beautiful tan blonde, who's perfect—except, as I mentioned, maybe too damn smart. "Got to go and see about a new gig." I check the time. "Three-thirty. Can you be even more beautiful by six, if that's possible?"

"I can put myself together. I don't know about beautiful."

"I do, and you can go to the Golden Steer in your bikini for all I care." Then I pause a moment and add, "Come to think of it, I don't want to beat up every guy in the place, so maybe you'd better wear something showing a little less of that beautiful bronze skin."

She smiles and bats those lovely gray-greens at me. "I'll be ready at six."

I grab a three-minute shower, the half inch of hair on my scarred noggin needs only a pat down, and pull on jeans and a polo shirt. And, since I'm meeting a Hollywood guy, loafers with no socks, and jump in my classic fifty-seven Vette and buzz over to Signature. The fixed base operator is a high-class operation, surrounded by a half-billion-dollars' worth of private jets. I immediately spot Mort Meyer in the waiting area. Who else would be in a tan kid-leather jacket with a neon blue silk shirt with the top three unbuttoned, showing tufts of gray chest hair? His coiffed silver—dyed I imagine—hair looks as if he takes his makeup artist along to touch him up. And the Cuban he's puffing—the size of a Great Dane's leaving—puts a perfect topping on the sundae. I muffle my laugh as I see he too, has on sockless loafers. I called that one right.

To his credit, he does stand and offer a hand as I approach. I'm complimented.

"I've seen your picture," he says.

"And I've seen yours in the *Hollywood Reporter*, the *New York Times*, and the *National Enquirer*." We shake. I'm sure he's pulled a full report on me before offering me a job, so I'm not surprised if he knows my every scar and where it came from.

"Let's get out to the jet," he says. "More privacy there."

He says it, but I know damn well it's the Hollywood shtick thing, 'see what I got and what I'm worth.' I don't give a damn as I'd like to see inside the Citation. Most of my flight time was in aluminum metal military seating. Don't get me wrong, I've got a lot of rich Jewish clients and love them, and I actually got to make this one wait on me. It's usually the other way around. Making you wait is a Jewish power trip…not that many goy execs are not equally vainglorious.

She's configured to seat eight in the rear with a pair of tables between the front-facing seats—soft blue and brown kid leather seats—and it looks as if the interior was done by Ralph Lauren, blue trim around brown walnut, mirrored bar in the rear, masculine but plush as hell. A nicely dressed young man sporting a thin patterned tie and striped shirt, wearing his sunglasses inside, which doesn't surprise me, pours us three fingers of single malt—that they screw up with cubes of ice, but I don't complain. Mort doesn't bother to introduce sunglasses and me, so I presume the young man is a flight attendant. He looks me up and down like he'd enjoy seeing me as I was when I climbed out the pool, so I don't give him a wink as he might melt.

Seated across from me, Mort again wastes no time. "My daughter, Sally…"

"I thought it was Simone?"

"Stage name. I'm on a short leash here, got a supper appointment with Steven in Phoenix, another movie deal, so let me finish."

I nod, not asking him if he's having supper with Spielberg, which I'm sure disappoints him, but he continues.

"Sally has booked a cruise, kind of a public thing for us and I'm concerned."

"So, you want a babysitter. Not my bag."

"I want a down-and-dirty bodyguard who has no compunction about chucking some overeager a-hole overboard if need be. And I'm always worried about kidnapping."

I laugh. "Did Al tell you my terms?"

"He did. Six weeks, a hundred grand, ten up front..."

"No, sir. Half up front."

"Fifty up front. A cabin for two. All incidentals. I can get a cabin directly under my daughter's suite, or close."

"A cabin with a king size, a desk and veranda?"

"No problem."

"The first incidental will be shipping a crate to a buddy in London as I can't fly with what I'm carrying on board the cruise ship."

"Expected."

"And I'm working for you. I won't be shagging drinks for your daughter. I'll be watching her back."

"Yes, sure. You are licensed to carry?"

"Of course, but no one is supposed to carry on a cruise ship. And London, France, Portugal, and Spain sure as hell don't recognize my Wyoming concealed carry permit, even if thirty-six states do."

"And that matters?"

"Not in the least. I have baggage that will allow me to board with enough fire power to repel Somali pirates. That's the crate I'm shipping."

"That's what I hoped you'd say. And I assume you're proficient."

"Well, sir, bad guys in several countries can attest to it—or could if they could talk."

5

I'M CONVINCED, AS WHO CAN'T USE A HUNDRED GRAND? BUT I HAVE a couple more questions.

"Your daughter isn't travelling alone?"

"No, a hired lady in waiting, if you will, Gretchen Sorensen, will be in the cabin next to yours, and Sally has a classmate from UCLA, Patty McCallister, who'll share the suite with her."

"When do we sail?" I say.

"One week, the Crimson Cruise ship *Blue Pearl* leaves from London." He rises and extends a hand.

I stand and shake with him.

"You'll get a delivery tomorrow, packet with tickets, et cetera. Your travelling companion?"

"Constance Nordstrom."

"Any relation to the department store Nordstrom's?"

"Never asked her."

He laughs. "You don't much give a shit about money, do you Reardon?"

"She's ex-CIA. She earns her way and is part of the deal. As to money, I only want to be paid for what I do and as agreed."

"Fair enough. A check will be in the material."

I stick out my hand, but he doesn't take it. Instead, he gives me a hard look.

"Reardon, I don't tolerate failure." I take it as a threat.

"Mister Meyer, as a bodyguard I take the bullet if necessary. If trouble comes, it's my middle name. That's all I can offer."

He pauses a minute for effect, then in a low voice, "If she takes a bullet, you'll have one coming."

I give him a sardonic one-sided smile. "So, if the worst happens, you'll become the enemy? You don't want me for an enemy, Mister Meyer."

His face falls, and he sighs deeply. "Okay, okay, I'm a little anxious about my little daughter insisting on this cruise. In fact, more than anxious...very concerned. It's that little bitch she runs with, McCallister, who talked her into it."

"It's not the hundred g's that has you rattled?"

He smiles. "Not at all. In fact, I'm her manager, and she makes me a hell of a lot more than that. And, even with this new tax crap, you're deductible."

"So, we'll take it all as it comes?"

"Like you say, just do your best."

"I always do."

I head for the ladder and pass the steward, who bats his eyes and says, "Bye." The kid is obviously Hollywood old-queen fodder...makes me wonder about ol' Mort.

I nod at the pretty boy and beat a trail. I forgot to mention that I haven't said anything to Miss Nordstrom as yet. I've committed, unconditionally, so I guess it's time to test the lady.

The American jihadist now known as Mohamid left the United States with his real name on his passport, Sean McCord. Living in Ohio in a nearly all-white neighborhood, he was raised under what he perceived as racism. He was dark, as his mother was full-blooded Nigerian and his father a former Irish IRA radical who fled Belfast to Canada when only twenty, then illegally into the USA. Sean was easily radicalized although his father thought jihadists insane. Sean travelled to Pakistan when only twenty-two, crossed the border to Afghanistan and joined the Taliban. Having a father who took full advantage of American's right to bear arms, he was raised from the age of ten on a gun range. He could break down and reassemble a Glock or AR15 nearly as quickly as any SEAL.

His talents were soon put to good use by the Taliban, until he fell under suspicion and fled to Somalia where he joined Al-Shabaab and fought against the TFG, Somalia's Transitional Federal Government. After the TFG captured all of Mogadishu from Al-Shabaab, and many of the senior commanders were assassinated, he fled to and became a favorite of the new Al-Shabaab leader Mukhtar Abu Zubair and was luckily sent out on an errand when Zubair was killed by an American drone. Mohamid fled to from there to join in the planning and execution of the Westgate Shopping Mall attack and the October Mogadishu bombings, after much training and indoctrination he was posted to London, to lead a small cell made up of only himself and two others. The others were killed by police as a result of their success in the 2015 Paris bombings, and now enjoy their seventy-two virgins in the company of Allah.

Al-Shabaab has learned to remain as anonymous as possible, and they now operate on a need-to-know basis.

Mohamid Ahmed—Sean McCord—is a disciplined and dedicated terrorist, enjoying a monthly stipend, a Libyan wife who is subservient to his every whim, and two children who attend London schools that are nearly one hundred percent populated by Muslims and respected Sharia Law.

This current mission is to be his most important and will raise him to become one of the most respected Al-Shabaab leaders.

He's made few mistakes, until he made a cell phone call with that pay-as-you-go phone he was instructed not to use.

The fact is it's identical to the flip phone he keeps for his personal use, and since the call was dialed from his memory, not in the phone's memory, he didn't realize he'd pulled the wrong phone from a jacket pocket.

I'M a little surprised and pleased at how receptive Connie is to this proposed trip. I know she's expecting a call from Harrah's as she sent them a resume looking for a job in their security department.

I give her my most convincing smile. "Okay, since you're getting a free trip with a dude to carry your luggage, me, then you can do us both a solid?"

"And that solid is?"

"A nanny, or lady in waiting as Mort calls her, by the name of Gretchen Sorensen, will be travelling with us. Simone will be accompanied by a Patty McCallister who was her roomy at UCLA. Let's know all we can about them."

"No hill for a stepper," she says.

I laugh as she gives me back one of my sayings, then continues, "How about the crew and passengers?"

"You can do that?" I ask.

She laughs. "You think I'm nothing but a pretty face? If I can't, friends at the Company can. Crimson Cruise line, The *Blue Pearl*, leaving Greenwich, right?"

"Are you a hacker, Miss Nordstrom?" I ask. She never ceases to amaze me.

"Not the best in the west, but damn sure the best in this condo. Can I work with the kids at Weatherwax Internet Services?"

"Pax is already pissed he's not coming along, and he'll bitch and moan but always helps. He's a sucker for a good hack."

"Cool, I'll go over in the morning."

"And he's a sucker for a beautiful blonde, so don't turn your back on him."

"Ha, I can whip you both."

"Ha," I repeat. "I saw your workout. Yoga does not a killer make."

"And, ha again. You knock-down-dirty street fighters probably never heard of Krav Maga. It's the Israeli hand to hand. Pretty darn good. But I'll tell you, having had some touches of all of them I have a lot of respect for good old American boxing and wrestling if you add the illegal aspects to it...hit 'em in the throat and the nuts. Jujitsu, karate, and that most effective of all, shoot the fuckers between their pig eyes. Use what works, that's my style. Let me know when you want to go a few rounds."

"Fuck me. Sorry I asked." Like I said, she never fails to amaze me. Then I laugh, and add, "Let's keep the battles to the bed, babe."

"Good by me. But right now, we've got to meet Pax and Ji Su. I'm starving."

"Then home for a few rounds of horizontal exercise?"

"Or standing up or hanging from the rafters. Your call, big boy."

God, you gotta love a woman who accepts a challenge.

6

In a conference room in Langley, Virginia, at CIA headquarters, Frazier Mendleson, a senior case officer assigned to JTTF, the Joint Terrorism Task Force—that's made up of over fifty agencies—leans back at the head of the table, comfortable in a swivel chair at the twelve-chair conference table. He's addressing five others—one of whom is not present other than on screen—including, three from his section and Hortense Appleby from the U.K. desk at the State Department. On a secure line is FBI Special Agent Harry Weinstein, from the London LEGAT agency office, the Legal Attaché's office, one of forty-six worldwide that conduct bureau business out of the country. Weinstein is also special liaison with the CIA for terrorist activities.

Mendleson's addressing Hortense, in particular, "NSA sent over an interesting text of a cell phone call made by an unknown caller to Abu Mansoor Mukta, who, as you may know, is on our terrorist watch list and the kill list. As soon as we glean some actionable intel from following his activities. He's a Tier One player."

Harry Weinstein speaks up. "He's a special interest of mine.

Mukta was likely a player in the Paris magazine Charlie Hebdo shootings. We've yet to develop enough proof but SO15 has a group with Mukta as a primary person of interest. Have you communicated this text to them? I'm surprised they didn't pick it up on this end."

"No, Harry. You're the first one read in. We don't know if they picked it up but doubt it as they've never mentioned Mukta having a throwaway—a pay-as-you-go in the U.K.— phone. Hortense Appleby is here now. I presume you'll get a written copy from her office. See what you make of it. Here it is, translated: Manny, I will not be at Mosque for a while. I am going cruising. Then he laughs and adds. I will be serving the infidel. I hope to see you on my return, unless I'm martyred. Then Mukta replies, do you love death more than the cockroach loves life? Then the caller laughs again and replies: I do, and the passengers are cockroaches, but will not be so successful as that species. I had hoped for a hard target, not a bunch of blue-haired fat Americans. Mukta replies: *Inshallah,* may Allah welcome you with open arms, even if your fatwa is a soft target. The caller*: ma'a as-salamah*. That's a standard goodbye. Mukta: May Allah be with you. And that's it."

Harry, on the speaker phone, asks, "That's it?"

"That's it. Both phones are throwaways. We know of Mukta's, of course, and will forward you what we know of the callers. Likely bought from some cigar shop in East London. And likely for cash so there'll be no tracking it. Please coordinate with Angelina Lara in our London office. She's out of pocket or would be read in on this call."

Harry asks, "And SO15?"

"Not read in yet, but NSA is waiting for our clearance to feed a copy to their terrorism desk at Thames House. I've asked them to give it to Nigel Watterson."

"Everyone there at the moment are your unit people?" Harry asks.

"And yours," Frazier replies.

"Then I can be frank. Watterson is a real asshole."

Frazier laughs. "Yeah, pretty much, but he's a cooperative asshole and that's way better than an uncooperative sweetheart of a limey who pays for the pints."

"True," Harry agrees.

Hortense, who seldom if ever smiles and has earned the moniker of Horrible Hortense, offers, "We'll follow up on cruise ship bookings on our end, but you should too, Harry. Our only real lead is American passengers and a near departure date. If he's not making Mosque, it's likely within a week. That should narrow it way down."

"I'll put some people on it. But until I get a handle on who the caller is, I've nowhere to start other than Mukta's known associates, of which there's damn near a hundred on our list, particularly all those in the East London Mosque. Does anyone have an asset there?"

Frazier Mendleson clears his throat, then offers. "The company may have some help in that department. I'll be in touch with London and get back to you. Let's go to work." He stops them all before they reach the door. "It's long been a fear of mine that these bastards will hit a cruise ship. Some of those babies have thousands of passengers with nowhere to run. And if it's a ransom thing, and they ask for millions for a freighter with a crew of twenty, what do you think they'll ask for if it's three thousand Americans? Let's nip this one in the bud."

He gets a collective nod and they all leave.

My packet arrives by courier while Connie is at WIS, putting her hacking skills to work.

There's a beautiful color brochure with our itinerary: Day 1 and 2, Greenwich, England; Day 3, Honfleur, France; Day 4, Saint Malo, France; Day 5, day at sea; Day 6 and 7, Bordeaux, France; Day 8, Bilbao, Spain; Day 9, day at sea; Day 10 and 11, Lisbon, Portugal; Day 13, Malaga, Spain; Day 14, day at sea; Day 15 we awake in Barcelona, Spain. Then we fly to Cannes, France for the Cannes Film Festival that begins on May 14 and extends through the 25th.

Tough life, but someone must do it. I'm sure I'll be sick of seeing beautiful women in bikinis on board ship, then of them wearing the latest fashions in Cannes, which if I remember from seeing pictures of the festival, the latest fashion is mostly well tanned skin. All I can say is it's a good thing I'm more attracted to Connie Nordstrom than I've ever been to any woman. Otherwise a fella might hurt himself on a trip like this.

But I must remember it's a work trip, so Connie is the one who'll do most of the vacationing.

I do not like the fact I won't meet Simone 'Sally' Meyer until we arrive at London's Heathrow Airport, as I'm sure I'll need to coach her as to helping me help her stay out of trouble. If she's the normal twenty-five-year-old who's only been exposed to Hollywood muscle-fuck bodyguards who are mostly see-how-tough-I-look and are probably light in their loafers, she'll need some education...and, more than likely, will have no interest in getting same. I'm sure she's smarter than anyone in the room or on the ship, in this instance. Or at least thinks she is.

As well as our flight and cruise tickets, the packet contains detailed maps of the airports—London, Barcelona, Cannes—maps of each city; emergency phone and email addresses for the police and hospitals for each city; contact info for Mort Meyer and his attorneys in Hollywood, New York, and London; and, to my surprise, some spare medicines. For the first time, I learn my charge is a diabetic. I'm instructed that it's Gretchen Sorensen's job to make sure Simone is properly medicated and has her insulin, but I'm sure we'll all get the blame if someone screws up. So, I'm glad I was advised. I can study up on the subject a bit.

Connie calls just before lunch to tell me she's eating in the office with the kids and working on into the afternoon. I'm glad, as I've got a week's work to do and only three days to accomplish same. I've got to study the layout of the ship, its systems, the schedule, our transportation arrangements for each shore excursion, which I'm changing as they are depending upon ship-arranged transportation. I'll reschedule with private cars. The hell of it is, I see the girls have booked every excursion, even if three or more of them are scheduled at the same time. As money is no object, I guess they want to make up their mind when the time comes. That means my work is triple or more. Thank you very much, ladies.

I can only begin to imagine what a clusterfuck I've gotten myself into. The good news is, Connie thinks it's the hot tamale, or the cat's meow, or whatever the current 'oh boy' term is.

In addition to my normal equipment, I decide—since cell phones don't work at sea—that I need another toy and call a buddy who has a medical supply company and who I know has personal alarm gear. He has a wireless system that will work either WIFI dependent or via radio wave up to five hundred feet—the *Blue Pearl* is six hundred ten feet long so we're close. Simone pushes a button on a matchbook-size transmitter, I get a squeal. I buy three transmitters and one receiver. Mine fits my wrist like an Apple watch and will remain with me except for the shower. Simone, her friend and travelling companion Patty, and her lady-in-waiting

Gretchen will each receive a transmitter. The latter two in case Simone is incapacitated. My job is to not let the subject out of my sight, but I won't be in the same cabin with her or accompany her into the ladies' room.

I also will carry a satellite phone, into which I program all the phone numbers Mort has provided, and a few of my own.

No matter who you ship goods with internationally these days, your packages are subjected to x-ray and explosive sniffers—particularly since Al Qaeda operatives in Yemen tried to ship a pair of computer printers with their large ink cartridges loaded with TATP, triacetone triperoxide. Either cartridge would have blown a 767 jetliner in half. One of those was loaded onto a FedEx cargo plane, one on a Qatar passenger liner. Luckily, due to a tip, both were discovered but not until after being missed by police and company inspectors.

I hope my shipment is missed and I'll do all I can to make it so.

7

So, I have a big challenge—shipping my munitions.

I have some wooden crates I've used before, one marked with International Harvester and one with John Deere embossed logos. When disassembled, my fully auto KRISS Vector 9mm machine pistol and my two fully auto Glock 19's will fit nicely and disappear among twelve-inch gear wheels and engine parts. Gear wheels with teeth nicely shield firearm components, and loaded magazines taped together with steel tape look like heavy-duty brake linings to match bills of lading. I'll repack them in my personal hard-sided bags, among my computer and camera gear and toiletries, before boarding the ship. Shipboard inspectors are busy greeting new arrivals and not nearly as due-diligent as international shippers. I have to hustle to my mini-storage and retrieve my weapons from safes. I maintain mini-storage units in Vegas; Ventura, California; Sheridan, Wyoming—my place of birth—and Salt Lake City, Utah. One never knows when one won't be able to return to any given location. It's happened to me more than once. While I'm there I look my gear over. For some reason,

I'm compelled to pick up a small pair of night vision goggles. What the hell, they don't take up much room.

Connie carries a Ruger .380, mace canisters disguised as hair spray and perfume, and a stun gun fitted out as a make-up compact. While employed there, the CIA fitted her out in high style. While she's powdering her nose, she can bloody yours from shock and knock you colder than a frozen flounder with a half-million volts deftly applied to your belly button.

I have to chuckle when I pull out my good Armani suit and a Saville row black sport coat and matching slacks, as well as a gray pair, and realize I haven't worn them, or my shiny black Cole Hahn tassel loafers, in a month of Sundays. They're covered with dust and I hope not moth eaten. I hustle them and white and blue dress shirts to the cleaners for an overnight.

My general attire is jeans, pullovers, and either hiking boots or running shoes, but I've been informed in the packet that I'll likely be attending a couple or more black-tie affairs. Black suit will have to do. Besides, I'm not the belle of the ball, but rather my job is to remain unobtrusive and stay observant in the background. My attire should be of little concern.

We leave for London the day after tomorrow, and my crates go out tonight to be picked up by a contact of Connie's in London, Carlos somebody, who we'll meet for lunch the day before boarding, to collect and repack our gear.

Hell, as soon as I pick up my clean duds, I'm ready to rock and roll.

Connie had a pizza for lunch with the kids from WIS, so I don't get her company, and this is Pax's poker night with a bunch of hot shot computer nerds with whom I have little in common, so it's Ji Su, Pax's squeeze, who is a former Navy helicopter pilot, Connie and me for sushi.

Ji Su put us in country and handled the ex-ville from North Korea on our last big gig. She's now doing a temp job flying sight-seeing types over the Grand Canyon. CO-Star EC-130's she can fly in her sleep after the wicked bird she flew to get us in and out of country. It's currently not a bad gig as the Navajo don't shoot at you, although the counter-rotating spots to sit down if in trouble are few and far between.

The lady has a bobbed haircut, raven-wing-black hair, of course, with ebony eyes that sweep the room like she's watching for incoming MIGs. Perfect teeth, a sincere smile, and absolutely perfect unblemished skin, with lips red enough that no paint is required. She's tall and thin, for a babe with Korean ethnicity, but has bulges in all the right places. I'm wondering about my buddy Pax as I am about myself. We both seem to not want to be out of sight of these ladies.

As soon as our food comes, Connie launches into how tough it was to develop background on the passengers and crew of the Crimson Cruise Line ship, *Blue Pearl*. She informs me there is a full load of three hundred sixty passengers and a crew of three hundred plus. And the crew represents a huge variety of countries. Indonesians, Chinese, Nigerians, Irish, Scots, Algerians, Libyans, Brazilians, Iraqis, and more. Even a few Americans, including the head chef, a photographer and videographer, and a crew chief in the engine room.

The only commonality she could discern among them was the ability to speak English.

Something niggles at me as there are a lot of Muslim Arabic names, and most of my dealings with Muslims have been unpleasant. But I laugh it off as being paranoid. How dangerous can waiters, bartenders and room stewards be?

THE SWAHILI TEA Room in Tower Hamlets, East London, is more crowded than the last visit when Mumin arrives early and opens his laptop. Using Snapchat, he contacts Amir Al-Karim, his contact in Algeria—both he and Al-Karim are under the control of Sheik Ali Hassan—and verifies that the mission is still a 'go' and that the small cargo vessel belonging to Amir, barely a ship at one hundred two feet, is loaded and ready for departure. Halfway between Malaga and Cadiz, inside the Straits of Gibraltar, near where they will rendezvous, is the course to be taken. Mumin quickly closes his computer when he is satisfied. Abdul has arrived, a few minutes early, then right on time, Mohamid strides in with the confidence and arrogance many Americans demonstrate with almost every motion.

As soon as they're seated and served tea and kanafeh, the sweet cheese dessert favored by many middle easterners, Mumin asks for the phones he's given them.

"Why?" Abdul asks, a little offended.

"I must program in another number and want to make sure it is done correctly."

Both hand the phones over and Mumin enters the number of a second pay-as-you-go he's acquired but then also checks recent calls.

He reddens slightly when he sees that Mohamid has made an outgoing call and mentally notes the number. He returns the phones, then excuses himself to the restroom and enters the number Mohamid has called in his own throwaway.

Deep down, even as much as the American jihadist has proven himself, Mumin doesn't trust him—after all, he's American. Before he confronts him with the affront of using the cell phone, he will determine who owns the number called, if possible. That will determine if Mohamid needs to be killed and the mission called off as it's been compromised.

Mumin's very angry but doesn't show it as he returns. Rather than go into more detail, he makes small talk, concealing his anger, and they agree to meet same time same place tomorrow. The day before they are to report to the *Blue Pearl.*

It's very likely Mohamid will not be among them.

As soon as they part, Mumin punches in the number Mohamid called.

He's is pleased it's not MI5, SO15, or the CIA that answers, but rather a man he's worked with many times, a devoted subject of Allah and Mohammad, Abu Mansoor Mukta.

He greets him, "*As-salām 'alaykum.*"

"It is your old friend. May Allah be with you."

"Ah—" Mukta starts to respond.

"No names please. You are a friend of a friend who called you yesterday?"

"I am?"

"He was using a non-traceable phone, so do not worry. And you discussed?"

"Why do you ask?"

"He is part of Allah's larger plan. I need to know he's among the faithful."

"I have no reason to think not."

"The task begins tomorrow, so it's imperative I know he's a true disciple."

"I have no reason to doubt."

"Thank you, old friend. You are among the blessings from Allah."

"*Inshallah*, God willing," he says.

They break the connection, and Mumin pauses for a moment. He is almost sorry he has no reason to kill Mohamid, the American. But he is sure he'll give him the most dangerous tasks in the coming operation. If Allah calls him to paradise, so be it.

8

FRAZIER HAS JUST WALKED OUT OF A MEETING WITH THREE OF HIS team, one of whom has been working closely with NSA. The only viable leads they have are the fact two cruise ships carrying primarily Americans are leaving Greenwich, England. One, the *Blue Pearl,* tomorrow with a few over three hundred Americans and fifty or sixty from scattered other countries, totaling three hundred sixty plus passengers, and one the following day with nine hundred Americans and nearly two thousand from other countries, mostly the U.K.

In addition, ships are leaving Amsterdam, Holland, and Stockholm, Sweden, day after tomorrow—all heavy with Americans. Any of those ports could be easily reached from London in a short time. So, they are no closer to pinning down the target than they were two days ago.

As he studies the itineraries of the five ships, his desk phone rings, and he immediately recognizes Harry Weinstein's voice, calling from the LEGAT office in London.

"Frazier, we're on with Nigel Watterson."

"Good afternoon, Mister Watterson. I guess it's actually good evening there."

"We've had another call to Mukta, but it, too, is from a pay-as-you-go," Nigel reports in his officious manner. It did confirm the cruise ship in question is leaving, or loading, tomorrow."

"I just had the call laid on my desk from NSA," Frazier adds. "No trace there either, except the same tower in East London."

"We are picking Mukta up before dawn and will sweat him, but the bugger has been under hot torches before. I'd give a hundred quid if they'd let me use the cables from my boot on him."

"Jumper cables?"

"As you rebels call them. But no, we're far too hospitable to the bloody wogs."

Frazier laughs. "And you're obviously not in your office?"

"I'm in yours, so speaking frankly."

"Read me in, if you'd be so kind, when you know anything—or even if you don't."

"Jolly good," Nigel says. "In fact, Harry can sit in on the indoctrination if it suits you."

"Harry, please do," Frazier requests.

"My pleasure. I wish we had Mukta in Guantanamo. I'd fry his *huevos*. Come to think of it, I can't sit in. I've got a lead on a tearoom in the London Borough of Tower Hamlets. I've had a waiter there on the pad for nearly a year. He thinks he may have something. I was about to give him the boot, but it's worth wasting a pound on some of their lousy slop tea. Besides, we're on a short leash and likely better dividing resources."

"*Huevos*?" Nigel asks.

"Nuts, but the literal translation is eggs."

Nigel chuckles. "That's a bloody good picture, your jumper

cables on his bollocks. I'll bring you up to speed by noon our time tomorrow."

And they break the connection.

PAX IS NOT TAKING the nerd's money with Texas hold 'em tonight, and I want to keep working and talk him into staying in so he and Ji Su, Connie and I, can keep digging into the passenger and crew information. I do have to promise to go to In-N-Out Burger and bring back a load of burgers, fries, and shakes, even though it's a fair haul over to Sahara and normally a thirty-minute waiting line to get served. What I won't do for a buddy? Besides their shakes are manna from heaven. So, I moan a lot, particularly when Connie says she'd better keep working and not go with me, but I don't really mean the moan other than the fact I won't have her company for the hour it will take me to get there and back.

Luckily, the Cruise line has fingerprints as part of each crew member's employment file, and Connie has a friend at the CIA who has agreed to run a dozen or so sets through IAFIS, the FBI's Integrated Automated Fingerprint Identification Service. It's a big favor to ask, but she says this gal owes her big time.

Needless to say I select a dozen with Muslim names to take advantage of the offer. Connie says she'll have answers by the time I return from my burger run, and she's a woman of her word.

As I'm gnawing the last bite of my animal-style In-N-Out, I'm fascinated by the only report returned that has shown up in the extensive FBI files. The employee name is Mohamid Ahmed, but his prints say he's Sean McCord, an Ohio lad who left the country after following his mother's Muslim faith. It's not abnormal for a Muslim convert to change his name and can cite Mohammed Ali as an example. So that alone certainly does not a terrorist make. Still, it's nice to have some background on at least one of the crew members, and he'll be worth special notice. I'll make it a point to identify him when on board.

We work until after midnight and, as we have a 10:00 a.m. departure on British Airways to Gatwick Airport, London, that means a 7:30 a.m. appearance at the counter.

Connie's mace and compact stun gun are packed in her checked luggage, and my only weapons are my hands, feet, elbows, knees and teeth, except for a tricky little faux ballpoint ink pen that shoots a stream of some concoction that will knock a big man on his butt and likely unconscious. Like Connie's toys, the pen was a gift from the CIA before my last op.

As much as I'd normally have another kind of sleeping pill on my mind, I don't mind a bit when Connie suggests, with a big yawn, that we cuddle ourselves to sleep.

9

I'M MORE THAN JUST SLIGHTLY PISSED WHEN CONNIE AND I ARE bumped to tourist class, not the minimum of business class I'd settled on with Mort, but the girl at the gate swears it's a booking error. Then I'm doubly pissed when the plane chatter stirs, and I overhear two young girls in the seats ahead of us ooh and aah over the fact the famous young singer Simone is up in first class with another young woman and two young men, members of her band it seems. I wonder if those two young men were the reason we were bumped to the cattle car.

I'm tempted to deplane while calling Mort Meyer and telling him to shove this gig where the sun don't shine, but Connie is so happy to be going and tells me to quit pouting, so I do. Even if I don't have my glass of bubbly before the engines even fire up.

It's a ten-hour-forty-minute flight to Gatwick, and we're nearly an hour getting off the plane and to the British Airways lounge, where, since we're not first-class passengers, Connie and I are forced to wait in the waiting room while the attendant fetches Simone or Gretchen Sorenson.

It's 3:00 a.m. London time when I discover neither lady is anywhere to be found. We were to meet here then ride together to the Amba Hotel Charing Cross, on Trafalgar Square. I have arranged for a limo to haul the five us there. But it seems we may be seven, if the two boys mentioned earlier are now part of the party.

I have Simone's cell, so I immediately hit the dial.

"Who's this?" she answers, and yawns.

"This is your bodyguard, Mike Reardon."

"Oh, yeah. I guess I should have called you. Change of plans. We're going to the Ritz. Mort is such a cheapskate."

"The Ritz?"

"The Ritz. You're booked into that Amba place."

I take a deep breath. This is likely going to be even tougher than I imagined. So, I advise her, "I'll be at the Ritz tonight and at 10 A M will expect to meet with you and Miss Sorenson to get a few things cleared up regarding my responsibilities and yours."

There's a long silence, but I outwait her, then she seems fully awake. "Look, muscle brain, who the fuck do you think..."

"Ten A M, got it?"

And she hangs up. It's not ten minutes as we're heading for our luggage and the limo I booked, when my unknown caller ring rattles.

"Reardon," I snap.

"You and Sally didn't hit it off, I guess." It's Mort.

"I don't work for Sally, Mort. As I made clear, I work for you. I told her I'd be at the Ritz at 10 A M to meet with her. For your information, I'll either get some things straight between her and me so I can do my job, or I'll have my people in Vegas FedEx forty grand to you. Connie and I will enjoy this cruise without worrying about your daughter."

"Calm down, Reardon. I'll have Gretchen meet you at ten…"

"Fuck that, Meyer. You'll have your daughter and Gretchen meet with me or you can expect a forty grand FedEx."

Now he's silent for a long moment, but I outwait him as well. Then he finally speaks up. "I'll have her at lunch tomorrow in the Ritz dining room if that will work for you?"

"Is there a room near hers at the hotel?" It's not all right with me, but it does involve a hundred grand, so even though I'm pissed I bite my lip.

"The Ritz?" he asks, his voice a half-octave higher.

"Of course, the fucking Ritz. I can't do my job if I'm at the fucking Holliday Inn a fucking mile away."

Connie hooks an arm though mine and, with the other, places a gentle hand on my forearm and gives me a pat. She's smiling as we stride along and seems about half tickled that I'm so pissed.

Mort sighs so deeply I hear it all the way from Phoenix, or wherever the hell he is. "My London attorneys book people in there damn near every day. I'll call you back."

"We'll be on our way to the Ritz."

Mort rings off and calls me back by the time we're loaded into the limo. I advise the driver. "New plans, pardner. The Ritz, please."

He shrugs and says, "You're the bloke with the purse." We're off.

What a cluster fuck. The good news. There's a cold bottle of some Dom knockoff in an ice bucket.

"Pop it. It'll help us sleep," she says and giggles that giggle that makes my loins heat up. However, the odds are, this is another cuddle night.

The lobby of London's Ritz looks like a morgue, a very fancy morgue, but you could shoot a cannon through it with little risk of hitting anyone at 4:30 a.m., with only a doorman and a single clerk at the desk. I'm pleased to discover Mort has redeemed himself and we have a room, not a closet, not a pair of sleeping bags in the parking garage, but a real room with a king-size bed.

I'd normally describe the room by saying, "It's not the Ritz, but..." But the fact is, it is the Ritz, with gold fixtures on the lav and bath and marble trim like I'd imagine Windsor Castle might enjoy.

I'm secretly glad Mort put off my meeting with Simone and Gretchen until noon. I dozed on the plane, but mostly reviewed the crew and passenger info. As it is, I'll only get four hours of shuteye, if that, as sleeping in daylight has never been a talent of mine.

HARRY WEINSTEIN WAS a lifer with the FBI, having signed up after graduation from Stanford University in Palo Alto, California in the late eighties. This is the beginning of his thirty-second year with the Bureau. He's risen slowly having never been a shooting star, but rather was a plodder who could always be counted upon to complete an investigation carefully with all i's dotted and t's crossed.

His office for the last six years has been ensconced in the American Embassy at 33 Nine Elms in London, assigned as liaison to the FBI in their LEGAT office. That LEGAT office covers the U.K.: England, Northern Ireland, Scotland, Wales, the Channel Islands, and the Republic of Ireland. He enjoys his job and plans to retire somewhere on the Atlantic coast of Ireland, probably near Dingle or Cong. He is not a practicing Jew although his heritage is obvious by his name if not his demeanor. He's not a lox and bagel

Jew, more a pizza pie kind of guy. His first overseas position took him to Israel, shortly after agent training at the FBI Academy near Quantico, Virginia, and liaison training at The Farm, the CIA facility on the nine-thousand-acre military reservation near Williamsburg, Virginia. He met his wife, Sarah, a graduate of Brown University, at The Farm, as she was training as a result of being hired by Defense Intelligence Agency's Defense Clandestine Service. They stayed married for over twenty years even though apart eighty percent of the time. His first job—he wondered if due to his ethnicity—was to join the recently opened legal attaché office in Tel Aviv where he became an expert in cybercrime. He was happy to eventually land a position as Liaison to LEGAT in London and get out from under the specter of bus bombings and suicide vests. Until he discovered he'd transferred to a city which soon grew to six hundred thousand Muslims, elected a Muslim mayor and was now under the same specter. Now, he was eager to retire and flee to Ireland where he could fish and sip Guinness and watch Fox News on the internet.

One of his primary functions is to develop clandestine contacts in the Muslim community and he has a six-figure budget to do so. He has a dozen informants on his payroll, including Omar Al-Amed, a waiter at the Swahili Tea Room, which is only five kilometers from his top floor—fifth floor—office at the embassy, but the morning traffic is horrendous. Luckily both embassy and teahouse are on the north side of the Thames and he doesn't have to worry about bridge congestion.

He arrives before they open at ten o'clock, has his driver and assistant, Angelina Lara, drop him, and stations himself between the Bow Road Tube Station and the teahouse, only four blocks apart. He knows Omar makes that walk morning and evening every day except Tuesday.

At ten minutes to ten, Omar tops the Tube stairway and Harry slips back in a doorway and whistles at him as he nears. He pauses and looks over, and the frown he suddenly acquires makes his displeasure clear.

"You don't seem pleased to see me, old friend?" Harry says.

10

Omar glances both ways, as if he can tell if he is being observed by any of the hundreds on the sidewalks, then steps into the doorway. "I am not pleased to be seen seeing you," then greets Harry. *"As-salam 'alaykum."*

"And good morning to you, Omar. There has been abnormal telephone activity from the cell tower in your neighborhood...the teahouse neighborhood. Are you earning your money?"

"I have nothing to report, my friend. You are here to bless me with my twenty-five quid?"

Harry digs in his pocket and produces two tens and a five-pound note and hands it over. Again, Omar looks up and down the street before snatching and pocketing it.

Harry cautions him. "If I'm to continue to 'bless you' you must bring me some actionable information. And soon, or my superiors will insist I find another source." He's actually using the old pass-the-buck ploy as he makes all decisions regarding informants.

Omar pauses a moment, then says, "I will text you a name, maybe two, possibly three, this afternoon. There are three men meeting at the Swahili regularly. They quiet each time I near and always sit apart from others, if possible. There is little other than that, but it seems they are planning something."

Harry shrugs, but is interested. "Names?"

"No, but I will attempt to obtain them. I overhead them talking about working together and it seemed on something they wanted no one to overhear. Of course, they could be planning a falafel street stand."

"Get me those names, and if possible, use your cell phone for a picture and include it with your text."

They part and Harry waves to Angelina, who is double-parked across the four-lane. He has three other assets to touch bases with before returning to the office, all likely within cell phone range of the tower where the call to Abu Mansoor Mukta had originated.

Harry always wants to look his informants in the eye when communicating with them. First, for their sake and safety, he doesn't want his number easily located on their cell phones, and second, he can far more easily discern if they are lying or only working him for a few quid, if he eyeballs them.

He thinks Omar sincere. Maybe he has something actionable? But the fact is, there are probably fifty thousand Muslims in the radius of the cell tower in question. Still, he trusts Omar's instincts.

I'M NOT surprised that I awake before 8:00 a.m. and am showered, shaved and downstairs for coffee by eight fifteen. The lobby still is nearly vacant other than, in addition to the same guy behind the desk, there's a mature gray-haired lady there and a bellman helping a high-class lady out with a half-dozen matching flowered bags that likely cost more than my Ford 250 diesel.

"Coffee?" I ask the lady, who shrugs before she answers.

"Ten o'clock in the tea-room, love." And gives me a tight smile as if she doesn't think much of my USA red-white-and-blue bill cap. Then she adds, "Starbucks across the lane."

I give her a wave and thanks and head out. Connie was in deep breathing hard sleep when I left, so I kill time at Starbucks, then walk a half mile up Piccadilly and back the other side, admiring the one red double-deck bus I see and missing the many that were here twenty years ago when I was a wet-behind-the-ears jarhead, and the iconic black taxis are now LEVC electric vehicles. Good for the environment, I guess, but too neat and clean to go with the cockney accents of the drivers.

I wander through the nearby Royal Green Park and enjoy the birds and greenery, then stop in another Starbucks and buy a London Times to read while I knock down a Latte, then stroll back to the hotel. This time there are a dozen well-dressed folks milling about. I look like I might be there to sweep the chimney. Before I go up, I cross again to Starbucks, get a crumb cake and coffee for Connie and check my iPhone. I see it's just after ten when I enter the room and hear the shower going. I'm tempted to strip down and climb in with her, but she turns if off before I have a chance to do so. She comes out with a robe covering that beautiful body, barefoot with red toes to match her fingernails, her hair wrapped in a towel, and flashes me a smile when she sees the coffee and cake. A brilliant smile that makes me extra happy I thought of it. And sorry I wasn't back in time to try out the shower for the second time this morning.

"Don't ruin your lunch," I caution. "We're meeting the famous Simone, her friend Patty, and her chamber maid or whatever the hell she is, for lunch here in the hotel."

"You are, I'm not," she says.

"Why's that?"

"Because you're pissy. You will likely ream them out and you don't want to do so in front of another woman. Particularly one they don't know. You need to get off to a little better start and embarrassing this twenty-five-year-old who thinks her caca smells like roses is not the way."

"This is CIA Psychology 1A?" I ask.

"Actually, this is mature woman common sense. Trust me in this. Besides, I have to meet Carlos and collect our gear. We have to repack."

I'm silent for a moment, watching her unroll the towel and begin to blow dry those long beautiful blonde tresses. I have to raise the volume. "This Carlos isn't an old boyfriend, is he?"

"Yes, I go for the five-foot-six, two-hundred-seventy-five-pound Latin lovers. Nothing like them. If they stand on their head so their belly falls the opposite way normal, they can actually find that chubby little love muscle."

I laugh, feeling better. "Okay, you're probably right. Where are you meeting him?"

"At his condo with a couple of our bags. He's driving me back here after we load up the gear, then you are going to repack it, so I can blame you if you end up in London Tower."

"Smart girl. I hope he's a good driver, and you don't get stopped on the way here. They'd call out SWAT and the bomb squad."

"Be gentle with the ladies. We've got two or three weeks with them, if you don't get canned at lunch time."

"If I do, we've got two weeks without them, and with a vacation, so I don't much give a damn which way it goes."

"A hundred grand?"

I laugh. "There is that."

I go back to my paperwork until she comes out looking like a million bucks in a brown business suit and white silk blouse with matching white high heels and purse and kisses me on the back of the neck.

Turning, I give her the once over. "You look too good to turn loose on London Town."

"And you look too good to turn loose on three chicks for lunch."

"Hurry back and stay safe."

She leaves, and I work until a quarter past noon then have a talk with myself on the way to the dining room. I reach the elevator, then realize I read that the dining room requires a coat, even at lunch. I hustle back and change into slacks, a long-sleeve shirt, and my Saville Row sport coat, which should be appropriate this close to Saville Row.

I walk in at twelve-thirty-five and am not shocked to discover no ladies in sight.

I'm seated at a table for four, order coffee and wait. At twelve fifty, Gretchen Sorensen, a bobbed blonde with piercing blue eyes, wanders in. She's in a patterned yellow and black mini-skirt mid-thigh, a black silk blouse, and a Gucci scarf matching the skirt, and is shown to the table. I stand and extend a hand and we shake. She has a strong square jaw and perfect teeth, but piercing ice blue eyes are her most prominent feature. I'm all business so don't let my eyes sweep a compact and well-formed body...maybe just a little.

"Sorry I'm late," she says.

"But not as late as the other two young women," I say, and it's obvious I'm not going to be obsequious. I've never been good at hiding my anger.

11

Gretchen, who's joined me for lunch, laughs pleasantly, not allowing me to queer her good nature. "Simone is not known for being prompt and Patty follows close behind. They'll be along."

"Let's order," I say.

"We'd better wait," she says.

"Nope, the lunch was for twelve thirty. Please join me as I'm going to order."

She shrugs but looks a little fearful like she's risking her job.

I order a veal marsala and she nervously orders a salad. We're served when a strawberry blonde and a striking brunette float into the room, followed closely by two loud men of about the same age, both in kid leather jackets, one in leather pants and the other in something I'd call pedal pushers were they on a woman. The pants are cuff-less just below mid-calf—I guess to show off the tattoo of a drum set on his ankle. Both wear ankle-high sport shoes that are probably as expensive as Air Jordans, and no socks. And both have on L. A. Laker jerseys.

Just looking at them makes me want to slap them silly.

One is taller than me and about the same weight, the other

even shorter than the brunette, who it appears he's hooked up with. The tall one is shaved bald, the other has shoulder-length dirty-blond locks.

The strawberry blonde, I presume, is Simone, as Gretchen immediately rises and eyes her as she nears.

And the blonde gives Gretchen a snotty look and snaps, "The table's not big enough for all of us."

I stand, even though I would rather remain seated. "My fault. I didn't know you were bringing the band."

"You must be Reardon. Mort said you were a smartass. We'll get another table and you can join us."

"Actually, I have my lunch and will finish it, then come over."

"What the fuck ever," she says, and spins on a heel and waves the maître d' over and points to a table across the room.

"Sorry," Gretchen says, and rises and follows.

The waiter strides over and asks, "Is everything all right, sir."

"I'm fine. You might take the lady's salad and iced tea to her."

"Yes, sir," he says, and follows Simone and her entourage across the room.

I don't hurry as I finish the delicious veal marsala, then for dessert have coffee and some pudding concoction that's equally wonderful. It was hard not to hear the three women and two young men across the room. They're loud and, I'm not surprised, obnoxious. Unfortunately, when I'm in a foreign country I'm almost always reminded of where the term "ugly Americans" comes from.

I take a deep breath and remind myself that this gig is worth a hundred g's. I wipe my mouth, fold my napkin, fill my coffee cup from the little silver insulated pitcher provided, rise and cross the room.

Dragging up an empty chair from a nearby table, I position it between Simone and the larger of the two-millennial a-holes. I straddle it, leaning my forearms on the back.

"I need to bring you up to speed," I say, directed at the little diva.

She eyes me like I'm something stuck to her shoe that smells bad and laughs.

"Really, I didn't know I was going slow."

"You may want to meet me after lunch for this conversation..."

"Anything you have to say to me you can say in front of my friends."

I shrug. "Okay. First, you should know I don't work for you. So please pay me the courtesy of treating me as you would any other business associate. That includes being on time."

"Okay, you're fired anyway."

I'm silent for a moment as everyone at the table, other than Gretchen, laughs as though she was one of those lousy late-night TV comics.

I wait until they quiet. "Like I said, I don't work for you. I work for your father."

"Who works for me, so I guess you work for me after all?"

"No, Sally, I don't."

"You may call me Simone."

"I may call you a spoiled little twit, but I'll refrain until I know you better."

"Hey," the big blond kid snaps, "you're a real smartass. How about you getting the hell out of here and leave us to eat our lunch."

I take another deep calming breath. I give him a polite nod. "Young man, I'm working here. I'll excuse myself soon enough."

"The fuck you will. Get the hell..."

I can feel the heat creep up my backbone, which doesn't bode well for me keeping this gig or him his teeth. I interrupt but quietly through nearly clenched jaw, "Hold on, sonny. You're getting in way over that shinny chrome dome of yours."

He stands and puffs out his chest like a parrot fluffing his feathers. "Look, fuck head, I played lacrosse at Yale..."

It's all I can do not to laugh, but I contain it. "Put your ass back in that chair. I played cross also, all over this tough old world of ours. Only mine was crossing assholes like you off the living list. I'd hate to end this job by throwing your ass through that window, but I'm getting close to doing so."

He's turning red in the face, his fists balled at his sides.

Simone may be smarter than she's acting so far as she jumps into the exchange. "Bryan, take a seat. I have been provided with Reardon's background and he's not a nice man. I'm surprised he's not eating raw meat for lunch."

"Fuck him," Bryan says, but retakes his seat.

"Bry," I say, "I'm sure you're a nice young man, but the fact is I'd look funny getting fucked and you'd look even funnier trying to fuck me after I ripped your dick off and stuffed it in your mouth." I give him a smile. "Bry, do you know what tinnitus is?"

He shrugs, staring at me with his mouth hanging open.

"It's when your ears are ringing. It's not a communicable condition. However, I'll give you a case of it if you think you can screw with me. Your ears won't stop ringing for a month."

"Shut up, Bryan," Simone snaps. Then eyes me. "Let's talk up in my room. Say two o'clock...no, two-thirty would be better?"

"Fine, please be on time. Not that it matters much from now on. Just so you know, you won't be out of my sight for the next six weeks except for going to the john. Then I may check the potty room first. We don't have to be buddies, but I'll do my job. Got it?"

"Not much fucking chance of us being buddies," she says. She gives me a phony smile, adds, "I got it," and nods. I get up and cross the room with coffee cup in hand. Unfortunately, the waiter has removed my little thermos pitcher.

I retake my seat and wave the waiter back over and order a cup of Earl Grey. After all, Mort is paying.

I'm half-finished when Connie strides in, looking like a real woman, and crosses the room. I jump up and pull out her chair, and she joins me.

"Tea?" she asks, seeming surprised.

"No Jack Daniel's until I put my charge to bed."

She gives me a devious smile. "I didn't know bedding her was part of your duties."

"Very funny. She's about as sexy to me as Little Orphan Annie. How was Carlos?"

"Smart, capable, and still a good friend. Our bags with gear are in the room when you're ready to repack. I presumed you wanted those crates, so they're shipped back to Vegas."

"Super. However, I'm now at work. Until little Simone and her lady entourage is up to speed with the alarm, and locked in her room, I won't be leaving her side."

As I say that, the kids are finished and rise to leave. The others head for the door, but Simone crosses the room and sidles up to our table.

"You...uh...work fast," she says, and sticks out her hand to Connie.

"Hi, Connie Nordstrom," she says, shaking daintily. "I'm Mike's back up."

"I'll bet. I'm Simone," she says, and cuts her eyes to me.

Connie overrides her as she starts to speak. "Of course, I know who you are. I love your music, and what a delight that last video was. *Moonlight* was the song, right?"

Simone actually seems pleased and gives Connie a sincere smile. "Thank you," then she can't seem to help herself. "It was a little on the rap side. I didn't know older people..."

I interrupt. "What's up?" I don't say 'what's up, asshole' as I'm tempted to, nor do I suggest that the older person—Connie's thirty-six—could kick the dog-do out of all four of them should she feel insulted.

Simone continues. "We're headed out to go shopping so I won't make our two-thirty."

"Then please wait in the lobby until I can go to the room. I've got a small alarm you need to carry everywhere." Then I smile. "Even into the loo. We can go over details and how to keep you from being overrun by fans or worse when we get on board. Right now, the alarm will do."

She laughs and turns and heads over to join the others, giving me a wave over her shoulder and saying, "Five minutes."

I yell and stop her, then move to her side. "I need the names of your two boyfriends?"

"Not boyfriends, but they're Bryan Cox and Terry Von Riche. Why?"

"Terry or Terrence?"

"Probably Terrence, why?"

"My job, that's why." I turn to Connie as Simone wanders on. "Sign the tab, please. See you in the lobby. Then we're going shopping."

"I'm going?"

"Damn right, I look a lot more innocuous with you on my arm. In fact, no one will even look at me. By the way, the two metrosexuals or millennials or whatever the hell you call them these days are Terry, maybe Terrence Von Riche and Bryan Cox. A little background on them would be good. You're strapped?"

"Of course."

"Stay with them, please, until I catch up."

She gives me a nod and notes the names in her iPhone. So, I head for the room to gather up the alarms. Connie follows the kids.

12

I've worn out shoe leather following this crew up and down Sloan Street and in and out of every high-class shop I've ever heard of and many I haven't. I'm happy to say Connie cares little about labels, but she's amused as she watches the girls and young men ooh and aah over tee-shirts that cost a hundred pounds and goofy shoes—some of which are over a thousand—and some purses the size of my fist over four thousand pounds. Simone explains they are works of art, which also amuses me. My neck hurts from shaking my head, and my awe is not over the looks or quality of the goods, but only the price and garishness of most. Being a Carhartt kind of guy, I don't impress easily.

I grab a sandwich from room service, but Connie goes to supper with the kids, with her .380 in her purse. Since they're only three floors below, have their alarms, and have Connie at hand, I take the time to repack my gear.

The client and her entourage have, so far, not decided if they want to report to *Blue Pearl* tonight or in the morning, but since they're nighttime types and as the ship sails at 1:00 p.m. tomorrow, I'd imagine we will board tonight, and I must be ready. And am, when Connie shows back up at 6:30 p.m. and informs me we're off to board, then the kids are off again. The kids have Googled and discovered British Music Experience, a concert hall of twenty thousand square feet in what's called the O^2 Bubble. It has a show, a Beatles retrospective by a tribute band called the Cheatles, in Liverpool but not far from the dock, and once aboard they can go back out to party it up. Oh, joy, I get to club it tonight with a bunch who sleeps in until lunchtime.

And we're off.

MUMIN GOES to the Swahili Tea Room, buys a paper and takes a cup of tea, then wanders out and pulls his phone from a pocket.

Omar Al-Amed is just getting off work, as he's worked the early shift, and follows as he'd like to get a picture and earn his fee from the American but can't quite get near enough. He watches Mumin from a distance.

Mumin makes one more important call prior to the three of them boarding the *Blue Pearl,* and that's to Mohamid who he arranges to meet in a small park in East London, a park with lots of trees and shrubs where a body can be easily hidden. Mumin is carrying a small .22 caliber revolver than fits easily in the palm of his hand. One doesn't need an AK47 for a single traitor.

Unknown to him, Omar has followed him the two blocks from the teahouse, hoping the man will stop so he can act as if he's taking a picture of something else, or merely looking at his iPhone.

The man enters a park, wanders to a bench, takes a seat and unfolds a newspaper, which unfortunately covers his face as he reads. Omar crosses the park then turns and heads back and sees another of the three he'd been watching as the man joins the first one.

"As-salām 'alaykum," Mohamid says as he approaches Mumin, who's on a park bench reading *Al Ahram al Duwali*, the largest Arabic newspaper, which is published in Egypt but distributed worldwide.

"*Wa 'alaykum as-salām,*" Mohamid replies, with an unusual wide smile. "We are soon to be smiled upon by Mohammed, the messenger of the one true God, Allah."

"*Inshallah,*" Mumin replies, with a tight smile. Then, it faded, "Let me see your phone again," Mumin demands, holding out his hand.

Mohamid shrugs and hands over the throwaway. Mumin takes another look at the recent calls and sees the phone hasn't been used since the call made to Abu Mansoor Mukta.

"You failed me," Mumin says with a hard tone.

Mohamid throws his shoulders back. "I have never failed you or our holy mission."

"You used the throwaway. You called Abu Mukta."

Mohamid's face falls and his mouth drops open. Then he recovers. "Abu Mukta is my dear friend, and, yes, I called him, but it was on my personal..."

"No, it was not."

Mohamid looks embarrassed, then confesses. "The phone you gave me is exactly the same as my personal cell. If I called him..."

"You did."

Neither of them notices another Muslim who passes as if he's enjoying the park, but like most, his attention is focused on his iPhone.

"If I did so it was a mistake," Mohamid says with a little gasp. "A terrible mistake and I'm sorry. I apologize to you and

Mohammed and our gracious God Allah. Please, I am without shame as it was an honest mistake."

Mumin slowly pulls the little revolver from his pocket and points it at Mohamid, covering it with his other hand so only his target could see. "Had that call gone to anyone other than one whom I know is faithful..." He almost growls the threat. "It is your one mistake on this mission. Another and you will be food for bottom feeders in the wake of the *Blue Pearl*."

"It will not happen again," Mohamid stutters.

"Swear to Allah?"

"I do, I do."

"Then return to your home and the next we see each other it will be on board. Do not even nod your head to me for the next weeks. Understand?"

"Yes...Yes, I understand. I will not fail you."

"*Inshallah*. Go."

And Mohamid hurries away. A friend will drive him to Greenwich, a few miles down the River Thames, to report to his new job and his calling.

Mumin finishes his newspaper and lets his anger recede, then drops the paper in a trash can as he exits the park.

13

HARRY WEINSTEIN'S DESK PHONE RINGS IN HIS FIFTH-FLOOR embassy office, and he's a bit surprised when Omar from the Swahili Tea Room greets him with an English hello.

"Mister Weinstein. I have pictures of two of them. I do not have names, but I have a newspaper and a cup one of them used."

"Can you e-mail me the pictures?"

"Of course."

"And the cup and newspaper."

"I presume there is a bonus for fingerprints?"

"Would have been, had you gotten their names."

"Will not fingerprints provide you with a name?"

"It will, Omar, if they are in the system."

"Then my bonus?"

"Look, I'll give you another twenty quid. When can I get the cup and paper?"

"I am off work. Meet me at the mouth of the tube near the embassy. In a half hour."

"Ten four."

"I beg your pardon?"

Harry laughs, then translates. "Got it. You bet I will."

CREW REPLACEMENTS, a normal occurrence at the cruise line's London, Greenwich stop, report to the *Blue Pearl* at least eighteen hours prior to its sailing time. There's some settling in involved as well as a few hours extensive training for new employees, even those with former experience on other lines.

The majority of Mumin's ten associates have been on board for some time, some many months, working in various positions; laundry, waiter, bartender, steward, deck hand, and cook's helper. Abdul will report to Stores. His responsibility is stowing and maintaining inventory, reporting shortages, which seldom happens, and maintaining the proper supply of fruit, vegetables, spices, and meat which he needs to pull for thawing per the chef's orders. Orders for each ship in the line are compiled near Rome at Civitavecchia, the port serving the city, then packed in containers for delivery to harbors called on by the particular cruise ship. Even meat, which is shipped frozen, arrives by container. Among the employees at Civitavecchia are Enrico Sansivio and Paulo Pierucci, both half-Syrian on their mother's side, both associates of Mumin.

Mumin's last phone call is to Enrico to confirm that his order has been filled.

Another, a bar manager, is responsible for liquor and mixes. A housekeeping manager for soaps and linens. Other associates will join later.

Mohamid reports as a roustabout, who will work in general maintenance and repair, which will give him access to the ship's shop and chemical supply rooms. He will work closely with Marco and Rajah, on board in maintenance and specializing as gas welders. Both of them are Abu Sayyaf and although he wonders if he can trust them, they were recruited by Sheik Ali Hassan, and it's not his place to question the Mullah.

Mumin goes on board as a passenger, in the least expensive cabin on Deck Four, but still travelling in style as compared to the homes of most of his Muslim brothers and his own background having been born in Somalia. Like many of his brethren, he's very thin with pronounced cheekbones, a high forehead, and nearly blue-black skin. But he's taller than most at over six feet. He will stand out among other passengers, although, as usual, there will be other Blacks from America—all more generous in girth than Mumin. The joke about most Somalians and Ethiopians is they can wear a leather watchband for a belt. Mumin has been well fed since he travelled to England, so it no longer applies. He has been provided with funds so he's well-dressed when necessary with a dark suit or sport coat, slacks, decent cotton shirts, as well as an expensive silk tie. His suitcase, however, contains camo shirt and pants, and web belt and ankle high boots.

Mumin's English is more than merely passable as he worked at a U.S. drone base in Somalia, swamping in the kitchen when he was very young and drones were the newest technology and used mostly for observation. A year in England has helped.

Luckily, Abdul and Mohamid are placed together in one of the modest crew cabins deep in the bowel of *Blue Pearl*, a cabin that has a bathroom, which earns the on-board crew joke: you can sit, take a piss, brush your teeth by bending slightly over the lavatory, and shower all at the same time. It has bunkbeds, each with a small storage shelf, and one pace across the room is eighteen inches of closet for each of the two cabin mates. They enjoy an equal amount of shelf space above each closet. The only luxury is a floor-length mirror on the bathroom door, facing out. Abdul thinks it's paradise; Mohamid, the American, is not impressed. There is, however, room and privacy for both of them to pray, with shoulders touching, without attracting attention to their religion.

They, as will the passengers, have their bags scanned as they board.

Of course, they carry nothing to arouse suspicion, not even a Quran. What they need to complete their mission will arrive in crates of lettuce and fruit, and in boxes of frozen meat.

Revenge is sweet, and best served cold.

SIMONE, who knows one of the public relations people who works for O^2, is able to get five of us comped. Which means I will have to buy a ticket for Connie. The show, of course, is sold out. She says to hell with it and decides to stay aboard the ship and get us settled in. Our bags have yet to be delivered, although they were x-rayed, and passed, as we boarded.

My seat is, of course, ten rows apart from Simone and the kids, which means I will have trouble doing my job. She is mobbed by a bunch of groupies in the foyer. That means an attack would be almost impossible to defend, but once they get them seated in the sixth row from the stage, she can watch in relative safety. When the lights dim, I move to the outer aisle and down near the end of their row, where I can respond quickly. I'm only there five minutes after the lights dim when an usher strides down and informs me, I can't stand in the aisle just to get closer to the stage.

Trying to be as nice as possible, and having trouble understanding the nasty little prick's cockney accent, I explain I'm on the job. I have my bounty hunter, bail enforcement officer's badge, which says Bail Enforcement in large and Wyoming in small print. He seems adequately impressed at first, then doubting.

He retreats, but by the middle of the third song, *Yellow Submarine*, a beefy dude with a flat-top haircut, and no neck, in a black and yellow printed security jacket strides my way and taps me on the shoulder. He's got a spider tat on a cheekbone, which tells me he's likely not ex-military. More likely a local tough who impressed the O^2 manager who likely wouldn't know a tough guy from a gumball. I've seen him coming, of course, but had high hopes he'd wander on by.

He doesn't. His shoulders are thrown back and hands combat ready at his sides. His see-how-tough-I-am stance.

"On the job, pardner," I say, and turn my attention back to the stage.

"Let's talk in the lobby," he says, and has me by the elbow and tries to pull me to follow.

I politely break his grasp and repeat. "I'm on the job, like you, and can't do my job outside."

"You're bloody cheeky. Look, mate, you're coming if I have to drag you."

I show him the brass as a last attempt to leave me be.

"Fucking," it comes out 'fookin', "badge don't mean piss. Come on," he again tries to tug me after him.

I'm getting a little irritated and hold back. He tries to put me in a come-along, wrist bent backward, but I spin, give him a short one just under the rib cage and hold him up to keep him from doubling. I'm close enough that no one in the crowd seems to notice, and he 'oofs' and his eyes bulge as he tries to catch his breath.

14

WHEN BUTCH, THE SECURITY GUY, FOCUSES AGAIN, I SUGGEST, "Pardner, you're making a scene."

"Piss off. My name's...name's not pardner," he says, gasping.

I move close to him and speak barely over a whisper. "Okay, Butch, I really don't give a flying fuck what your name is. I'm working here, and it would be very embarrassing and probably cost you your lousy job if I mopped the aisle up with you. Most of these theaters hate blood on the wall and carpets, and you should hate it, particularly if it's your blood. I'm no threat to you or your crew or your patrons, unless someone accosts my client. Now, the good move would be to leave me the fuck alone to do my job and maybe you'll keep yours. You won't be able to do yours if you're sucking oxygen in the emergency room."

We've caught the attention of a few in the crowd, including Simone, but she remains seated and only gives me a pissed off glare and shake of the head.

Rather than him heading back up, I admire the security guy for going six rows down and taking a seat on a short stairway that leads to the stage. I'm sure the Cheatles are his first responsibility. I give him a nod, but he ignores it.

I'm on my feet, leaning against the wall, watching the show but mostly eyeballing the crowd seated around my charge, until the show ends. I'm not overly thrilled as there are two curtain calls as the crowd gives the Cheatles standing ovations.

Then it's over and the crowd starts out. I see it's eleven and the ship is due to sail at 3:00 a.m. It's only a half hour away, but of course Simone and her hangers-on head for the stage. Butch stops them, but Simone hands him a card that apparently is an invitation to come backstage. Of course, I haven't been informed of this possibility. I still haven't had a real heart-to-heart with Simone, so I take a deep breath and hustle to sidle up with her as Butch steps aside to let them pass. But, of course, he puts a hand in the middle of my chest and stops me.

"Card says four," he growls.

"Simone," I call after her, but she turns and gives me the finger and Patty, Terry and bald-boy Bryan all laugh. Which pisses me off totally...not quite totally or I'd drop Butch in his tracks.

"You're working for her?" Butch asks, with a curl of his lip.

"You ever bodyguard?" I ask.

"Some," he replies.

"Then you know what pricks these rich, spoiled bitches can be. Now, do me a solid and let me do my friggin' job."

He gives me a knowing smile, I don't know if it's because he does understand or because he remembers the poke to his solar plexus, but he steps aside and lets me pass.

I stay unobtrusive as Simone and the shitheads knock back a few shots with the band, then, when I see it's midnight, move over to Simone.

"Gotta go. The ship sails."

She gives me a dirty look. “We have time.”

“Gotta go. The ship sails,” I repeat.

“Go, we’ll catch up,” she says, and reaches for another shot.

“Is that on your diabetic diet?” I ask.

She glances around to make sure I haven’t been overheard, then snaps at me, “Shut the fuck up about that. No one knows. It wouldn’t be good for my career.”

“If you don’t gather up your gaggle, I’m going to shout it out to all these creeps and drop a note to the London Times.”

She gets red in the face, but then turns and yells at the rest. “Ship sails soon. Let’s go.”

After hugs all around, we leave and catch cabs.

Connie’s and my suite is on Deck Seven, a Category Two cabin with veranda—fairly modest but plenty for two weeks—Simone and Patty share a two-bedroom Grand Suite above us on Deck Eight, only two cabins away at the bow end of the ship. Beside us is a small suite like Connie’s and mine but occupied by Gretchen. Across the hall from Gretchen, Terry and Bryan share a cabin identical to ours but with twin beds, I presume. But they spend so much time up in Simone's suite they might as well have all their things there. Come to think of it they may share a queen bed. And may be queens. I remember Simone did say they weren’t her boyfriends.

Whatever the hell we all are, I’m glad we’re sailing soon. It will be hard for Simone to get very far from me on board ship.

As is normal when we board, or bags are taken, and I know will be scanned. We pass through a metal detector so anything that is untoward has been packed and well disguised as computer or camera gear.

We're also photographed, and each given a credit-card-sized ID card which will identify us as we disembark and return to the ship. Each time it's scanned the computer will flash our pictures. I've studied cruise ship protocol and know not only when leaving or returning to the ship, but when entering a dining room, you're asked for your suite number. Then you're highly complimented when the host or waiter calls you by name. Of course, when they plug in our suite number, your name and picture appear on the computer in front of them. You think they're looking for a table to seat you, but actually they're identifying you, so they can personalize your visit.

Not only that, but each crew member in the service areas are given pictures of all guests and quizzed as to their names.

Among the first pieces of business aboard the ship is a lifeboat and life preserver drill, where we're all called to our respective stations and instructed how to use the preserver, even down to blowing the whistle. I already knew how to blow a whistle.

WE AWAKEN, docked at Honfleur, France, on the Atlantic. We're just inside the mouth of the Seine River. Just looking out at the historic city I'm already wishing this was truly a vacation and that I didn't have to concern myself with a gaggle of snot-nosed brats. But a hundred grand is a hundred grand, and more importantly Connie wanted me to take the gig. I've made arrangements to meet little Miss Simone for breakfast, with the threat of quitting and ratting her out to the world regarding her diabetes. For some reason she fears that, and I finally have a wedge I can use to move her. She fears the world knowing; she fears her father knowing she's an abhorrent patient.

Connie has come down as well but taken a seat across the main dining room on Deck Four. She wisely advised me to conduct this dressing-down without anyone else within hearing. I already have a short-stack with a side of ham and two over easy when Simone arrives—a combination I had to give strict instructions to the waiter in order to achieve. I'm at a table for two, and even though I told her this conversation was to be private, she shows up with big boy Bryan in tow.

"Let's get another table," she says as they approach, nearly twenty minutes late, of course.

"No. You and I are having breakfast. Bry baby can go over and join Connie if he needs his hand held or jump the fuck overboard for all I give a rat's ass."

"Wow, did ol' Mikey ever get up on the wrong side. I think I'll eat with Bryan."

She starts to turn and walk away, and he's grinning like he just won the lottery.

"London Times," I say, and she stops short and turns back.

"You're a real prick," she says, low enough that other diners don't hear.

I point at where Connie is seated with a couple of blue hairs. "Over there, Bry."

"Go," Simone snaps at him, and his face falls but he strides away, and she takes a seat.

I wave the waiter over and she orders. When the obvious Arab waiter—his name tag says Hussein—pours her coffee then hurries away, I lay into her.

"How many times have you had a half dozen stinking, sweaty, barely-human fat men hold you down and ravish every opening you have?"

She glares at me. "What the fuck kind of question is that?"

"One you need to consider. I'm on the payroll to guard you.

You have to take that seriously or I'm quitting and going on the TV talk circuit. How's that?"

She takes a sip of her coffee and stares out at the city, then turns back. "Look, this is going to be a long two weeks. How about we try and get along?"

"Maybe three weeks. Your old man wants me along to Cannes, too."

"No fucking way!" She looks totally exasperated.

"Way."

"Bullshit."

"No, no bull. I can always give your old man, the BBC, and the National Enquirer, a call and rat you out." I can't help but smile.

"All right, all right, I surrender."

"Good," I say. "And this is how we get along. And I'm signed on for three weeks. The Cannes Film Festival and all. You read me in on everything you do outside the privacy of your bedroom and bathroom, and I want to know who is in there with you."

She laughs. "You some kind of freak?"

I nod. "Damn right I am. I'm a freak for doing my job.? I had a young lady much like you get kidnapped before I reported for my first day of work. Kidnappers are not nice, particularly to beautiful young women."

"You noticed. I thought maybe you're gay?"

15

I THINK SHE THINKS SHE'S OFFENDING ME. SHE'S NOT. I HAVE SOME gay friends and even served with a very tough gay Marine.

"I don't give a rat's ass what you do in the privacy of your bedroom. I don't want it in my face, so to speak. Sally, I've known some very tough gay guys. But no, Connie is my lady and you're my job. Do you have your alarm?"

She rolls her eyes but reaches down and snags it out of her purse, and holds it out, showing it off like a cat who's brought a mouse to the lady of the house. "It's Simone, not Sally."

"Good. Don't go anywhere without your alarm, and even if you're in the sack with some good lookin' dude, it's on the bed stand. Understand?"

"Yes, Mikey."

"I don't give a damn what you call me, so long as you let me do my job. Does Mort know you drink like the proverbial fish?"

"No, and don't tell him. He'd go crazy."

"Good, I have another hammer over you to keep you in line."

"Don't let it go to your head."

"Just follow the rules. I have your phone number. Give me your phone."

She hands it over and I program my number in, with an AAA before Mike, so it goes to number one on her contact list.

"I'm AAAMike, top of the list. Don't use the alarm unless you feel threatened. If you use it, and I'm not next to you, I'll come like a freight train, and it's likely to be anything but pretty. The phone will work most of where we'll be when in port. If you hit that alarm, know I'll come like a Sherman tank, and I don't want to hurt someone for calling you a name or short-changing you. Got it? You put me on the wrong trail, I could end up in a cell, and I can't keep you from getting dragged off by that half-dozen filthy throwbacks if I'm the guest of the boys in blue."

"I got it, and I get it."

"Good, I'll leave you alone in your cabin, but when you're ready to leave it, call me so I can flank you. Every time, even if you're only stepping down the hall."

"Flank me. Well, flank you too, futher mucker," she says, and laughs.

"So, I can be close by."

"Hell, I'm hoping over here I'll just be another strawberry blonde."

Before she can get it out, two teeny boppers stop at the table, breathlessly, and ask for her autograph, which she gives graciously, I'm happy to note. Happy she's not a total asshole.

"I guess that answers that," I say.

The waiter arrives with her granola and some frozen concoction.

I take the last bite of hotcake and rise. "I'll send Bryan over. I'm finishing my coffee with Connie. Don't leave the room without touching base with me, from now on."

She gives me that phony smile, but nods.

So, I add, "The captain has invited a few to view the bridge, and if I'm going to do my job, it's important I know every crack and cranny of the territory I'm working. The visit is scheduled for 9 A M and I'd like to go. Please don't plan to leave your suite until ten or after."

"Nowhere to go that early," she replies, with a shrug.

Before I leave, I give her an honest smile. "I'm glad we had this heart to heart, and hope you are?"

"It'll have to do," she says, and again I get the phony smile.

I guess she's right. It'll have to do.

I start the day out pissed as Simone and crew decide Rouen, a winery and ancient town tour, is their excursion. I've decided not to express my opinion in these matters unless asked—and I'm not asked.

The reason I'm silently seething is Normandy is an alternative destination, where 156 thousand brave allied soldiers stormed a handful of beaches to begin freeing Europe from Nazism. On a plateau above Omaha Beach, 9,386 marble crosses and Stars of David are aligned, where our dead are buried. It's a somber but historic place I'd love to see, and one these kids should see.

I will come back, I promise myself.

To play it safe, I've had to rearrange our transportation to a limo as opposed to the tour buses arranged by the ship. And for 10:30 a.m., after I've had my tour of the bridge.

I enjoy meeting Captain Van Groot, in a most perfunctory manor, and his First Mate Armundsen who actually conducts the class, and seeing the workings of a modern cruise ship.

We are off on an hour-and-a-half drive to Rouen, a town of towers and spires and the capital of Normandy. A happy place I'm told, if you consider where Joan of Arc was toasted at the stake in 1431 a happiness.

Connie and I stay as far front in the limo as we can place our backsides, and I guess Gretchen identifies with us older types as she sits forward also. That's fine as we get to know her. I've read some of her background that Connie was able to gather. There was nothing in any of Connie's reports on Gretchen, Bryan or Terry of any consequence.

Connie and I are able to drift ten paces behind the kids and follow them without being too obtrusive. I'm happy to say, my client does not try to ditch us.

It's a good day. We're back on *Blue Pearl* safely, and Simone is in her cabin dressing for supper as are we.

The food aboard is great, and you can get damn near anything you want, lobster or a fat rib steak with every meal, should you so desire.

If the rest of the trip is as easy as this, it will be the proverbial lark.

MUMIN IS ENJOYING HIMSELF. His cabin is modest but far nicer than any apartment he's ever had and a thousand times nicer than the hut in Somalia where he was raised. Mumin, along with his associate Sa'id, did visit Sheik Ali Hassan, the Mullah in charge of this mission, in his palace deep in the Libyan dessert near Wadi Al Hayaa, and near Ubari Airport. Ali Hassan is the mastermind behind Operation Bloody Blue. But even it wasn't finished as nicely as his cabin. Even though it was five hundred times larger.

He's spent his first day on board wandering from place to place to check on his charges. He has not made contact with Abdul as he will be almost constantly on the lower decks and will be working nights. This concerns Mumin as Abdul is responsible for unloading and hiding the munitions that come on board in foodstuffs. He does find Mohamid, who's repainting some trim on an upper deck. He's happy to note that Mohamid does not acknowledge him in any way. Mohamid, born an American, is a valuable asset. Hussein is working as a waiter, and Alia, the only female operative, as a bartender. Mumin is happy to see they seem to fit right into their jobs and as instructed ignore him. He also sees Habte, who's a steward on the same floor he occupies. He has yet to see Gama, a cook's helper; Omar, who's working in the laundry; Rajah, a floor steward; Sa'id, who's been a longtime associate of Mumin, also a steward; Enrique and Salazar, both welders; but he will come across them eventually. Long before their mission becomes known to the infidels.

All of them carry pagers that work off the ship's WIFI, hidden in their clothing. These will call them to the service of Allah.

I'M NOT unhappy that Simone and crew decided to have a cocktail or two prior to going to supper. Connie, worn out by sightseeing, has asked to beg off and remains in the room. The kids take a table next to a large window in the bar overlooking the city and as I want to always maintain some distance from them, but not more than ten paces, I see three old boys at a table with an empty chair. One of them has a Navy bill cap with U.S.S. Ranger embroidered across the front, and the other two proudly display their military affiliation on bill caps, both former Marines.

"Can I join you, gentlemen?" I ask, and they all wave me down.

We introduce ourselves and I'm proud to be in the company of retired Master Sergeant Elroy Filson, a broad-chested Texan; Master Chief Willard 'Willy' Porter, a Black from Alabama who may have missed his calling as a professional tackle for the Rams; and by-God two-star Marine Major General Maurice Tolliver, a survivor of the Lebanese bombing. Tolliver, after being severely wounded by falling masonry, served mostly on the East Coast, supply for Desert Freedom and other ops, and prior to that in both Somalia and Kosovo, and I'm just as pleased we never crossed paths. I have no idea how he'd feel about my General Discharge. All these old boys are at least in their seventies, Major General Tolliver's probably in his eighties, I'd guess. Interesting thing about the Corps, a Major General must retire five years after attaining the rank unless he's promoted. This old boy looks like he might be one who pushed back against the system—like I did—which could be a reason he didn't make Lieutenant General.

They immediately ask me if I served and I report my former ten-year service in Marine Recon without mentioning my General Discharge or the reason, therefore. I'm proud to report my ten years a Marine, my early years serving in Marine Intel, HUMINT or Human Intelligence. I was particularly proud to end my service a Warrant Officer reached at the end of my eighth year, as soon as I possibly could after reaching E-5, sergeant, and—which I don't mention as we Marines don't crow—after receiving the Legion of Merit for distinguished service in Somalia. That particular engagement was unknown to American civilians, so I don't mention it either. I do mention I applied for the appointment in Force Recon and was accepted. I then attended Warrant Officer Basic at Quantico and was given additional leadership and management training—that's SOP for non-coms. I don't often get to relate my Marine years, and seldom relate the reason for my General Discharge, known to many as less than honorable—sending an Iraqi general and some of his armed male family members to their paradise. And I'd do it again, as they were stoning to death a couple of young women. I didn't save them, but I saved my self-respect.

I truly enjoy hearing these old warhorses relate tales of their service—including Tolliver's experiences as a teen at Chosin Reservoir in Korea—and standing them to a round of drinks, which is a joke as all drinks aboard are free. I'm enthralled until the Simone party heads for supper. I excuse myself, follow, and take a table not far from theirs.

Tomorrow is a day at sea on our way to Bordeaux. So, I can sort of relax. With luck, it'll be a something-cold-by-the-pool day.

With luck, but on this gig, I'll always be waiting for the other shoe to drop. Nothing is ever merely lollypops and roses.

16

Harry Weinstein is in his London LEGAT office with Nigel Watterson of SOI5, the counterterrorism command of the London Metropolitan Police Service, across the desk, both on the speaker phone with Section Chief Terrorism Frazier Mendleson at Langley headquarters.

"So," Frazier asks, "the guy talking to Mukta and inferring he was going cruising and may be on his way to his seventy-two virgins, is Yazid Al-Saud."

"And Yazid Al-Saud's prints match those of a new employee of the Crimson Cruise line, going by the name of Mumin Amir?"

"That's it. A very vague threat," Nigel says.

"It would be unless you've read the folder on Al-Saud. He's Al-Shabaab and MI5 or SO15 would bust him right now except I'd think we'd want him to lead us to his cell members. This guy has enjoyed Pakistan, Iran, Somalia, Libya, and God knows where else. He's an old hand and is now high on our most-wanted list. Particularly now that we know he's in the west."

"Even leave him be," Frazier says, "at the risk of whatever they're going to do on the *Blue*?"

"He's already on board," Harry reminds them.

Frazier clears his throat. "Well, Nigel, old man, how about you fellas get someone on board..."

"Bollocks," Nigel snaps. "She's out of our waters, she's an American registry, she has ninety percent American passengers. No way in bloody hell. Besides, James Bond is busy."

"Okay, and you can count on us to not mention the UK harbored him there in East London." It's obvious Frazier is being facetious. He doesn't wait for a response. "Harry," Frazier asks, ignoring Nigel's attempt at humor, "who do you have who might want to work this, who might fit into with a bunch of old farts on a cruise? And who can nail this bastard before he straps on a vest or whatever is up."

"Everyone is out of pocket or involved in a mission that is more insistent. And this guy is not the vest type. He sends others to take a trip to paradise. Let's hope he's on a recon mission or trying to travel somewhere without showing his face at London's well watched and videoed airports."

Again, Frazier clears his throat. "Harry, I guess you need a little sun. I'll clear it with your director." It's not a question, but rather an order. And Frazier knows the FBI Director will go along.

"I guess a fella could pull worse duty," Harry groans, "...unless, of course, Mumin or Yazid or whatever has a half ton of C4 on board. That could screw up a vacation."

"Exactly why," Frazier says, "I want you to meet the *Blue Pearl* in Bordeaux. We've already made arrangements with Crimson for a new passenger. I know it will break your heart but the only accommodations..."

"Fuck, I'm in the bilge?" Harry moans.

Frazier laughs. "Right. The only accommodations left are a grand suite. It's booked after Malaga, but that'll give you a few days in style to recon the situation. Take a good suit and your wife along. Crimson is giving us a hell of a deal. Zero."

"My wife zeroed me out five years ago, chief."

"I'm sorry. I forgot. Girlfriend?"

"Not one I want to offer up as possible fish food."

"Good point. You have a passport as?"

"Not James Bond. Harry Drummond, with cards as a fertilizer salesman from Columbus, Ohio."

That's the shits," he says, and laughs, then continues, "I guess spreading b s is appropriate," Frazier says, and laughs again. "I'll advise my contact at Crimson to look for you in Bordeaux, tomorrow."

Then it dawns on Harry. "How big is this suite."

"Two bedrooms," Frazier says, "but I don't think you want to take the grandkids."

"No, but my assistant, Angelina Lara, is qualified for field work. And she can get places and answers I might not be able to reach."

"She is a distraction," Frazier says. "Hard not to notice her."

"But she speaks French, Farsi, Arabic and Spanish. She could be useful. I can get her a passport as Angelina Drummond by morning."

"Take her. She'd likely be twiddling her thumbs until your return anyway. Only problem is no one will believe an old fart like you could attract a Latina fox like her."

"We'll make it work," Harry says, used to Frazier's sense of humor.

"Bring back the bacon," Frazier says.

"Weinstein's don't do bacon."

"Oh, yeah, I forgot," Frazier says. "But likely Drummond's do."

"I'll order a side, and pack my Speedo," Harry says.

Again, Frazier chuckles. "That's a picture that will haunt me. Okay, that's it until we get a field report from you, Harry."

"We'll be around to pick up the pieces," Nigel says, with his own low chuckle.

"Harry," Frazier continues, "ask for John Chung when you get to the ship. He's number one security on the *Blue Pearl* and he'll escort you aboard, so you don't frighten the natives with whatever you're carrying these days."

"John Chung, it is."

I'M happy I'm on the major city side, the left side, of *Blue Pearl* as we steam up the Garonne River to dock. I'll enjoy this couple of days, except missing Omaha Beach. I'm a Jack Daniel's guy, but I like wine and it seems Simone and her charges are going to charge off to a number of wineries and enjoy lunch and supper and lunch again with wine pairing feasts. Feasts I can do. Again, I've cancelled their mass transportation provided by the cruise line and lined up a limo that will transport the seven of us.

As always, I brush up on the area. Bordeaux is a city of over a million population if you include adjacent villages. It's the premier wine growing region of the world, according to *Bordelais*, as the inhabitants are called. California, Argentina, Chile and Australia disagree, but it does host the world's major wine fair, Vinexpo, and is renowned as an outstanding urban and architectural ensemble of the eighteenth century, according to UNESCO. After Paris, it has the highest number of preserved buildings in France. I like history, food, and wine, so expect to enjoy Bordeaux.

We leave before the coach. Until the first stop I ride up front with Jacque, our driver and guide, as I want to get the feel of the guy and make sure he obeys the law and doesn't put my client at risk. Jacque has ear buds and a microphone which projects through the limo's speakers, and asks if we want narration as we travel, and Simone says, "Please." I'm pleased at her politeness.

Simone and party want to cruise the old city before the thirty-minute drive to Chateau Smith Haut Lafitte where Connie and I tag along at a respectful and propitious distance, but also enjoy the tour of vineyards and winery, a sixteenth century tower, and two underground cellars. The owners have reintroduced horse-drawn plowing, which kind of amuses me but thrills most of the tourists, including Connie so I keep my amusement to myself. It's good show but wouldn't fly in Wyoming. Unless, of course, you had lots of paying tourists.

The lunch with wine pairing is magnificent and I'm a little sorry I'm working, so it's far more swill and spit than swallow.

I do get braced by Simone as she complains about my booking private transportation. She claims she wants to be plebian and ride the coach with the folks, which surprises me and makes me like her a little more. Then again, she may not be getting enough adulation from her intimate crew. I'll reserve my judgment.

The driver, Jacque, is knowledgeable of the history of the area and takes us on a long tour before returning. Simone has us booked into a five-star joint for supper, with Connie and me at a separate table per my request. She always seems a little peeved when I want to sit separate from her, as if I'm insulting the diva, but the fact is, I can better do my job if I'm not identified as protection. A wise attacker would take out protection and bodyguard first. Surprise is a great advantage. So, it's best to be the surprise rather than the surprised.

Le Chicoula is one of those fusion joints and I'm hungry. Every bite is exquisite, but there's just not enough bites for a two-hundred-plus-pound guy who's been stomping vineyards and wineries all day. But I resign myself as I need to stay alert and a full gut is counterproductive. Besides, I can chow down again on the ship where portions are geared for American chowhounds.

So far, I've been more than pleased that even those folks who seem to recognize Simone keep their distance, that is until we've finished our meal. I've asked Simone to let me lead when we're entering or leaving someplace, at least a public place away from the ship, and so far, she's been pretty good.

She does hesitate and let me pass before walking out onto Rue de Cursol, the narrow street. I quickly discover that someone has ratted us out, as there is a half-dozen photographers in a semicircle awaiting her exit.

Shouting and pushing.

Not good.

17

I've been down this trail before and know you must give paparazzi their space so long as they don't invade the clients to the point of possible injury. And that, to me, means a little more than an arm's length.

Closer can be dangerous.

Simone is wearing a shoulder bag, larger than she would normally have as a clutch—what she'd normally take to a nice supper place. And as she's not particularly concerned with theft, it's open.

I am concerned and watch carefully as the paparazzi crowd around her. She's laughing and trying out her rudimentary French when I step forward and make sure they don't get right in her face with video and still cameras. I've seen lips busted and eyebrows requiring stitches from the sharp rims of camera lenses.

She growls at me, seemingly enjoying the attention and not wanting me to queer the moment. I notice a hand snake into her purse and come out with a wallet. He's a good grafter as he hunkers over hiding his crime as he picks the goods, and had I not been carefully watching the invitation of a wide-open target, he'd have been long gone. The little worm of a guy quickly fades back into the crowd—bystanders have gathered to see what the attraction is—and I shove between a couple of photographers and see the worm striding away. I charge, quietly in soft-soled shoes. In ten strides, I've caught up and use the ball of my palm to smack him behind the head. He goes to his face on the pavement. I expect the prick to leave a grease smear, but there's only a smear of blood. I reach around him and snag the wallet from his front pocket as he's trying to get to his knees.

The last thing I want is to spend half the night at the *gendarmerie*, or the *police nationale*, as it's hard to do your job if you're miles away being interviewed.

Rather than hold the prick for the police, I give him a swift boot in the butt as he's trying to get up. He shoots another six feet forward, comes up with a skinned nose to match the abrasion on his cheekbone, which I only see as he looks back as he's beating feet down the street.

Simone has broken free of the gaggle of photographers, and as usual is eyeing me like I'm dog-do, and yells at me, "What was that all about? That won't look good in the local papers."

I serve her the wallet on the flat of my hand as if a waiter serving hors d'oeuvres, and she looks sheepish, starts to say something but chokes on it, as I suggest, "Keep the purse zipped, please." I don't add 'and keep your mouth zipped' no matter the urge.

The limo was unable to park nearby. I called Jacque when we were finishing up supper, and he now arrives.

I laugh as Simone holds the door for Connie and me and gives me a sincere, "Thank you," as I crawl in.

She's learning.

I do talk her into attending a 'meet the crew' function in the show lounge as we're back in time. Captain Van Groot is introduced by the hotel manager and we learn there are twenty-five officers on board, half ship-operation, half hotel, all subject to the orders of Van Groot. We meet a half dozen of them, most on the hotel staff that deals with passengers.

Then it's off to the casino as the ship is again at sea. Simone is a terrible blackjack player and contributes at least five hundred bucks before the kids hit the bar for a nightcap.

"I CAN'T RISK IT," John Chung says as he and Harry Weinstein, now Harry Drummond, and Angelina Lara, now Angelina Drummond, meet in the privacy of Chung's small *Blue Pearl* office.

Chung has the round face and hooded eyes of an Asian, and is on the squat side, but Harry evaluates him and his thick chest and heavy shoulders, deciding he's a lot more muscle than fat. His heavy upper body is well anchored by a thick belly and legs. His furrowed brow suggests his intense interest.

Chung continues, "All ships must comply with the ISP—International Ship and Port Facility Security Code. I'm obligated to report any security issue to next port authority prior to arrival."

"Your call," Harry says. "Also, it'll be your responsibility if this guy who now calls himself Mumin Amir is only the tip of a very dangerous iceberg. I have the feeling he's not working alone. If he is, he's only travelling, and we'll have no problem on board. If not, your legacy could be six hundred dead. And these folks are normally technologically very efficient. I guarantee all your ship-to-shore communications are being monitored and if they think they're discovered, it's very likely you'll have to deal with a major incident long before you dock."

Chung sighs deeply. His jaw is set. He's not happy, but he understands the problem. "Okay, so what's your next move?"

"Mumin is on board as a passenger, so, easily watched. While we keep tabs on him, and every employee he comes in contact with, you keep a close eye on any of your people with Muslim, Arabic or other names."

"Hell, there must be two dozen," he snaps. "We've got Muslim Indonesian and Pilipino as well as those from the Near East. All of our employees are vetted and of course have passports so were evaluated by their home countries long before hired by us."

"As were the couple of dozen who flew planes into the Twin Towers."

He sighs deeply. "Point well taken."

"Then you watch two dozen. But if it were me, I'd closely watch only those employed by the line in the last eighteen months. I'll bet there're not more than a handful."

"Makes sense," Chung agrees. "What else?"

"Let us know if Mumin has any excursions booked so we can go along. Other than that, it's watch and wait. You should know that our people and London's are working on the background of all your onboard employees. If anything turns up, we'll be the first to know."

"We?" Chung questions.

"We. You, me, and Miss...oops, Missus Drummond here."

They exchange cell phone numbers. Then Chung suggests, "You know we can run pretty fast and loose with surveillance. No F.ISA court to worry about at sea. How about I have a bug put into this Amir's cabin and in the passenger Mumin's?"

"How about video?" Harry suggests.

"That may be a step too far, but audio?"

"Do it."

Chung rises and extends a hand. "Enjoy your cruise," he says, with a shake of the head.

"Nice ship. We'll do our best. I'll phone, or you do so the instant you have anything."

"You bet, you too. Let's not let this get out of hand."

Harry leaves happy with his meeting and thinking that Chung is a competent and cooperative security guy. That has not always been his experience with security types.

MOHAMID KNOWS this is a critical moment in the mission. The receipt, unloading, and hiding of munitions.

Mohamid has a cook's helper who's one of the jihadists, Gama, assist him on-loading cases of oranges, lemons, lettuce, spinach, crates of grapes, and more from a local supplier. A supplier who's unknowingly employed two of the faithful for more than six months. Later in the day they'll unpack cases of frozen fish, beef, lamb, and pork and dry goods from the company shipping container that meets them in various ports. It's their job to stow all.

As they are working, another young cook's helper, Luma Al-Faraj, a Sudanese like Gama, appears.

"Chef sent me to help," he says. Unknown to Mohamid, had Gama and Luma been anywhere else they would be mortal enemies, as Luma is of Sudan's Gimar tribe and Gama of the Beni Halba.

This use of someone not a member of their group is not in Mohamid's plan, as one slip, one spilled case, could reveal an AK47, a KRISS automatic pistol or it's detachable stock, one of the dozen Russian F1 hand grenades, or one of the half-dozen American Claymore mines stolen from the Egyptian military.

Luckily, they are working far from others on Deck Two in the bowel of the ship. Mohamid notices that Gama and Luma work without speaking. He thinks nothing of it.

They are down to the last four cases of citrus, three of lemons and one of grapefruit, when Luma stumbles and the case of grapefruit falls, and grapefruit roll across the deck.

"Oh, I am so sorry, so..." Luma begins, then stares at six Russian hand grenades spread across the deck among assorted grapefruit.

18

"OH...OH...OH," HE MUMBLES, STARING WIDE-EYED AT THE LITTLE fist-size purveyors-of-death, then turns to Mohamid. "Do you see? Do you see? The fruit merchant must..." But he doesn't get it out. An eighteen-inch wrench, removable from a valve on a refrigerant line traversing the wall, is in Gama's hand. Swinging it like he's driving a spike with a sledge, it crashes on Luma's head, splitting it with the force of the blow.

Gama stands over the boy, smiling, white teeth flashing. He glances up at Mohamid. "Filthy Gimar," he says, reveling in what he's done.

"I don't care what he is. Hurry." Mohamid only wants to remain undiscovered.

Luma's flat on the deck in front of the door to Cold Room 3, blood pooling beneath his crushed skull.

"Hurry," Mohamid says, grabbing the boy's arm. Gama grabs the other and they drag Luma into the cold room. They quickly hide him behind cases of citrus and vegetables, after stripping him of his shirt and wrapping his head to try and quell the bleeding, unnecessary as the dead don't pump blood.

"Get a mop," Mohamid instructs Gama. "I'll continue to sort. Hurry." And Gama runs, disappearing into a passageway.

A garbage cart, wheeled, three-feet-wide and three-deep-by-five-long, is the vehicle they're using to hide the armaments, under vegetable and fruit trimmings and peelings. Mohamid is busily stowing automatic pistols, a half-dozen AK47's and fifty thirty-round clips when he hears someone coming. He palms the wrench but drops it when he sees Gama with a mop and bucket.

They've just finished when the sous chef, a Frenchman who goes by the name Pepe and is disliked by most, appears.

"Where the hell is Luma?" he asks. He's egg-shaped and stands with one fist on his side. Had it not been for his chef's hat, his *chapeau de chef*, in his white chef's outfit, he looks a little like a squat porcelain tea pot with a handle.

Mohamid, thinking quickly, "He was ill. He threw up and we have just cleaned up. He said he was going to his cabin."

"Damn, damn, damn. Gama. When you have cleaned this floor with a twenty percent bleach mixture, you report to me. I will make a saucier of you. Clean it well. We don't want sickness to run rampant. What is that pink crap you are using?"

Mohamid stutters when he realizes some of the liquid he's using is mixed with blood. He shrugs. "Pink soap from stores."

"Use bleach and water."

"Yes, sir," Gama says, and the fat Frenchman, Pepe, disappears heading back to the kitchen.

"Close," Mohamid says.

"How do we get rid of the scum Gimar?"

"I'm compacting cartons when we finish here. I'll dismember him and will squash him up with the cardboard."

"Do you need help?" Gama asks.

"No, I'll be alone near the compactor."

"Good," Gama says, and truly means it as he cannot imagine the horrid job, even as much as he hates the Gimar.

MUMIN HAS STAYED on board while other passengers visit Bordeaux. He has much work to do. He carefully cuts the bottom lining out of his large suitcase and recovers the one-half-inch-thick by two-foot-by-three-foot layer of C4 explosive, four detonators, and four cell phones. The normal C4 charge is thirty-four cubic inches; he has only twenty-seven cubic inches per charge to work with, but it will be more than enough. The Iranian version of C4 is equally explosive as the American version. After an excellent breakfast, he spends the balance of the morning constructing four bombs that will be detonated by a call to one of the four cell numbers assigned to the throwaways.

For the first time since boarding he is able to speak to one of his fellow jihadists. Sa'id is the steward taking care of his cabin. Mumin purposefully leaves the do-not-disturb switch off so Sa'id will enter when it's his cabin's turn.

It is nearly noon, their second day in Bordeaux, when Sa'id enters.

"*As-salam alaykum,*" Sa'id greets him.

"Speak English, always, when on board."

"You have packages for me?"

"I do. And you have a safe place to store them?"

Sa'id smiles. "Crew cabins are not searched, and we clean our own. As I told you, they would not be safe in your cabin, as I will rotate to another post after Lisbon."

"Then they must be entrusted to you. Should you leave them here for a while?"

"No, my supervisor may check my work anytime. They do white glove inspections and are liable to look anywhere. You only have room for a couple in your safe. In fact, I think they look to see if employees are hiding anything. We have a small safe, but a Glock will barely fit there."

"Then you must hide them."

"*Inshallah,*" Sa'id says.

"English only," Mumin corrects, and they roll each bomb in a towel and stow them in Sa'id's supply cart.

Mumin is enjoying his position as guest, and as he gets ready to leave Sa'id to his work cleaning the cabin, hands him his loafers, "Shine, please."

Sa'id looks a little irritated but takes them.

It's a beautiful day and lunchtime, so he goes up to the swimming pool, orders from the small cafe adjoining and takes a spot on a chaise lounge near the pool. Most passengers are ashore enjoying their second day in Bordeaux, but a few have stayed behind. A European or American in a nylon track suit, wearing a Doncaster Rovers red and white football jersey, takes a chair at a small table nearby and is soon joined by a beautiful woman, maybe Arab.

Mumin eats slowly, enjoying the view of three young women in bikinis and the beautiful dark-skinned woman seated nearby.

He's wondering if the woman is Muslim, married to an infidel, and even if so, she should be wearing a hijab with her face, and particularly that tanned body, covered. If so, she'll be one of the first to receive Allah's wrath.

As he rises to leave, he pauses near the man in the tracksuit.

"You are a Rover's fan? English, I presume."

The man glances up from the novel he's reading. "American, but yes, I'm a Rover's fan. I live in England."

Mumin extends his hand and the man shakes. "I am Mumin Amir. My English friends call me Moony."

"Harry Drummond," the man says. "Nice to make your acquaintance."

19

MUMIN NODS, THEN EYES THE LONG-LEGGED WOMAN ON A NEARBY chaise lounge—a woman dressed in no more than a pair of hankies and inviting the hands of a man. "Your wife?"

"Yes," and he speaks a little louder. "Angelina, say hello to Moony."

She glances up from the magazine she's reading and gives Mumin a little unconcerned wave.

"Spanish?" Mumin asks.

"Mexican," Harry says, with a smile. "You're not going ashore today?"

"I have seen Bordeaux and, like you, I am enjoying the wonderful weather. Enjoy your book," he says, and walks away.

When he disappears into an elevator, Angelina folds up her book and moves to a chair across from Harry. "That was unplanned," she says.

"She's a small ship, and with others ashore, I'm not surprised. Might be easier to keep track of him if we're buddied up."

"Guess it couldn't be helped."

"Young lady, with that bikini I'm surprised half the males on board are not circling you like hungry sharks. He looked at you like he was about ready to exercise his so-called rights as a Muslim man with any infidel."

"Thank you, for almost a compliment, I think. Are you saying I shouldn't have…?"

"No, no, besides it won't do any harm. Like I said, watching him might be easier. It's good you got his attention. Just don't wander down a dark corridor in that outfit with any Muslim man within one hundred yards."

Mumin returns to his room. It is time for his Dhuhr prayer. As he works the lock, he thinks back on the Mexican woman. She is as beautiful as the most beautiful Somalians although her skin, of course, is not nearly so dark. He has only been with whores in Somalia and Libya. What would it be like to be with this Mexican westerner?

Maybe she will favor him with her body or be somewhere he can favor himself, no matter her wants. She'll likely offer it freely when she is wondering if she is one selected to be beheaded.

He laughs. If he offers her life, he is sure she will think black is beautiful.

HARRY'S PHONE rings almost as soon as Mumin leaves.

"We've got something," John Chung says.

"Your office?" Harry asks.

"As quickly as you can," Chung says.

Harry folds up his book. "Angelina, I'm headed to Chung's office. Suggest you get dressed and join us."

"I have a robe."

"Then let's go."

Chung is at his desk, his fingers steeple under his chin. He's deep in thought when they enter. He stands immediately and can't help but eye Angelina up and down. She has on a wrap, but it's slightly translucent.

"Sit, please," Chung says, and they do.

"I want you to listen." He pushes a small recorder forward and hits the play button. "This is the passenger Mumin and his area steward, a fellow named Sa'id, whose file says from Yemen. Not concrete, but good enough for me to bust them."

The recorder reports,

"You have packages for me?"

"I do. And you have a safe place to store them?"

"Crew cabins are not searched, and we clean our own. As I told you, they would not be safe in your cabin, as I will rotate to another post after Lisbon."

"Then they must be entrusted to you. Should you leave them here for a while?"

"No, my supervisor may check my work anytime. They do white glove inspections and are liable to look anywhere. You only have room for a couple in your safe. In fact, I think they look to see if employees are hiding anything. We have a small safe, but a Glock will barely fit there."

"Then you must hide them."

Chung stops the recorder. "Obviously, something they want hidden, and the only reason they do is it's against our rules. And it must be something dangerous. I've got to search this Sa'id's cabin and arrest him or at least sack the wanker."

Harry sits forward. "Hold on, John. This might be something dangerous, or it may be porno tapes or marijuana. If it's something dangerous then, like I said before, it may be the tip of the iceberg. You want my suggestion?"

"Your suggestions and my responsibilities may be at odds...but go ahead."

"Search his cabin when he's at work. I'd like to help in that effort. Both I and Angelina are well trained in surreptitious searches. Let's not upset the proverbial apple cart. Then if we locate something, we can decide our next step."

Chung is quiet for a moment then nods. "Done. Let's give him tonight to hide whatever the 'packages' are. You meet me here in the morning, eight-thirty, and we'll do our shake down."

"We have two ways in and out and Angelina can stand guard on one end and your man the other, if that works for you?"

"Perfectly."

"Then we'll get back to observing Mumin Amir."

OUR SECOND DAY at Bordeaux turns out to be a breeze.

I'm a little curious to see one of the crew, a tall thin brown man, take a seat at a far end of the bar, and be brought a beer in a can by the pretty bartender. She glances around as if she doesn't want to be caught doing so. I judge them both to be Middle Eastern. I'm a little surprised to see a crew member at a passenger bar, but presume he's off work. The pretty bartender looks nervous to have him there. He leaves quickly, but not without paying her a compliment of some kind, I presume, as she bats her pretty eyes at him, and I overhear her say, "Thank you, Sa'id."

I'm not unhappy that the kids have decided to stay aboard rather than take in more of Bordeaux. It's a perfect day and they've decided to work on their tans. Lying by the pool, with a much better than average café only yards away, a beautiful blonde by my side, is what I pictured this job to be. I only have to glance up once as a couple of teenagers beg Simone for autographs.

We have supper in the *Blue Pearl*'s gourmet restaurant, El Greco, hit the show, which is a great retrospective on Abba, the casino for an hour, then the sack.

HARRY AND ANGELINA split up to wander the public areas and look for Mumin, when Harry steps into the Deck Five bar, his cell rings the theme from Paladin's *Have Gun Will Travel.* He knows it's his immediate superior, Frazier Mendleson.

"Yes, sir," he answers.

"Getting any sun?"

"Not much today, yesterday was beautiful."

"Well, I've got another beautiful boy for you to look for. I've texted you a photo of a guy who signed on the *Blue Pearl* as Mohamid Ahmed. We made him from the picture you got, facial recognition. However, he was formerly Sean McCord."

"Irish? Or Brit?"

"Nor Australian or Kiwi. He's a bloody American, to borrow some English slang."

"And?"

"And a bad son-of-a-bitch. He's on the Company's hit list. And you know how bad he's got to be to make the enemy of America's hit list. Maybe he's calmed down now as MI5 has reported he has two brats by a wife in London."

"When did kids slow the pricks down? What job?"

"He's on as a roustabout. He's liable to be anywhere. But Chung can put you on him."

"Chung keeps wavering. He wants to bust these guys at the

drop of a hat. I've held him in check so far. We're onto another who may be a player. Sa'id Al-Gharsi is the name he signed on under."

"I'll get back to you on him."

"We're onto some packages that Mumin must have carried aboard. He's passed them to Al-Gharsi. We've got Sa'id's cabin bugged and Chung and I are going to toss it in the morning, and he'll bug Al-Gharsi's as well."

"Stay alert."

"You bet your ass. I'm retiring next year."

Frazier chuckles. "And miss all this fun?"

20

WHILE WE WATCH THE KIDS LOSE A FEW HUNDRED AT THE TABLES in the ship's small casino, Connie orders her second dirty martini, which portends good things for me when I get the kids locked into their cabins and Connie into the suit God gave her at birth.

There's nothing like a little horizontal exercise to make one sleep well, and I do.

Morning is another day at sea. As Simone and I have come to an understanding that if she is going to leave her cabin she'll call and wait until I knock on the door; one knock, pause then two knocks, pause, then another. Knowing she won't be up and about until at least ten, and having my alarm receiver strapped to my wrist, I decide to take advantage of the gym. I'm there at dawn, an overcast day with a rip of bright orange on the eastern horizon. It's damp out, and the rails are peppered with dew. I get a drop on my nose from above as I enter the door to the bow-facing gym. There is a dozen or more Life Fitness machines, free weights, and a dozen walkers facing forward with floor to ceiling windows looking out on a gentle gray sea reflecting the dappled pewter sky. The floor under the machines is well polished wood, except for the free-weight area that is thick carpet. Dropping free weights on a wood floor is not good.

To my surprise there are a dozen passengers already there. I do some stretches then find the carpeted area and a bench. I load two-hundred-fifty on the bar and get ready to do a few sets of presses, when someone speaks up, "You want me to spot you?"

I glance over and see the backlit full head of gray hair of General Tolliver.

"Good morning, sir," I say, and place the bar back on its hook. "Actually, this is just warm up weight. If I get serious, I'll impose on you."

"I'll be on the treadmill, watching the sea go by."

"Have you had breakfast?" I ask.

"Meeting the squid, Porter, and Elroy in a half hour. Join us."

"Honored to do so," I say, and he heads for a treadmill.

After working up a good sweat and then a sponge bath, I exit to see the General standing by.

"Let's eat," he says. And I give him a loose salute.

As we head for the restaurant, he makes a request. "Mike, do me a favor?"

"You bet, sir."

"Knock off the sir and the general. Friends call me Tolly or Bull and I prefer it. Damned if folks don't treat you differently when they know your rank."

"Yes, sir...I mean, you bet, Tolly."

He laughs. "Thanks. Actually, most my Marine buddies call me Bull."

"Then Bull it is, sir. I mean Bull it is, Bull. May I ask how you got that moniker?"

"Long story, over a tall Scotch sometime soon."

"Yes, sir. But it's Jack Daniel's for me, if it's all the same."

"Hell, Sergeant, you're buying, so drink what you want." He guffaws like a bull snorting and I have to laugh as well. We both know drinks are free on the ship.

We join who I've come to know as Rockin' Roy Filson and Willy Porter and have a great time, until Filson gives us a little pause. "I'll tell you; I love this boat and most the folks, but some of these ragheads..."

Willy laughs. "No headdresses allowed on board, or so I understand."

"None the less," Filson continues. "It doesn't take much moxie when you get their names to know their persuasion."

"And that is?" Tolly asks.

"I've seen a couple of the sand fleas whispering and looking over their shoulders like they wanted to make sure no one was in earshot. After five tours in the sandbox, I hate turning my back on the goat fuckers. I mopped up too many buddies from IEDs."

I must agree. "I don't have the time in you do, Sarge, but I've had enough AK47's buzzing me to feel the same, and saw enough buddies buy the farm to feel your pain."

Tolly speaks up and has a commanding presence as do most staff officers. "I've got to trust the hiring practices of a cruise line like Crimson. I'll bet they do cavity searches. In fact, a few of the employees look like they'd enjoy cavity probes."

We all laugh at that. And all say, "Hope you're right."

Another fella, trim for an old fart, with gray hair shorn in a tight flat-top, stops at our table and glances from one of us to the next. "Yanks, I'll bet a quid. Any takers?"

"No," I say as the others eye him. Then ask, "Liverpool?"

"Not a bad guess, bloke. But I'm no Scouser—Manchester, east of Liverpool. You boys bloody Marines, I'll bet."

Bull takes over. "And damn proud of it. You look old enough to me that I might have run over you in Desert Storm."

"And then some," he says, and extends his hand. "Alistair Nelson."

He introduces himself around the table. Then turns back to Bull. "SAS, mate, greatest fighting force in the world as you damn well know. We were so far out in front of you blokes it would only have been a camel run over us."

We all laugh and tell him to take a seat. He's going to fit right in.

HARRY AND ANGELINA report to John Chung's office at 8:15, and together they head to Sa'id's cabin. Nothing of consequence has been heard over the bug they placed in his cabin.

Neither he nor his cabin mate are in, as expected, so while Angelina stands guard at the elevators, and Peter Zucker, who works security under Chung, watches the stairway at the far end of the corridor, Chung and Harry toss the place.

Chung is the first to be shocked by his find. He, of course, has a master key to all the small employee safes, and is taken aback by the two rolled tubes with what looks to be plastic explosives enclosed, both wired to cell phones.

Harry continues to hunt while Chung carefully exposes the cell phones and their connections to the detonators.

While he works, Harry discovers another pair of bombs behind a row of books in Sa'id's upper bunk. He, too, carefully unrolls and shoots pics with his cell phone.

"What do we do?" Chung asks Harry.

"Roll them carefully, remove the batteries, return them, and we'll get instructions from our bomb people. If we can disarm, I say leave them."

"Jesus Christ," Harry stammers. "That's four pounds of C4 that could damn near blow this ship in half."

"So, let's disarm it further and make sure there's not another forty pounds somewhere else. The only way to do that without docking this ship and putting passengers and crew ashore is to keep doing what we're doing."

"I think you're fucking crazy," John says with sincerity.

"The hell of it is, John, if we deviate from the normal, they'll very likely decide it's time to collect their seventy-two virgins. It looks to me the intent is not to merely blow us to fish bait, or they'd likely have done so already—if there is that forty pounds elsewhere. Let's get some instruction and disarm these and keep with the Sherlock Holmes."

"We have three of them. This Mumin and Sa'id, and your people have made Mohamid—that could be the lot..."

"Not a chance in hell. I'd guess ten at least. Do you regularly check crew's quarters?"

"No, but it's not unheard of. Every couple of voyages we might wander through."

"Then I'd start doing so, when the occupants are at work, if possible."

"Fine. Get in touch with your people. I've got to report this to my home office and make sure I'm doing the right thing."

Harry moves up a deck but can't get a cell signal, so he returns to his cabin while Angelina and Chung's man watch the cabin to make sure no one returns to distribute those nice two-pound packages over the ship. They may have another way to detonate, even manually if strapped to their bellies.

Harry has to resort to his satellite phone, and soon is placated by the fact two CIA bomb experts will board later tonight at Bilbao, Spain, their next stop, and will not only properly disarm the bombs, but will bring a harmless substitute—probably play dough—aboard and replace the explosive so the 'bombs' can remain in place, and safely so.

John Chung is on the phone with his home office the same time the CIA was, and he is instructed, after much discussion about the risk, to stand by and let Harry take the lead, but to watch closely. So, he is off the hook.

Of course, off the hook doesn't matter much if you're all blown to hell.

21

A DAY AT SEA, ANOTHER TOUGH DUTY AT THE POOL, EVEN THOUGH the now flat lead-colored sky stays with us. The pool is protected from the wind, even so, it's a little chilly so the kids are drinking hot Irish coffees while they soak up sun.

I am more than a little amused when Terry and Bryan wander by, and Terry gives Connie a yell. “Hey, Connie, you tired of that old man yet?”

“He is getting pretty rickety,” she says, looking up from her book.

“I’ll bet you ten bucks Bry can take him in an arm wrestle.”

She gives him a polite smile, and I look up from the *Wired* magazine I’m reading. She says, “I wouldn’t want Bry to hurt him. He promised to dance with me tonight.”

“I did?” I say.

Then Terry turns to me. “How about it, old man?”

“Connie doesn’t want him to hurt me,” I say, and pick my magazine back up.

“I thought so,” Bryan says.

"He was the champion of our frat," Terry adds. "Smart of you to chicken out."

Connie eyes me. "Don't even think it," she says.

I can't help myself and fold up the magazine. "Did you say ten bucks?"

Terry laughs. "How about twenty?"

I dig in my wallet for a Jackson and fish one out. "That table over by the girls looks pretty sturdy," I say, and rise and walk over.

"What's up?" Simone asks as we plop down at the table.

"Frat champion wants to lose his crown," I say.

"What?" she says, looking puzzled.

"Left or right," I ask him as he takes a seat, and offers his right.

We lock up and Terry counts down. "Three, Two, One."

And he humps it to me, but I merely remain vertical. "When are you going to start?" I ask, and I can see the doubt in his eyes.

"Let's call it even," I say, not having given an inch.

"Fuck no," he says, and he humps again and his eyes bulge and the veins on his temples protrude.

I try my best to sound like I'm begging, "Come on, Bry, I don't want to pull a muscle or something."

"Okay, okay," he says, slightly panting. "You gotta fight off those hundred-twenty-pound wallet thieves and need both arms."

He relaxes and we break. "Thanks, Bry," I say, and he knows better where we stand and who's the alpha wolf.

As they head for the bar, I overhear Terry, "What the fuck was that?"

"Didn't want to hurt the old man," Bryan says as they disappear inside.

I glance at Simone and Patty as I get up to return to my chaise lounge. Simone mouths, "Thank you," and I give her a wink and half-hearted smile.

"Aren't you the nice man?" Connie says as I return to my magazine.

"Not really. I thought about putting his knuckles through the tabletop," I reply. "But you said he was a drummer and I was hoping for his version of *sing, sing, sing*. He actually looks a little like Gene Krupa."

"Showing your age," Connie says, and laughs.

"One of my old man's favorites, actually."

"Good, you had me worried there for a minute. How the hell old are you?" she asks, and I'm surprised she doesn't know.

"Yeah, I know, I probably look fifteen years older than you, but I'm not even five. I've just been ridden hard and put away wet too many times."

"Thank God," she says. "I was afraid I was the old one."

"You sweet talker," I say. "I will dance with you tonight."

John Chung picks up his desk phone and finds Pepe, the sous chef, on the other line.

"What's up," he asks.

"I had a helper not show up. A couple of others said he got ill and headed to his cabin. I took pity on him and took him a container of soup, and guess what?"

"Tell me, Pepe?"

"No one in his cabin. I checked with the doc and he hasn't seen him. I asked around and no one's seen him. He was as faithful as the sun rising, so I'm concerned."

"I'll issue an employee bulletin. He's probably tired of you ragging him."

"Not so, Mister Chung," Pepe has taken umbrage at John's remark.

Then it dawns on Chung. "Who reported him sick?"

"That new roustabout was helping Gama from stores. I sent Luma to help them and I guess he threw up and went to his cabin."

Chung takes a deep breath. "Okay, Pepe, we'll get right on it."

He hangs up and dials Harry's room.

"We've got a man missing and the last one to see him and reported him missing was this guy Mohamid."

"I'm glad you called. We're taking on two CIA bomb guys at Bilbao. And they're staying aboard to help out."

"I'm worried. Mohamid was helping another Muslim crew member, Gama Suliman. And Suliman has only been on board a little more than a month. I don't like it."

"Let's bug his cabin," Harry says, "and Mohamid's."

"Hell, I'm out of bugs."

"I'll have the guys in Bilbao bring a dozen aboard."

"God willing, we'll make Bilbao."

"Look, I'm as nervous as you are about those four packages. Can you do anything to keep that part of the ship vacated?"

"I confiscated some sulfur bombs from some kids on the last voyage. How about I set them off in that section of the crew's quarters and we report a pipe failure."

Harry chuckles. "Sounds good. Do it. We can block the area off and those crew members near will have to bunk elsewhere tonight."

Chung sighs deeply again. "Damn, it may take a month to get the stink out."

"Better some stink than ending up under five hundred fathoms of sea water."

"I'm off," Harry says, and goes to his storage closet and is thankful Chung had forgotten to get rid of the kid's rotten bombs.

He returns to the floor, advises Angelina and Peter Zucker of the plan, and they agree to help him evacuate any crewmember in quarters after he's literally raised a stink. He commandeers a wastebasket and uses it to contain the sulfur bomb, and when smoke fills the corridor, goes back into Sa'id's cabin and flushes all but one of the sulfur bombs down his toilet.

Then they begin evacuating. In the dozen crew-cabins, only two night-workers have to be rousted out.

In short order Zucker has returned from John's office with yellow "keep out" tape, and the C4 bombs are protected from handling and distribution, although without batteries in the phones they should be safe. Should be.

Unless, of course, the detonators are also susceptible to radio waves?

22

Harry Weinstein is waiting at the lower departure cabin when the ship docks, and is surprised to see one of the CIA agents who boards is a woman. Felicia Washington shakes with a stubby fingered hand, and gives him a serious grin, but one that shows pearly white teeth that look even whiter in her coffee-colored face, and the fact she wears even darker sunglasses. They called her Flossy-round-bottom at the Farm, but soon learned that prodigious mass was mostly muscle. She did as many pull ups as most the men, and even as short as she was, barely over five foot two, she was in the top sixty percent of her class, men included.

So, what is the white cane with the red tip all about?

Short doesn't really matter except in practical matters in the Company. Jobs in the National Clandestine Service require eighteen years of age, being a U.S. citizen, a bachelor's degree with a minimum GPA of three. You're more likely to be hired if you're fluent in a foreign language, have a history of living abroad, and some perceived 'sensitivity' to other cultures. When hired, you go through extensive background checks, medical and psychological evaluations, a polygraph exam, and a year and a half training for either the clandestine service or a headquarters-based job.

So, if you're hired, you've been put through the ringer. And Felicia came through with flying colors and still smiling.

She introduces him to her partner, Ronaldo 'Ronnie' Alberto. Harry is even more surprised to have her release the handle on the harness on a German shepherd and place the cane in the other hand in order to shake.

"That's Buster," she says.

Harry glances over his shoulder to make sure the desk attendant is out of hearing range, and asks, "I presume you haven't gone blind since we last met."

"No, thank God." Her deep chuckle is almost a rumble. "No one suspects a sight-impaired person and I can bump into them and pick their pocket," she laughs. "Buster is incognito, too. He'll alert us to any explosive."

"Outstanding," Harry says.

"I remember you, Harry. You're the FBI guy who trained with us. Don't know if you know it, but they called you, Hermy, not Harry, the hermaphrodite at the Farm, FBI hanging with CIA."

"I've been called worse."

"We're only on board until just before *Pearl* leaves Bilbao." Felicia says.

"That won't work," Harry says, furrowing his brow.

"Got to. We're off to Riyadh on special assignment. Higher priority, I guess. Have to catch a company Citation at midnight *mañana*."

"Higher priority than three hundred fifty passengers, mostly Americans, plus the crew?" Harry snaps, shaking his head, then resignedly mumbles, "Then let's get to work." But he can hardly hide his disappointment.

"I don't set the priorities, Harry," she says.

COMMON AREA for the crew is their mess. Even though the jihadists worked different shifts and even though they'd all been warned to act as if the others had leprosy, they couldn't help but acknowledge each other in small ways. Even if only a glance. Sa'id couldn't help but do more. Alia is beautiful.

Most, on the coming shift, have finished their breakfast and left.

They had trained together nearly two years ago in Libya, lived together as soldiers for three months, so each knew the other, even if instructed to not acknowledge the fact. Alia is the only female among the *jihadi's,* and very attractive as Yemeni women can be.

She's alone at a crew mess table when Sa'id enters, fills his plate with rice and salad and sits across from her. He's been attracted to her since they all trained together but had been warned against even recognizing the fact she is female. At the moment, no one is firing an AK47 over his head as he crawls on his belly beneath barbed wire—so he decides to be bold. Still, he keeps glancing over his shoulder to make sure no one is watching.

"I am from Sana'a," he says, and she glances up from her iPhone.

She surveys the room before answering. "My home is...was...a small village near Ta'izz."

"You left for what reason?" he asks.

She glances around again and lowers her voice. "A drone, killed an Al-Qaeda leader, but also killed my family who were following in another car and ran into the wreckage."

"Sorry," Sa'id says, then whispers. "The infidel will pay, *inshallah*."

"*Inshallah*. If Allah wills it. We must not speak more." Then she returns her attention to her phone.

"Do you have shore leave?" he asks, persistently.

She glances back up at him. "I do, beginning at nine this morning, but…"

"There is a nice mosque in Bilbao. I could take you there. There is a square near the pier. Three blocks. I will be in the square."

"Only if none of our group are about," she says, and flashes him a quick smile.

"I will wait there."

"Mumin will kill us," she says, in a mutter.

"Mumin will not know. He doesn't leave the ship."

"Inshallah," she says, but doesn't look convinced.

WE AWAKE DOCKED AT BILBAO, Spain. When the little princess rises, we'll be off to see the Guggenheim Museum, have lunch, then take a driving tour of the city. I like having a client who sleeps in as it gives me time to enjoy my travelling companion. It's almost as good a workout as going to the gym.

All my retired military buddies are off with their spouses to take in the wonders, so I breakfast with Connie and kill time until I'm shocked by my wrist alarm going off. I haven't heard it since I first tested it, and it makes me leap out of my chair.

I bolt for the stairway, take the stairs four at a time, reach our deck and palm the Glock 19 that's in my middle-of-back holster under my loose shirt. I am surprised to see the kids all gathered around the door to Simone's suite, and they're laughing it up. The heat begins creeping my backbone.

"What the hell," I growl as I slide to a stop.

Terry, the short dirty blond sax-player, is looking at his iPhone. "I win, one minute thirty-three seconds."

"Bullshit," Bryan says. "You had one and a half minutes, I had two and a half, Simone had three and Patty six. I win because it was over the time you choose."

"So," I interrupt. "Y'all had a little pool going on how fast I'd show." Then I get in Terry's face. "You win a friggin' knuckle sandwich if you don't get that stupid smile off your face."

They all laugh, if a little nervously. Simone sees how tight the skin is drawn on my face, and my jaw muscles working, and speaks up. "Hey, no biggie, Reardon. Just checking to see if you were on the job."

I give her a fake smile. "Okay, but let me tell you, fuck with me once and you're a fool, fuck with me twice and you've made a fool of me. I don't do fool well. So, do I have to mention that I'll put you all across my knee and blister your asses if you make a fool out of me?"

"You might be pretty tough," Bryan mumbles, but back steps as he does, "but you can't spank me."

"Don't be such an a-hole," Simone mutters, before I back Bry baby out onto the veranda.

I turn to her. "You saw me re-holster that Glock?"

"So."

"So, if some stranger had been in the hall near your doorway, looking like a bad guy, and scratched the side of his hip, I might have stitched four or five .40 cals up his sternum. Would you all have thought that real funny?"

"Okay, okay, okay," she says. "I get it. We won't..."

"You're fucking A right you won't, or you'll see a shit storm like you can't begin to imagine."

There's silence for a moment.

"Can I have that spanking now?" Patty says with a purr, I guess trying to lighten the mood.

23

I KNOW SHE'S TRYING TO BE FUNNY, BUT I STILL HAVE NOT SHED myself of the shot of adrenaline. "Patty, when I spank you, it'll be blisters and the last thing you'll feel is sexy."

"Kidding," she says, and pouts.

"Are y'all ready to go?" I ask.

"Give us ten," Simone says, and I leave and slam the cabin door behind me hard enough to blow the curtains on the sliding glass door out fluttering over the veranda.

I check my phone, see I have a signal, and call Connie. "Ten minutes," I say, then look up to see her at the end of the corridor, her phone to her ear, her hand in a slot in her purse, I presume caressing her .380. She's backing me up.

I do like that woman.

Bilbao is a north-facing harbor at the mouth of a river that winds through a wide canyon surrounded by hills. A beautiful city, but one with its share of spray-can art, much of which proclaims, "no king." I guess that's the current cause in Basque country. Painting is better than bombing, which Basque separatists have been known to do.

The Guggenheim, in a serene location next to the river, was designed by renowned architect Frank O. Gehry. The museum is flowing titanium tiles and limestone, more a sculpture of a roiling surf than a building. The plan was to have it reflect Bilbao's heritage with its suggestion of maritime shapes and sails. I read the building is covered with more than 35,000 titanium tiles and pieces of glass strategically placed to catch the natural light. It's wild and fascinating. I've always heard the first rule of Architecture is form follows function, but I guess if a building is supposed to be a work of art itself, that doesn't matter so much.

It's well worth seeing.

As has become our normal, the kids stay together and the hired help follows at a discrete distance—Gretchen, Connie and me.

There's a spindly sculpture of a spider, twenty feet tall, outside the museum and walking under and between its ugly legs sends chills down my back. I'd prefer a butterfly, but that's just me.

That said, when it comes to art, give me Degas—who the museum also features—Winslow Homer or Andrew Wyeth. Those guys knew a camelhair brush from a whisk broom.

I'm glad I tolerated the modern scribbles as the day redeemed itself with a late lunch at Zortziko, and I love Basque food. Nevada is also blessed with it, as, it too, is sheep country. My baby squid with peppers and scallops, washed down with a good red, mellows my mood. And Connie stroking my calf, snaking toes up under my pant leg, fires my mood back up again. My appetite is rekindled, but not for food.

However again we are sabotaged as a gaggle of paparazzi awaits when we exit.

So, it's back to work. Luckily, the gaggle is made up of fairly-respectable jerks who keep some distance. And none of them dive a hand into Simone's purse.

HARRY ADMIRES HER. Felicia is onto something with the German shepherd doubling as a seeing eye dog. She begins working the ship a deck at a time, one end to the other. Tonight, they've arranged for Chang to escort her through the crew living area, the kitchen, laundry, shops, and engine room. He's violating ISP rules as no one, other than assigned crew, is allowed in the engine area.

The only hit the dog shows early on is sniffing Mumin, who's dozing on a chaise lounge near the pool. The dogs sits and barks, six inches from the man who comes violently awake and lurches to his feet. He's holding a hand to his chest, panting, as if he's having a heart attack.

Harry and Angelina are nearby, acting as if they, too, are merely enjoying the sun.

"What the fucking hell…" Mumin shouts.

"Sorry," Chang says. As Mumin is wearing a see-through net shirt and swimming trunks, it's pretty-obvious he doesn't have a vest stuffed with explosives ready to detonate.

"Get that filthy animal away from me," he commands. Chang is not surprised as he knows Muslims will tolerate dogs only if they function for guarding house or livestock.

"So, so sorry." Chang says, and acts as if he's helping Felicia away.

When they are out of sight, Felicia turns to him. "That was a hit. What's up?"

"He's one of our three known, and who we know handled the C4, so the hit obviously was residue."

"Then let's keep moving."

While they work all the public areas, Chang's number two, Peter Zucker, has used the sulfur bomb scam again to clear the crew sleeping area, and he watches the corridor while Felicia's partner, Ronnie Alberto, replaces the C4 with four pounds of yellow play dough that's nearly the same color.

They all meet later in Chung's office. While Angelina keeps tabs on Mumin, Harry continues the argument with the head of security. Since Buster made no more discoveries, he wants to immediately arrest Sa'id, Mumin and Mohamid. Harry again talks him out of it, with Felicia and Ronaldo 'Ronnie' Alberto chiming in.

Ronaldo, who's the explosive expert, explains, "The C4 is an easy hit for Buster. Cartridges, hand grenades, or even cannon shells, not so much. Isis and Al-Qaeda love to construct their IED's from artillery rounds, well-sealed, scrubbed and dried and scrubbed again, hard to detect. I don't know how much you know about the problem?"

"Not much," Chang admits.

"Okay, here's the quick and dirty. IEDs and other bombs are constructed and activated in a number of ways.

"Radio controlled, the trigger for a radio-controlled improvised explosive device is controlled by radio link. The receiver is connected to an electrical firing circuit and the transmitter operated by the perp from a long way off. One of those cheap handheld Motorola radios will do the job but are not desirable as the signal is much too common. A signal from the transmitter causes the receiver to trigger a firing pulse that operates the switch. Usually the switch fires an initiator; however, the output may also be used to remotely arm an explosive circuit. Often the transmitter and receiver operate on a matched coding system that prevents the device from being initiated by random radio frequency signals or jamming. A device can be triggered from any number of different mechanisms including car alarms, wireless doorbells, cell phones, pagers and radios. Even those hot new Ring doorbells would work nicely.

"Mobile phones, like the ones you found, are common actuators and receivers. A radio-controlled IED incorporates a mobile phone that is modified and connected to an electrical firing circuit. Mobile phones operate in the UHF band in line of sight with base transceiver station antennae sites. In the common scenario, receipt of a paging signal by phone is sufficient to initiate the IED firing circuit. Not likely at sea as you're out of range of towers, but when close to shore, as we are now...

"Then, of course, there are victim operated. A booby-trap. Sometimes operated by simple movement, sometimes a trip wire, sometimes pressure such as a butt in a car seat. Or releasing pressure by opening a mailed well-wrapped package.

"Then we have the infrared devices. Perfected by the IRA in the early nineties, many used against the invading forces in Iraq... actually thanks to our friends, the Brits, who inadvertently passed the method to the IRA who, in turn, trained the PLO, the Palestinians, who of course trained the rest of the Muslim world.

"And, of course, hardest to defend against, is the suicide bomber. Enough?" he asks Chang.

"Damn sure enough. More than I wish I knew. I've now got my bachelor's degree in IED's, thanks to you. Now I hope I don't get my masters by being the victim of one."

"Buster is our first line of defense," Felicia says, then adds, "tonight let's see what, if anything, he hits on in the crew's quarters, the storage areas, or the kitchen and cold rooms. Then we talk again."

24

CHANG SIGHS DEEPLY. "YOU SPOOKS HAVE YOUR ROW TO HOE AND I have mine. Yes, my office tells me to play second fiddle in this and, against my wishes, refuses to evacuate the ship. But, I God-dang guarantee you, if this all goes south, the pricks…I mean the ladies and gentlemen…in the home office will scatter like quail when blame-time comes."

Felicia smiles and gives Chang a pat on the forearm. "Then let's circumvent anything untoward happening. I'd like to make another round of the ship."

Chang nods, "I fear disarming these four bombs is only the beginning. And that lecture only elevates my fear."

"All the more reason…" Harry says, "…to keep hunting without putting the enemy on notice we're on to them."

"Go to work," Chang says, and puts his face in his hands.

Harry, the last one to leave, turns back and asks, "How is this tub powered?"

"A pair of Wartsila dual fuel engines. Why?"

"What do you mean, dual fuel?"

"She carries three hundred fifty thousand gallons of diesel and three hundred cubic meters of LPG."

"LPG?"

"LPG, liquid natural gas. Why?"

Harry takes a deep breath. "Because she's a fucking bomb, that's why?"

Chang immediately goes into a canned speech. "No way. The onboard LPG system consists of two bunker stations, two horizontal LPG storage tanks, cryogenic, vacuum-insulated, stainless steel, total gas volume three hundred cubic meters. She has double-walled bunkering lines, pipelines that are acid-proof stainless steel, special pipe fittings, gas distribution system, steam boilers. All the electrical equipment is certified explosion-proof. This is the safest..."

"Are you through with the corporate bullshit?" Harry asks.

Chang shrugs and looks a little sheepish.

Harry continues. "So, what happens with an explosive strapped to one of those LPG tanks?"

Harry is not surprised when Chang flushes and suddenly looks heated. His hands ball into fists. "We have lots of failsafe..."

"Nothing I've ever come across in damn near thirty years of this kind of duty has ever been proven fail safe."

"No one's allowed access..."

"I hate to keep interrupting you, but let me ask you a question? Do you think your number two, Zucker, will hand over a key if a *haji* has an AK shoved up your ass, or his? Or maybe has the ship's captain hanging upside down with jumper cables hooked to his gonads."

"You're right. Nothing is failsafe. I should arrest those three..."

"And not find the guy who has the next bomb. We've neutralized the first threat. Stop with the CYA and let's save this tub from a visit to Davy Jones' locker."

"With luck there's only those four bombs," Chang says.

"From your lips to God's ears," Harry says, quietly. "I'm going back up to relieve Angelina watching Mumin. Any word on the missing crewman?"

"I may have to report him overboard if he doesn't show by the end of the day."

Harry shakes his head. "I presume that's protocol?"

"Twenty-four hours, since no one saw him go overboard, if he did. Let's hope he snuck off the boat here after hiding out. With luck he filched some old fart's Rolex and beat a trail."

"But it won't change the day-to-day onboard ship?"

"No. The *Maritime Gendarmerie,* the French Coast Guard, will search north of Spain, and the Spanish Coast Guard, *La Guardia Costera,* will do a search from the line to here in Bilbao, but we'll charge on, on schedule."

"How many access doors are there to the LPG storage tanks?"

"Two watertight fire heavy duty hatchways with key locks."

"So, you could station a man inside with instructions not to open under any circumstance?"

"Keys work both inside and out. We could chain the doors from the inside and prevent easy access. The hell of it is, the fuel lines run through that compartment's walls to the engine room and if those were blown, they'd become the world's largest blow torch and melt everything for yards and yards. We'd likely all be blown to hell."

"Let me check on Angelina then maybe you could give me a tour?"

"I'll be right here, worrying."

Harry chuckles and hurries out.

SIMONE HAS MADE friends with the kids doing the shows, impressed with their ABBA retrospective she hunts them down and they are thrilled to join her for a drink in the aft bar. I'm not surprised when she agrees to go on stage tonight and sing a couple of the songs from her new album.

And I see another reason for Gretchen, as she doubles as wardrobe and makeup.

Simone's a good promoter has the crowd loving her, and I'm not surprised. It will, however, make my job even more difficult. Half the folks on the ship have no idea who she is—and a few of the older ones wouldn't know her from Adam's off ox if she introduced herself—but now nearly everyone on board will know a famous young singer is among them.

Anonymity is my friend, but no longer.

Actually it's kind of a hoot as Connie and I have to go backstage to watch over our charge, and the kids in the show and stage crew are great.

For the first time I see what Simone sees in Bryan Cox and Terry Von Riche. I wouldn't be surprised, after hearing Bryan on the sticks, that he could do a damn good job with *Sing, Sing, Sing*. And the short dude with the stringy dirty-blond hair wails on the sax and could give Kenny G. a run for his money...maybe even Charlie Parker. And Simone is surprisingly generous, giving both long solos. And Patty, along with the four kids employed, sings backup. I'm impressed.

It's a night at sea between Bilbao, Spain, and Lisbon, Portugal. I don't have to worry about several million Frenchmen or Spaniards or even a few Basque terrorists, only about three hundred plus passengers and three hundred or so crewmen.

The kids and their new friends close up La Terrazza, the Deck Seven Italian restaurant, and are safely tucked in just before midnight. Connie has been in our stateroom reading and I'm surprised is still not only awake, but dressed, and invites me back to The Promenade Lounge for a nightcap. And I'm pleased to see General Bull Tolliver and the limey, Nelson, are still at it. He waves us over and we join them.

They both rise, as true military gentlemen would when a lady approaches the table.

"Glad you stumbled in," Bull says, then leans over and whispers in my ear as Alistair and Connie engage in conversation. "Can I talk frankly in front of your lady?"

"Anything you can say to me you can say in front of Connie."

He clears his throat and gets all our attention. "I heard a couple of ship employees talking, and it seems we're missing a crew member. Likely overboard."

25

"That's terrible," Connie says, just learning the ship is missing a crew member, likely gone overboard.

"What's terrible about it is they think it was foul play."

"Funny you should say that," Connie says, "as I overheard some interesting comments. Of course, being a blonde, they'd never suspect I speak Arabic..."

"The devil you say," Alistair says.

"And French, a smattering of Breton, and passable Farsi. I can understand a bit of Mandarin but couldn't find the loo on a bet."

We men all laugh, then she continues. "These two were blathering on, continually glancing over their shoulders as if concerned about being overheard, and said something, in very low voices about meeting up with a freighter. Why the devil..."

"That's bloody strange," Alistair says.

"I don't like it," I say, then add, "how about we all pay a little extra attention. I'd hate to play *Achille Lauro.* That would screw up a nice trip." I turn back to Connie. "Do you remember exactly what they said?"

"All I got was 'when we meet with the freighter.' Then I heard a name, Amir Al-Karim, I think."

I nod. "Suggest you run that by some of your old chums."

"Old chums?" Bull asks.

"Connie was fifteen years with the Company—CIA."

Alistair offers, "And I have a mate with MI5. Should I…"

"Better safe than sorry," Bull says, then laughs. "What the hell do we pay taxes for?"

"Let's meet in The Restaurant for breakfast," Bull suggests. "Say 0900?"

"I can," I say, "presuming my client is not yet up."

Bull nods, then cautions us. "Let's keep this to ourselves, other than Willy and Elroy—the other military types."

We all nod and agree.

Bull adds, "We're probably being paranoid, but what the hell. It doesn't pay to be blindsided."

As Connie and I are taking the elevator to our cabin floor, two dark skinned fellows join us. They look as if they could be Syrian or Saudi, and both are in work clothes, uniforms. So, I can help but ask, "Working aboard."

I get a smile from them and, "Yes, sir. Welders."

"Aw, a great trade. Electric or gas?" I ask.

"Gas, sir."

"Good for you," I say, in a complementary fashion, then ask, "Philippines, right?"

"Yes, sir. And you?" one asks.

"Nevada, USA."

"Aw, Las Vegas, always wished to go there."

"Exciting place," I say, and we reach our floor and wave as we exit.

Connie and I head back to our stateroom, and she steps out on the veranda and gets on the SAT phone to her old friend at the CIA.

"It's a little after nine P M in DC," I caution her.

"Janice is a night owl. I could call at midnight."

Her friend Janice Toynbee answers on the first ring.

Connie must know her very well as she doesn't even bother with hello. "Big favor, you up for one?" she asks. Then throws out the name. "Amir Al-Karim." Pauses listening, then adds. "Yeah, I'm on a cruise ship, *Blue Pearl,* with that hunk I told you about." Pauses again, "Owe you, kiddo." Pauses again, eying me with a wink. "Yeah, he's a stud. Talk tomorrow." And rings off.

"Stud hunk, eh?" I say with a laugh. "I guess it's not too late to prove it?"

She flashes me a smile that's a good enough answer.

LISBON IS a way up River Tejo. I've heard and read quite a bit about Lisbon, knowing it was neutral during the big war. Hell, I watched Casablanca and know half the world was trying to escape the Nazis by reaching the Portuguese capitol. I've travelled quite a bit, but usually with an AR15 at hand. Other than the sand box, I've been to North Korea, Estonia, Latvia, Russia, Montenegro, Italy and Paraguay, Mexico and Canada, of course, and a few of the Caribbean Islands. This is the first time I've traveled as even a semi-tourist. I hope the trip ends that way.

We're docked, so no tender necessary to transport us ashore.

Simone, via her travel agent had hired a guide for the four kids, ignoring Connie and me and, Gretchen, her own lady-in-waiting.

Luckily, I learned of her failure to accommodate her bodyguard well ahead of time and was able to book another car from the same provider. We are to tour the city, all seven hills of Lisbon and several of their monuments. Portugal is, or was, the home of the great navigators including Vasco de Gama who discovered Europe's first sea route to spice-rich India. I will tell you that was a hell of a feat, rounding the horn of Africa in a ship pegged together and glued with stuff made from horse hooves.

I'm impressed with the city with its mix of the historic and the modern, and with the people, who everywhere have a smile and helping hand, if asked.

We lunched at a local's joint by the harbor and if anyone recognized Miss Simone no one so much as took a picture, so it was an easy day.

We're back to the ship for a welcome nap after stomping over cathedrals and monuments and ending up with a stroll down a high-end street where Simone drops a couple of thou and Connie buys a blouse for thirty-five Euros. That's my girl.

I'm glad we wore the kids out, and that Connie and I had a rest, as tonight it's Fado in the old city, thankfully near the ship.

I challenge Simone before she disappears into her cabin as to how we're getting to the clubs and am surprised. "Walk," she says, and closes the door in my face.

We're scheduled out at 8:00 p.m., so Connie and I get an hour of shuteye, then order in the room. The ship will bring you anything, anytime, to your cabin, so I knock off a filet and fries and she downs a slab of salmon and a salad. We both refrain from boozing as we'll be shadowing the kids until they crash.

The last two ports have been lax with security and have had screeners, but we've walked right past them. I'm tempted to shove Connie's little .380 in an ankle holster but decide my stun gun and mace, backed by Connie's, will be more than enough should we get mobbed.

Fado is American blues but even more morose. I happen to love jazz, really like the blues, and am impressed with what I hear. The singer, Fadista she's called, is accompanied by a twelve-string guitar but with a round body like a mandolin and other instruments, all strings, that must be of Portuguese origin. Simone seems to be studying every vocalization and riff. The singer rolls into the first word of the next verse as if bemoaning every word of the last one. To be truthful, I didn't know there were as many sad songs as we heard in the first two bars we passed through.

The third is much larger than the first two intimate ones, and I see Simone slip a hundred Euro bill to the bouncer, and, of course, she, Patty, Bryan and Terry are escorted to a table next to the dance floor, which also serves as a stage. A singer in a bright red full skirt and blouse that hides little is moving around the floor from table to table while the three-piece string pickers are seated nearby.

She finishes one song, moves to Simone and stops and stares, and I can't hear but can see her mouth Simone, which makes our girl smile as if she just won the lottery. The singer grabs Simone by the hand and pulls her to her feet. She's wearing a wireless mike and even though there must be a hundred and fifty people in the room, she commands them to silence, and is quickly successful. Then she introduces Simone in both English and Portuguese. The crowd applauds and the singer gives Simone a little bow, asks her something and gets a shake of the head—I presume asking if she wants to sing--then lets her return to her seat as a round of the strong Portuguese cherry liquor, ginjinha, is served.

It's a dozen songs, with me having to pay much closer attention as now everyone in the place knows there's a famous American singer in the place. So, I've left Connie and Gretchen at a table, six tables from the stage, and positioned myself near an exit that's only separated by one table from the kids.

The singer and the three string guys take a break, and I'm surprised by a Benny Goodman recording of *Moon Glow* blaring from a Deejay that I can now see behind a glass across the room. His little cove was dark during the Fado, but now is brightly lit.

Many of these Portuguese guys are built like the proverbial brick outhouses, and I quickly learn are not shy, as two rise from a table of six across the dance floor and move to Simone and Patty. It's clear they want to dance.

26

THE DANCE FLOOR HAS A DOZEN OTHER COUPLES BY THE TIME they've extended hands to the girls. Asking for a dance is no harm, no foul, but I'm surprised when Simone jumps up, giggling, and follows a guy with a bull neck, a square head with flattop haircut from the fifties, equally my size, onto the floor. Patty is not to be left behind, and she's quickly nuzzled up to some longshoreman from the nearby docks in stretch jeans so tight his unit is outlined. Both guys are in muscle-fuck tee-shirts and wear them well.

There's one empty chair at a table near the kids so I sidle forward and motion to the couples at the table. They wave the chair away. I drag it between Bry and Simone's chair.

"Where the fuck have you been?" Bry snaps.

"Near, why?"

"Because some lout dragged Simone on the dance floor, that's why."

"The lout asked her to dance and she accepted. Should I shoot him between the eyes?"

He puffs up but shuts up, and I keep an eye on the girls. The song ends and Simone gives the no-neck a smile and nod and starts back for the table, but he has her by the wrist and jerks her to a halt.

I rise but wait to see how it plays out. Patty's partner is more polite, and she returns, but the longshoreman remains standing near no-neck and Simone, and she's beginning to look less than happy.

Another Benny Goodman song begins, but this one is not exactly a dance tune. One of my favorites, *Sing, Sing, Sing,* with Gene Krupa doing a long drum solo.

Simone tries to pull away, but no-neck hangs on and begins to drag her toward the table where another four muscle-fuck tee-clad dudes are laughing and pointing at no neck and my charge.

Before I can reach them, Simone is actually looking over her shoulder as if she's happy I'm dogging her trail.

She sees me coming and sets her heels, but the big boy is easily dragging her along. He's three quarters facing away when I catch up, and my short punch to his kidney with my right doesn't drop him, but he releases Simone and turns to face me. He's a little green in the gills. It's not him, but his longshoreman buddy who tries an overhand right at me. I see it coming and see the other four at the table leap to their feet.

I slip the longshoreman's wild haymaker, step into him and have pulled my little stun gun—smaller than a pack of Lucky Strikes—from my pocket as the odds are bad. He catches me with part of a backhand as he recovers from the roundhouse, but it doesn't keep me from stepping into him and upper cutting the stun gun into his crotch. It's that electric welder screech and turns everyone's eyes our way. His eyes roll back in their sockets and his head bounces on the wooden dance floor—a rat tat tat—as he hits the floor like a felled pine tree. Had it been concrete he might never have gotten up. His girlfriend, if he has one, is going to be disappointed with their love life for a month or so.

No-neck is pretty damn tough as he's recovered and catches me with a glancing right to the cheekbone that rocks me a little, but I duck the roundhouse left—this guy doesn't know from a straight punch—step in and catch him on the side with the stun gun. Quickly two of the offenders are on the floor, wondering what hit them.

But there are four more closing from across the dance floor, then to my surprise I think one of them has slipped on something as he hits the floor flat on his face. Then I see Connie is behind him, now looking for another target with her stun gun. One of the other tee-shirts has seen her drop his buddy and charges her but is stopped six feet away by a spray of mace, and he joins the other three on the floor, but he's squirming like a cat with its tail under the rocking chair. The two-remaining tee-shirts have wised up and are backing away.

As quickly as she appeared, Connie has slipped back into the crowd. As I get to Simone's table all of them are on their feet.

"Let's go," I snap.

"Look out," Simone says, and I turn to see the bouncer who'd been at the door, closing the distance like a torpedo. I hold out my hand, giving him a flat palm and a sign to stop, and he does.

I zap zap zap the crackling stun gun with one hand, which lights up the room like a small burst of lightning, and he extends both hands flat palm out and backs away.

Just to give him some comfort I flash the brass, my bail enforcement officer's badge—worthless as one from a Cracker Jack box here—and would yell "police" but I've failed to learn what the cops are called in Portugal.

And who the hell cares, as we're moving to the door and are

out in the street without further discussion, and Simone says, "Enough for tonight."

She leads the way the six blocks back to the ship.

Connie sidles up to me and dabs my cheekbone with a hanky.

"You're bleeding," she says, and I realize he split my cheek a little with that lucky backhand.

"Keeps you healthy, cleaning out the pipes," I say, and give her a wink.

"You know, hot shot, you could likely have talked us out of that one. You weren't showing off for the little girls, were you?"

"No, to the second and 'maybe' to the talk our way out, and I could have worn one of those chairs like a horse collar if I hadn't moved quickly."

But she's shaking her head. "Discretion is most often the better part of valor."

She's pissing me off as I'm pretty damn happy we got out of that whole. "You be discreet, I'll be deadly, if you don't mind."

"Everybody's got to be something," she says, and I realize she's a little pissed as well.

My tone is a little harsh, "Would you be chastising me if we were driving, and I swerved the car and avoided a head on collision?"

"What kind of silly question is that?"

"Answer the silly question."

"Of course not."

"Well, I likely avoided us, at least me, getting the dog do kicked out of me with me ending up in the hospital and you pining away at the end of my bed for a month, which is the same thing as avoiding that head-on collision."

She shakes her head. "First, I don't pine. Second, did you graduate from UFUL?"

"UFUL?"

"Yes, the university of fucked-up logic."

"Summa cum laude," I say, but she merely shakes her head, still pissed.

SHE'S PISSED, but she does take time to fashion a butterfly bandage and close the half-inch split in my cheek before we turn in. But I get nothing but her back when we hit the sack.

We sleep a little far apart for the first time since the first time.

Connie has an encrypted text before we have our morning coffee. Janice Toynbee reports that Amir Al-Karim is the owner of the one-hundred-two-foot cargo vessel *Bit Tawfīq*, whose normal range is the North African coast from Alexandria to Casablanca.

"So," I ask, "what does *bit tawfig* mean? Death to America?"

She laughs, and I'm glad she's got her sense of humor back. "No, actually it means good luck."

"And what does *Bit Tawfig* haul? Nuclear arms, biological weapons..."

"No, silly. Wheat and other grains. Cotton...harmless stuff."

"Well, the food is damn sure too good on this tub to be loading wheat for gruel and the mattresses don't need another stuffing of cotton, so are you sure you heard something about meeting up with this small cargo tub?"

"Pretty darn sure."

As we're talking, another text arrives from Janice. Connie reads it, then re-reads it, then looks up, biting her lip.

"What?" I ask.

"Janice was called in to the Director's office and questioned about why she'd done a search on the ship. Then when our names came up... It seems someone there knows you and your, to use her term, questionable activities."

"So what?"

"They've asked me to get in touch with another passenger, Harry Drummond."

"For what reason? Why the hell would the CIA..."

"I don't know, he's been advised I'll contact him."

"Then let's go find Harry."

"Just me."

Now it's my turn to laugh. "My feelings are hurt. After all I've done for the Company."

"You've got work to do. The girls will be at the pool. Looks like a beautiful day."

"Fine. You go find Harry Bond...Bond, Harry Bond," I do a lousy imitation of Sean Connery, "and I'll go to breakfast and wait to be summoned by the little princess, but come find me and fill me in."

"I didn't say he was an agent."

"Okay, you didn't say. I presume he's the pizza cook on board. Go find him."

"If it's anything..."

"Why don't you just call and ask the desk to put you through."

"You really think I should have this conversation on a ship line?"

"Like I said, go find Harry."

I'm pleased she heads for the bathroom and not out the door in her skimpy nighty. I'd have to fight off half the ship.

27

LIKE MIKE AND CONNIE, HARRY AND ANGELINA HAVE JUST climbed out of the sack, but in separate rooms. Harry was awakened by the telltale ring of his office calling on his SAT phone, which he's left on the floor near the slightly open slider. He's quickly informed of Connie's presence on board and of Mike Reardon and of Reardon's former association with the Company—even though he'd been operating as a private mercenary and covered with the cloak of plausible deniability. As Connie is a former trusted employee, Harry's told to read Nordstrom and Reardon in on a need-to-know basis, without letting anyone else on board know they have any relationship to Harry. He's texted a picture of each of them and informed that Constance Nordstrom will be having coffee at the Panorama Lounge at 0830, expecting contact.

Angelina showers and dresses quickly as Harry has suggested she alone makes the meet—the less obtrusive they can appear, the better—and arranges for all of them to get together when and where it can be accomplished without calling attention. Reardon included, if and only if, Nordstrom feels it safe to read Reardon into what intel Harry is willing to share. While she's gone, he contemplates advising the ship's security officer, Chang, and decides not to do so.

The Panorama lounge is high on Deck Eight and forward, a half-round room that serves only coffee and sweet rolls in the morning, and the first place on the ship to serve anything. However, you can get anything in the ship's larder as room service any time day or night.

Angelina enters to see only seven others in the Panorama Lounge, all of them older blue-hair couples except for one beautiful blond who she immediately recognizes as Constance Nordstrom. Only one table separates her from another couple, and as Angelina gets coffee and a roll from an informal self-service counter, she listens carefully and notes the couple nearest are speaking English—U.K. accented English at that. As she and Harry were texted a quick background on Connie, she knows Nordstrom is fluent in Farsi, so she approaches and asks in the Iranian language, "You seem to be alone, may I join you?"

"Of course," Connie answers in Farsi, and Angelina sits, and they make small talk for a while. The rest in the room pay little attention, including the two attendants who are serving and bussing tables.

When Angelina is sure no one is close enough to hear, she leans close, "When and where can we get together to talk?"

"Mike is working, as I'm sure you know..."

"We know little of your reason to be on this cruise."

"He's got a bodyguard gig. A young very, well known singer."

"I saw her at the pool, signing a few autographs. When can Reardon get free...that is, if you think he should be read in on our mission?"

"He's as trustworthy as it gets, but he's tethered to his client whenever she's out of her cabin."

"Then it might be best if only you meet with Harry and me?"

"Fine. Time and place?"

"We're in suite 717. The sooner the better."

"Fifteen minutes?" Connie suggests.

"I'll take the forward elevators. Suggest you take the aft."

Connie stands and sticks out a hand and says, in English loud enough for others to hear, "Nice meeting you. Enjoy the cruise."

Angelina shakes hands without rising and finishes her coffee as Connie leaves.

When Connie finishes and gives herself five minutes to make her appointment, she waves to the attendants and hurries out to the aft elevator. She's not surprised that the door is ajar when she reaches 717. She glances both ways, then quickly enters and closes the door behind.

Harry and Angelina await, and Harry meets her with an extended hand.

"Have we met before?" he asks, with a curious look.

She studies him a moment, then, "Three years ago, a conference on Israel, Iraq and Syria. You gave a presentation, as Harry Weinberg."

He smiles. "Well, nice to be remembered." He nods Angelina's way. "We're both Drummond on this cruise. Coffee?"

"Sure."

They take seats around a small coffee table, with a view of the passing ocean out the sliding glass door.

Angelina smiles and reassures her, "You can speak freely. I sweep this cabin twice daily."

"So, what's up? What's got Langley's panties in a twist?"

"First," Harry replies, "this Reardon chap has never been part of the family?"

"Independent contractor, but who's done great service to the country. I worked with him when he made an incursion into North Korea and kicked some serious ass for Uncle Sam. Trust me, you can trust him."

"Trust, but verify," Harry said, with a smile and a nod.

"I'd bet my life on him," Connie said, returning the smile, but a more serious one.

"You may be doing so right now. We are onto, we believe, a plot to either blow this boat to hell or possibly to hold all passengers hostage."

"Perps?" Connie asks.

"Arab, Muslim, terrorists, as usual. Al Shabaab, we think."

"A high-jacking from outside, Somali style? We're to be stormed by pirates?"

"Inside, at least to begin with. The crew. We're onto three of them and have subverted four of pounds of plastic, without them knowing it, but think there's more, maybe much more."

"So, why haven't you called in the cavalry?"

"These are crazies as only these Al Shabaab types can be. If they see it coming, they'll trigger whatever is still out there. The good news is John Chang, ship security, is up to speed and is protecting the obvious..."

"Which is?" Connie asks.

"This ship is dual fueled, diesel and LPG, the diesel, of course, is as safe as fuel can be. The LPG is another story altogether."

She's quiet for a few seconds, contemplating that. "How many infiltrators do you think there are?"

Harry gives her a tight smile. "The crew is over two hundred fifty strong. Both our folks and MI5 are working hard to vet them, but we have over twenty possible...maybe more."

"Interesting, as I overheard some comments by the crew that may be of interest."

"And?"

"I have reason to believe they plan to meet up with a small freighter and could board a hundred more if so."

"Name?"

"I overheard the name Amir Al-Karim, checked with a friend who was called in by the director and who instructed us to get together. Amir Al-Karim owns a small freighter..."

"We have it all," he smiles, "just verifying it came from you."

"And," Connie asks, "we haven't sunk that tub because?"

Harry laughs again. "You're not a hawk are you, Miss Nordstrom? We don't normally sink vessels from other countries unless we're attacked. And this ship has not done so. We do have a drone watching her every movement or will as soon as she's located."

Connie shrugs. "So, should I advise Reardon to get his client off the ship? After all..."

"If we start bailing out, I'm sure these crazies will put this vessel on the bottom if they still have the capability. Even if not, if they have twenty shooters on board, this could make the thirty-two innocents in Brussels or forty-nine in Orlando look like a cake walk. We have six hundred souls on board, including the crew."

"We're planning to ease folks off at Malaga, our next stop. Over two hundred passengers have shore excursions scheduled. Fifty or more of the crew will be ashore. Spanish authorities have been asked, without any indication it's a true operation, to invite our people in country, but will not allow our Special Ops boys in, so that means we rely on them if and when we're forced to do so. So far, we don't feel we can chance a leak from either the cruise line or Spanish. The cruise line has been advised, but only the very top people."

"I have to read Reardon in on all of it."

"Your call. But remember, loose lips sink ships."

"Between you and me, he goes nowhere without hardware. He has refrained from carrying anything that would be picked up by scanners going on and off the ship."

"Good," Harry says. "God willing, no one will need to palm anything more than an ID to disembark."

"God willing," Connie repeats, thanks them for the coffee and heads for the door.

Harry calls after her, "Keep your ears open and watch for anything out of order."

"I will. By the way, Mike's been hobnobbing with some ex-military types who may be old but are damn sure experienced and likely willing."

"Keep them in the dark for now. Loose lips and all that."

She nods, and leaves.

28

Sa'id & Alia were able to meet in Bilbao, both found themselves infatuated with each other, and had to be very careful not to make that fact obvious to Mumin. Sa'id, in particular, knew Mumin to be a zealot, and it is not wise to upset a zealot, even if you're fairly zealous yourself. Still, Sa'id could not help but occasionally have an excuse to pass the poolside bar where Alia was busy bartending. He tried and tried to think of a way to speak to her without Mumin or anyone else seeing them together, but he could not figure a way. They were both off at the same time while the ship was docked in Lisbon, so maybe there. Sa'id's thoughts were wandering. Did he really want to give his life to the cause when for the first time he had a woman—a woman of virtue—who might spend her life with him?

Amir Al-Karim and the small one-hundred-two-foot cargo vessel *Bit Tawfīq* had enjoyed almost a month in the Algerian port of Oran, two hundred fifty miles west of Algiers, while being painted and refitted. She now had a deck house that extended twenty feet farther out onto what had been cargo area, and a new deckhouse on the aft. Her masts and outriggers that had served as cranes to move cargo had been removed, and one repositioned far aft. Her bright green paint, which had enjoyed the name Al-Karin, in bright blue and covering the loaded-freeboard in letters six feet high on both starboard and port had been painted out. Aft, her ship's name Al-Karin had been painted over and she was now *Bit Tawfīq*, the Arabic word for good luck, and under that name was the port of origin, Casablanca. Although Amir Al-Karim was still captain of the *Bit Tawfīq*, she was now owned by Sheik Ali Hassan. All was in preparation for *Azraq Zaraq*, Bloody Blue, the operation Hassan had been five years planning and executing.

Even though she was a rusted tub, Ali Hassan was over five hundred thousand American dollars into the ship, *Wahran*, and the armaments she now carried, and over that amount again in wages and arms for those aboard the *Blue Pearl*, the two who'd now been working for Crimson Cruise Line in the supply facilities in Civitavecchia, near Rome, and the produce broker in Bordeaux.

Well before the Blue Pearl reaches the mouth of the Med and Gibraltar, the *Bit Tawfīq* has moved out of her berth and headed for the planned rendezvous south and west of Malaga, Spain. She'd be at sea two days before she goes dead in the water at a spot ten miles southeast of the Spanish town of Sitio de Calahonda.

Peter Zucker, John Chung's number two security officer is on the other end of the line when John picks up the phone in his cabin. He checks the clock on his bed stand and sees it's a few minutes before 4:00 a.m.

"You must come to the office," Zucker says, his voice terribly strained, and John is immediately awake.

"What's up?"

"I can't say over the phone. Come quickly." Zucker disconnects.

John pulls on a track suit and running shoes without socks and hurries out. He jogs to the stairway and takes them three at a time. His office door is closed, and he bursts in. Zucker is face down on John's desk, face turned toward John, eyes open, but he's in a pool of blood.

Before John can speak, the door is slammed, and he realizes there are two crewmen behind him. He spins, but both fire suppressed handguns and he's blown across his desk but sinks to the floor as blood begins pumping from his chest wounds, then stops.

CAPTAIN HANS VAN GROOT is in the chartroom, just behind the bridge, when his First Mate appears in the doorway. His face is as white as the background of the chart the captain bends over.

"Yes?" Van Groot says, looking up from his chart. "How could we have had both engines shut down?"

"We have an event." And the first mate steps aside so the captain can see the tall thin black man standing behind, with a semiauto handgun leveled on his side.

"What is this?" Van Groot says, rising to his full six feet four inches.

"To the bridge, Captain," the black man commands.

Van Groot stomps on by, noting the two crewmen with long guns following the black man, and moves onto his bridge, where a helmsman is looking confused and says, "I was just coming for you, sir."

Before the helmsman sees the man with the gun, he eyes the captain and shrugs. "She doesn't respond to the helm, captain."

Mumin steps onto the bridge. "Your rudder controls have been destroyed. Your automatic systems have killed the engines as your fuel supply has been cut. You will now make an announcement."

"Get the hell off my bridge," Van Groot foolishly commands.

Mumin extends the handgun, and the roar of the Koch reverberates the wide thirty feet of glass overlooking the bow and sea ahead and fills the room with the stench of gunpowder. Van Groot stumbles back against his GPS screen, his hand on his chest, blood already seeping between his fingers, a very surprised look on his ruddy face, his ice blue eyes wide. He sinks to his knees then to his back. Blood bubbles from the hole in his chest as his hand slips away.

"Jesus Christ," First Mate Arnholt Armundsen says, stepping forward, but the muzzles of all three weapons wave him back.

"Go face the windows," Mumin orders, "Jesus Christ has no influence here." The first mate and apprentice officer retreat, but Armundsen cannot help but look over his shoulder.

"You will make an announcement," Mumin orders him.

"And if I don't?" Armundsen snaps, his face reddens with anger.

29

MUMIN STEPS FORWARD, STOOPS, AND PLACES THE MUZZLE OF HIS weapon against Van Groot's forehead, and pulls the trigger. The blast splatters gore—blood, bone and gray matter—in a semicircle over the deck behind Van Groot.

"My god!" Armundsen shouts.

"Your God is not in charge, praise Allah. Now, you will make an announcement! Ship wide. All males are to report to the showroom, all females to the main restaurant. Announce this is an emergency. They are to report immediately or will be shot by those who have taken over the ship."

There are two microphones on metal snakes and Armundsen moves to one and switches it on. "Emergency, emergency." Then he turns to Mumin, "Crew also?"

"Crew also."

Armundsen repeats. "Emergency, Emergency. All passengers and all crew report as follows: All females report to the main restaurant. All males report to the show lounge. Repeat, all passengers and all crew. Men to the show lounge, women to the main restaurant. This is not a request. This is an emergency order."

"Good. You will live a little longer," Mumin says.

Armundsen turns. "Many will be confused, and some will go to their lifeboat stations. Some will sleep through even this loud announcement. Some will refuse to leave their companions."

"And many will die," Mumin says, his sardonic smile returning.

WE'VE HAD two days and a night at sea and aren't due to arrive in Malaga until late this afternoon. I'm back to my normal pace as the kids are soaking up the sun, which seems to tire the little darlings and they hit the sack, or at least their suite, by ten. So, I'm awake at four and as usual can't sleep in—some say guilty conscience, but I prefer to think good old American initiative—so I'm up. This morning, I decide to make my darling happy—her conscience must be free of guilt as she can sleep until ten—and take our light laundry and head for the Laundromat. I should have no competition for the machines at this hour. The passenger laundry occupies a small area on Deck Three near the hatch to the engine room. That area off limits to us passengers.

The muffled roar of an explosion rocks the room slightly and I can feel the normal small shudder of the ship slowly grind to a stop. Not good. However, the washers and dryer still function so I go on with my task.

I hear the engine room hatch open and turn to see a ship's crewman, dark skinned, in coveralls standing in the doorway to the laundry.

It would not be disconcerting, except for the fact he's carrying an AK47 and motioning to me with the barrel, that and the familiar smell of cordite that's billowed out of the open engine hatch are both as unexpected and unwelcome as a cockroach in your shrimp cocktail.

"Back to suite," he says, motioning with the gun barrel again. He's a head shorter than me and I outweigh him by fifty or more pounds so I'm considering passing close and relieving him of the automatic and shoving it up his skinny ass, but then another AK47-carrying dipshit appears behind him.

I nod and give him a phony grin as I point to the machine. "My laundry?" I say, as if he doesn't have a weapon and I'm more concerned about my socks and shorts and Connie's pink and blue lace valuables than I am the rifle.

"Leave. Go now," he says and is growing a little impatient. So, I move. He's no experienced law enforcement or military officer as he has to raise the muzzle of the rifle to let me pass. I could have easily booted him back through the door or into his amigo, and stuffed them both into a dryer, but I have other responsibilities—Connie and my charge, Simone, not to speak of the other smartass kids.

So, I head for the elevator, with the two armed crewmen close behind. Are these crewmen part of ship security? If so, I could understand sidearms, but AK47s on an American-registered ship? Don't think so. They ride with me in an elevator so tight only one of them can keep the barrel in my gut, then to my cabin door and let me disappear inside, with an admonition, "Wait for instructions. Do not leave suite, or you will be shot dead."

Wow is that ever bad public relations for Crimson Cruise Line. I can't wait for that form asking how I enjoyed the cruise.

"Connie," I yell, as the door shuts behind me. "Time to rise and shine."

She rubs her eyes, stretches, then eyes the clock. "What the heck? It's five A M."

"Yep, time to lock and load."

"What?" she questions, rubbing her eyes.

I don't have to expound. About the time she sits up in bed, the announcement to report to the show lounge for the men and the restaurant for the ladies, rings through the ship, awaking most who are vacationing, not expecting to be awakened at proverbial gunpoint.

Then even to my surprise, the announcement continues in another voice. "We are soldiers of Allah. You are all infidels and will die by gunfire or beheading if you don't do exactly what I command. Women shall have their heads covered and scarves over face as appropriate for the faithful. And all garments shall be buttoned at the neck. If you have no long garments you will devise them from bedclothes upon your return to your cabin, or you shall not leave the cabins again. Men shall wear no coats and have shirts tucked in. Your suites will soon be searched and all alcohol, identification, and valuables, confiscated."

Of course, closely following the announcement, my wrist alarm goes off. I'm pretty sure Simone and crew will have a different attitude than the last time I showed up, if I can figure out how to do so.

HARRY AND ANGELINA, traveling as the Drummonds, come awake with the announcement and are in their robes, meeting in the living area of the suite.

"Looks like we waited a little too long," Harry says.

"Water under the bridge. What now?" Angelina replies.

He grabs the phone and tries John Chung, head of ship security, and gets no answer. "Looks like we're on our own," he mutters, then adds, "better at least wake some folks up." He digs into the desk drawer, palms the SAT phone, heads out on the veranda, and gets the emergency response number in Langley. A recording of course, so he announces, "Harry Weinstein aboard the cruise ship *Blue Pearl*. We have an incident. Ship is under attack. I presume by those we've been tracking. This may be our last transmission." He disconnects then asks Angelina, "Where can we hide this damn thing?"

"Do we go out of here armed?" she asks, ignoring his question.

"Not unless we want a running gun battle. Let's tape everything under the bed up against the bedrail."

"Tape?"

"Men never go anywhere without duct tape and cable ties. In my bugout bag."

"Let's get to work. No telling how much time we have."

"Not much. They'll be taking a count, and time will depend upon how many assholes are involved." He glances out and is silent for a second, then turns to her. "Don't look now, but there's a freighter coming along side, and there's a couple of dozen camo-clad boys aboard. I'd say we're in deep shit."

"Then hide the weapons. Let's comply and see what's coming down. Play the dumb tourists."

Harry grabs his bugout bag and goes to work.

"Don't be a hero," she cautions.

He replies, "Wrap your face, young lady, cover your body best you can. Don't make eye contact with any of them."

She hurried to her room, puts on long pants and a blue man's work shirt, grabs a scarf she'd bought in Lisbon and covers herself.

"Let's hope they let us return and don't find the weapons."

"God only knows," Harry said, confidence seeming to fade.

She's silent for a moment, then crosses her arms. "I'm not going, Harry."

"They will search the cabins for holdouts."

"I'm not going. I'll slip around the veranda petitions and hide in the cabin next door while they search this one, then slip back. I'm not going, I'm not giving up my weapon."

"Well, you got gonads, girl. See you when…if…I get back."

30

There's no way I'm going into the hallway as armed hostiles are patrolling, but there's another way. Simone's suite is one floor above ours and two toward the bow.

"I'll be back in short order," I say. I head for our little veranda, climb up on the rail, grab the floor of the deck above, kip up and get a foot in the space below their railing. The deck railings are open so I can grab a stile and pull myself to the railing, then easily get both feet in the space below and vault the railing.

A woman in the cabin screams and I put my finger to my lips, hushing her, then even more easily I broach the partition, swinging around, and drop to the floor of the next deck. Even if I slipped and fell the forty or fifty feet to the water, the ship is unmoving, and I'd likely find a way back aboard. Almost as soon as I hit the floor, the sliding glass door opens, and I'm face to face with General Bull Toliver.

"Fucking ragheads," he says.

"Suggest you comply, General. Let's recon the battlefield, then talk. I've got to move on." And I quickly swing out and around the next partition and am on Simone's deck. A wide-eyed Bryan runs to the door and slides it open. He's white-faced.

"What do we do?" he stammers.

"Exactly what they command until we know the odds and what we're up against." I walk to Simone and place my hands on her shoulders.

"I don't want to go out there," she says, with a choked sob.

"Again. Do exactly what they say to do. I've got to go back to my cabin and square some things away. Be brave, but don't be stupid. I'll get us out of this, but not before I know I can do so and keep you safe."

She nods her head, but tears are streaking both her and Patty's faces.

Then I charge back out, broach both partitions until I'm over our cabin, swing back down, get my feet on our railing and am quickly back in our cabin.

The KRISS Vectors are still in hidden compartments at the bottom of our suitcases. I know by the instructions they plan to search us. I can only hope there's only a few of them on board, and with my old military buddies we might overwhelm them.

I hide the handguns and our toys in a panel I discovered in the ceiling of the bathroom. It's an access to the wiring and some of the plumbing in the suite above, and I can only hope the infiltrators don't know of its location.

When I'm out of the bathroom, I see Connie has used a long scarf to both cover her head and wrap her face. She has on an ankle-length skirt, and a nonmatching long sleeve tee-shirt.

"What do you think this is?" she asks through her scarf.

"Hopefully a kidnapping for ransom. If so, we have time. You have your .380?"

"On my inner thigh. Hopefully they'll have some restraint about searching the women."

"From your lips to God's ears," I say, then add, "And I don't mean Allah as he'd likely rat us out."

I give her a wink. "And here I thought you were a slave to fashion. Your top and skirt don't match. Brown and blue, how gauche."

"You might consider getting serious," she says, and she's not smiling.

"I've always figured I'm gonna go out laughing," I say, and give her another wink.

"I don't plan to go out for a hell of a long time. And I'm not leaving until I put some makeup on. So..."

"So, what are the advantages of being a Muslim look alike. Veil, no makeup necessary."

"Under this veil is a Christian who will not sit on the right hand of God without her makeup. Hopefully we'll meet back here."

I grab the SAT phone, step out of the slider and make one call. My buddy, Pax Weatherwax, who, of course doesn't answer, so I leave a message. "Hey, pard, looks like we've got some raghead invaders on the ship. We're in the Med somewhere short of Malaga. Call the cavalry." I disconnect and hide the phone in the ceiling panel in the bathroom, then return and give Connie a hug.

"Let's see what we're up against," I say, and open the door. Only a few other passengers are in the hallway. At each end of the hall stands a crewman holding an AK47. Again, as I pass on the way to the main stairway—I have to go down a floor to reach the showroom—I pass the crewman who stands only two strides away and could be easily taken. But not until I see what I'm up against.

I head for the showroom and fall in step with two dozen other men whose expressions vary between utter fear and red-faced anger.

There are two crewmen/guards at the entry doors to the show lounge, another pair flanking each side of the stage below, and the room is filling with all chairs taken and men lining the walls and sitting in the aisles.

I'm not surprised that the tall Black I've seen around the pool, a passenger, is at the microphone. He has an Uzi slung over his back and he's not in cruise or pool garb, but rather desert camo.

He smiles and his white teeth flash in a very dark black face. "Gentlemen, as you have probably guessed, you are under the complete control of Al Shabaab. My name is Mumin Amir, and your lives and those of your women are in my hands. Yes, there are only five armed men you can see, however, there are many others, and some of you may have noticed the small freighter on the starboard side of the ship. As we speak, she is tying up alongside and our many other soldiers are assisting another thirty well-armed soldiers aboard. You may wonder why you don't merely charge the few of us. You think if you do, only a few of you will perish." Mumin laughs, then adds, "You may have noticed the devices in the hands of my friends here on the stage and those at the doors as you entered, or the fact they appear overweight. Those are explosive vests..."

The men in the room can't contain themselves and shout out a variety of insults. The man at the microphone swings his Uzi up, pans the crowd, and most of them silence. Then the few that don't are silenced when he fires a three-shot burst into the ceiling.

"You will be silent when I speak, or I will empty the rest of my weapon into the crowd. My soldiers are more than willing give their lives in service of Allah." There's some slight stirring in the crowd that immediately silences as he again pans the crowd with the muzzle of the Uzi. "Quiet, or quickly go to infidel hell." And they quiet. "Those devices are what is known as dead man switches. Should they be released, the vests will detonate. And, of course, if my soldiers are attacked, they will be released. There are five hundred steel ball bearings backed by some very fine explosive. If my experience means anything, each vest, in an enclosed area such as this large room, will kill at least twenty and wound many, many more."

Murmurs run through the crowd, but not so loud the Black man is disturbed.

The man who calls himself Mumin continues. "Now, know if you comply, and if your government and the Crimson Cruise line comply, you will be able to return to the sins of the infidel soon. If all comply. If not, the vests will be inconsequential, as the ship itself will become all our tomb. Over one hundred pounds of high explosive are situated next to the LPG tanks near the engine room on Decks Two and Three." He holds up a device in his hand and pans it so all can see. "I have a controller that will blow this ship into very small pieces and you and your loved ones with it."

Again, low murmurs, then absolute silence.

Then he commands, "I have a passenger list. I see there are several Jews aboard. We will now rearrange the room. All Jews will go to the aisle on the starboard side. Those of you not Jews seated there give up your place and move elsewhere.

Soon there are thirty men in that aisle. I'm sure those Jews with names not normally attributed to Jews have been smart enough not to move. And I'm sure they're wondering if they have any indication of their religion/heritage in their cabins or the ship's passenger records, or in their room—things like jewelry with Stars of David.

31

I SEE THE OLDER GUY WHO I'VE YET TO MEET, HARRY DRUMMOND, who Connie has told me is an FBI operative but loosely tied to the CIA, and slowly sidestep, inch by inch, the twenty feet to where he stands. This guy looks to be in his sixties, and I wonder how much help he'll be if a little war starts aboard the *Blue Pearl*. He glances over at me as I sidle up to him.

"Drummond," I say, under my breath without turning my head his way.

"Reardon," he replies, also facing straight forward.

"SAT phone, if we get a chance."

He nods. Then adds, "A shipload, coming aboard."

I'm silent a moment, digesting that, then say, "More targets."

He gives an almost indiscernible smile. I think I'm going to like this guy.

And beyond Harry I see my drinking buddy, Marine Corps Master Sergeant Elroy 'Rockin' Roy' Filson. Then I notice next to him is Navy Master Chief Willard 'Willy' Porter. I scan the room, but don't see Major General Bull Tolliver. He's among the missing.

However, across the room is the Englishman, Alistair Nelson, former SAS, eyeing us as if he's being left out.

So, I continue my slow sidestep while the sand slug, Mumin, rattles on, until I'm alongside Filson, and out of the side of my mouth, ask, "Sarge, you in for a little revolt?"

"Bet your sweet ass," he replies, also under his breath.

"I've got some thoughts, but let's recon some more. I'm sure they'll have to feed us, so stay close at chow, if possible."

I get a slight nod from both he and to his right, Master Chief Willie Porter.

That means there are a least four of us, against maybe forty of them—five if we can tie up with Bull Tolliver. And who knows who else.

HARRY HADN'T MADE a move to join the other Jews on the side aisle. He was aboard as Harry Drummond and nowhere was his true name, Weinstein, available to the insurgents…at least so long as he knew.

He made a slight glance at the guy who was slowly moving his way while the terrorist asshole who called himself Mumin let the crowd know he was in charge. Then he was pleased to realize it was Constance Nordstrom's cohort edging alongside, the guy his superiors had said was slightly batshit crazy but good to have on your side. He judged the guy to be over six feet tall, two hundred twenty if an ounce, not more than forty years old, and confident. Maybe too confident.

MUMIN CONTINUES AS SOON as the Jewish passengers have gathered, and as another half dozen soldiers, each carrying an AK47, all dressed in camo and combat boots, file into the back.

"Ah," Mumin says, with a smile. "My fellow faithful have arrived. You should know that there are now over forty faithful combatants aboard this ship. They, and the over one hundred pounds of explosives strategically placed against many thousand pounds of LPG, will ensure your cooperation. You will now return to your cabins. Three of my fellows will appear at your doors to search all you own. You will gather your valuables and place them in the wastebasket in your room. And I mean all rings, watches, cell phones, cash, credit cards, and other identification. We have your passports from the ship's safe. Your cabin safes will be open for my men's inspection. All medications will be..."

An immediate roar of complaint sweeps through the room.

"Silence," Mumin snaps. "Medications other than pain killers or antibiotics will be returned. You need not worry. We want you healthy. You are of no use to us if dead and dumped overboard. As soon as things are in order, you will be called to lunch. We will not starve you."

The crowd quiets. "First to be escorted out will be the Jewish passengers. You will be led by one soldier and followed by three. Our brothers in Palestine would be pleased if you tried to rebel as we'd be forced to butcher and dump you overboard, so don't give my men the excuse."

There is a quiet murmur as thirty or more Jewish passengers disappear out the showroom doors.

"Now," Mumin continues, as soon as they are clear of the room. "You will be escorted to your cabin floors by two soldiers, two rows at a time. You will not use the elevators but rather the stairs. Those of you who cannot manage the stairs will wait near the elevators until we have a soldier stationed at each floor to make sure you exit and return to your room. If your female companions are not already in the room, they soon will be. One last thing. Your life means nothing to me or my soldiers. I do not wish to harm you but will do so as easily as I smash a cockroach. Do exactly as you're told, and you may live to see your infidel loved ones."

To their great dismay, the Jewish passengers were not returned to their suites but rather led to Deck Three, past the small laundry room, and into the engine compartment. It is now quiet, at least not the usual roar, as all engines other than generators are still. A crewman stands near a closed door—a door with a sign that says, CAUTION LPG FUEL TANKS—which attracts their attention as against the door are two green tanks, ten inches in circumference by five feet in height, which might normally be filled with acetylene and oxygen for a welding job. However, these tanks have a cellphone and a yellow substance that resembles clay attached just below the gauges that normally would be telling the pressure.

"That's plastic explosive," one of the men mumbles as they pass.

"And thousands of pounds of liquid propane in tanks two decks high inside. I'm a boiler maker and used to work in the shipyard."

It is deadly quiet—other than the hum of generators—and dank in the engine room as they make their way down ladders only to be told to relax, their women will be joining them soon.

One soldier, a very large man with a missing eye who calls himself Zahir, is left atop the ladder, looking down on them. The other three leave, slamming the engine room hatch behind them.

One of the men yells up to the soldier. "What the hell are we supposed to do now?"

"Sit," the soldier says, "my name is Zahir and you will do as I say," motioning them down with the muzzle of his AK. "Your women will be along soon. No talking."

"But..."

The soldier immediately draws a bead on the man who spoke and yells, "No talking! But now pay attention." He turns and opens the door marked, "Danger LPG Storage." And wheels the tanks inside. He removes one end of a small chain from the mechanism on the tanks and attaches it to the inside doorknob. Then he closes the door, encircles the outside knob with a chain, runs it over the nearby landing railing, pulls it tight and clicks a hardened padlock shut. He walks to the rail, looking down on the Jewish contingency of passengers. "Those tanks are not filled for welding. They are filled with explosives. Our leader, Mumin Amir, a faithful subject of Allah, has the controller. You should pray no one attempts to take over the ship as he will, without fear, detonate the tanks and the LPG. If anyone opens this door all of us die. We have demands, and if those are not fulfilled, we all die."

To their credit, not a sound comes from the Jews. They plop down on the deck and remain quiet.

32

General Tolliver and his wife awake with a start when the first announcement rings through the ship. His wife, Martha, has been by his side for fifty years, and, since his retirement, they've been inseparable.

"What's happening? Are we sinking?" she asks, sitting up in bed and rubbing her eyes.

He's on his feet by the time she finishes her question. "We might be better off sinking."

"What...what are you saying, Bull?"

"We've had our eyes on some of the Muzzies on board and wondered if something was coming down. They know I am a General. Our butler, Malik, won't stop calling me General and he's a Yemini. I'm not gonna have those worthless bastards' hand you my head."

"Bull, calm down. This, too, will pass."

"It always does, Martha. Just remember I love you. If something happens, tell the kids and grandkids papa will save a place for them in heaven."

The General walks to the wide sliding glass door in their suite. "Jesus," he says.

"What?" Martha asks, stopping on her way to the bathroom.

"Son of a bitch," Bull says, shaking his head.

"You're scaring me, Bull. What is it?"

"The ship is dead in the water. Some junk heap of a freighter with Arabic writing on the stern is pulling away from the ship. No telling what…or who…they transferred to us."

Martha disappears into the bathroom, but Bull walks to the little bar sink and combs his hair, then goes to the closet and begins dressing. In fifteen minutes, Martha sticks her head out. "I'm going to shower. Bull, you have your uniform on? And you left the slider open."

"Yes, darling, I have my uniform on. I'm not facing some foreign scum in my pajamas. And I'm enjoying the fresh air."

"But Bull, won't they be offended by your uniform?"

He gives her a look that would wilt a rose, clears his throat, and says in a calm tone, "When was it you saw me unwilling to offend someone who hates the United States of America?"

She can't help but give him a tight smile. "I guess 'never' would be the answer to that."

"Go take your shower. You'll want to comply with their demands to wrap your face and cover your head. Hijab, remember. Like you did the last time we were out of the compound in Saudi."

"I remember." She gently closes the door.

He's just finished tying his tie, when the doorbell jingles.

He takes a deep breath, and under his breath he says aloud, "Probably not smart to mess with an old man who's way past his life expectancy. Old men don't fight fair."

Bull throws his shoulders back and walks to the door, he opens it to see Malik, his butler, and behind him, two uniformed men in desert camo. Dark-skinned men with hair much longer than he would have tolerated in his troops.

“Malik,” he says, in the way of a greeting.

“I’m so sorry, General, Sir. These men have weapons and say you have to come with them.”

“They came on board the ship from that freighter?” the general asks.

“I believe so.”

“That ship that just pulled away." Then he smiles. "That ship that is sinking?”

“I…I don’t…” Malik turns to the two armed men. One of average size, one much larger but still not as large as the General. Malik rattles something off to them in Arabic, and they look at each other in astonishment, then both run past the General and out to the deck and lean on the rail to peer at the *Bit Tawfīq*.

They are both turning back, when the General hits them like a Steeler’s linebacker, his arms spread wide, he sweeps them in front of him over the rail. The three of them spiral to the sea, forty feet below. Only the General goes into the water feet first. He has toes pointed, one hand cupping his personals and one over his eyes. The other two hit hard, flat on the back for one, the stomach for the other. They won't fare well from forty feet to water seeming like concrete.

Malik runs to the railing and looks over to see all three surface, one of the two soldiers is slapping the water as if he cannot swim. The other seems unconscious.

Bull Tolliver has one by the collar and is dragging him to the other, who claws at the General as if he’s trying to climb aboard. But the General spins him around, throws a beefy arm around his neck and pulls him close. Then the second man who’s facing away is sucked in close.

Bull has an arm locked around both their necks, with them both kicking and waving their arms slapping the water as he forces them under. All three of them go below the surface, then resurface, then go down again.

Malik is shouting as loud as he can and Martha runs from the bathroom, a large towel circling her body. "What's happening," she yells.

"The General Sir, men with guns come and pointed guns at him and ordered him to come with them. He dragged them over and all falled to the ocean."

She leans over the rail in time to see them surface one more time, then all three disappear under the water. She screams a scream that reverberates and makes Malik retreat back into the suite.

"Report that," Martha yells to Malik, who runs to the phone and dials, then turns to her.

"The phones, they dead."

She looks back at the water, and begins to sob, then shakes her head in defiance as she watches for a couple of minutes, bites her lip, dries her eyes, then turns to the butler. "Get out of my room. Go somewhere and report my husband is overboard."

"And the two..."

"Fuck them," she says, and goes back to the bathroom, pausing only to chastise Malik again. "Malik, I said get out."

"Yes, ma'am," he says, and is quickly out the door, moving like a turpentined cat.

She goes to the mirror and says to herself. "Old soldiers never die; they just fade away. And the good ones take a few enemies with them."

She returns to the railing and stands staring at the surface, hoping against all hope that Bull will reappear.

33

I ENTER OUR SUITE ONLY MINUTES AFTER CONNIE ARRIVES AS SHE'S just now removing her scarf.

"Have they searched the room yet?" I ask.

"Yes, I'm fine. Thanks for asking."

"I can see you're fine."

"Right. Okay, some female terrorist who called herself Alia, with two armed male guards at the doors, gave us some instructions and more threats. The bad news is they separated all the Jewish women, called them out by name, and took them somewhere."

"Same with the men. I've got to check the SAT phone and see if Pax has called back."

"Don't get caught with the phone. We'll need it."

"I hope Simone and her ladies were there. I didn't notice her boys with the men's group."

"The girls were there, eyes like saucers and even with the veils I could see they were white as sheets."

"And they're safe back in their suite?"

"They went upstairs, and I stayed on six. So, they were good that far."

"Block the door. These guys will have passkeys and won't be knocking. I have to step to the open slider to use the phone and it could be too far back to the john to hide the phone in time." I fetch the phone from the space above where I've hidden it, go stand near the open slider, and see the call light is blinking. I immediately call Pax.

"What's happening?" he answers.

"Raghead terrorists, maybe as many as three dozen. Hell, maybe more. They claim to have the ship rigged with a couple of hundred pounds of explosive, and she's a dual-powered vessel with thousands of pounds of LPG. She's a floating bomb."

"I've called Matt Patterson, our buddy in the local Federal Marshal's office and he's contacted the CIA. He's already called me back and said they are already on it. I'm sure the fleet is already steaming your way. What can I do?"

"From Vegas? Not a damn thing, I imagine. I don't know if this ship is totally disabled or what, but she's dead in the water. They brought a tramp freighter alongside and offloaded many of the bad guys who are now on board. The tramp has retreated but only a couple of hundred yards."

"How far are you from Taj?"

"Malta? A long way but he's likely our closest asset." Taj is an old buddy, former Brit military but now running an electronics shop on Malta, an island south of Italy. He lost a leg in Libya, so his mercenary career is over. He has three sons, however, and knows every operative, legal and otherwise, in Malta, Italy, Greece and North Africa."

"I'm calling him," Pax snaps.

"Can't hurt. See what he can learn."

"You can't come in. I'm not dressed," I hear Connie shout.

Shouting, in Arabic, rings through the door.

"Bogies at the door," I say, and quickly disconnect and hustle into the bathroom to replace the phone. I'm tempted to snake a handgun out, go ahead and deep six a couple of these pricks, but I still don't know what we're up against and don't want them panicking and blowing us all to hell if they truly have explosives that will detonate the LPG tanks.

I've got to bide my time. I have an idea, but need all my military buddies, or anyone capable on board to participate. Right now, we have a communication problem.

What do you do when you're outnumbered? You separate and eliminate. The objective is to get them separated so the odds are even or at least closer to even.

Connie sees me in the bathroom doorway and removes the desk chair she's propped under the knob.

"Sorry, she says. I was not dressed." I can see her slip her compact into her pocket and know it's the compact that's actually a stun gun. I hope she doesn't have to use it.

The door slams open, back against the wall, and a couple of very irritated slime balls dressed in camo and holding AK47's step inside. We've emptied a small wastebasket and filled it with some jewelry, a fat chunk of cash—over two thousand U.S. and three hundred Euros— our driver's licenses, and some credit cards.

That should make them believe it's all we have. I've made a pair of fine slits in the mattress, only a little over a dollar bill wide along a bead where it won't be noticed, and have slipped over twenty packs of twenty-one hundred-dollar bills and ten one-ounce gold Swiss francs in a fan around the slits. I never travel without dough, and this is something over fifty-four thousand bucks—only nine thousand of which is declared to keep from filing a ton of paperwork. Dollars are normally good around the world, but gold always seems to work.

Connie, sitting on the bed, points to the wastebasket.

"Out," one of the hostiles says, motioning for us to retreat to the outside veranda. We do, and he closes and locks the slider behind us. Then they begin toss the suite, dumping all drawers, they pull our suitcases from under the bed and open them but don't lift them. Had they, they'd likely notice the weight of the pair of KRISS Vector's in the secret panels inside. But they don't, only running hands through every zippered pocket and then kicking them aside.

We have tense moments as they go through the luggage, and one throws the mattress off the bed. It's a silent moment as one of them disappears into the bath. But he comes out and continues to rifle the room.

They don't spend more than ten minutes shaking down the room, then dump the contents of the wastebasket, the valuables, in the pillowcase. One walks to the slider and unlocks but doesn't open it. He yells through the glass, "Wait move, we leave."

So, we do. We wait until they've left the room.

Had they discovered our toys I'd have had to try chucking them both overboard.

Now, I've got to check on Simone, Gretchen, and the kids.

But things are getting goosey, so I retrieve a Glock and its canvas holster from the compartment above the toilet, then decide it might be a little loud, so I grab a K-bar as well. In seconds I have them both on my belt.

“Stall them, if you can, while I'm gone,” I say to Connie as I exit the room and mount the railing.

“Good plan. Tough execution,” she yells after me as I kip up to the deck above, then work my way to the side and realize I'm facing Bull Toliver's room. The slider opens and it's Mrs. Toliver in a robe. She has a hanky in one hand and waves me her way.

I throw a leg over the rail. She puts a finger to her lips, shushing me.

"Bull dragged two of them over the rail and drowned the bastards."

"And the General?" I ask.

I can see her jaw clamp, then she gets it out. "He went with them. God damn their black hearts. Our butler saw it all."

"Is he with the terrorists?"

"Malik? I don't think so. They treated him like dirt as well."

"Play dumb. Stay tough. We'll get through this. I gotta go."

She merely nods, but with tear-filled eyes. I hustle back and swing around the partition onto the kids' deck.

I'm happy to note the slider is ajar and drop silently onto the veranda of the two-bedroom suite, expecting to be greeted by the kids.

Nothing, and the reflection of the sun on the glass doesn't allow me to see inside. I creep to the six-inch opening where the door's ajar, then realize the blinds are drawn. I ease the curtain aside, then hear Patty's panicked voice. "No, no, no don't."

And a male laugh, followed by a husky voice in Arabic.

I slip the curtain aside just enough to peek inside and see the back of a camo-clad soldier. He's pulling his shirt off and staring down at Patty who's on her back on the living room couch, both arms extended trying to fend off her attacker. Her blouse is ripped away, her breasts exposed, and her pants torn open.

No one else is in the room.

34

As quietly as I can, I open the slider enough to slip through.

As I do, I palm the K-bar. Unfortunately, some light floods the room as I slip through the drapes. He's a big raghead but blinded by the light as he turns. He's holding his trousers with one hand and trying to shade his eyes with the other to see if it's merely the wind that has blown the curtains—or something else. Patty sees me coming, but to her credit, merely shakes her head and grits her teeth at her attacker. I detect the hint of a smile and a glint in her eyes. I know I'm welcomed by one of the two in the room.

Before he can determine the source, *something else*—me—is bringing the butt of the K-bar down directly on his pate with all I can put behind the blow. His skull indents as his jet-black eyes roll up in their sockets. Happily, he only makes a little grunt and hardly any impact sound as he hits the carpeted floor. Very little blood seeps from the crater in his noggin. When your heart stops, so does the flow of blood.

"Simone?" I asked with a whisper, and Patty points at a bedroom door. "Only one?" I ask, again whispering, and she nods.

This soldier is atop Simone on the bed, his pants down, his shirt thrown aside, covering his AK47, which is on the carpet.

She's fighting him, her legs together and twisted to the side as he's holding her shoulders down and trying to force a leg between hers.

"You fucking bastard," she says, and he laughs.

But his laugh is cut short, turning to gurgle, when the K-bar goes to the hilt through his side, and I'm sure, through a kidney. This kill isn't as clean as the first. Blood sprays from the wound as I hang onto the hilt and the blade slips out as he scrambles away toward his rifle. He bends to retrieve it, a weak screech coming from him as he does. I give him a shove with my running shoe on his butt and he slams headfirst, and hard, into the wall, and collapses holding his side. He has one hand down on the floor propping himself and glaring at me, holding the other hand over the spurting wound in his side.

Like I'm going for a three-point field goal, I give him all I have with a kick under the chin that lifts him a foot in the air. When he lands, He's out cold, and he'll be totally cold soon as no one can bleed like that for long. He blows a few bubbles of blood. Guess he bit his tongue half off. Then he rolls back and forth, gurgling, then stills.

"Motherfucking pig. Goat-fucking cocksucker," I hear from the obviously very offended young lady behind me. She turns to me, "The asshole took a selfie...a friggin' selfie, holding me down. I want to cut his penis off and stuff it in his mouth."

I turn to her and shake my head. "Where the hell do you learn stuff like that?"

She's standing stark naked, with her hands on her hips. I have to glance away to keep from looking her up and down, and do, still shaking my head.

Then I turn back to Simone. "Get towels." I grab a top sheet off the bed and try to get it under him so blood doesn't cover the floor, but as soon as I do, he stops spurting and I know his heart has found little to pump and has stopped.

Simone, still naked as she was when born, is quickly back from the bathroom with hands full of towels. I grab one and try to get the blood soaked up, but the carpet is a mess.

"You worthless piece of shit," Simone says, and spits on her attacker.

Patty is in the doorway, half put back together.

"Get dressed," I snap at Simone.

"I have to take a shower," she says, and starts for the bathroom. I grab her and spin her around.

"Get the fuck dressed. You two have to help me heave these assholes overboard. In case you don't know it, there's another three dozen of the pricks on board."

To her credit she nods, but still heads for the bathroom and is quickly back in a robe. We head for the living room first. The girls each grab a leg and we struggle through the room and out to the deck.

"Wait," I command, then look up and down the length of the ship. At least no one is hanging over a rail checking things out. "Now," I say, and we heave the smaller soldier over. It's forty feet to the water and he hits with a splat. Again, I scan the ship, bow to stern, but see no one, thank God not even a pointing finger on the end of a camo-clad arm.

The larger of the two has two grenades on his belt, so I relieve him of those. Then we drag him out to the veranda, and again I check and see no one hanging over a rail.

This asshole has been too well fed and must go two-fifty. It's all the girls can do to get their third of his weight up and over the rail, but they do.

"*Sayonara*, motherfucker," I say, as he hits the water. Again, I check to see that no bogie is hanging over a rail, and luckily no one is. He splats so hard I can't imagine no one has heard.

No one seems to have.

Then it dawns on me, the boys are missing. "Where the hell are Bryan and Terry?" I ask both girls.

"These two assholes came and took them away, then returned to have their fun."

I couldn't help but smile. "Turned out not to be much fun for them," then I get more serious. "I hope they just moved them and didn't move them overboard."

I know we're pressing our luck, chucking terrorists overboard. That won't fly for long. Where the fuck is the Marine Corps?

THE PRESIDENT of the United States is at his desk in the oval office. On the two upholstered sofas in the center of the room are perched the Chairman of the Joint Chiefs of Staff, Vice Chairman of the Joint Chiefs of Staff, the Military Service Chiefs from the Army, Marine Corps, Navy, and Air Force. In addition, the Director of Homeland Security, the CIA, and of the FBI are in attendance.

"What's next?" the President asks.

"May I?" General Robert 'Butch' McKniffin, Commandant of the Marine Corps, asks.

"Shoot," the President replies.

McKniffin turns to the Navy admiral at his left, "Correct me if wrong, Jack, but the majority of the Sixth Fleet is all the way across the Med off the coast of Turkey, putting on the show to discourage Iran from moving against the Turks. NATO flexing their muscle, and we are their muscle."

McKniffin continues, "Mister President, Task Force 62 is the nearest combat-ready ground force composed of a Marine Expeditionary Unit of approximately eighteen hundred Marines. Transported in Task Force Sixty-One ships. The unit is equipped with armor, artillery, and transport helicopters that enable it to conduct operations ashore or off or evacuate civilians from troubled areas. They are stationed in Italy. We can move on this cruise ship in three days, maybe less, given Jack's transport."

The president shakes his head. "Gentlemen, there are not only Americans aboard the *Blue*, but citizens of at least six other countries, a dozen or more if you include the crew. Even if we were willing to risk American lives, we must think twice before risking the lives of citizens of other countries. So how do we accomplish this with the smallest possible loss of life?"

Again, it is McKniffin who speaks up. "SEAL Delivery Vehicle Team Two based at Little Creek, Virginia, is already en route to Gibraltar, with the acquiescence of Rear Admiral Jeremy Sanderson, commander of British Forces Gibraltar. The Virginia Class sub SSN-794 Montana is steaming for Gibraltar at the moment and will be ready to move near the *Blue Pearl* in less than twenty-four hours. Those SDVs are the small underwater boats, Mister President."

"Once they're in position and the team of twelve SEALs on three SDVs have deactivated any explosive devices, we can follow up with a deploy via chopper and put an overwhelming force aboard."

35

THE PRESIDENT LOOKS DOUBTFUL. "SO, YOU DON'T BELIEVE THEY have done what this contact aboard says they've done. Explosives?"

It's the Director of the CIA who speaks up. "We were watching this potential situation and have a man, actually an FBI liaison, from the London LEGAT office. He's FBI but special liaison to the CIA. He and his assistant are aboard, as you know. He's an experienced operative and still in touch via SAT phone. It's his belief that it is likely they have what they say they have. We eliminated the use of four pounds of plastic so far but feel there may be lots more. And the *Blue Pearl* is a dual-fuel ship. Many hundreds of cubic yards of LPG are aboard. It won't take much of a charge to set off a secondary that would level half of Malaga were she in port. And we don't know what this small freighter standing off her starboard side is all about. Our man says that ship, with Arabic markings, deployed a large number of terrorists aboard. Maybe as many as three dozen, but she's standing by. We don't know if there're more bodies aboard and if so, how the ship's armed. We were on to her earlier, but it appears they have renamed, repainted, and reconfigured her deck houses. They did a good job throwing us off. We're working on the origin of this obviously Arab ship. So, maybe she'll be taking hostages or maybe they intend to blow the *Blue Pearl* all to hell with all on board."

The President is silent for a moment, then asks, "I understand there's someone else on board who's in touch with us?"

McKniffin, the Marine, gives a low laugh. "Former Marine Warrant Officer, sniper qualified, Michael Reardon. Actually, I stayed close to his General Discharge from the Corps years ago..."

"General?" the President asks.

"Administrative General Discharge, sir. Not an honorable, not a dishonorable. He was in Iraq and killed a Major General in their Iraqi Army and a few others."

"Wait," the President says, then questions, "not a dishonorable?"

"Extenuating circumstances. These Iraqi's were stoning two young female members of their own family. They fired on him first, and he followed the rules of engagement at the time—ludicrous as they were. Reardon was a squad leader who took a little umbrage at this so-called rite of honor. He was quietly drummed out."

"And killed them?" the President mumbles.

"And is not apologetic, sir."

"So, can he be useful?" the President asks.

Again, McKniffin chuckles. "Mister President, if what I've read of his activities since, mercenary work, including some work for the CIA, is true. The guy is a wrecking ball. In fact, he's been in and out of Russia and North Korea—in Russia with some NATO involvement, and in North Korea to extract that NK ambassador no one has talked about. Happened under the prior administration. There are also some other retired military types aboard, including Marine Corps General Bull Toliver retired, and a Brit, a former

SAS major. Alistair somebody. But reading his background, he's no Alice. A real bad ass, pardon the term." The President merely shrugs, so McKniffin continues.

"I'd be surprised if those boys aren't getting ready to take some terrorists with them, even if they all go down with the ship."

The President shakes his head. "Let's make sure those on board, most my age, stand down and let the young proven capable SEAL team handle this. There are more than five hundred lives at stake, and I don't want the loss of five hundred lives to be my legacy."

All in the room agree and nod.

"Get back to me when our SEAL team is in position, and we'll see what's transpired."

"Yes, sir," they all say in unison, and file out.

Mumin Amir is in Captain Von Groot's plush office, across the captain's desk sits Akim Musa, who enjoys the title of Colonel in Al-Shabaab, and is in command of the squad delivered to the *Blue Pearl* by the *Bit Tawfīq.* They speak in Arabic.

Mumin eyes him and is not smiling. "Akim Musa, this is my operation and you will not give orders to me or my fellows. It would take all day to deliver one meal to the suites. The men will eat from the kitchen on the pool deck where they can be easily watched from above. The women will be seated in the main restaurant. It may take two servings, but the food will be simple and not to order," he laughs at that, but it's now Musa's turn not to smile.

Akim gives Mumin a hard look, his voice angry. "I am missing two men I sent to bring the American General here so we can make an example of him. His cabin is 718. Go see what is detaining them."

Mumin is so angry, spittle flies as he speaks. "I am not your man, Akim Musa. I am my own man and the blessed Prophet Mohammad's. Do you see this?" he holds out a controller almost in Musa's face. "This will vaporize this ship and all on it. So, unless you're ready to be a martyr, as I am, then it's you who will go and see what detains your men. And you will not speak down to me again. This is my operation, and I am in command. Do you understand?"

Musa stares at the controller for a moment, then shrugs. "The sheik said you were a hard man, but a faithful one. I and my men will do as you say, unless I deem you are making an error, then I must interfere."

"I do not make mistakes, Akim, Musa. Go find what's happened to your men. I have two men on each cabin floor, at each end of the hallways. You will have your men take three six-hour shifts to spell them. I'm waiting for contact from both the Crimson Cruise Line and the American government. We will begin loading the freighter as soon as I make the sheik's demands. We will take as many hostages as we can carry on the freighter. The rest will be left aboard, all the Jews, to find their way to hell. It will be our greatest victory since the Twin Towers."

"Then let's feed them." Musa says. "It will give them false hope," then retracts his order, "If you are ready, of course. Women to the restaurant. Men to the area around the pool."

"That's right. We can station men at the railings above the pool and it will be easy to watch and less risk of the infidels trying something. Go now. I will inform the kitchen to prepare something simple that will feed all."

Musa disappears out of the office. Mumin picks up a SAT

phone and walks out of the office, down the hall away from the office and out a side door. SAT phones only work where you can see the sky.

It's time to make demands. He dials a number he has already programed into the phone. The call is to Sally Ann Maddison, Chargé d'Affaires at the U.S. Mission to Libya, in Tunis. He enjoys talking down to an American and a lowly woman.

The receptionist says she's busy and will return his call.

He's silent for a moment, then says in a quiet voice. "This is Mumin Amir aboard the American cruise ship *Blue Pearl*. I am a soldier of the Prophet Mohammad, peace be upon him, and have four hundred Americans as hostages. If my demands are not met in ten hours, I will begin killing one every ten minutes. Are you sure your American bitch is too busy to talk with me?"

"One second, sir."

In only ten seconds, the Chargé d'Affaires is on the line. "Who are you?" she asks, without bothering with hello.

"Mumin Amir, a soldier of Allah. I am aboard the American cruise ship *Blue Pearl* with six hundred passengers and crew, mostly infidel Americans. Do you have a pen or is this call being recorded?"

"Go ahead, Mister Amir."

36

"FIVE HUNDRED MILLION DOLLARS IN GOLD WILL BE DELIVERED TO A place of my instruction beginning in ten hours from the termination of this call."

"All right. But that's a lot of money, Mister Amir. Obviously, I don't have the authority to agree and certainly not to begin delivering, even if we had one hundredth that amount here at the mission. And five hundred million? I'm sure it's impossible."

"Woman, I did not expect you to have any authority. Talk to whoever does and call me…have them call me…back on this SAT phone. Now, listen."

"Yes, sir."

"If you do not comply with my demands, I will kill a passenger every ten minutes, beginning at midnight tonight, that's ten hours. Do you clearly understand?"

"Yes, sir."

"Then get to work."

And he disconnects, looks at his watch, and laughs. It's now 2:00 p.m. his time which means it's 8:00 a.m. in Washington, D.C.

The lazy Americans will probably not yet have had their coffee. Now there will be many with stomachs too upset to take a cup.

As soon as he's checked his watch, he dials another number, and this time the answer is in Arabic.

"My Sheik, now."

"Who is this?"

"Mumin Amir, and I need to speak to my Sheik."

HARRY WEINSTEIN, Drummond on board, has been on and off his SAT phone since the first announcement came over the ship intercom. His last call resulted in him being instructed to comply and to inform the wild card, Mike Reardon, and any others he suspects might be rebels, to stand down, as a SEAL team is on the way. Harry was forced to tell the Director of both the CIA and FBI that he was not sure the ship wouldn't be destroyed with the first indication of a SEAL incursion, but both insisted the President was adamant to let the teams handle the problem.

Harry's two-bedroom suite, which he shares with Angelina Lara, on Deck Eight, has a number of good hiding places for their phone and weapons. However, they were moved at Cadiz to a small suite—both Glocks are now in pots under artificial plants—and the short hallway on the pool deck has only one guard. Even at over sixty years of age, Harry thinks he could take the pissant guard, and wishes he'll have the opportunity to give it a try.

He is bemoaning the fact to Angelina when the next announcement rings throughout the ship, "You will now be fed. Men report to the pool deck, women to the restaurant. Women remember to cover yourselves. Be out of your cabins in ten minutes."

Harry eyes her, "God speed. Don't get caught." He has only a short walk out to the pool. Angelina moves out to the veranda, praying she can hear the terrorists as they search one of the cabins on either side. Then she'll know which way to go. She pulls off the low heels she wears, figuring she can negotiate swinging around the petition far better in bare feet. Then waits.

SIMONE AND PATTY have been madly cleaning the blood from the carpet and wall of the bedroom. They finally give up and remove the only throw rug in the suite from under the living room coffee table to cover the bedroom carpet blood spots with it. It looks very clumsy as it is up against a wall, not spaced out as a normal throw rug would be, but it will have to do. They have just thrown blood-soaked bath towels overboard and are in the bathroom washing their hands. They hold their breath as their suite door is suddenly swung open and smashes against the wall. They hurry into the living room and a terrorist, this one slightly gray and stooped with a pockmarked face, enters. He wears a sidearm and carries an ugly rifle with a long magazine.

"I am Colonel Musa. Lie to me and you die. Have you seen my men? Two men were stationed on this floor?" he demands.

Both girls are taken aback but remember to keep their eyes down as Reardon had instructed.

Simone recovers from another threat of death first. "No, sir," she lies with some expertise. "You're the first man we've seen since two terro..." She decides to change her description of the men who'd taken Bryan and Terry away—the same men who returned and tried to rape them. "...soldiers came and took our...our brothers away." She knows Muslims would chastise them or worse if they knew four unmarried and unrelated people, of different sexes, are sharing the same suite most of every day.

Simone gets a chill as the Colonel looks her up and down, as she is barefoot and barelegged in her bathrobe. But he merely snarls. "Did you hear anything…anything unusual outside?"

"No, sir. We were called to eat and are very hungry. May we go now?"

"Go," he snaps, then walks from room to room checking, and stomps out.

They take a quick sponge bath with washcloths, dress appropriately, and hurry out to eat. As they enter the restaurant, the male guard at the main door continues to chastise the line of women.

"No talking. You will not be fed if you talk."

It is 'serve yourself' with canned soft drinks, water, and juice. Plates are piled beside flatware and serving trays are filled with pasta. The only attempt at variety is half the pasta has white sauce and half marinara. The female guard who'd called herself Alia stands near the serving line. A male guard stands at the main entrance door and one each at the doors that lead outside to the deck.

Simone can't help but find it amusing that the room is filled with Frank Sinatra songs at a high volume.

"Jesus," she says to Patty, "elevator music."

"No talking!" the female guard yells at her. Patty eyes her, then remembers what Reardon had told her. Keep your head and eyes down. She fills her plate, grabs a canned diet Coke, takes two rolls, and finds a seat.

No one talks.

MEN FILE out to the pool deck from forward and aft. I've climbed the stairway and manage to fall in beside Master Sergeant Elroy Filson and Master Chief Willy Porter and notice that the SAS guy who's introduced himself as Nelson is only a few feet behind us. As we shuffle out onto the deck surrounding the pool, I manage to get him closer and to voice a low, "stay with me," and he does.

Walking through the doors leading outside, we're cautioned by a guard. "Talk and you'll be shot and fed to the sharks." He keeps repeating it and I wonder if that's all the English he's been taught.

As soon as we are outside, I do a quick recon. There are six armed hostiles with automatic weapons on the pool level, and on the walkways of the deck above, four are stationed at each edge of the overwatches. They're alert, continually scanning the men below with weapons.

Trays full of pasta rest on both the bar and a serving area on the far side of the deck. Barrels with soft drinks and some with bread rolls flank the pasta. We queue up and fill plates and I try and space myself as far from guards as I can, then plop down on the deck with my back against the rail. The nearest guards are forty feet forward and aft.

As soon as we're all seated on the deck, I cough and cover my mouth and ask though my fingers, "Show of fingers, what floor you on?"

Each of them spreads fingers on the deck. Filson is on four, Porter on five, I'm on six, and Nelson is on seven. Perfect as eight is the only floor without a military guy, although we certainly haven't met all among the over three hundred passengers.

We eat a while, then I do the cough trick again. "I can isolate each floor, so we only have two guards each to deal with."

I get curious looks from each of them, but a guard is passing, patrolling around the pool, so it's shut-up time. When he's at the furthest distance he'll reach, I cough and cover again. "Fire-doors. Just after dark. Be ready to clear your floors."

37

I GET A NEARLY IMPERCEPTIBLE NOD FROM EACH ONE OF THEM. I'VE got to take that as a commitment to act.

As we're ordered to return to our suites and being escorted by guards—I've now counted even more as sixteen have appeared and are being fed—I'm disturbed to see the junk freighter is again coming alongside. Is he offloading more hostiles or loading something?

When I get back to our suite, I'm a little concerned that Connie has not yet returned.

MUMIN HAD ONLY BEEN DISCONNECTED from his phone call with Sheik Ali Hassan for a half hour. Hassan, the head of the snake. The airstrip can accommodate his Citation Jet, thanks to the American company Interco Petroleum. Interco had constructed the airport for their own use.

In only a half hour after his disconnect, the encrypted phone on the desk of Frazier Mendleson, CIA section chief Terrorism, rings. NSA Director General Fred Quinn is on the line.

Mendleson immediately recognizes General Quinn's southern drawl.

"A call originated from the *Blue Pearl* to another SAT phone in the middle of the Libyan desert. We have the originator as a Mumin Amir, the recipient as Sheik Ali Hassan, another oil rich son of a bitch. I'm sure your Libya desk knows far more about him than we do; however, we're doing a deep investigation of all his email and international phone data and will bring y'all up to speed with what we learn soon. We'll stay on it."

As soon as he disconnects, Frazier checks the number of the *Blue Pearl* originating call against that which State had provided him from the number their Libyan mission Chargé d'Affaires, Sally Ann Maddison had recorded.

He immediately buzzes his secretary and instructs her, "Conference call, Director of the FBI, the President's Chief of Staff Harley Forrest, Director CIA, and General McKniffin at the Pentagon."

"Yes, sir."

In moments he has them all on the phone, all at work even though it was not yet nine AM.

He has one question. "Gentlemen, do we have a consensus that I'll take the lead in stalling his Amir until we can act?"

All concur except Forrest, who replies, "It will take me ten minutes to get to the President, then I'll get right back to you."

"Standing by," Frazier says.

In less than ten minutes he gets his call. "The President suggests you have an FBI profiler and hostage psychologist at your side. But don't wait for them. Make your call, then send us a recording. This guy does speak English."

"Miss Maddison at the mission in Libya says his English is as good as hers. First report is he's a Somali. I have an expert from the Somali desk at State on the way here. We believe he's Al-Shabaab, so I have a Marine Colonel who served in that Mogadishu mess coming in as well. We should have all bases covered."

"Go for it, Mendleson."

Frazier takes a deep breath, waits for a nod from his equal at the CIA, the section chief of the Terrorism Analysis desk who has coordinated the recording and analysis of the call, and dials the number. It is not necessary to go outside to make a SAT call in most Intelligence buildings as they have an antenna array that can reach most the world.

The party who answers has only a slight accent, but a very smartass tone to his rather thin voice.

"You have called to save infidel American lives?"

"Mister Amir."

"You took your time."

Frazier answered quickly. "We get many crank calls. You know, illegitimate calls of the nature of your call to our mission in Tunis. We never know what's real."

"You may assure yourself mine is not a crank call. I'm sure you have your satellites watching the *Blue Pearl* even as we speak. You will note she is dead in the water."

"Not yet with our birds, but I'm sure they are being reprogramed. My name is Frazier Mendleson and I've been authorized by our President to discuss this matter with you."

"There will be no discussion, Mendleson. You will not call me again until you're ready for instructions as to where to deliver the five hundred million in gold."

"I understand, but..."

"No buts, Mister Mendleson. The first American passenger's body will hit the water at one-minute past midnight should I not hear from you before with the word that a C130 is loaded and ready for my instruction. The gold should be on pallets for delivery via parachute in North Africa at GPS coordinates per my instruction. Call me when your delivery is ready."

"Mister Amir..." Frazier begins, but realizes Amir has disconnected.

Frazier can't help but give a sardonic laugh, and thinks, *I wonder if this damn fool has figured out that five hundred million dollars in gold, at today's price of around $1,400 an ounce would weigh over twenty-two-thousand pounds.*

We can sure as hell drop it from a C130, in fact she'll carry twice that weight, but who the hell is going to haul it off?

NOW I'M REALLY WORRIED. Connie has still not returned, and the junk freighter is tied alongside, unfortunately on the far side and I can't see what's going on.

I've checked our hiding place and she must have her little Smith and Wesson .380 semiauto with her. She has a thigh holster and, if worn in the inside, which is how she's worn it before, it's undetectable unless someone gets very personal. And knowing Connie they'll only try to get that personal once, and she'll either use the stun gun makeup compact or they'll be well ventilated with the .380.

I'm tired of waiting, so I make the climb up a deck on the outside again. I rap on Mrs. Tolliver's slider and get no answer, then transfer to the kids' veranda. No one there either. Jesus, what's going on? My alarm has buzzed off and on, but I can't respond to someplace if I don't know where someplace is. It's driving me a little batshit. I finally take it off my wrist and stuff it in a drawer. I should have found one with voice.

I hustle back to my suite and dig out a Glock and a KRISS. I have two magazines for the handgun and four for the KRISS Vector, if I abscond with Connie's. Even if I make a kill with every three-shot burst from my KRISS, I'd likely not clean up the bad guys.

I hate impossible odds.

I have a plan to isolate the guards on each floor, and know exactly how to do it, but I inferred to the boys at lunch that I would wait until after dark.

Things change on a battlefield, and this ship is rapidly about to become one. A soldier must adapt.

No matter the odds.

When I studied the ship while back in Vegas, I took a hard look at fire protection, and part of that system is the ability to close all fire doors from the bridge. There's no opening them—sans explosives—when closed, except from the bridge. And now closing them seems my only move. Isolate each floor and hope those on that floor can overpower the two guards there.

Of course, the first problem is getting to the bridge and activating the fire doors.

38

I've pulled on my combat trousers with multiple pockets and a camo shirt, and I sling the KRISS Vector on my back and holster a Glock. Maybe some hostile will hesitate ventilating my hide if he mistakes me for a fellow terrorist? I'm carrying the semi-auto's suppressor in a thigh pocket since it won't fit in a holster if screwed onto the muzzle, pocket the two grenades I lifted from the guy who attacked Patty, and am about to scale the outside of the ship when my SAT phone rattles. I grab it up off the floor where I've left it near the open slider so it 'sees' the sky.

"Reardon." It's a voice I don't immediately recognize.

"Make it quick," I reply.

"Harry Weinstein, on board as Harry Drummond, FBI, special liaison to the CIA."

"Make it quick," I say again.

"You said call you but didn't leave your number. I got it from DC."

"I have a plan and it's time to get on with it."

"You realize they've loaded the women aboard another ship? At least most of them. My associate hid out and is still aboard. The

Jewish women they isolated were not among those offloaded. I watched from my veranda until I was threatened and forced back inside."

"No, I didn't know, but I suspected something like that as my lady has not returned from lunch. And my alarm has been running over. My client had a... Doesn't matter. I gotta go."

I'll have to relax to speak again. The heat floods my backbone and my jaw is knotted so tight it's already beginning to ache. Both my charge, my responsibility, Simone, and my lady love are among the missing. I'll fix this, or never be able to fix anything again.

"DC has instructed me to tell you to stand down. A SEAL team is being staged."

"Nice, but as good as they are, it will likely get us all killed. We've got to move from the inside, disarm these explosives, and methodically kill all these pricks. Are you armed?"

"Sidearm only, two actually, as Angelina has hers, and a couple of other defensive toys, but they only work in arm's reach."

"Do these assholes have any demands?"

"Gold, lots of it, delivered to North Africa by parachute."

"That's good news. If it was purely political, killing would be the only result. Where are you?"

"I'm on Deck Eight."

"One deck below the bridge."

"Correct."

"Are you ready to assist if I make a move?"

"Are you sure you won't be the death of us? Bad pun, I guess."

"Hell no, I'm not sure. But if these jihadists see a team coming, I'm sure that will be the death of us. It's a long way from the garbage deck or other opening that an underwater team can breach, or from a deck that a chopper team can rappel to, in order to get to this Mumin. He'll know they're coming long before they reach him and can likely blow this ship with the push of a button. We have to get to him from inside."

Weinstein is quiet for a second, then agrees. "So, what's the plan?"

"Isolate each floor so those of us who are combat-willing can act against reasonable odds, but only after I remove the threat of the destruction of the ship, which means this Mumin. Eventually disarming the explosives. This Mumin claims he has a dead-man switch to detonate, but it's bullshit. I saw the dumb bastard change hands with the switch, and he took no special care."

"Remove the threat how?"

"The fire doors are activated from the bridge and can't be opened other than from the bridge. That will mean only two guards on each floor, then it's up to those on each floor to neutralize them. Mumin is on the bridge or has been and I can only hope still is. I'm headed for the bridge."

"How, with guards on every floor?"

I don't know this guy, so I'm not eager to let him or anyone know I'll be like a fly on the wall climbing up the outside of the ship. I'll be too easily swatted. "Don't worry about it. I can get there. We have players on nearly every deck, so we have a chance. I'm counting on the fact I can reactivate the cabin phones and advise our people we're moving before I close the fire doors. Have you contacted DC regarding the women?"

"I have, but they already knew most of it. Eyes in the sky."

"I gotta go."

"Go with God, young man. You realize you're depending on a bunch of old farts?"

I have to laugh. "I'd rather have willing old farts than pussy millennials."

I disconnect without a reply and begin my climb.

I'm on Deck Six, and this will be by far the biggest climb to date. Three decks up the outside of the ship. And it's warm, my hands sweating, much more weight with the KRISS Vector, grenades, Glock, and eight magazines—four of thirty cartridges each for the KRISS Vector, four extended twenty-four cartridge magazines for the Glock. Normally they'd hold fifteen plus one in the chamber.

Passing Deck Seven there's no one in General Tolliver's suite. I climb on. On Deck Eight, as I light on the veranda, the slider opens. I palm the Glock, but it's an older wizened gentleman I can remember seeing.

He's not bashful however and demands, "Who the hell are you?"

"When you hear the fire doors slam shut, it's a call to arms, disarm and control...hell, throw overboard...there are, or should be, two guards left on your floor. They'll be locked in until the doors are reopened and that can only happen from the bridge."

"I'm no soldier...no hero...I don't want to get involved in this," the watery-eyed old boy says.

"Sir, you are involved. Is your wife with you?"

"She was. She hasn't returned from lunch."

"And likely won't. They offloaded the ladies onto that freighter that's been hanging around. Our only hope is to take back the ship and dispatch the invaders, which means every one of them, one or two at a time."

"They better not hurt my Margaret," he says, and I see a little fire in the old boy's brown eyes.

"We'll never know the fate of the ladies unless we get the ship back. If you're not going to help, stay out of the way."

He nods, and the door slides shut.

So, I continue my climb. There is only a half-dozen suites, all high end, on Deck Nine, and you pass them on the way forward to a door marked 'NO ENTRANCE – CREW ONLY' in bright red letters. The bridge.

As I get my feet on the top rail, reach for and grasp the deck above, my sweaty hand slips and I'm hanging by one hand. Before I can regain my handhold, I feel the old man below wrap his arms around my legs.

"I'll hold you," he yells.

"Thanks," I yell down. "But please don't. I'm okay. Boost me if you want to help."

"You sure?" he asks, then adds, "I'll do what I can."

"Thanks. Let go, please."

He does, puts feeble hands under my feet, tries to lift, and I kip on up, get a foot on the deck, then hand over hand up the three rails and vault the railing.

My feet no more than hit the deck of the veranda on Deck Nine, when the slider opens. I'm reaching for my Glock, then realize I don't have to do so. Tall, still thin and fit if totally white haired, stands former SAS officer, Alistair Nelson.

"Hallways a wee bit crowded?" he asks, with a wicked smile.

"Yes, sir, and we can't wait until dark. I'm headed to take back the bridge." I have to smile as he has a long thin lamp in hand, shade and cord removed, heavy base on the bludgeon end. I can't help but add, pointing at the lamp, "That standard SAS issue?"

He smiles. "UCIW, the short version of the M4 was my favorite, but I forgot mine. You need both those weapons?" he asks.

39

A PETITE GRAY-HAIRED LADY IS SEATED NEARBY. I'M AVOIDING answering his question, trying to poach one of my firearms. I turn to her. "Sorry about the intrusion, ma'am."

She actually works up a smile and a nod. "I'm used to such things, young man. I've followed that bloke over half the world."

"Yes, ma'am," I say, then turn to Nelson, "You coming along?" I ask.

"Wouldn't miss it. Queen Lizzy Two would be a little miffed if I let you bloody Yanks have all the fun."

So, I reverse the Glock and offer him the grip, then take it back before he grabs it. I slip the KRISS Vector off my shoulder and hand him it, reach down and pull the Glock's Gemtech suppressor from a pocket and screw it on. "You're familiar with the KRISS Vector so you back me up, but don't fire that loud prick," then I turn to the lady, "pardon my language, ma'am," and back to Alistair, "unless we're in trouble. I'll take the lead and the suppressed weapon."

"You boys try and come back safe," Mrs. Nelson says and glances at her watch. "It'll be teatime soon."

Then I realize a woman is left on board. "They didn't take you?"

"Age seventy-five seems to have been their limit." She laughs, "Maybe they were short on Depends. There were nearly thirty of us they left behind, and I didn't see any of the Jewish ladies being loaded."

Alistair interrupts. "Social hour is over. There's only been one guard in this short hallway. I might be able to lure him in."

"Go for it." I step back into the bathroom, only leaving the door ajar a couple of inches. The bathroom door is only two paces in the entry hall from the entry door.

Damned if the old boy couldn't have been a Shakespearian thespian. He swings the door open, drops to his knees, grabs his chest with one and leans out propping himself up with the other, looking up and down the hallway. "Help, please, help, I think I'm having a heart attack," then he moans, falls to his back, and scoots a little farther away from the door so the guard, if suckered in, will have to come even with the bathroom door. Alistair's on his back, grasping his chest with both hands, rocking back and forth and moaning.

I hear footfalls in the hall, then see the barrel of an AK47 appear in the hall. The guard is entering slowly.

"Please, please help him," his wife says. She could have starred in Romeo and Juliet, but she stays seated across the living room of the suite.

Finally, the guard steps in and puts the muzzle of the AK in the middle of Alistair's chest. "You...you faking?" he challenges.

When I fling the door open, he tries to swing the muzzle my way but isn't nearly fast enough as I crack him on the left jawbone with the Glock and grab the AK out of his hands with the same motion. Luckily the dipshit has the safety on, so an errant shot doesn't alert any in earshot.

I didn't finish him with the blow, and he starts to yell, but my knuckles driven into his Adam's apple squish his scream. It drives him back against the wall, I pistol whip him one way then the other, and this time he goes down hard and unmoving.

He's chewing something, and I've knocked some leaves out of his mouth.

"Khat," Alistair says. "It's a narcotic. I hope they're all chewing away."

"I remember seeing some of it in Iraq."

"Overboard?" Alistair asks, nodding at the guard while climbing to his feet.

"Later maybe. We've been lucky as hell that no one has spotted a couple others dropped overboard, or me swinging like an orangutan up and down the ship. You got the cord from that lamp?"

"You bet." He fetches it and throws it to me. "And a gag?" I ask, and Mrs. Nelson crosses the room and hands me the silk scarf around her neck, which I imagine she's been using for a hijab. I tie his mouth so tight I hope he's got stuffed up nasal passages and can't breathe.

"Thank you, ma'am," I give her an encouraging smile. The cord is long enough to tie his wrists then fold his legs up and hog tie him.

Alistair hands his wife the lamp. "If the bugger twitches give him your best five-iron on his ugly head." He smiles at me. "She's still a hell of a golfer."

"My pleasure, dear," she says, taking the lamp, pulling a chair away from the desk and positioning herself within swinging distance.

I see the soldier has a small two-way radio clipped to his belt. I snatch it up and clip it to my belt.

"Now," Alistair says, "how about visiting our new captain and setting a new course for this tub?"

"My pleasure," I say, then bend and relieve the guard of his AK and two extra magazines, now happy to leave the KRISS with Alistair.

I take a look out into the hallway. Aft, only fifty feet, is an elevator and a door outside to a deck overlooking the pool. No one is in the hall, so I head for the doorway with the red letters. I pause at the doorway and glance back.

Alistair has the KRISS Vector in present-arms position and is two paces behind me. I leave the AK leaning against the door jamb, so he'd have the most possible mobility.

"Bloody well ready," Alistair says, and gives me a nod.

The damn fools have left the door unlocked. Confidence will kill you. Before I can quietly shove it open, the radio I've purloined crackles. I reverse direction and close the door quietly.

A stream of Arabic rattles out of the radio. I don't get a word of it.

"It's that Mumin, telling his guards to check in. He's asked for two by name."

"Not unless they've got com at the bottom of the Med. They were busy raping a couple of young ladies and forgot to watch their back. They won't be answering. Is he done?"

"Done," the radio crackles again, but it's his guards checking in. I switch the radio off, so it doesn't announce our coming.

I slip the door open and am proud of the ship's maintenance people as, well oiled, it opens without a squeak.

There are two sets of doors off the short hallway, facing each other across the hall. The first door on the left is open, the other's closed. The end of the hallway opens onto the bridge and all I can see are some electronic screens and, above them, six feet height of glass. Beyond that is clear sky.

I creep the hall to the first door, then make a SWAT team entrance, going in low, sweeping the room with the suppressed muzzle of the Glock.

There's a handheld radio perched atop a large desk. A bottle of scotch is beside it along with a glass half full.

The tall thin black man behind the desk, Mumin, is leaning back, feet propped up on the desktop. Another hand-held radio is in his hand. His eyes widen, like fried eggs with black yokes, as he sees me.

"Don't say a word. Don't move," I caution. He doesn't speak, but drops his feet off the desk, leans forward and closes an Apple laptop as if hiding something. There's another device on the desk, far enough that he'll have to lean forward to reach it. I see his eyes cut to the device, it's like a small, square, garage door opener. He cuts eyes back to me. Then he goes for it.

The Glock roars and bucks in my hand. He's suddenly on his side on the floor. Nothing like a head shot to change your mind from whatever mischief you might have been thinking about. I move forward and, just for safety's sake, gather up the device, then look back to see Alistair in the hallway, motioning up with the muzzle of the KRISS Vector.

I check the Mumin guy, just to make sure the 9mm took out a chunk of skull and see gray matter mixed with the pooling blood on the carpet, then turn back to Alistair.

He's speaking in Arabic and motioning with the muzzle. When I make the door, I see another raghead. This one is in a traditional white robe and even has a jambiya, the traditional dagger, stuffed into the sash wrapped around his waist.

Alistair obviously knows his stuff and has stayed back from the creep with his long arm. So, I close. Shoving him with a hand in his chest and with the other and the dagger from his belt. It's a nice piece with a jeweled grip.

"Where's the fire control box," I ask.

"Fuck you," he says, in perfect English.

He's sorry. My instantaneous reaction with the butt of the Glock has shattered his front teeth. He's bent over, hands on knees, spitting blood and shards of teeth, but it doesn't keep me from asking again. "The fire control box?"

But all I get is a gurgle from the haji with the perfect English. But then I understand as he straightens. He's pointing to his own chest. "American, McCord...Sean McCord," he's trying to say.

Then I realize this is the guy Connie turned up when she was hacking sites to check out passengers and crew on the *Blue Pearl*. This is the first time I've come face to face with him. It makes me angry with myself that I wasn't more diligent.

"No shit, a true-blue American?" I ask, and he nods as hard as he can, looking hopeful, hand over mouth, blood seeping between his fingers.

I can't help myself from hitting him face-on with the butt of the Glock, bust his nose which sprays like a garden hose, and he tumbles to the floor. "Fucking traitor," I manage, glad I'm not impeded by rules of engagement.

Alistair taps me on the shoulder, and I turn to see a wall-mounted panel with a Plexiglas cover. Under it is a series of switches under little individual fold-up Plexi covers, and each of them is numbered to match a deck.

"You see any reason to wait?" I ask my new running mate. "Shall I close them?"

"Jolly good," he says, and I flip them all.

If we're going to take the ship back, it has started here.

40

Sa'id Al-Gharsi, a Yemini, has been serving as a floor steward, a butler, on Deck Five. He is stationed at one end of the long hallway and Marco Hernandez, a Pilipino who's on board as a welder—and was instrumental in bringing the explosives aboard in the welding tanks—stands guard at the opposite end of the hallway. Deck Five has suites only in the front half of the ship, only thirty-four total, so Sa'id and Marco have been trading off guarding, taking two-hour stands. Only two suites, nearest the casino, are luxury suites. Next to the suites aft is the small casino and casino bar. The lobby/reception and hotel crew occupy the center but are isolated by fire doors. The aft end is almost totally show lounge—descending theater seating but with small tables, and below them is the stage.

Virgil McIntosh, an American from West Virginia has been stationed at the reception desk since the terrorists took over the ship. He has not been allowed to leave his post and has been sleeping in the small purser's office in his desk chair.

The balance of the crew, other than cooks, has been confined to their quarters on Deck Three.

Sa'id is already unhappy as Alia has been assigned to accompany the women on *Bit Tawfīq* and he has no idea if he'll ever see her again.

Most of the passengers under his guard are the typical retired older folks, average for cruises, except for one. The Black man in 533, next to the large suite, is twice his size and has the look and bearing of a military man. His gray hair is cropped close. He walks with shoulders thrown back and eyes that seem to be scanning all around him.

So, Sa'id is wary when the fire doors slam, and he can't open the one at his end. He strides to the end that Marco has been guarding—he is off and somewhere else on the ship—and tries that fire door. Passenger doors begin to open, and they step into the hallway, yelling at him.

"What's happening? What was that noise?"

Sa'id screams and threatens them with his AK47. "Back in your room. I will shoot. It is just the doors closing. Get back!" He moves up and down the hallway until all suite doors are closed again and quiet is restored.

Then he moves to the door on the far end from his bow station. Closed tight, nearly impenetrable. What is happening?

Then pounding and caterwauling rings from a room—the room occupied by the big Black man.

Master Chief Willard 'Willy' Porter is taken by surprise when the slamming of the fire doors vibrates through his cabin. Damn, he'd been thinking of how to face the two guards, then discovered they've been alternating at their stations. With luck, he'll only have to confront one. At least one at a time.

Now he must implement a plan. He has already made a bludgeon out of the bedside lamp, but he wants something that will solve his problem without facing the muzzle end of an AK. When he'd cut the electrical cord away from the lamp it gave him an idea.

The hallway electrical outlet is near enough. He strips the insulation away from the end of the cord, grounds one of the two exposed copper ends to the door jamb with a Band-Aid and wraps the other around the doorknob. He prays it will work. The door has a peephole. He waits until the guard has threatened the other passengers and he hears their cabin doors slam, then he plugs in his makeshift device, backs away nearly to the sliding glass door, and starts making all the weird noises he can conjure up, screaming and banging on the walls, but distant from the door, so the guard will believe he is not lying in wait just inside.

SA'ID IS FRIGHTENED. He is locked in the hallway alone, with at least thirty-four passengers—more if you count the old women—behind doorways. They can lock him out, he can't lock them in. He gets on his handheld radio and yells, "What is happening? Hello?" and is answered by other guards, but not by his commander, Mumin. Where is Mumin?

The wailing and pounding coming from the room of the big Black man is driving him even more crazy than the fact he doesn't know what is going on, so he stomps to that door. He makes sure his AK is armed, and off safety, and that the sounds are coming from deep in the cabin, then uses his universal pass keycard and plunges it into the slot, when it flashes green he reaches for the knob.

He stiffens as if he's been hit by a lightning strike. All goes black as he collapses, smelling burned flesh.

Willy Porter hears the guard hit the floor and runs to the plug, pulls it, and cautiously opens the door. The guard is in a heap on the floor. Willy scans up and down the hallway seeing no other guard and drags the prostrate man inside, along with his rifle.

He checks for a pulse with an index finger on the man's carotid artery and finds a weak one, so he binds the man's wrists behind him, relieves him of his sidearm and two grenades on his battle-rattle belt, then carries the AK as he goes out into the hall. He can't help but smile at the blisters and blackened streak on the guard's hand that had grabbed the doorknob.

Sucker.

He strides out of his suite with confidence. First, he checks the fire doors at each end of the hallway. Locked tight. It would take explosives to breach those doors.

Then he goes from room to room, beating on each door, talking to each occupant to see who, if anyone, might be willing to help. More than half the rooms are occupied by men who are crazed with worry over their wives. A few, the much older ones, have their wives with them. Willy gets four volunteers, all former military who offer to help no matter the consequences.

Willy arms them as best he can, keeping the AK47 and two extra clips for himself. One passenger, Paul Whittington, proudly exclaims he is an ex-Navy Seabee, in addition, shooting is a hobby, so he gets the guard's sidearm and the single extra magazine, two of the others are armed with grenades after they proclaim their former proficiency with the weapon, and after he's cautioned them.

Then, all they can do is wait.

Army Master Sergeant Rockin' Roy Filson is on Deck Four, with even fewer suites, as it's the work deck with anchoring and docking equipment forward and the main restaurant aft. Fire doors on that deck seal off one end of the suite area, between it and the reception area outside the main restaurant doors. Another fire door closes off the forward work desk, which is always closed to passengers by another locked door.

However, open decks surround the restaurant on three sides and extend slightly past the restaurant reception area.

Filson, a hundred forty pounds but lean and in fairly-decent physical condition for sixty-seven years old, has been beside himself with anger and angst, as his little sixty-year-old ninety-pound wife, Joy, has not returned. He is on the side to see the freighter being loaded and is sure she's been forced to leave with the *Bit Tawfīq*. He's been pacing the floor, angry that nothing is going to happen until dark. Who the hell is this Reardon anyway to act as if he's running the show—the revolt show? Roy is about to step outside and confront the single guard assigned to their short hallway when he hears, and feels, the shudder of the fire door being slammed. His only weapon is a can of his wife's hairspray. In his small suite—actually a single room, but all cabins on board are called suites—there are no table lamps, only ceiling lamps over the bed.

But he's had his eyes burned before when he walked by while Joy was messing with her thinning hair. It's a weapon, of sorts.

So, as soon as the slamming door reverberates up and down the hallway he steps out. The guard is at the fire door, only twenty-five feet from Roy's cabin.

He moves quickly, spray can in hand. The guard, who's monkeying with the door, hears or senses him coming and spins, bringing the AK47 up. At the same time, Roy aims and sprays. The guard reels back against fire door but pulls the trigger as he does. and Roy feels a burn on the outside of his thigh and takes another 7.62 bullet through his side, but it doesn't do more than clip bone and Roy keeps staggering forward, spraying.

The guard drops the AK, putting his hands over his eyes. Roy snatches it up and empties the clip into the dark-skinned man, who spins to the side and grabs his chest. But wounds are spurting blood from his groin to his collarbone, and he's dead, hamburger, as he hits the floor.

It's not Roy's first rodeo and he collapses to the floor, sets the AK aside, pulls his belt and puts a tourniquet on his deeply grooved thigh. Then he's trying to get his tee-shirt off to tear it up to stuff the through-and-through wound in his side, when men start sticking their heads out of rooms.

He waves at the nearest one to come help and the man hurries to his side. The man answers with an Australian or New Zealand accent.

"You serve?" Roy ask the man as he assists in tearing the tee-shirt into wound stuffing material.

"Serve?"

"Military?" Roy asks, a little insistently as he's getting a little dizzy.

"Damned if I didn't, mate," the man says, and Roy decides he's an Aussie.

He hands the Aussie the AK47. Then instructs him, "That prick has two grenades on his belt, one of them fancy daggers in a sheath, and a sidearm." The hall is filling with men. Roy motions at them. "See who's willing and distribute."

Then he fades from consciousness.

Deck Four, at least the passenger section, is secure...at least for the moment.

41

CONNIE NORDSTROM IS ARMED.

Her little semiauto .380 is strapped to the inside of her thigh. In her purse is the brass compact with mirror, face application, with a small pair of nubbins that will deliver millions of volts when switched on—the women have been allowed to keep purses after being searched. Everything resembling a weapon, including fingernail files were removed. Her small can of hair spray is actually mace and was missed. But when confronted with a dozen well-armed hostiles, and among more than one hundred women—mostly blue hairs—the last thing she'll do is risk pulling a weapon and responding rifle fire when surrounded by dozens of innocents. She'll bide her time.

The cargo area of the freighter has been turned into a jail, with four large containment areas only fifteen feet deep by eighteen feet long enclosed with hog wire fencing. Each cell is packed with forty women, plus or minus...just over six square feet per prisoner. A long walkway three feet wide runs the length of the cells on the port side with ladders to the deck on each end. Each cell is provided with cases of plastic bottled water and four five-gallon plastic buckets to be used as toilets. A six-foot-high stack of folded blankets, twenty-five total—fewer than needed—rest in a corner. The floor is a cold metal deck with a cold bilge below and the sea beyond that.

Connie makes a quick count and figures there are one hundred twenty-five women, more or less, all under 65 years old; four are teenagers, two only seven or eight, maybe only a dozen under thirty. She has positioned herself to be in the same cell as Simone, Patty, and Gretchen.

Simone and Patty are so frightened they seem catatonic, Gretchen far less so, but still wide-eyed and fearful.

Now that the male guards are absent, the women can undo their scarfs and face coverings, and do.

Connie crosses the cell, hoping she can give some comfort and encouragement to Simone, Patty, and Gretchen.

"Calm down, girls. There's nothing much we can do with a dozen or more armed hostiles aboard. Stay calm, hydrate, get as much rest and nourishment as possible…"

But Simone interrupts her. "I don't have my meds."

Only then does Connie remember that Simone is diabetic. "No insulin?" she asks.

"No. It won't take long before I'm sick as hell."

"Rest and calm down…it's the best we can do for a while. Half the United States military will be after us very soon."

"Soon may be too late," Gretchen cautions, with a low voice so only Connie can hear.

The only guard below is the woman who introduced herself as Alia, and she wears a battle rattle belt with two grenades, a can of mace, a Taser, a sidearm and extra magazine, and three magazine holsters for the AK47 she carries with some obvious competence.

She occupies a stool near the forward ladder leading to the

deck.

Connie has counted an even dozen hostiles topside, four of whom have escorted them to their cells. There were also large plank boxes on the decks fore and aft, and hostiles were tearing them apart as the women boarded. It was obvious to Connie that some kind of cannons have been concealed in the planks. The superstructure is only twenty or so feet high on the freighter, which she determined to be one hundred twenty feet or so in length. On both port and starboard sides, hostiles were mounting what looked to Connie to be fifty-caliber machine guns. At least four, maybe six. She was below before she could make sure.

There were no ports below, so she had no idea where they were headed when she felt the vibration of the engines.

She'd bide her time, but if one of those filthy fuckers dared to lay a hand on her or the girls under Mike's protection, he was going to get a hell of a surprise.

The hell of it is, Simone may die from neglect, not too much unwanted attention.

As soon as we've secured the asshole who kept yelling he was American—as if I give a rat's ass and, in fact, it only makes me hate him more—with cable-tied wrists in the back, feet folded and bound to wrists, he's thrown in the captain's closet. I decide it's time for the second part of our plan.

Now I must figure out exactly what the second part is?

"Any ideas?" I ask Alistair.

"We now have radios, which obviously are on channel with lots of other wogs all over the ship. So, we change channels. How about twenty-three? A lucky number for me as I was chest wounded and it missed all the vitals when I was that age. Smashed a rib, but missed heart, vessels, and barely nicked a lung."

"Sounds good to me," and we reset the radios.

"Now," I suggest, "it's a floor at a time. Let's trade weapons," and he gives me the KRISS Vector and spare magazines. The KRISS is much shorter and a more viable weapon in urban battlefields. The close quarters of the ship qualify as urban. He keeps Mumin's longer AK.

"Now what?" he asks.

"I'm going floor to floor. I'll radio the floor number and you open the doors when I'm locked and loaded."

"Yes, Alistair cautions, "but first let's activate the intercoms and tell all to stay in their suites."

And I caution back, "We don't want to alert these assholes that we're on the bridge."

"The way the radios have been crackling, I'm sure they know this Mumin guy is out of pocket. I'll be surprised if they aren't on their way. I've got a smattering of Arabic."

He makes the announcement in Arabic then broken English, as if he's one of the hostiles. So many Arab countries are represented among both terrorists and crew, including an American, his accent won't be questioned. Then he turns to me. "You get out of this area and I'll reclose the fire doors leading here."

"Good thinking. Make damn sure they don't get in. Watch those big windows. They can get over the top and drop down to see what's going on."

"Ten four," he says, then adds, "Get going, let's not let them start planning. Take the Glock, too—I've got Mumin's AK—and the suppressor may come in handy."

"One thing first." I go to the desk and grab the device that we presume was to detonate the explosives that would have destroyed the ship. The wings of the bridge extend out six feet past the hull on either side, so bridge occupants can see some of the ship behind and following seas. I investigate the device and see it has a battery compartment on the back and pray that these pagan bastards are not smart enough to program the device so if the battery compartment is opened, it signals.

But I also don't want the device to short out and send a signal when I do what I plan to do. So, I hold my breath, open the battery compartment and pop the nine-volt battery out.

I'm able to exhale, so I presume that means I'm not fried in LPG hell. Then I walk to the edge of the wing and open a small slider and drop the device into Davy's locker. I only hope they don't have a fallback with another haji holding another device somewhere else on the ship. I guess if I see a ball of flame enveloping me, I've miscalculated.

Then I suggest, "Turn the phones back on. We may need to communicate with someone locked in their suite."

"Good idea," he replies and starts searching the control panels, finds a switch near the intercom systems and gives me a nod.

"I'm out of here," I inform Alistair, and head down the hall and out of the bridge. No one is in the short hall outside between me and the fire door, so I head that way, get ready taking a combat stance, and radio Alistair. "Deck Nine."

The door swings aside and in ten strides, I'm passing the stairway that only goes down from Deck Nine. In a few strides I'm at a glass door looking out at the deck that overlooks the pool, one deck below.

I drop low and creep on elbows close enough to the edge to peer down. Four hostiles are enjoying the pool, splashing and laughing. I find that a bit strange, but so far damn near everything that's happened has been more than merely a 'bit' strange. Then I realize that outside they have no way to know the fire doors have closed. And no one can get outside to tell them. Since they're swimming, radios are with their clothes in a pile at the far end of the pool.

I go prone and decide to ruin their fun. I think about trying my luck with the suppressed Glock then remember how water muffles explosive sounds.

My next decision is one grenade or two? This likely is one of the few opportunities to use the explosive devices without compromising passengers.

Hell, one should do. They're intent on taking a small beach ball away from one another so the timing is good. It's a foreign grenade, maybe Russian, and I presume works the same as its American cousin, so I pull the pin, count to two and lob it. They don't even notice the splash. It erupts like a miniature sub depth-charge with a four-foot-high bubble, ten-feet in diameter. The two nearest the blast are immediately floating face down, the two furthest are bleeding and confused, so I put one suppressed 9mm in each of their chests; I'd be ashamed to miss at no more than fifty feet. Now there are four floating face down. One I didn't see, as he was under a sunshade, runs to the side of the pool looking very confused that the swimming pool exploded. Then he seems to get it and shades his eyes and looks up as a nine mil takes him about the bottom of the rib cage and knocks him to his back. He rolls and is crawling as I put another between his scapula. I'm embarrassed about the first not being chest center but then, hell, two out of three ain't bad.

These dummies are too damn easy, I think, just as a three-shot burst stitches the wall behind me and as I scramble back as far as possible from the edge, another three-shot burst blows the glass door all to hell.

42

I DIVE OVER THE, NOW GLASSLESS, LOW TRANSOM INTO THE hallway, crab the first twenty feet, then crouch and run a few feet to the stairway, descend four stairs at a time to a landing, then slow, and creep the second set. There's another glass door out to the pool, but I see no one, so I hustle to the fire door leading to the forward suites on Deck Eight, then pause to count my expended Glock cartridges. I had one in the chamber and a twenty-four shot extended clip. I fired four, so twenty-one left. I recall that there are over thirty suites on Deck Eight forward, so I imagine there are at least two guards.

I radio Alistair. "Deck Eight," and crouch with the Glock extended in a two-handed grip.

A guard is standing just inside, looking very relieved that the door is finally open, then his mouth drops open as I put one in his chest, knocking him to his back, and one in his head as I pass. One is good, two are better—double tap my Marine Corps instructor drilled into our heads. I have to jerk his AK47 hard to get it free as his full weight is on the sling. I figured using his weapon was better than taking the time to unsling my KRISS Vector, but I was wrong. Another guard at the far end of the hall, at least two hundred feet, already has his long arm shouldered. I dive behind the fallen soldier and use him for a rest, flip the safety and the selector to three shots, as three shells splatter the fire door behind me. Then another three hit the jamb on the far side.

I pull one off, then realize the dumb bastard didn't have one in the chamber. I work the slide as shells thump into the body beneath me, splattering me with goo. I fire a three-shot burst and he spins away, crawls a little, then all I can see are his legs extended out from the indentation where he's leaning on a suite door.

On my feet, I close the distance between us until I'm less than a hundred feet from him. I shoulder my weapon and put three into his extended legs. He screams and throws the AK he's carrying out into the hallway. I see his stretched arms as if he's surrendering.

So, I move forward. But as I come up on him, I see his eyes roll up in his head and he slumps forward. He's through, as a four-foot circle of blood surrounds his legs, permeating the hard hallway carpet. I must have blown away both femoral arteries and he bled out like pouring water from a pitcher.

Another hallway down.

A couple of the more adventurous passengers are peeking out of their suites, so I yell, "There are grenades, two rifles, and two side arms here. Arm yourselves. We're taking the ship back." Then I have an afterthought. "You'd be wise to hide these bodies."

Deck Seven next.

I get down the stairway to the Deck Seven mid-ship fire door without incident, get in position, and radio Alistair.

The door flies open, and I flatten myself against the sidewall, surprised to be confronted by armed men then realize they're passengers, I yell, out, "Friendly, hold your fire," and am pleased to see muzzles lowered.

"We got one wounded, but two dead Muzzies," one of the AK47-wielding passengers calls out, and I see an older gentleman leaning against a hallway wall, obviously with both a thigh and a torso wound. But he struggles to give me a thumbs up and I give him a quick salute back. It seems Deck Seven is already in good hands.

"Stay locked and loaded," I yell to the crowded hallway, then spin on my heel and head back to the stairway only to hear Arabic chatter and footfalls.

More firepower called for, I unsling the KRISS, and wait. I know there's more than one, but only one rounds the bottom of the stairway and has his AK going to his shoulder. He should have tried a hip shot as I stitch him from belly button to broad grimace. He reels back, and I hear yelling and retreating footsteps. I reach the bottom of the stairs in time to see another soldier rounding the landing halfway up. I'm not fast enough to blow his legs away but rather take a few stairs, just enough to be able to reach through the stiles and heave my second grenade up to the top of the stairs.

I retreat as the roar rips through the stairwell and don't wait but rather go down to the Deck Six fire door. I radio Alistair on the run. It opens, and I'm greeted by the slap of passing 7.62 lead, so close it makes my left ear ring. I hit the floor on a knee and empty my clip down the hallway, then stand and grab for the Glock as I can't get the damn thing free without standing. I've failed to remove the suppressor so the frickin' thing is hard to handle with the length, but I get it raised as a guard peeks around from a door indentation. I snap a shot and he fades back into the doorway, unharmed. Another at the far end of the long hallway has taken a knee and is firing away. I'm knocked ass end over teakettle and momentarily think I'm cut in half, then realize a shot has hit the magazine on my belt. I spin with the impact, hit the deck, and, prone, manage to hit the far guard. But the other one is still hidden in the doorway.

I'm surprised to hear two muffled shots and that guard spins out of the recess to the far side, hits the wall and slides down it, leaving smears of blood.

"Who's there?" comes a voice from that doorway.

"Reardon, American, friendly," I yell back and am pleased to see the old CIA guy, Drummond or Weinstein, or whatever the hell his name is, stick his head out, then step out. He's shot the guard through the door. Following him closely is his travelling companion, the strikingly beautiful Hispanic chick. She comes out in a crouch, her handgun held in both hands as she pans the hallway.

Then I catch a movement down the hall.

"Watch it," I yell, and jog past them. "The other guard is down, but maybe not out."

When I come even with the second guard, he's on his hands and knees, blowing blood from a fatal neck wound so I put him out of his misery with another to the back of his head. Again, I'm pleased I'm not hindered by rules of engagement. I do take the time to strip away his two grenades to replace those I've used. I throw his AK and sidearm to Weinstein and his lady.

Then I limp back to the stairway end of the hallway.

My hipbone is hurting like hell, but I realize it's only from the bruising of my magazine being blown away and my belt half ripped off. No time to stop and whine. With a yell to Weinstein, "More weapons here. Organize your people," I head for the stairway. I can't help but add, "Sorry, couldn't stand down." He smiles and gives me a thumbs up as men begin to appear out of the cabin doors.

Deck Five is next.

Descending the stairs to Deck Five is a new problem altogether. It's obvious by now the bad guys are totally alerted to the rebellion. I must presume they've been chattering on other channels on the handhelds. I can only hope and pray some zealot is not figuring a way to detonate the LPG tanks and blow us all to hell. The stairway to Deck Five lands next to a wide-open lobby, that will be on my right, and beyond it is the casino, casino bar, and a couple of shops. Then there's the main bar, which is also ship-wide, and a seventy-foot deep room.

To my immediate left is the fire door and, on the bow side, are some thirty to thirty-five suites.

I wish I had some good old flash-bang grenades, but I have only frags. I fear chucking them ahead of me into the lobby or the bar. If I'm to be one of the good guys, it would tar my image to take out a few old blue-haired passengers.

I know only about ten words in Arabic, I knew more years ago while serving in Iraq, but have tried hard to forget them.

So, I yell out, "*As' salam alaykum,*" in greeting, thinking I might fool someone.

"Fuck you, infidel," is replied, in an accent, and it's not a Brooklyn one. I guess my accent is not so great.

Now what? I can't chuck a grenade as I have no idea who's in the lobby.

Then the voice rings out again. "Throw out your weapon or we blow the ship up."

Discretion is the better part of valor I decide, so I spin around and haul ass back up the stairs and to a side door leading to an area where the shore boats—tenders—are stored, then go over the rail and drop down to a deck just outside the lobby, an area from which boarding and departures are normally made.

I drop as combat-ready as possible since I'm facing a glass door into the lobby, from which I was being cursed. But I see no one.

As stealthily as possible, I open the door and slip inside. The hotel counter is to my right and beyond that, across the hall leading to the casino and bar, is the concierge counter. I can't see who might be behind the hotel desk, but the far one is empty. I know there are offices beyond the counter space.

I creep forward, and a desk attendant comes into view, still in his nice hotel uniform. He looks very frightened and is standing behind the counter with both hands conspicuously flat on the countertop as if ordered to remain that way.

He cuts his eyes at me, then looks down, back at me and down again. Without lifting his hands, he points down the index fingers, both left and right of him. I can only surmise that bad guys are hiding behind the counter on either side of him, awaiting him greeting me as I wander into the lobby from where I was on the stairway. He remains silent.

43

It's time to take a risk, so with the KRISS in one hand and the Glock in the other I step out directly in front, so I can ventilate the counter without hitting the hotel guy.

I put three shots from each weapon, spaced a foot apart from just beyond the width of the deskman out. Screams, slamming, and banging erupt as I drop back, and the deskman flees into the office behind, slamming the door so hard the counter vibrates.

From behind the counter, a clip is emptied through the wooden face, but I'm back behind the adjacent wall and it merely shatters a couple of waiting room chairs and a glass case beyond. I'm surprised to note the fire door itself, across the room, has taken a couple of hits that appear to have penetrated.

Then moans and gurgles come from behind the desk. I'm peeking around but can't see down behind the counter when the desk clerk reappears in the office doorway with a heavy paperweight in hand. I can see him swing it hard. It sounds like he's beating a watermelon. Then he places the bloody paperweight on the counter, returns his hands flat there, and looks at me with a white-faced big-eyed barely perceptible nod.

"It's safe now," he mutters, a little Orphan-Annie-eyed as if in shock.

I can't help but smile. He's finished a terrorist off with a snow-globe, snowflakes still swirling around a cherubic angel inside. Christian revenge.

"Collect their weapons and stay locked in the office," I instruct him. "Can you use those AKs?" I ask.

He gives me a nod. "I was an Eagle Scout."

I can't help but shrug and smile. So, satisfied, I limp for the fire door leading to the cabins.

I'm sure the guards behind this fire door are well forewarned with the amount of gunfire just outside their posts.

I get on the radio and announce to Alistair, "Deck Five."

He starts to say "Ten," and I presume he was about to give me a ten four, when I hear nothing but automatic fire over the radio. Then it goes dead.

I back away from the door and call again.

ALISTAIR HEARS the clattering on the bridge roof as Reardon is calling him to switch open the Deck Five fire door. He's reaching for the switch and about to give Reardon a ten four when a pair of combat boots appears outside the windows, dropping down to a narrow ledge above where he can get a foothold. He's only dropped to his waist when another pair appears next to the first.

So, Alistair steps back into the doorway. He wants to take out both of them, so he waits until the second set catches up with the first. The windows are six-feet-tall so both hostiles don't have to bend to see inside. He waits until both are in place, then sprays the window with a half clip and both hostiles disappear, falling backward. Alistair knows it is at least a twelve-foot fall to the roof of Deck Seven.

He is smugly congratulating himself, when an arm extends down and a grenade flies through a break in the now shattered glass. It is obviously safety glass and the thrower has to beat the glass twice to get enough of an opening, but does so.

Luckily that delay gives Alistair time to scramble back and through the first available side door off the hallway—the chart room.

He slams the door behind as the explosion roars down the hallway. He wastes no time in jumping back to the hallway, praying they haven't followed with a second grenade, when two more sets of legs appear. He doesn't wait this time. He shatters the window with the rest of the AK's clip. They both appear for only a second as they follow the other two to the roof below.

He doubts they will try breaching his position via the forward windows again, so grabs up his radio.

"Slight interruption," he transmits. "Four more wogs done bit the dust, to use a John Wayne-ism." Then said, "Oh, bollocks."

"What?" Reardon came back.

"They chucked a grenade and the bridge is half destroyed. The switch panel is caved in, as well as much of the other gear."

"No more fire doors operable?"

"Not right away. I'll get the front panel off and see if I can short the other switches."

"Advise when and if. I'm headed for the engine room to do my bomb squad act. Stay tight and out of the line of fire."

"Ten four, you too."

Zamir, the huge soldier who was left atop the landing overlooking the engine room and the now nearly seventy Jewish passengers, both men and women, was tired. His head was hanging. He was one of Colonel Musa's favorite followers and had been kept very busy while this attack was planned, and even on the cruise to join the *Blue Pearl*. He had slept little. The quiet rocking of the ship, now dead in the water with movement only subject to the wind and waves, was hypnotizing, particularly in the growing heat and humidity of the engine room.

The only thing keeping him from dozing off was the intermittent crackle of the radio. The chatter of other hostiles was beginning to worry him as many had been summoned by others and were not responding. Mumin Amir, the leader of the shipboard faithful, has not responded to the calls of Captain Yasim Al-Jamil, now in command aboard the *Blue Pearl* as Colonel Musa had left with the freighter and women. He'd heard the captain order a squad to the bridge to see what was happening, now they had not been heard from.

Zamir was dozing, even as concerned as he was becoming. He had heard chatter about fire doors being closed and attempts to open them unsuccessful. He wanted to move out of the engine room to test the door just beyond the laundry room, but it would mean not watching the Jews, and he'd been ordered not to take eyes off them. He'd been delivered a plate of rice and pot of tea. The Jewish passengers had nothing, not even water. Earlier, when he'd radioed Colonel Musa regarding the Jews' complaints, Musa had replied, "Where they are going, they will not need full stomachs."

More than one of the Jews spoke Arabic, overheard the radio, and the message passed among them.

44

As had been the plan, Colonel Musa, was aboard the *Bit Tawfig* with the women, who would be the primary bait for the payment of the huge ransom. He left the *Blue Pearl* under the control of his next-in-command, Captain Yasim Al-Jamil. Yasim has established his command post in the Panorama Lounge, aft on Deck Eight, with a protective guard of ten of his finest soldiers. The Lounge has a fire door separating it from the pool. And like others, it has been closed and is impossible to open except with explosives or from the controls on the bridge. Al-Jamil is incensed he's been locked in. He has, among his armaments, eight Claymore mines. His last order on the radio was, to anyone near on Deck Eight, to stand clear of the fire door closing off the Panorama Lounge, as he is preparing to blow the door with a Claymore.

As the Claymore is activated with a wire pull, which often serves as a trip-wire on a trail or in a dark building, he loosens it and ties a longer cord so he and his men, and the two servers he's allowed to remain in the lounge, can take cover out of the line-of-sight of the mine and its killing shrapnel. The explosion knocks over tables and chairs, destroys hanging chandeliers, and shatters two of the large plate glass windows fifty feet away, looking aft of the ship.

The Colonel has not heard a word from the men he'd formerly ordered to the bridge. Colonel Akim Musa's parting orders, as he'd boarded the *Bit Tawfīq* was for Yasim to take over command of the ship from Mumin Amir, even if it required sending Amir to his seventy-two virgins. Musa wants all credit for this mission—second only to September 11th—to be his and is ferociously jealous of Mumin Amir's admiration in the eyes of Sheik Ali Hassan. If Mumin is disposed of, he would still be a hero in the Sheik's eyes, but no longer competition for any reward the Sheik would pay. And future admiration would be Musa's alone.

Yasim is a leader; he's not gotten to his position as a captain without showing his skill in many previous encounters with other factions of Al-Shabaab, Al-Qaeda, and Isis, not to speak of his former encounters with Americans, Brits and Poles in Addis Ababa, Ethiopia, Syria, and Iraq. He is a well-seasoned soldier.

He's led his ten men, seven of them carrying Claymores, at a dead run to the stairway and up to floor nine where the bridge occupies the most bow-forward position on that deck.

Of course, they've discovered the fire door shut.

Yasim tries his radio one more time, but none of the four he'd sent to take the bridge answer, nor does Mumin Amir or his fellow faithful.

So, it is time to gain access, even at the risk of destroying much of what is inside. But first he sends two men outside with a Claymore, to mount the roof and see what they might see through the bridge's large front windows.

It is less than five minutes when they radio the message that they can see three dead and one badly wounded comrade on the roof of a lower deck below the bridge, and shattered windows of the bridge itself.

"Can you gain access?" Yasim radios back.

"Of course," one of them, an Ethiopian named Omar, replies. Like Yasim and Musa, he is eager to gain favor with a superior. He removes his jacket, has his fellow hold one sleeve, and lowers himself down across a solid, slightly tilted window next to the shattered one.

His last vision is of a tall wild-eyed ruddy-complexioned white man with white hair, aiming a rifle at him.

That window, too, is blown away and he joins dead comrades on the roof below.

His comrade who's been holding the other sleeve of his jacket scrambles back, crabbing across the bridge roof, as three gunshots poke holes in the metal roof just behind his retreat. Had he not tripped over an array of antennas and rolled away he would have been accompanying his partner on a trip to stand before Allah.

He quickly radios his commander, who's already heard the gunfire.

ALISTAIR IS DOWN to one magazine, thirty rounds, and takes a deep breath as he inserts his final one into the AK. He steps into the hallway, the door to only six suites separating him from that hallway and the fire door beyond. He picks up the radio.

"Reardon, acknowledge," he calls.

Mike comes back immediately. "What the hell's going on? I heard a hell of an explosion. I was afraid it was a precursor to the big boom."

"I don't know, but the bastards are trying to access the bridge. I guess they want to open the fire doors. There's a surprise for them —" He doesn't complete his sentence as the door between hallway and bridge explodes inward and hits him as if it had been dropped off a four-story building. However, it hits him flat on—would likely have killed him if it hit on edge—but knocks him flying onto the floor of the now glass-and-equipment-scattered bridge.

Yasim had positioned not one but two Claymores in front of the fire door, and even though it was seventy feet from the door marked 'CREWMEN ONLY', the explosion was concentrated down the five-foot-wide hallway and blew the 'CREWMEN ONLY' door off with such force that it flew past four offices and into Alistair.

He'd, luckily, had the AK slung on a shoulder, and it stayed with him.

Equally lucky, the force of the explosion has shocked the ten remaining hostiles and Yasim, and they have to spend a moment getting their bearings. But in less than a minute, Yasim yells, "Follow me," and charges down the hallway toward the bridge.

Yasim spots the old man on the floor, rifle raised, too late. The rifle's muzzle spits fire and Yasim spins with blood splattering those behind. One of them is hit as well. But the following two go prone and fire indiscriminately as do the standing two behind.

Many of their rounds splatter the walls, some ricocheting like angry wasps, but enough of them strike home to silence the tall Australian and send him rolling across the bridge floor as his magazine empties harmlessly into walls and ceiling.

I HEAR THE EXPLOSION, then the transmit button on Alistair's radio is released. I try him several times in a row, then decide he is either out of commission, his radio destroyed, or worse, the bridge has been retaken by the terrorists. I fear the latter. For the short time I knew the Aussie, I am sure if the bridge has been retaken, it is over his dead body.

With Alistair not responding I have no way to access the Deck Five forward area of suites but move to the fire door and listen where the shots from the two hiding behind the reception desk had poked holes about chest high. The funny thing is I hear a man inside moaning and crying out in Arabic. I can only smile as I hope he's been taken out by friendly fire. I presume he ran to that door when he heard my gunfire and was hit by the reckless return fire through the reception counter. God works in mysterious ways.

I've been avoiding going directly to Deck Three and the entrance to the two-story engine room as I'm sure it's full of the Jewish folks who'd been removed from their cabins, both men and women, and placed there—I'd like to say for safekeeping but know the opposite is true.

And, attempting to access it could be the trigger that pushes the terrorists into detonating the LPG tanks and putting us all in Davy Jones' locker, not that we'd care as we'd likely be long cooked before reaching there. I presume there is more than one fire door on that deck as it, and part of Deck Two, are the housing for the whole crew in the forward two-thirds of the ship, engine room, and fuel storage in the aft one-third.

If I have to destroy a fire door to get access to the engine room, and if there's a guard or several there, then they'll have lots of time to detonate.

45

But I have no choice if I'm to keep them from vaporizing us all. It's a catch 22. You're damned if you do, likely damned to hell if you don't.

So, I skip Deck Four and descend directly to Deck Three. Deck Four's fire doors remain closed, so if guards are there, they are still locked in. That could be a good thing.

I realize in passing outside glass doors that it's getting dark. Unless there are automatic controls on the ship's interior lights, it will soon be very dark, with the exception of moonlight through ports and glass windows and doors.

That could be to my advantage, if I can get back to my room where my night vision is hidden. A big if!

And I'm right with my remembrance of Deck Three. There's a fire door between me and the base of the stairway, the passenger laundry room, beyond it the engine room, and the other way between the landing and the crew quarters.

Now, how to get the damned fire door open.

A HALF DOZEN of the Jews have military experience—four of the men and two of the women. Two couples had emigrated from Israel where all citizens must spend time in the military. Both couples are in their early sixties. The other two men served in the American Military, one a clerk in a supply unit, but the other in the tank corps. They all met prior to being imprisoned in the engine room and had migrated to a spot as far from the guard as they could get to plan their escape. Those plans were accelerated when they heard, and the four who'd emigrated from Israel understood, the radio message in Arabic which said, "Where they are going, they won't need full stomachs."

As they watch the big guard up on the stairway dozing, they decide to implement their plan.

Even in her sixties, Gertrude 'Goldie' Goldstein is an attractive woman with flashing dark eyes and an easy smile. She weighs no more than ten pounds more than when she'd graduated high school in her hometown of Krakow, Poland, just before her family immigrated to Israel where she'd married Abraham. She is a shapely woman, with generous breasts, and proud of her womanhood.

"I'm ready," she says in a low voice to the others. She'd unbuttoned her blouse down two buttons below the ravine that is her cleavage.

"God go with you, Goldie," Abraham says, and gives her a restrained hug with an arm around her shoulder.

"Yahweh has always been at my side," she replies seriously.

She moves through the sitting and sleeping men and women to the base of the stairway, then, barefoot, begins to climb. The guard is more than twice her weight and armed with both an AK47, a sidearm, grenades on his belt, and one of those wicked curved daggers many Arab men wear with such pleasure. Goldie is a nature lover, and an environmentalist, and hates the vanity of Arab men who relish the destruction of Rhinos, causing their near extinction for their horns to adorn the vanity of daggers. She knows many Arabic men pay thousands, some hundreds of thousands, for a dagger with Rhino horn grips. Almost more than the fact these *hajis* are holding them prisoner, she hates this guard for his dagger—even if the grip is likely cheap bone—and the fact the man who'd searched her purse had taken a golden locket with a picture of her daughter whom she'd lost to breast cancer. She believes in the sanctity of life but is rapidly coming around to the concept of 'an eye for an eye'. Arabic-speaking men have taken so much from her people. All of these things go through her mind as she ascends the rough treads of the expanded metal stairway. It hurts her bare feet, but she barely notices.

And what she planned is particularly heinous to a man who's already lost one eye.

She, on the other hand, has no weapons other than a pair of tweezers. They had been overlooked, or ignored, when the guards rampaged through the women's purses.

Abraham, and the other three Jewish men, gather, seated and acting as if they are dozing, at the bottom of the stairway, but ready to charge the guard should Goldie be able to divert the muzzle of the AK47 long enough. Five of them should be able to control the huge man. Particularly since Abe had been able to find an eighteen-inch pipe wrench and hide it up his coat sleeve. The head of the heavy wrench is too big to fit along with his arm, so it is cradled in his hand. If he can only get close enough.

Goldie makes it to within three steps of the dozing guard, who is seated and leaning back against the door to the LPG storage, when his eyes flutter, and open. His milky eye is particularly ugly up this close.

He grunts and has to roll to his side to get a hand under himself and push up to his feet. Goldie instinctively puts her back to the entrance door, at right angle to the LPG door, and smiles, as she pulls her blouse and bra away from two large cantaloupe-sized breasts.

Zamir, the engine room guard, is not the sharpest needle in the sewing box and stands for a moment, gaping at the nakedness of the woman in front of him, then with one hand, without hesitation, he reaches out and caresses a melon. The other hand holds his AK dangling at his side. She giggles like a schoolgirl, reaches up as if to caress the side of his face, in return, and with the butt buried in the palm of her hand, drives the tweezers deep into his only good left eye.

He stumbles back, at first gripping his eye with both hands, the tweezers appearing between his fingers, and as tall as he is, teeters back over the rail. Goldie pushes as hard as she can, but he drops the AK and grabs onto the top rail.

Just as he is about to recover and land back on his feet, Abraham tops the stairway and slams the heavy pipe wrench onto the fingers clasping the railing. He jerks back, releasing the other hand to grab for the Jew man, but Goldie shoves hard again, with both hands.

The big guard goes over the rail and falls twelve feet slamming onto metal deck below. Even had he survived the fall, he wouldn't survive the dozen men who fall on him with punches and kicks.

Abraham stands at the railing above for a moment, looking down, satisfying himself that the guard is no longer a threat. Then he turns to his wife. "Goldie, cover yourself, have you no shame?" but he is smiling broadly.

YASIM'S second in command is an Uzbekistani Muslim, Vlad, whose father had been a Russian bureaucrat. Vlad followed his mother's faith and soon fled to Afghanistan to join the Taliban before fleeing again to Algeria, where he eventually ended up with Al-Shabaab. He is eager to take command of the remaining four soldiers of the ten who'd attacked the bridge.

He and his men all concur their most important mission is to get the fire doors open. One of his men had been an electrician and with the help of another who both spoke and read English, immediately they recognized the fire panel and it's Plexie-covered switches as their target. The bad news is the panel is fairly-well peppered with shrapnel. They pry it open and the electrician immediately begins jumping the switches.

They are happy they have accomplished what they know will free soldiers all over the ship.

They wouldn't be happy to realize they'd also released the crew from Decks Two and Three, and passengers who'd already dispatched guards.

NO ONE COULD HAVE BEEN MORE surprised than me when the fire door swings open as I am considering rigging my two grenades in hopes of blowing the door hardware away.

Almost as soon as the fire door swings aside, I see the door twenty feet away on the other side of the laundry room swing aside. I drop to a knee, ready to drop a guard, when two gray-haired passengers with generous waist sizes push their way out. Neither of them is armed and both slide to a stop with hands extended.

When they realize I'm not emptying a magazine into them, they yell out, "Passengers here. Passengers."

"And the guards?" I reply, worried one was right behind them.

"Only one and he's a putz. He's in a pile, stomped to a grease spot, and no threat," says one of the men.

"You have his weapon?" I ask.

"An AK and a fine SIG Sauer handgun. He had a dagger, but my wife just ran down and shoved it in the goat fucker's gut," he says, and gives me a big smile.

"They said they had the LPG tanks…." I don't get it out before one of them interrupts.

"The door to the storage tanks is chained and locked with a hardened chain and padlock. One of the other bastards rigged it when he closed the door. I think if we open it, it blows."

I give him a grimace of a smile. "Then I guess we shouldn't open it."

"All good, except," he says.

"Except what?"

"I heard them say it had a timer, a failsafe in the event they couldn't detonate remotely."

"Fuck!" I can't help but exclaim. "How long?"

46

THE MAN MERELY SHRUGS. "COULD BE MINUTES, COULD BE HOURS."

"Okay," I say. "I've got to get back to my suite where I've got a SAT phone. One of you go below and shake the crew out of their quarters and tell them to prepare to launch the tenders and lifeboats...anything that floats. Two of you, whoever is ready to take the guards' weapons and fight, come with me. We've got to take the bridge back and finish these bastards off, so I can communicate with the ship."

I'm somewhat surprised, and pleased, to see the boys, Bryan and Terry, appear behind the men.

As I head for the stairwell to climb to my suite, two passengers, with weapons, fall in behind. And behind them, unarmed, follow Bryan and Terry. I'm proud of the boys. As I climb, I'm not surprised to be joined by the CIA operative Weinstein, then by Master Chief Willard 'Willy' Porter and four others carrying guards' weapons.

Damn if we ain't becoming a formidable force.

We go straight to my cabin and, as I recover my SAT phone

and head for the veranda to call, the seven of them recon their situation and take inventory of the weapons.

I phone my buddy Pax, who picks up before the first ring finishes.

"You're still alive?" he asks.

"No, this is my poltergeist calling."

He, for once, doesn't have a smartass reply to my smartass reply, instead continues. "I'm in New Jersey, stopped for fuel, on our way. We have four friends about to re-board the G5 for Mal..." he starts to say his destination then thinks better and adds, "...nearest airport. We have a State Department type on board, no names. I'll call the instant we touch down."

"We're still down range," I tell him. "I have a hunch we're headed into Morocco, Algeria or maybe Libya from the direction the freighter left." I'm sure the 'State Department' statement is total b.s. but said for the sake of NSA who listens, no matter what they claim, to all foreign calls. Then again, I wouldn't put it past Pax to have forged documents.

"Freighter?" Pax asks.

"Most of the women on board were offloaded to a tramp freighter that headed south."

"All of them?"

"Plenty, including Connie and my charges."

"Our Apache friend told me something odd was going down. He's on it."

I smile. Our Apache friend is Taj in Malta, an India Indian by heritage who we've ragged in the past about being a take-no-prisoners Apache.

Pax continues. "We'll be near as soon as we can get near. Enjoying your vacation?"

I knew he couldn't resist being smartass.

"Too much lead in the air," I say. "Must be global warming."

"Must be. Keep your head down," he advises.

"Ten four." I disconnect and the FBI or CIA guy or whatever the hell he is, Weinstein, reaches for the SAT phone.

"Let me see what the status of the cavalry is."

I hand it to him. We don't want to shoot at or, sure as hell, get shot by an invading SEAL team.

He makes a quick call, then while still on the phone, gives me a crooked grin. "They say to stand down."

We both laugh, then I ask. "SEAL ETA?"

"Classified. But hours away."

"Tell them in case we're not waiting with supper, not to board. We'll either be dead or gone and the ship could be ready to blow any time."

He relates the message, and, as I suspected, they reply, "Stand down."

"A little late for that good advice."

He disconnects.

"Okay," I say, "gentlemen, we've got to get to the bridge, announce all to the lifeboats, and get rid of the back shooters. We don't want fire or hand grenades raining down on our escaping lifeboats, or worse, the ship exploding and blowing us all to hell just as we think we're safe."

As I finish, a uniformed guy I've seen around the ship steps into the doorway. "I'm Kevin Connerly, Staff Captain and second in command of this ship. You fellows are now under my command."

I stride over and get in his face. "I don't see your automatic firearm, Connerly. Your bridge is under the control of terrorists. Your captain is lying dead on the bridge. You gonna rush it with those stripes on your shoulders and overpower them with your authority?"

"No, but..."

"No buts, Connerly. If you want to help, make sure the tenders and all lifeboats are launched. Women and children first, of course. Then the old men passengers, then the men and your crew."

But he's still adamant. "No one is abandoning this vessel."

"Everyone is abandoning this vessel, except for the dead and soon-to-be-dead terrorists on board, and as soon as you can get it done, as if the ship was already sinking."

"You don't have the authority..."

I shake the KRISS at him. "This is my authority and as soon as I inform the rest of the crew and passengers of the explosives attached to your LPG tanks, which we can't get to, they'll likely be happy to leave you aboard if you stand in their way. Now get the fuck out of my way."

He looks over his shoulder at two other uniformed lesser officers. One of whom says, "I'd say get the fuck out of his way, Staff Captain."

The man looks totally crestfallen, but steps aside. I wave for my new troops to follow but turn back to him as we leave. "If you don't want 'hundreds of lives lost' carved on your gravestone, then get those boats launched."

To his credit, he gives me a nod.

Now, to take back the bridge.

Frazier Mendleson, CIA section chief terrorism and member of the Joint Terrorism Task Force, and the individual appointed to communicate with the terrorists has tried and tried to get this terrorist, Mumin, on the SAT phone.

To no avail.

He is not particularly surprised when he gets another call from the State Department, who's had a call to their Libyan mission Chargé d'Affaires, Sally Ann Maddison from a second terrorist. They give him a new number for a terrorist who calls himself Musa.

So, the officer from the Algerian desk—where they have calculated, by course, is the destination of the small freighter—the officer from the Spanish desk, a CIA negotiation expert who's watching a voice stress analysis machine on a nearby desk, and a Navy liaison officer who's in direct contact with the 6th Fleet—which is only hours from the *Blue Pearl*—are seated in a semicircle around the desk Mendleson is occupying in the COM room of The National Clandestine Service section of the CIA in Langley, Virginia. Mendleson puts on a headset to await the answer of the terrorist.

It's 1400 in Washington, which means it should be 2000 on board the *Blue Pearl,* only four hours before the time the terrorist Mumin said he would begin killing passengers—one every ten minutes.

Mendleson is getting very nervous by the fifth ring, then a husky voice answers:

"Yes."

"Mister Musa?"

"Yes. Is the gold in flight?"

"Mister Musa, we have not been able to contact Mister Mumin so have not received a location. We're staging the flight in Gibraltar."

"The imbecile Mumin. Is it ready to take flight?"

"Mister Musa, that's thousands of pounds of material that has to be collected from half the countries in Europe, delivered to Gibraltar, placed on pallets, and rigged to parachute. It's not only a complicated process to acquire, which we're in the process of doing, but complicated to execute. I hope you'll consider..."

"No. No extension of time. I will call you back with the next waypoint when you tell me the shipment is in the air over the oceanfront village of Melilla, Morocco. We have people in Gibraltar and will know if your plane is in the air. If you lie to me, I start the beheading."

"That's it? Melilla?"

"You will then be given another village waypoint. Not until you're less than thirty minutes from dropping will you be given the exact coordinates."

"You will be patient?"

"No, I will not be patient. I will behead the first passenger..." He hesitates a minute and Mendleson presumes he's looking at his watch or cell phone. "...in exactly three hours and fifty-three minutes."

"But we're complying with your demands."

Musa disconnects.

47

MENDLESON TURNS FIRST TO THE CIA NEGOTIATOR. "WHAT DO you think?"

"His voice was not particularly stressed. In fact, I was amazed how calm...."

Then he turns to the Navy. "What's the status of the load?"

He laughs, sardonically. "Hell, that much gold would be impossible to collect in that short timeframe. Or probably a week. We still don't even have enough lead put together to resemble gold."

"How long?"

"Before their deadline."

"And the fleet?"

"ETA six hours."

"And the SEAL team?"

"They and their equipment are aboard the sub. The *Montana* is well beyond the straits and should be a thousand yards off the stern of the *Blue Pearl* in a little over fifty mikes. It will take another thirty mikes to launch the team, then fifteen or so for them to board the ship, if the garbage deck is open to the sea and ship. They can blow the door, but it will likely alert the enemy."

"Then the crap hits the fan in an hour or so. Of course, the team's been informed about this explosive device on the LPG storage tanks?"

"They have, as least as much as Weinstein knows. They have plans from a sister ship and, as long as the *Blue Pearl* was built to specs, they'll be able to breach the LPG storage room and go after the explosives. I don't envy them cutting their way into a room hosting tons of LPG. They have welding gear from the Montana and can cut through the walls without touching the door. There's a demolition expert with them."

"An expert who can disarm this device?"

"He's good at building them, so let's hope."

"Hold on," Mendleson says. His cell is ringing. He picks it up and says, "yes?"

Then disconnects. "We're not sure what's going on. But the eye-in-the-sky folks report lifeboats are being launched from the *Blue Pearl*."

"Weinstein?"

"Haven't been able to raise him."

HARRY WEINSTEIN IS ONLY two paces behind me. He's sent his lady associate to her lifeboat station. I've sent Master Chief Willard 'Willy' Porter to the outside to climb to the roof of the bridge and take out any guards there. He has my second KRISS, a spare magazine, and is accompanied by two other Glock-armed passengers.

The ship is dark except for emergency lights, I presume battery-operated, dimly lighting the hallways. I have my night vision goggles, but they aren't needed. You can see enough to negotiate.

I'm followed by four who carry AKs we've recovered from dead guards.

I've been worried that the fire door leading to Deck Eight's suites and beyond the bridge, may still be locked, but am not particularly surprised to see it blown to a twisted mess, and easily passed. Beyond it, the door to the bridge is completely gone.

We step over two dead terrorists as we move forward.

Also, I'm saddened but not surprised, to see Alistair Nelson in a bloody heap on the bridge floor and the windows shot and blown out beyond. I pause and whisper, "Rest easy, partner. God loves warriors who give their all."

As we move forward, as silently as possible, a soldier peeks out of one of the rooms off the hallway, then jerks back seeing us and the machine pistol going to my shoulder.

I have a bit of a quandary. I'd like to clear the room by chucking a grenade through the doorway but have no idea who might be inside. My problem is solved by a white flag waving and a man with an Arabic accent yelling, "Surrender, surrender, surrender."

"Throw out your weapons," I yell. Two AKs, two battle rattle belts with daggers and grenades, and two sidearms land in the hallway.

"Step out with hands on your heads," I yell again.

Two soldiers exit the room, as ordered.

"No one else inside?"

"Two dead men," he says.

"Lie to me and you die."

He holds up six fingers and points at the blown-out bridge windows.

I wave my people forward and carefully enter the bridge, panning my KRISS until I'm satisfied no one's there if you don't count the dead captain and terrorist, then move to the windows. Twelve feet below on the roof of the next deck six hostiles are standing, with their dead scattered around, seemingly planning their next move. I duck down and wave my people forward, giving them six fingers and pointing.

I need not have doubted any of them as all line up.

I count in a loud whisper, "One, two, three," and as one we rise and begin sweeping those below with fire. Only two of the six hostiles get any shots off, and luckily, they have no accuracy.

We have the two living hostiles secured and I'm quickly on the ship's intercom.

"This is an American, currently in control of the *Blue Pearl.* This is not a drill, I repeat, not a drill. Report to your lifeboat stations, with your life preservers, if possible. No one, I repeat, no one will be left aboard. This ship has been rigged by terrorists to blow all to hell. This message will not be repeated. I'm heading for a lifeboat." And I disconnect.

I turn to my crew and point at the secured guards. "Untie them. They, along with us, are carrying the captain's body and that gentlemen on the bridge floor to the lifeboats. No man left behind."

We meet up with Master Chief Willy in the stairwell. "No one above," he reports. "Many dead on the deck below the bridge."

"We're moving out, chief," I say, and we double time it down five decks to Three, the lowest deck with access to the ocean's surface. But I don't pass Deck Seven without going to my suite, retrieving my gold coins and forty grand plus in good old American greenbacks, and packing my bugout bag and backpack with a few necessaries.

I've got to make two stops to check on ladies. I find General Toliver's wife sitting on the edge of her bed.

"We've got to go, ma'am," I say, as gently as possible.

"I don't have to, young man. I believe I'll just stay here."

"Sorry, ma'am," and I lie, "but the General asked me to make sure you were safe. So, even if I have to carry you."

She eyes me with some fire in her eyes, then melts. "If the General said so." And she walks out ahead of me, shoulders thrown back, erect. The General would be proud of her.

Then I turn her over to Master Chief Willy and head for Alistair Nelson's suite. I'm not surprised to find Mrs. Nelson in a chair out on the deck.

Before I can speak, she's at the sliding glass door and asks, "My husband gave his life?"

I have to take a deep breath before I answer. "Yes, ma'am, bravely, saving all our lives by taking out a half-dozen terrorists. Your husband was a hell of man."

"I know that, young man," she says. Then adds, "That was you ordering us to the lifeboats."

"Yes, ma'am, where's your life jacket?"

She grabs it, follows me out, and we join the others near the stairway.

As we descend the stairs, on Deck Five, a camo-dressed soldier hops down the hall. Master Chief Willy chuckles. "That's the raghead that was guarding my room." The man hops our way, his wrists and ankles bound.

"Please," he calls out, "I cannot feel my hands or feet."

"Tied him a little tight?" I suggest to Willy.

"Should'a tied it tight as I could pull around his skinny neck," Willy says with a snarl.

"We might get some info from him. Loosen his wrists. In fact, untie his ankles and wrists. He can help carry our mates."

In thirty mikes, there are over four hundred of us, nearly all men, packed into four seventy-five-passenger shore tenders and several inflatable lifeboats. I've managed to get Mrs. Nelson on a tender with her husband's body, with Mrs. Tolliver along to commiserate with her. The ship is disappearing behind us in the darkness.

We didn't take the time to search the ship and have no idea if more terrorists are aboard, but if so, they're going nowhere unless they float off on ship furniture. So long as they don't pop up firing at our escape, I'll ignore them. We'll let the SEAL team sort it out if they insist on boarding, and I'm sure they will.

Harry Weinstein and the still camo-dressed soldier who informs me his name is Sa'id, is on my same life raft, and Harry is on the SAT phone as soon as we push away from the ship. He's giving intel to the CIA to pass along to the Navy.

I'm not as gung-ho as I know the Navy will be, so can't help but advise him to pass along to his people, "Tell them to stand down. Let the fucking tub blow to hell."

He just shakes his head. Knowing the SEAL teams, they'll disarm the damn explosives...or die trying.

We managed to clear the ship, at least of enough of the threat to get our people headed for sure. I glance at my iPhone, which I've managed to hang onto, and I see it's a few minutes before midnight.

FRAZIER MENDLESON IS happy to be able to report to this Colonel Musa that the plane is loaded, the 'gold' rigged, and ready to depart Gibraltar, and snatches the SAT phone up as soon as it rattles. He's been waiting for the call, waiting to hurry to the CIA airstrip as soon as it's complete.

"Colonel," he answers. Several others are in the room, hopeful he's successful.

"No aircraft of adequate size to deliver the ransom has departed Gibraltar. We will kill the first woman in seven minutes. I am sure you will enjoy receiving a video that I will also send to American news agencies."

"No, no, the plane is nearly ready to depart."

"Ready? You've had many hours."

A rather heavyset woman, in her early fifties, had been randomly selected and brought to the aft deck of the *Bit Tawfig*.

Colonel Musa walked aft as he talked to Mendleson. The woman stood, her face and head covered as instructed.

"Colonel," Mendleson yelled into the phone.

"I am watching my clock. In one minute."

"Wait, the plane will be in the air within a half hour."

"Then at least two more will die," Musa says.

The sound of a gunshot rings over the phone.

It's silent for a moment, then Musa returns to the phone. "You have caused the death of one woman. In exactly ten minutes, another will die, then another, then another."

Mendleson yells at one of his minions in the room. "Tell them to get that 130 in the air."

Then he returns to the phone. "She's firing up now. Ask your people to watch."

They remain on the phone, the only sound, heavy breathing, for the next nine minutes.

Mendleson, watching the clock on the wall, covers the SAT phone with a hand, and yells at his minions. "Is she taxiing yet?"

"She is, tell him she's heading for the runway."

"Mister Mendleson," Musa finally speaks again. "Another woman is ready."

"But the plane is taxiing."

Exactly at the ten-minute mark, another shot rings out.

Musa returns to the phone. "You have caused the death of another."

"Talk to whoever you have watching. The plane is on the runway."

Musa is quiet for two full minutes, then returns to the phone. "A C130 is in position for take-off. Yes, it is rolling. Now, Mister Mendleson, you would be wise to do exactly what I instruct. I will call again when we know the gold has entered Algeria. You should know that when this load lands, if it is not gold, all women will be killed. They will be gassed where they are imprisoned. Do you understand?"

"Of course, we wouldn't risk..." But Musa has disconnected.

They have to move fast, or think of another ruse, or many women will die when the many thousands of pounds of lead are discovered.

As Mendleson heads for a CIA jet, he dials the White House to speak to the Chief of Staff. He doesn't hesitate, as much as he'd like to do so.

"I'm sorry to report it seems they have killed two women. Hopefully that's all, as the ship is in the air. All, at least until after we drop the ransom."

"We've made no headway with Algeria. How long before they discover they've been tricked?"

"No idea. The load is bound with hardened steel strapping and even after they get to it, it'll take special equipment to discover what's on those steel pallets. We're working on ideas, but until we know exactly where the drop zone is... I have a half-dozen people studying our options."

"Call, no matter the hour."

"Yes, sir," Mendleson says, and disconnects.

As the C130 nears the coast of Algeria, the *Bit Tawfig* nears an Algerian port.

"Melilla in one-half hour. Get them presentable." Connie hears a male yell in Arabic, down to the female guard.

Alia, the female, walks from cell to cell yelling. "Cover yourselves. We will leave the ship before light."

Connie walks, picking her way between women trying to sleep, to where Simone lies sandwiched between Gretchen and Patty.

With a toe, she nudges them all awake. Simone sits up rubbing her eyes.

"How you feeling?" Connie asks.

"Mouth feels like the Gobi Desert. Thirsty. And I gotta pee... again," Simone answers, with a pout.

Connie moves a few feet, then returns with a half-full revolting five-gallon plastic bucket.

"I can't pee in that," Simone complains.

"Then hold it."

"Help me up. I guess I gotta."

As she's pulling Simone to her feet, Connie turns to Gretchen, who also is climbing to her feet.

Then while Simone is situating herself atop the bucket, Connie says, "Seems okay?"

Gretchen shakes her head, worriedly. "Thirst, peeing lots, by tonight she'll be nauseous and soon upchucking."

"When was her last injection?"

"It's been nearly thirty-six hours. It won't be long before she feels really tired. Her breath will smell fruity. She'll begin throwing up. Then have trouble breathing. Another twelve hours and we'll be in deep caca."

"Stay close when they unload us," Connie instructs the girls.

The C130 crosses over Melilla, and Mendleson awaits a call. It's only two minutes until the SAT phone rattles.

"Your new course is one hundred forty degrees. I will call in twenty minutes." He disconnects and Mendleson calls Langley.

"You get that?"

"Of course, we're working on possibles."

And Mendleson disconnects, and worries.

48

THE SHIP ROCKS WITH SOME BANGING AND CLATTERING, AND THE engine vibration subsides to quiet stillness. Women are already standing and those asleep are coming awake.

Connie works her way through the women to as close as she can get to the guard, Alia. She finds her on her knees on her jacket, which Connie presumes is passing for a prayer rug.

She's bending face down to the east and not quiet.

It's morning prayer. "Prophet Muhammad, peace be upon him. We have awoken, and all of creation has awoken, for Allah, Lord of all the Worlds. Allah, I ask You for the best the day has to offer, victory, support, light, blessings and guidance; and I seek refuge in You from the evil in it, and the evil to come after it." She seems to pause, then adds, "Forgive me as there is no place to wash. Keep Sa'id safe from harm."

Then she rises. Connie has appealed to her twice during the voyage but decides to do so again. It's all she can do not to say you're the evil in it, but knows it wouldn't be wise, so instead, "You're a devout woman. Do you have a daughter?" she calls out. She points to Simone, "This girl is like a daughter to me."

Alia pulls her stool nearer, but not near enough to the cage to be reached.

"I had a sister, much younger. You killed her, my brother, my aunt and my mother and father with your drones. There was no medicine that would have saved them."

Connie is silent for a second, then with eyes lowered, lies, hoping to endear herself to the guard, "I'm so sorry. I marched with many other women against the wars."

Alia merely nods, unimpressed.

So, Connie continues. "My friend will die without her medicine."

"You have told me that many times."

"Is there a pharmacy where we're going?"

Alia laughs. "The Sheik can get you anything you wish."

"How long before we get there?"

"You ask too many questions."

"I must, or my friend will die."

"If you're among the chosen, you'll be there in three hours or less, Allah willing. If not *inshallah*."

"I pray Allah is willing," Connie says, and begins to turn away.

"Allah only answers the prayers of the faithful."

Connie can't help herself. "My God looks out for all, no matter to whom they pray."

"I have not seen you praying to 'your' god."

"Christians can pray anytime, anywhere, in any direction, without even bowing their heads or closing their eyes."

"Then pray for your friend, who is like a daughter to you, as my sister was like one to me." Alia turns and looks up as camo-covered legs appear descending the ladder.

"It's time," the first soldier of four says as he hits the deck and goes to the far end of the cells. Then yells back. "Release them one cell at a time."

Soon they are on a quay, lined up single file. At the end of the quay are a half-dozen military style trucks. As well as a van.

Colonel Musa stands where the line will pass with two soldiers at his side. He yells something, and the line begins to move.

As they pass, Colonel Musa pulls the occasional woman from the line. Connie watches and realizes he's picking the youngest and prettiest of the women.

Before she and the girls reach where Musa seems to be culling women, she notices the large Mercedes van, almost a bus, parked nearby under a metal-roofed shed. The other women are being loaded in the trucks, but the selected few line up behind the Colonel, guarded by the two who've been at his side. He has at least two dozen girls lined up when she, Gretchen, Patty and Simone reach him. He pulls Simone out of the line, then points at another girl among the two dozen. That girl leaves the group and takes Simone's position in the long line. Then he does the same with Patty, then Gretchen, then finally Connie. Only two more women are selected after them.

They are loaded onto the van, with Colonel Musa in a front seat near an armed driver, and Alia and another armed guard in the rear. Connie wonders if this isn't the best odds she'll get, but is sure that even if she can surprise and get two of them, AK 47s will spray through the van and the losses will be unacceptable. To her, the loss of even one of them is unacceptable. They only drive a few miles when they swing off a main paved road onto a two-track driveway, where she sees a sign in Arabic, French, and English. Aerogare Terminal. They soon brake to a stop far from any buildings. She recognizes the aircraft. It's a DeHavilland Otter.

The women are quickly loaded aboard the aircraft. Connie

counts the seats. Nineteen passenger seats and twenty-four women.

Pilot, co-pilot, and now two guards who sit across the aisle in the rear. Two passenger seats are taken by Alia and another armed guard, so that leaves seventeen seats for twenty-four girls. Fourteen have to ride double. It's a good thing all are slim and shapely. Connie notes that, by this time, it seems the women are so numbed out they don't give a damn if they have on seatbelts.

She notices that the pock-faced Colonel Musa does not board, and is picked up by a Land Rover as they taxi a long way to the south end of the runway then only use a fourth of it taking off. It climbs steeply. She knows the Otter is a STOL aircraft, particularly with the propjet engines this one has. It can also land in a very short area, so God only knows where they're headed. This damn Algerian and Moroccan desert is practically all airstrip. At least there's hardly a tree to get in the way, other than a few palms at the scarce oasis. As soon as they level out, she rises, knowing the small toilet room, hardly bigger than the toilet itself, is in the rear of the plane. Both guards have muzzles leveled on her as she nears. She points to the small restroom door and they wave her on by.

While in the restroom, she checks the .380 on the inside of her thigh, her single extra clip, her tiny can of hair-spray-mace, and her stun-gun-compact.

She's ready, but now wonders how wise it is to take out the two guards in the rear of the plane—easily done as they let her pass and she's behind them—but then she'll have to face the armed co-pilot and pilot. If a stray shot should take the pilot out, could she handle a large propjet? She once took lessons in a Cessna 150, which you could park inside this Otter—at least its fuselage. And she has no idea their altitude. A shot through the port or skin of the aircraft might cause such havoc they'd all die.

She sighs deeply.

She still must bide her time.

FAR TO THE SOUTHWEST, in Libya, Sheik Hassan answers his SAT phone.

"Aw, good," he says, then disconnects and dials his chief of security, Omar Al-Wandi, who is at the drop zone sixty kilometers from the sheik's palace. "It is time. Move quickly. You want to be waiting, watching, as the load is released. Wind, other factors, could impair our recovery."

"I will not let you down, my Sheik. I have four search vehicles ready and in place plus the six trucks. I am watching carefully."

"Do not err, Omar."

"No, I will not."

And he hurries for his vehicle, wondering how wise it will be to position himself directly on target. It would not do to be crushed under tons of weight, even if that weight was gold.

49

We're no more than four miles into the twelve or so miles to shore when we're met by two dozen craft. The largest a ferry of at least eighty feet, and many smaller craft. A miniature Dunkirk. I presume we're a long way from the Spanish Coast Guard as it seems half the private boats on the nearby shore have responded to what must have been an SOS from someone with a cell or SAT phone.

Our small rubber boat, one of many stored individually in large drums on the *Blue Pearl,* holds twelve of us. Harry Weinstein and his lady are in my boat, and, at my insistence, the man Sa'id. I mean to have a long heart to heart with Sa'id. Sa'id and I have both gone in the drink trying to help load folks aboard. I'm thinking maybe the Al-Shabaab soldier is having a come-to-Jesus, or more likely a come-to-Allah, moment. He's actually being helpful.

A fifty-foot sport-fishing yacht is the first to reach our boat and nuzzles up alongside. Soon we're enjoying a cocktail as guests of Señor Lucas Victorio Vicario. And he's operating the twin-engine diesel himself, with a crew of two: his wife, Imelda, and daughter, Paloma. Both beautiful Spanish ladies; that doesn't surprise me when papa is owner of a several hundred-thousand-dollar craft. What a surprise, big yachts and bigger bank accounts seem to attract beautiful women.

The tenders proceed on their own. Only folks in inflatables are being transferred to hard-sided craft.

As we're motoring in at twenty-five knots, Harry pulls out his SAT phone, steps out of the salon, takes a seat in a fighting-chair, and I follow. He starts to poke in a number as he speaks.

"Let's get a ride when we get ashore. I'm sure we have people on the way or nearby."

I cover the keyboard with a hand before he has a chance.

"A small favor, Harry?"

"And that is?"

"I don't have time to do three or four days in interrogation much less a few years in Leavenworth or another gray-stone hotel. I don't want to be met by the CIA or Spanish cops or military. I'm going after the ladies who were hauled off and I don't want to be told to stand down by a bunch of our guys with M4's, or worse a bunch of bow ties. I have no use for bullshit rules of engagement."

Harry gives me a slow nod. "They'll wonder why I haven't been in touch."

So, I twist the SAT phone out of his hand and flip it over my shoulder into the Med.

He looks a little surprised, then a slow smile appears. "I guess that's a good excuse."

"Hope that was a company phone?" I say, returning the smile.

He nods. We're good, I guess.

I shoved the KRISS into my bugout bag before I disembarked the ship, but don't want to be noticed and chucked into a Spanish *jusgado* by the first cop I run into. I know the shore will be crawling with them. So, I climb up to the flybridge where Señor Vicario is handling the wheel and sidle up beside him.

We chat for a while and I find he's in the import-export business, finally I ask, "Are you a man of discretion?"

He looks at me curiously before answering. "Of course. Discretion is a valuable commodity."

"Señor, I have a gift for you. I cannot land in Spain with the weapon I had aboard the ship. I was tasked with guarding the life of a young lady, but your authorities will only confiscate the weapon. I would prefer you have it."

"Weapon?" he says.

I drop the backpack and dig out the KRISS. "A beautiful firearm. May I gift it to you?"

He gives me a conspiratorial smile. "She is beautiful. Is this weapon known to any others aboard?"

"No, sir."

"Please slip it under the...how do you say...cushion. I accept *con mucho gusto*."

I slip the KRISS, and two extra magazines, under a nearby seat cushion, give him a smile and a nod, say, "May it keep you and your beautiful family safe," and return to the salon where his beautiful wife and daughter are pouring a rich red fruit-filled sangria for their thankful passengers.

When we arrive at Señor Vicario's private slip, I help him tie up, then thank him. "I'll see you again, Señor. I owe you one." I say, then grab Sa'id's arm as he disembarks. He tries to pull away, but I put him in a wrist-lock come-along, and he goes up on his toes. There's a cab under a streetlight after we exit a combination lock gate—locked to enter, not to exit—at the street end of the dock.

"Cantina, paisano's solomente, no gringos, deiz kilometers,

mas y minos," I instruct the cabbie. That's half my Spanish language vocabulary.

He nods and we're off. Thank God, the warm salon of the Señor's yacht has us nearly dry.

Sa'id is nervous and keeps glancing back over his shoulder. He should be. If he doesn't come with some actionable intel, I will rip his head off his skinny neck and piss down his throw-up hole.

I intend to get my lady back, and I took a job to protect Simone. I'm a little behind on that task.

I see by highway signs we've landed in Puerto Marina Benalmádena. The cabby seems happy to have a long trip and when he's gone ten clicks or more pulls off in a town with signs saying Churriaña and stops at a highway restaurant and bar—the motorcycles outside say biker bar, and the two semi-trucks say the food is likely good or at least cheap. The sign says Restaurante Loro Purpura. The purple bird or parrot, I'm guessing by the painting on the sign.

I take a moment before entering to recover my Glock from my backpack and shove it into my belt under my wrinkled shirt and make sure Sa'id watches me do so.

Already it's clear to me that my new best buddy, Sa'id, speaks English damn near as good as I do as he responds to my every command.

A half-dozen leather and tee-shirt clad toughs line the bar, but the rest of the place is empty, other than a bartender with a thin face and even thinner mustache and a waitress with thick calves, a pink ribbon in raven-wing black hair, and a wide smile. As requested, *paisanos solomente*. Only countrymen. Not a white European or American in sight.

The chubby but smiling waitress who comes to the booth brings a menu, but I wave it away.

"Dos cervesas y tapas."

"Tapas?" she answers, with a shrug.

"You choose," I say, give her a wink, and she understands.

She brings beers from the tap and places them in front of us. As she's walking away, Sa'id manages, "I do not drink alcohol."

"And you should not lie. Even though I know the Quran allows you to lie to infidels with impunity. And I also know all you Muslims drink alcohol when the Imam is not watching. Besides, you forget I watched you enjoy yourself on the ship."

This actually elicits a smile from him. "It is permissible to confuse the infidel."

"I'm confused, so drink away."

"Thank you," he says, and takes a long draw on his foamy beer, then wipes away a foam mustache with the back of his hand.

"Your mission is a failure so far. What will the Imam think of that?"

"It is a Sheik who directs our mission."

"The Sheik then."

He's haughty and arrogant as he snaps, "Our mission has only begun. Your many women are under our control…"

"Not yours any longer, you are under my control."

"Still, the women are under the control of the faithful. Americans will pay or many will die."

He gives me a nasty smile.

It's a narrow table. I come up off the table, leaning across, and slap him so hard his eyes spin. He's knocked aside and comes up slowly.

MENDLESON'S SAT phone rattles again and he grabs it.

"Now, ninety degrees. Prepare to drop your load in...one... two...three...twelve minutes."

"Exactly twelve minutes?"

"Now eleven minutes, fifty seconds." And he disconnects.

Mendleson dials and Langley picks up. "Did you get that?"

"Of course. We're diverting the course three degrees. There's a short but very high mountain range four miles north of their target. With luck, we'll put it atop a three-thousand-foot rock pile. Even if they have a chopper, they can't get there for hours...if we hit our target."

"Good, that just might save some lives."

50

ONE OF THE TOUGHS AT THE BAR STRIDES OVER.

I realize the Yemini Sa'id is dark, but not so dark he couldn't pass for a Spaniard.

"*Que?*" the tough says, wondering what the hell's going on. His hands are splayed out as if he's ready to rumble. Four more at the bar are turned our way.

I don't need trouble so, without saying a word that would give away the fact I'm a gringo, I flash my bail enforcement officer's badge. Hell, a badge is a badge, even in Spain. The tough looks a little confused, but then rolls his eyes and returns to the bar. I hear him say, as he shrugs. "*Policia*."

I turn back to Sa'id, whose eyes have stopped spinning. "As you will die, if even one of the women from the ship dies. Now, let's get you what you want and get me what I want. I saw you on board, at the bar by the pool many times."

I believe he actually blushes.

So, I continue. "The nice young lady there..." then I correct myself. "The young lady who was seen in camo carrying an AK47 by some of our people. I guess she's not so nice?"

I can see his hackles rise. It seems to me he has more than a military interest in the bartender who called herself Alia.

"Aw...Alia," I continue. "I will see she is on the CIA's kill list. You know of the kill list. They become prime targets for those drones you *hajis* love so much. At least she will not suffer as the flesh will instantly be burned away."

"You can do that?"

It's time for a propitious lie. "How do you think I came by the weapons that I used to kill a dozen of your fellow terrorists? Weapons are not allowed on cruise ships as you well know. Only we upper-level American agents of the CIA and FBI are allowed top secret weapons." I can't help but have some fun with it, so I add, "I have a ray gun that will shoot through walls and stop hearts. I've already killed more than a dozen of your so-called faithful. Do you think an average American on vacation is capable of that?"

He's silent for a long time, as the waitress brings us a plate of that wonderful thin-sliced Serrano ham, some pickled veggies, and a variety of nuts.

I can see him repel from the ham, and it gives me an idea.

I let him stew as I sip and munch. He's wringing his hands, then finally speaks up.

"She only joined Al-Shabaab because drones...your drones... already killed her family. She is a good person...a very good person."

"Then you would prefer she lived and not die a flaming death as her family did?"

"Of course. She is one of the faithful."

"But no seventy-two virgins for her, right?"

"Do not be silly..."

"You want her to live. I will do my best to see she does, but you will take me to where she's gone with all the women from the ship."

Again, he's silent for a long spell. "And you will take me to join her? And will free us both?"

"Only if you agree to take her and flee. And I mean flee not only the country but Al-Shabaab. If you do not agree to this, I will kill you out in the parking lot and order more of this fine ham, rub your naked body down with it, then drape you over the sign. Then I will take your picture and send it to my friend at the London Times."

I swear his dark brown skin flushes. His voice is up an octave, "Do you have electronic measures...abilities?"

"The finest."

"Then we go to Algeria and when there, I will give you the number of Alia's cell phone. You can locate her with that number."

"Of course. And, with luck, and Allah's grace, you will both live to grow old together."

That elicits another small smile.

Then my SAT phone, which is buried in my bugout bag, rattles.

Pax, again not bothering with a greeting. "Where are you?"

"Ashore."

"One hour to touch down at M. Can you get there?"

"Of course. Inside an hour. I have an...an associate."

"Fine, we've got a dozen seats and only five, including our pilot and co."

"How long on the ground?"

"Our State Department clearance allows us to refuel without immigration as our flight plan calls for Malta."

"Who's the fixed base operator?"

"Hold a sec..." he's back in a moment. "I hesitate to give you this over the air, but Aviapartner Executive Málaga."

"We'll be standing by near the coffee pot."

"Ten four," he says.

THE LOAD MASTER, Mike Gebheardt, and the crew on the C130 are sweating bullets. They've been advised that if they miss the target and the false load is easily discovered, there's a very good chance women will die every ten minutes for a very long time.

Not only that, but they are in Libya. A flight of F16s is circling five thousand feet above them, and the Libyans will be foolish to attempt anything.

Not only do they have the exact coordinates of the top of the tallest peak in the east-west range, they can see fairly-well thanks to a quarter moon rising in the east. They will be three clicks north of the demanded target, but purposefully so. Sure that no one in the Algerian or Libyan militaries could hit a target any more accurately, the mistake should be easily believed.

Even though they are attempting to hit a mountain top, they are using the LAPES procedure, Low-Altitude Parachute-Extraction System. A delivery method to deposit the load where landing is not an option, and it sure as hell isn't on a rugged range with nearly vertical slopes rising to sharp peaks.

Master Sergeant Gebheardt was trained by the 109th, who had developed the method, and the load is properly equipped with a drogue chute, which, when deployed, will pull out a cluster of larger extraction chutes. The array of deployed extraction chutes will then drag the load out of the plane. Floor locks hold the pallet in place until extraction time, then are overcome by the pull of the load.

As per protocol, Gebheardt waits nervously until the pilot has slowed nearly to landing speed, just above stall speed, a delicate maneuver over sharp peaks that they'll attempt to clear by no more than one hundred feet. He adjusts his speed, lowers the cargo ramp, which changes the altitude of the aircraft, which will change again when the load launches. There are a hundred things that can go wrong, not the least of which are the changes in altitude due to up or down drafts from the peaks.

When the pilot gives him a green light, the drogue is released. Gebheardt stands, tethered to the bulkhead so the wind doesn't suck him along with the load, with his jaw clamped as the drogue drags the supplemental chutes out, which deploy nicely. Then the shock of their pull overcomes the floor locks and tons of pallets began to leave the aircraft.

Gebheardt bows his head as the last pallet disappears and mouths a small prayer. He's dumped lots of loads with lots of lives dependent upon his accuracy, but for some reason these innocent female civilians, most of them seniors, particularly touch him.

He moves forward quickly as soon as he gets the cargo ramp recovered and enters and moves up behind the pilot. He has to balance with a hand against a bulkhead as the plane is banking sharply.

"Gonna try and get a visual," the pilot says as Gebheardt leans next to him. The copilot has binoculars, but the navigator is tracking the load with a much more powerful belly-mounted camera attuned to a tracking device attached to the load.

"Geronimo," the navigator yells. "Damn if more than half the load didn't hit a cliff side. Some is hanging there; some went to the bottom...but the bottom is twenty-five hundred feet off the desert floor. They'll be a while getting there. Probably all night even if they're tough as hell and experienced rock climbers."

Gebheardt expels a long breath. "Thank the good Lord," he says. Then adds, "Let's get the hell out of Libya."

51

THE G5 BARELY ROLLS TO A STOP AND POWERS DOWN BEFORE SA'ID and I are on the tarmac, walking to the dropping ladder.

Pax greets us at the hatch. "We're only topping the tanks, then we're off. Let's not hang for twenty questions."

"I think I know this ride?" I say, looking at the camel and blue interior of the forty-million-dollar aircraft.

"Old favors repaid," Pax says. "CalGeoCyber, thanks to the administrator of Prather Wedgeworth's trust. I'm sure you remember Tatya?" He laughs, knowing I remember her fondly, then continues. "Same ship you recovered from Paraguay."

I can't help but grin. "Past deeds do come back to haunt you. Who's on the stick?"

Now Pax laughs. "Charles Glascock, pilot, Tobias Bartlett's in the right seat. He's going along for the duration. Charley is taking a risk returning to Malaga alone, as you know a co-pilot is required on this ship. He'll wait out the mission there in case we need him back."

I recovered this airplane from a Colonel in South America who decided it was his. Got well paid for it even though the owner went to the gray-bar mansion. The lady now in charge of his estate, and I, were the best of buds for a while. Nice guys don't tell.

As soon as I'm buckled in, and after greeting some old buddies Pax has recruited, I have a Jack rocks in hand.

I noticed a guy with his back to us in one of the front seats, and am flooded with the warmth only an old buddy can bring to a brother-in-arms as he walks my way and extends a hand, "Semper fi," he says and I shake knowing he could crush my paw if he wanted to. Skip, Pax, and I wandered many a downrange Iraqi street together.

Skip is a hell of a warrior, a great guy and an even better friend, but he's got some dark places that he won't let even his best buddies visit, places carefully mortared together and shaped and shaded by dark deeds none of us want to recall, but few of us can forget. When one charges into a *wadi* or mud hut in Iraq or Afghanistan only to see an armed *haji* loose a few rounds in your direction before retreating into a back room, and rather than charge in blindly you chuck a grenade, yell frag out, hit the deck, and then charge in as the dust clears...and a back door stands open and the haji is gone. You stand shocked and shaking as a three-year-old girl and her baby brother are bleeding out on the dirt floor and the scent of hot blood floods your nostrils and utter heart-rending remorse and disgust fill your head while you puke your guts up in a corner. Well, those are sights, sounds, smells and dark deeds not easily put to bed until washed into unconsciousness with a bottle of tequila. None of us talk about what visits us in the night, but all of us who've puked our guts up over deeds done that can never be undone, have gargoyles creeping through our heads who laugh crazily, do back flips, and awaken us in sweat-soaked bedding.

I'm happy to see Skip's not among the many who couldn't live with the wages of war.

I'm not ashamed to say I love the guy and am not surprised he dropped everything and showed when Pax put out a distress call.

"Been watching the news," Pax says, with a laugh. "You're either a hero or a terrorist, depends on who's reporting. Good chance you'll get a bill for the damage to the ship as you were instructed, or so the BBC says, to stand down. And the CIA, Military, FBI, and various other anagrams want to chat with you about the reported death of a retired Army General whose body they are conducting a search for."

"First, dumb fuck, you mean acronym, not anagram."

"Fuck, I must be tired too, to have a Neanderthal like you correct my vocabulary."

"An anagram is when you say 'funeral', like the mission we're about to undertake, and rearrange the letters to read 'real fun'. Get it?"

"Yes, a-hole, I get it. Let's do word games back home."

"Second, Tolliver was a hell of a guy and took two ragheads with him. He'd be up for the medal of honor were it enlistment time. And they can take the General's demise up with Missus Tolliver. She knows more than I. Let's see," I offer, after a long draw on the Jack, "Couldn't be more than a few mil in damages. Maybe they'll ask for the burial cost of a couple of dozen jihadists? Nothing would surprise me."

"Likely," Pax replies. "Taj tracked the ship to a tiny port on the Algerian coast, thanks to marine location dot com and the fact the dumb fucks didn't disable the ship's GPS. The ladies were transferred to six canvas-covered military style trucks and are off into the desert."

I lean over and eye Sa'id. "Any idea where they are going?"

He looks a little perplexed, then answers, "The Sheik would not bring them to his compound in Algeria. He is a clever man and would not lead your drones there. There are over one hundred women and they will need shelter from the desert sun and cold, to be fed and sheltered. I would look for somewhere between this town Melilla and his compound. Somewhere with lots of space under cover, out of the sun. You Americans say follow the money, I suggest you follow the road between this town and his compound."

"It's time to give me Alia's cell phone number."

"Not until we are in Algeria."

I yell forward to Charlie Glascock, the pilot. "Hey, fragile dick. What's our altitude?"

Charlie leans out and looks back into the cabin. "Fourteen thousand, dipshit, it's a short hop."

I lean forward with my hands on my knees and give our guest a hard stare. "Sa'id, do you know what sixteen feet per second per second is?"

"No, I do not."

"That's the rate of acceleration you'll reach until wind resistance keeps you steady. You'll hit the surface of the Med after many mikes...that's minutes...in the air. You'll have some time to pray that Allah accepts you."

"You cannot throw me out of this airplane."

"The fuck I can't. The phone number?"

He eyes me, then cuts his eyes away as I have his attention. Then rattles off her number.

I nod. "That cell phone better be travelling across the Sahara or you'll be shark bait."

I turn to Pax. "How about putting Taj on it?"

"I was already dialing."

"And does Taj have any thoughts?"

"I'll call him, get him on that number, and see where we are. He is finding us ground transportation and a couple of locals. I'll be receiving an e-mail with some intel. You look like hammered dog shit. Get some sleep. I'll wake you before we touch down."

A good idea, so I put the seat back and am fly-fishing on the Tongue River in Wyoming in about a half minute. A much better dream that the nightmares I've been living. I'm now comfortable. Where I was basically operating alone on the ship, it will be a pleasure to go into action with *compadres* I can depend on, who'll watch my back as I'll watch theirs.

It seems like I've only made three or four casts into some ripples when Pax shakes me awake.

"This damned short airstrip is a bit of a challenge. Thought I'd wake you before he brakes it and throws you on the floor. Here's a cup of mud," he hands me some strong coffee and, as soon as I'm half done, calls me forward. There's a pair of tables between seats on either side of the passageway. So, four of us take seats while Pax and our co-pilot, Toby Bartlett, an old buddy I recognize, lean over the backs while Pax reads us in.

"Two Land Rovers will meet us at touchdown, one with a small two-wheel trailer. Or contact has hacked the eye-in-the-sky and our enemy SAT phones and will put us on the trail. Our guides and drivers are Tuareg locals, and speak both Tuareg, a variety of the Algerian Tamazight and the local Bedouin and Berber dialects. They speak some Wargli, which is the area into which we venture. Both guides are desert people, the Blue People they're called for what they wear and the fact it stains their skin. If Taj is right, and he's seldom wrong, we're going to an ancient ruin on a small mountain in a wide wadi southeast of Ouargla, a large city by desert standards, well over a hundred thousand population,.

a little over six hundred miles from our touchdown. This ruin, an ancient mosque and palace, some hundred miles beyond, is now off limits to tourists due to recent civil unrest. That's one of the reasons, and SAT phone intercepts. Taj says he's on the cell phone, although it's travelling in and out of service. He thinks it's our destination."

"What assets do we have?" I ask.

"What we have may not be near enough. Taj says the transportation could be thanks to the Algerian military."

"Too bad for them," I say, but, in fact, that worries me.

"We got Six M4's, night vision scopes for two of them, two with 37mm grenade launchers and a dozen frag grenades for each, two M72 LAWS rocket launchers, one light 60mm M224 mortar with a dozen rounds, two .338 Lapua sniper rifles with forty rounds each and one night-vision scope for them. Two DJI Phantom drones, four 28-minute batteries, in hard cases. Ten pounds of C4 with both time and phone detonators. One M249 SAW with two thousand rounds. You have a SAT. I have a SAT, and we have a dozen handhelds. Standard first aid with quick clot. Ji Su will leapfrog, stay no more than thirty mikes behind us for quick extraction should we require, as soon as she's checked out in the rent-a-Ranger, the Jet Ranger. We'll have to carry fuel if we have to leave the beaten track, so we're limited space and weight wise. Of course, we have desert camo and backpacks with standard gear, MREs to last two weeks, and our drivers have been instructed to load water and fuel in the trailer, so we can drive more than a thousand miles without a domestic fuel stop. Speaking of that, detailed maps with topo for Morocco, Algeria and Libya. Anything I missed?"

That's my man. So, I add, "dancing girls, Jack Daniel's and a Marine division?"

"All you want of the first two, when we return."

I feel the pilot throttle back and presume we're on the glide path.

SHEIK HASSAN GRABS his SAT phone as it rattles.

"They dropped it but missed. The load is somewhere near Goat Mountain," Al-Wandi reports.

"Can it be reached?" the Sheik demands.

"It is down, a huge load under many parachutes. It must be reached by hard climbing."

"How long?"

"An hour, maybe two."

"Then I must order more women killed."

Al-Wandi is silent for a moment, then suggests, "May I speak, my Sheik?"

"Do."

"I would wait. If you kill more, they might do something harsh. I heard other aircraft even after the big cargo ship departed. They have drones, they have eyes in the night. They could destroy the load…the gold…and us, should they not trust us. And they have dropped the load."

Now the Sheik is quiet for a moment. Then he concedes. "All right, Al-Wandi. I will wait two hours, but no more. Report your progress."

52

Our drivers, Abdallah Gatif, who says his nickname is Abby, is in the lead vehicle. Dawad Ziadi, who we quickly nickname Waddy, is in number two. They are waiting, as Taj promised—in fact more than he promised—with two Military Land Rover Wolfs, light utility trucks, and a two-wheel trailer. The trailer is loaded with a hundred-gallon fuel tank, with hand pump, centered over the axle, and five cases of one-liter bottles of water. It and the small compartment in the rear of each Rover are soon packed tight with our gear.

Our crew is Pax, my always partner, former Marine Recon sniper and a computer guru; Bojing, former SEAL, half-Korean half-Chinese, who Pax and I worked with in an extraction from North Korea; Skip, former Recon Marine who we've worked with many times including in the Corps in Iraq; Tobias Bartlett who is the G5 copilot and who I worked with in Paraguay; and our new mercenaries, Abby and Waddy. Taj, as always, is way ahead of us, even from his distant location of Malta. We soon learn Abby and Waddy are both former French Foreign Legion, and I raise my expectations of their value to the mission.

I'm not surprised to learn Abby and Waddy have their own weapons. Both carry German 9mm HK sidearms and French FAMAS assault rifles in standard 5.56 mm.

Of course, Sa'id is along for the ride and it may be a good thing as he has visited the lair of the head of the snake, Sheik Ali Hassan, the mullah in charge of this mission, in his palace deep in the Libyan dessert near Wadi Al Hayaa. Even Taj hasn't been able to get any detail on the Sheik's palace, much deeper in the Sahara out of Algeria in Libya. Hopefully we'll have no need of that intel.

Ji Su is in reserve and should be close behind in a Jet Ranger; Taj and his sons are standing by in Malta, hacking every military and intelligence asset in hyperspace; and Sol, Pax's number one at Weatherwax Internet Services in Las Vegas is using his big brain online.

I'm going back to sleep, as Pax will keep an eye on Sa'id, and Abby is driving. We've got at least fourteen hours on the road. Just as I'm about to doze off, stretched out as far as possible in the back seat of the Land Rover, my SAT phone rattles.

"Reardon," I answer.

"My daughter's not answering her cell and I see by the news the fucking ship is under attack or some goddamned thing."

"It was."

"You better have my fucking daughter with you or you're a dead man."

I clear my throat and my mind before speaking. "Mort Meyer, I presume. I wondered why I haven't heard from you."

"I've been in Tahiti on a shoot and just got back to this terrible news."

"Your daughter is among the missing..."

"Missing how?"

"All the women on board were taken."

"And, where the fuck were you?"

"Throwing two of the fuckers overboard after I killed them. I'm on Simone's trail now. "

He's silent for a long moment, then his voice waivers. "Where...where are you 'on the trail'?"

"I'm with a crew of mine, well-armed, well-provisioned, in country. We know the approximate location and we will extract the women."

"What country?"

"Algeria."

"You let them take my daughter to some shithole in Algeria, you prick. How long before you get her back?"

"Have no idea, Mister Meyer, but I won't stop until I get Simone...Sally back."

"I hope I don't see you until you deliver her safely to me."

"I'm signing off now. I'll bring Sally home to you."

"I trusted you. I paid you what you asked. I expect nothing less."

And he hangs up. It sounds like he might have thrown the phone against a wall.

FRAZIER MENDLESON CAUGHT the weekly CIA flight in the Company's Dassault Falcon 50. The jet masquerades as a private business flight, primarily for the covert movement of terror suspects, but when not involved in that effort makes weekly flights to Europe, normally landing in Schiphol International in Amsterdam.

Twice during the flight, he talked with Colonel Musa, his conversation relayed via Langley. He feared he was getting nowhere with the terrorist.

But due to the immediacy of the op, Mendleson was delivered directly to Malaga where he was met and briefed by Harry Weinstein. SEALs landed on *Blue Pearl,* breached the LPG room by cutting through a bulkhead, disarmed the device and cleared the ship. So far, they've found twenty-two dead dressed in camo, presumed hostiles, and two wounded who'd been flown to Landstuhl Regional Medical Center, LRMC, the U.S. Army hospital in Rhineland-Palatinate, Germany. At least one was expected to live. He would be turned over to the CIA for extensive interrogation.

The SEAL team had returned and was staging at Gibraltar, awaiting clearance to be the lead into Libya or Algeria to extract the women. Secretary of State William Prosper Williamson himself was landing in Algiers, along with his aide from the Algerian desk, Forrest Matson, and scheduled to meet with President Abdelkader Ouyahia to negotiate the necessity for our military to conduct an operation on Algerian territory.

The President had given Williamson forty-eight hours to gain Algeria's approval, then had instructed him to begin evacuating the mission and informing all Americans in country to leave posthaste.

He had no intention of having the legacy of his predecessor, the peanut farmer, and leaving Americans to rot in what he considered a shithole. Negotiations were underway with Niger, Mali, and Egypt to stage troops in those areas.

It wasn't going to be a simple negotiation with President Ouyahia. Algeria is deeply suspicious and has already assured POTUS and the Secretary of State that their own military, the Armée Nationale Populaire, the armed forces of the People's Democratic Republic of Algeria, is perfectly capable of handling the problem and would deliver the women back safely.

Except for clashes with Morocco in 1963 and 1976, the armed

forces have not been involved in hostilities against a foreign power. Their combat capabilities in defense of the country remain untested. And the military plays a major role in government and our Algerian desk is positive they will never allow the incursion of American troops, in any numbers, not even one, into the country.

And we know the military is not in control of their country.

The Secretary has been briefed by his aide: Al Qaeda and the Islamic Maghreb, the MUJAO—Movement for Oneness and Jihad in West Africa—as well as Al-Shabaab, are active in Algeria. Even those groups are divided. Al Qaeda has split into northern cells and southern cells, with the former sticking more closely to its jihadi origins and the latter increasingly turning to criminal activity. Many former tourist attractions are now closed due to the prevalence of kidnapping. Algeria and the wider region through much of Libya are affected by organized crime. Drug and arms trafficking, as well as cigarette and fuel smuggling, are a significant source of income. Kidnapping for ransom, particularly of Europeans, is a major source of funding for Islamist groups and is rampant. Protests in the cities erupt on a daily basis due to a lack of basic services and unemployment. The regime has taken steps to appease protestors, which has prevented the protests from escalating in the same way that they did in other countries in the Middle East and North Africa region during the 'Arab Sprint'.

To say Algeria is unstable is a great understatement.

And adjoining Libya is far worse.

The Sixth Fleet is rapidly approaching off Algiers, which, in fact, compounds the problem and the fear of the true intent of the Americans.

After all, Algeria is more and more, an oil-rich country.

United States Navy Task Force 62 is currently steaming along the north coast of Algiers. The combat-ready ground force is composed of a Marine expeditionary unit of approximately one thousand nine hundred Marines equipped with armor, artillery, and transport. They will lay up at the edge of the twelve-mile maritime limit and await the conclusion of negotiations.

It's not a wise move, as Algeria is martialing its armed forces in strategic locations, becoming adamant no American forces will enter Algeria.

Then again, this President is no peanut farmer.

53

I'M AWAKENED BY MY SAT PHONE, ABBY STILL DRIVING, AND SEE the sparse lights of Ouargla not far away. I yawn and stretch before answering, knowing it's likely Simone's worried daddy. I should have known better. It's Harry Weinstein and the CIA, likely wondering if I'm about to cause a major international incident.

"Where the hell are you?" he asks in a demanding tone.

"Playing Lawrence of Arabia. Where the hell are you?"

"I'm with Frazier Mendleson, CIA section chief terrorism and member of the Joint Terrorism Task Force, who's flown here in regard to this incident..."

"Harry, you may call a major terrorist attack against several hundred Americans and the kidnapping of over a hundred, an incident. I call it a fucking outrage that needs immediate retaliation."

"...and he wants to speak with you," he continues as if I haven't interrupted.

"I have no interest in a lecture from some spook." I offer in the same demanding tone Harry's been using.

"Look, Reardon, this is important. Hold on..."

A new voice. "Mister Reardon, this is Section Chief Mendleson..."

"What can I do for you, Mendleson?" I ask, with an equally officious tone.

"Stand down. These animals are killing innocent Americans."

That silences me for a minute. And strengthens my resolve. My trigger finger will move even more quickly now.

Mendleson continues, "We know you're in Algeria, without a visa, and about to cause an international incident. We have negotiations underway..."

"Without a visa?" I can't help but laugh. "Sorry, Chief. I have a job to do and it won't wait for negotiations."

"Reardon, you could be responsible for the deaths of more than a hundred American citizens. I don't know what you could be charged with, offhand, but I'm sure the list is as long as my arm. As would be your stay in Leavenworth."

"Could be. You keep negotiating and I'll call back in a few days and see how y'all are doing. In the meantime, I'll be having tea with the locals. Right now, I'm a little busy so stand by your phone. If you want to do something constructive as I may need a little help, how about loaning me a drone with a couple of Hellfire missiles, or maybe a Wart Hog A10 or two."

"Look, Reardon..." he manages before I disconnect. I think he gets the idea that I'm not going to 'stand down'.

The phone rattles again, but I ignore it.

"You gonna answer the damn SAT phone," Pax asks, yawning and stretching.

"Nope. Just somebody wanting to sell me health insurance." I flash him a grin.

"I'd grab it," he says, and adds, "You're damn likely to need it. Does it include burial insurance?"

"I figure that's a waste of money as you assholes would likely feed me to the dogs."

Abby joins in, "Damn few dogs in Muslim countries. A few hyena's way in the south. They would do the job."

"Thanks, Abby, for the help," I say, and PAX's SAT phone rattles.

He picks up. Says hello, nods a couple of times, then disconnects and turns to me.

"Taj has tracked this Alia's cell phone a hundred miles south east of Ouargla." Then he turns to Sa'id, who also has awakened. "Mister Sa'id, I believe you know more than you've divulged. I think you know exactly where you assholes are taking these women."

"I told you what I thought."

"And why did you think that?" Pax presses.

"I overheard Mumin talking to the Sheik, and that is what they discussed."

"And that was what was long planned?"

"I believe so, yes."

"Have you been there?" I ask.

He looks a little sheepish and I know he's been holding out.

Finally, he speaks up, "I have been there. I helped in the preparation of the palace for the arrival of the infidels."

"Sa'id, let me assure you, if you hold back anything more, I will gut you like a catfish and stuff you with hog fat. Understand?"

"Yes, yes, yes, I will tell all." His eyes are round and bulging like volleyballs.

I have a small notebook in my bug out bag and dig it out and hand it and a pen to him. "You will draw, accurately, all you know about this so-called palace. First the plan and location of all buildings, the surrounding territory, rocks, trees, brush. Then the plan, location of all rooms, where guards or soldiers will be housed. All you know. Take your time and do it correctly as your life may depend upon your accuracy."

"I will be accurate."

We skirt the large city of Ouargla passing lots of trucks and cars, mostly old and some packed with locals, then on the far side take a dirt track southwest into the Sahara. For the first few miles, we pass some patches that pass for farms, but mostly barren landscape with the occasional rock poking up through the sand like jagged logs floating on a flat pond. And the temperature rises with the sun. Abby even comments:

"It must be forty degrees already. It may reach forty-three or even more."

Of course, he means centigrade so by midmorning it's one hundred ten Fahrenheit. It could go to one twenty.

I can't help but smile as in the distance a couple of hundred yards from the road are a half-dozen camels, half of them mounted with riders pushing a few dozen sheep and goats.

I point them out to Abby, who explains, "Sanusi Bedouin. They are one of the most unique groups of our people. They observe the traditional nomadic lifestyle and the religious teachings of a prophet known as Sayyid Muhammad ibn' Ali as-Sanusi. They are a peaceful people, unlike many other tribes."

Then his attention turns to the job at hand. "We will arrive at our objective in the heat of the day. I will not approach on the road as they will have forward observers. I know of a small Oasis only two clicks from the main one where Ma'an Helu was built. Suggest we recon there and plan our attack."

"And rest up," I add, "and wait for the cover of darkness."

"Wise. Give these hostiles, who Sa'id has said are mostly

Yemini, Sudanese and Somali, time to chew plenty khat and get very peaceful before they go to meet Allah."

It's almost an hour before Abby swings off into the desert, due west, and only a few mikes before the green of a half-acre of palms appear in the distance.

"Sanusi are there," Abby observes. "They will be no trouble."

"Will they know anything?"

"Sanusi know all that goes on in the Sahara...the ocean of sand. They are said to have eyes in the back of their heads."

"You speak their dialect?" I ask.

"They speak Badawi. That was my aunt's native language."

"Good, we will invite the leader to supper with us."

"And he will accept as it would be rude to refuse and likely will bring a goat to roast."

SHEIK ALI HASSAN does not partake of liquor, but he is inclined to use the demon cocaine and the occasional Turkish water pipe, of hashish.

As he wishes to stay alert, this evening he's cut a few lines of cocaine.

When his SAT phone rattles again, he's travelling a thousand miles an hour and snaps. "Do you have it? Have you recovered it? It's been hours, hours, hours."

"I am sorry my Sheik," Al-Wakim says. "We tried to climb to the load one way and reached a spot we could go no farther, we..."

"You are cowards, that is the reason you have not reached the gold. You will suffer. I will call Musa and we must begin killing women again."

"My Sheik, the load is there. I was close enough to see much of it in the distance. We will reach it another way. Do not be eager to bring death to us from the infidel's drones. That would not get the gold for you."

Hassam sighs deeply, then snaps, "I will give you a few more hours. Call me when you reach it."

"Yes, my Sheik."

Hassam disconnects, looks at three more lines of cocaine, then decides he must switch to hashish. He unlimbers his water pipe and loads it.

Then after two pipes, decides he must sleep. There are two dozen young infidel women coming to please him. He will need his rest.

54

THEY OBSERVE US FROM A DISTANCE AS WE ERECT TWO lightweight tan ten-by-ten-foot sunshades and spread some small tarps around a fire pit, then Abby and Waddy wander over to their small tent camp. Like the other group we saw, these have a few camels, sheep and goats.

In moments, they return with two men in white robes, both carry old Lebel World War 1 rifles, at least one hundred years old and pretty-exhausted. Both weapons, however, are well oiled and the stocks, if scarred, finished nicely. They are followed by a woman with both hindquarters of a goat on her shoulders and a teapot hanging from an elbow, as well as an iron device with legs and a rotisserie bar in a sling on her back. We'd built a fire from the stubs of palm fronds and some wormy wood from sparse shrubs resembling our Mojave and Sonoran Desert greasewood. After our introductions, to the men who place hands over hearts, a gesture we return. But we are not introduced to the veiled woman. She's busy heating the tea and preparing the meat, and the hindquarters are soon turning. She leaves the roasting to another woman she waves over. The first woman fades away but shows one more time with several pieces of unleavened flat bread and a clay vat of some yogurt mixture, I presume from goat or maybe camel milk. We throw in some canned peaches and a box of Hershey bars.

We're soon around the fire sitting cross-legged and eating, while making nice talk with Abby and Waddy doing the interpreting.

Abby turns to me after dabbing his mouth with a neckerchief, "Now we will see what they know." And turns back and jabbers, gets answers, jabbers again, gets answers, then turns to me again. "We should reward them."

"What do you suggest?"

"Do you have Algerian dinar?"

"No, I have American dollars and some Swiss gold francs."

"Gold. A tenth will do?"

"Then a full ounce will do better as it's all I have."

He smiles. "We should get a camel and information for that."

"I'm happy to pay it, if it's actionable and accurate."

"Then that is as it is." He turns back to the two Bedos and jabbers, and I get a tight smile and nod from each. In a heartbeat, both are seated and drawing in the hard earth. The good news is what they draw agrees closely with what Sa'id has drawn.

The so-called palace is atop a cap rock plateau, covering nearly all the south end of the half kilometer long, quarter click wide flat top. The mosque, a much smaller structure, occupies the far end, smaller and centered. A double row of planted palms creates a two-hundred-yard walkway between the two structures. The edges of the cap rock are twenty to forty feet of nearly vertical basalt, with another twenty to forty feet of rough rock escarpment sloping away below the cliffs. A two-track trail that will likely accommodate the Rovers has been carved out of the south side, steeply rising to massive timber gates. I'm pleased to see a more easily breached human passthrough door near the huge ones. The palace is walled by twenty-feet-high stone with little fenestration, partially collapsed in a few spots, only a few slotted openings for shooters. They are only six inches wide by three feet tall, reminiscent of those I've seen in castles to accommodate archers. Sa'id has drawn the interior, which is a half-acre building only partially roofed. The rest collapsed. Two outbuildings consist of a barn and a water-well building. A few palms are scattered at the base of the escarpment. Lots of spindly brush resembling greasewood and mesquite is spotted around the escarpment. A small grove of ancient olive trees is a scraggly change from sand at the south, and two cypress grace the edge of the two-track trail halfway up the slope.

The good news is there are two smaller caprock basalt edifices flanking the larger, one only ten acres or so, the other only fifty feet wide and slightly longer. The smaller is almost tower-like and at least fifty feet taller than the palace walls. With luck, a shooter atop it will see into at least half the palace courtyard. Lots of loose rock and the same spotted brush will offer a plethora of sniper hidey-holes on both secondary caprock islands in the sand.

I dig a coin from my bugout bag and the Bedos excuse themselves, happy with their reward, as we are more than happy with the info they've provided.

More than happy if it's accurate. It seems they know of a tunnel leading from a nearby wadi under the walls of Ma'an Helu and into the main building.

The so-called palace itself is reported to be a wreck, as would any untended building be after ten centuries in the Sahara sun, and wind; Sahara simooms, as the storms are known. The Mosque, a separate building, is in better shape as it has been used by passing

Bedos off and on for the last centuries. Abby informs me that *ma'an helu* means sweet water in Arabic.

If necessary, we'll turn the water salty with blood.

It's time for a planning meeting.

THEY FLEW FOR AN HOUR, landed at an airport near a small town, and were fed and given water while seated in the plane. Four men in military uniforms, driving a military vehicle, were stationed nearby. The vehicle had a machine gun mounted in a top turret, and one of the soldiers sat nearby while the other three played some game. Then, three at a time, the women were taken to a nearby building and, even though the plane had a small toilet, allowed to use the toilet and wash up, escorted there by the pilot and the female guard, Alia.

They slept in the plane, then again were fed and taken to the toilet.

Connie has been torn. Pull the .380 and shoot it out with the four bogies on the plane as soon as it touches down or wait and see what transpires. She's sure the plane will be met by other soldiers, but if not, she's decided to make her play.

She dozes a little on the trip. Then the throttling back of the engines awakens her. Then one of the guards yells, in English, to tighten their seatbelts. They are obviously on a glide path, and soon the plane rocks and bounces as it touchesd down on a rough strip. Then she is thrown forward as the pilot violently applies the brakes. It is obviously a short strip they're on. The plane rolls to a stop, then the plane reverses direction and taxis back to near touchdown.

Connie studies those awaiting. Seven vehicles—three Toyota

trucks, three Toyota SUVs, and a Mercedes limo. The bad news is at least another half-dozen armed men are scattered among the vehicles.

As the stairway is dropped, a robed man of generous girth exits the limo and strides forward, his robe flowing behind. He's sandal-wearing, and a sash holds a large carved dagger in a jeweled sheath. His scraggly beard scatters below his receding chin. He's flanked by two men with more sophisticated arms, small automatic pistols with thirty-shot magazines as long as the weapons. Much smaller than the AKs the others carry.

The fat robed man stands with hands folded behind. Another man in a military uniform exits the limo and strides up but stands slightly behind the first.

The man in uniform is an ominous sign. Could the Algerian military be involved?

"Do not forget your belongings," the guard on the plane announces. Then adds, "You are about to meet Sheik Ali Hassan, who will be your host. He will explain more to you when you arrive at the harem."

"Harem!" several of the women exclaim.

55

"Silence," the guard snaps. "You will be silent unless the sheik asks you a question. Keep your eyes down, as is proper. Do not look him in the eye, even if he speaks to you."

Simone has managed to get directly behind Connie as they stand to exit the plane. "What the fuck is this?" she asks, in a loud whisper.

Connie turns and hushes her with a finger to her lips. "Quiet, do exactly what they say."

"I feel like shit. I need my shot. I won't make it much longer."

"Quiet. Just as soon as..."

"Who's talking?" the guard shouts, and the girls shut up.

As they reach the bottom stair, each is stopped, then led forward by the hand to stand in front of the sheik, whose hands are now folded on his generous belly. He seems unsteady on his feet. As the first one is brought before him, he speaks loudly to his men in Arabic, but Connie can hear as he commands, "Divert your gaze," and his men look away. Then he speaks to the girl who's standing with eyes down. "Remove your *niqab*...your face cover," and she unwinds the scarf she has wrapped around her face. He nods. She's led to a Toyota truck and loaded in the small bed. He continues the ritual for each girl.

When Connie is led forward and he commands her to remove the scarf she's using, she says, in English. "The young girl behind me is diabetic and needs insulin."

"She may need insulin, but you should be less insolent." His tone is harsh.

"I am so sorry, but my friend..."

"My sister is diabetic. We are not barbarians. She will receive what she needs in the harem."

"Thank you, sir," Connie says, keeping her eyes down.

The sheik looks to the side where the man in the military uniform stands and speaks in Arabic. "She has much mouth, maybe I'll put it to good use."

Both men laugh.

Connie shows no sign of understanding, merely stands with eyes down until she's led away to an enclosed Land Rover. But she hears the sheik as Simone stands before him. "You are very lovely. You will be cared for in your new home."

"Ukfa ouya," Simone says, with a bit of sass in her tone.

Jesus, Connie thinks, *I hope he didn't attend school in the U.S. and understands pig Latin. A 'fuck you' likely would not be well received.*

"I beg your pardon?" the sheik replies.

"Sorry, sir," Simone says, "I feel very bad and need my medicine."

Thank God, Connie thinks. *The girl has a brain. A small one, but a brain.*

The fat sheik starts to say something, then is distracted, digs in a pocket and pulls out a cell phone. He walks away a few steps and begins screaming into the instrument. "You fool, you fool, I will send someone else. You had best disappear into the sand!"

Then. He seems to calm down and says in a lower voice. "You will continue. I am sorry two of your men have fallen to their deaths. Be more careful but do not fail me." Then he slips the phone back into his pocket and returns as if nothing was amiss.

Connie and Simone are in one vehicle, Patty and Gretchen in another, as they speed away from the airstrip. It's nearly an hour and growing dark—and they've been on a dirt two-track for most of that time—when Connie sees what she thinks is an apparition in the distance. Atop a hill rising from the desert is a white palace with gleaming gold minarets. At the base of the hill is a grove of palms. The hill itself seems a kilometer wide, she has no idea how deep. As they near, they enter a wide road lined with palms and paved with brick-colored pavers.

The road winds around the hill as it rises, and Connie realizes the hill is almost a perfect bubble, as long as wide. The top is surrounded by a ten-foot-high wall, probably some kind of block but plastered and whitewashed. The gates are black iron topped with golden spikes, and open as they approach. Their caravan is led by the limo and it veers to the left while the vehicles containing guards and twenty-four young women go to the right. The entire courtyard is paved with the same brick pavers as the road leading there. A round fountain is centered twenty paces in front of double doors that appear to be sheathed in gold. The fountain is programed, sprays from five to twenty-five feet high, and dances with alternate sprays from several heads. Peacocks and Guinea hens roam the grounds.

They stop around a corner of the whitewashed building in a line twenty paces from a rose-colored door. The door is flanked by a white wall but covered with red bougainvillea. The exterior wall around the courtyard and on the face of the building has alternating red and yellow bougainvillea clinging to the whitewashed plaster.

The door opens as they exit the vehicles and the guards form a line as Alia leads the women past them and inside.

Most of the women gasp as they enter a courtyard of palms and well-tended flowers surrounding a twenty-by-forty-foot swimming pool. Plates of fruit, mostly dates, rest atop white iron tables surrounded by what, in the states, would be called veranda furniture, all rose colored.

Six women in black burkas are lined up and stand jabbering from side to side. Residents, Connie presumes.

Alia hands her AK to a guard who's followed as far as the door, then he shuts it, remaining outside.

"Gather around," Alia commands and stands atop a landscaping stone. As soon as the ladies are settled, she commands, "Listen closely. You will each have an individual room. Two rooms share a bath. You will bathe as quickly as possible then dress in the clothes provided. Attendants are available for anything you need..."

Simone interrupts, "How about a cell phone?"

Alia is not amused. "After you are here for some time, and should you please the sheik, you will be allowed to communicate with your family."

"I have to have medicine, or I'll not be here for 'sometime'," Simone says, and not in a kind tone.

"Your medicine will be provided after you are examined by the resident doctor. We have a fully stocked clinic on the grounds."

"Quickly please," Simone says.

"The ladies in black are your attendants and will assist you. Now, do as you're told. Help yourself to the fruit. Then you will be assigned your room."

Connie was wrong, she surmised, as the women in burkas were maids or whatever the attendants were called, not conscripts of the harem. As Connie and Simone dig into some grapes, Simone whispers to her, "Alibaba and the fucking forty thieves. Harem is horseshit. I'll bite that fat fuck's nuts off if he gives me the chance."

"Let's get out of here alive, kid."

56

We drive to within a click of Sheik Ali Hassan's depository of American women, Ma'an Helu. I'm pleased we have only a quarter moon, but it nicely backgrounds the three rock heaps rising out of the Sahara. The north one is about the same height as the main middle one, sixty to seventy feet or so, the south one well over a hundred.

Much to his chagrin, I leave Sa'id cable-tied to the steering wheel of a Land Rover.

As planned, Pax takes one night-scoped .338 Lapua sniper rifle and heads south to the highest of the flanking rockpiles, one he can climb and, if he reaches the top, see at least partially into the courtyard of the wreck of a palace. As I want Skip and Bo with me, muscle and brains, I send Waddy, who claims to have been a marksman in the French Foreign Legion. He jogs to the other. I will give them two hours to get cuddled into a hidey hole. All of us have handheld radios and Skip has a SAT phone, as well.

Google Earth has shown us a brush-lined ravine that will take Bo, Skip, and me the last three hundred yards to a position in the moon-shade of the rock that should allow us unseen access to the base of the escarpment, or, hopefully, into the tunnel that has an entrance only fifty yards from the base of the escarpment. It's said to be covered by planks, level for a hundred yards, then a long stairway ending in a stall in a stable building. If the tunnel is a dud, I plan to climb to a position only fifty yards from the road and the gates, move along the wall, and blow the passthrough gate if I have to. I have five pounds of C4 in my backpack, as does Skip. I pray I don't have to set a charge as I want to know the exact location of the women before any firefight or threat to life takes place.

I've left Tobias and Abby—who claims proficiency with the mortars and the LAWS Rocket Launcher—with the vehicles in case we need them relocated or us recovered from some other location. Tobias has a SAT phone as well as a handheld and is also in charge of all communication between us. Ji Su, who's now located with her rented Jet Ranger at a small strip only twenty clicks from us, Taj in Malta, and Sol in Las Vegas. All are standing by.

Bo, Skip and I are waiting in the ravine, no more than two hundred yards from the base of the escarpment, giving Pax and Waddy their prescribed two hours, when my SAT phone rattles.

"Reardon," I answer in a low tone.

"Taj here," he replies. "Sit rep. We have tapped into an American satellite they've diverted to do a flyover of Ma'am Helu and it seems all women are in the Mosque. We've counted a half-dozen vehicles in the walled palace compound but no more than a dozen hostiles. How are Abdallah and Dawad working out?"

"You did well. So far so good."

"Good. They are good men."

"It's about to hit the fan here. Got to go."

"The bird is due another fly-by at 2227. If anything changes, I'll sit rep again."

"Ten four," and he disconnects.

I'm all smiles hearing there are several vehicles on site. It was my plan to appeal to the CIA when we had control of the ladies and pray for helicopter transport, but if we have to drive out maybe we can haul everyone in eight vehicles. Haul to where, I have no damn idea, but I do know there are at least three U.S. oil company camps within forty miles of our position. And oil companies have their own protection forces in place. I know. I was offered a job doing same.

Even if the Algerian military is involved, as was indicated by the trucks used to haul the women, they would risk terrible retaliation by the U.S. if they interfered with their rescue after I have them in hand. I'd make damn sure everyone from the President to FOX news will know if they do. Of course, after the Benghazi fiasco, I would not be surprised by anything my own government is capable of doing—or ignoring. However, this President or this Secretary of State is not one to sleep through an emergency.

As hot as it was today, it's now cold enough to wear a jacket.

I check my watch and it's 2100. Time to call my shooters. This one's via the handhelds.

"Anybody got eyes on?" I ask.

Waddy comes right back. "In place, high as I can get but not high enough to see into the compound. Eyes on one bogie."

"All you can do is what you can do," I reply.

"What kind of fucking snakes are there around here?" Pax asks.

"All kinds. Are you in position?"

"Ten ticks of the minute hand. It's slippery as your old girlfriend's excuses for all those other guys. Damn if I didn't pass a wet spot, a bunch of olive trees, and then some cypress."

I was worried about asking him to climb with his one leg a bit shorter than the other, but if I'd questioned, he'd have offered to black my eye. "Keep it on biz, bud. You okay?"

"Something slithered away a minute ago. I almost made things even more slippery."

I have to laugh. "And smelly I imagine. Don't worry about the Nubian cobras, they spit several feet and don't have to gnaw on you. And you won't have to watch them sink fangs as the spit will blind you."

"You're just a frigging ball buster, you prick. Glad I didn't know that while climbing this last fifty yards, looking up over these damn ledges. Some friggin' bird came in my face and you damn near had to scrape me up with a spatula."

"Double click me when you're in place."

"Yes, Bwana."

In less than ten, he calls back. "I'm topped out. Can see seventy-five percent of the courtyard and into a few archways in the main building. I have eyes on two ragheads leaning on the wall, having a smoke. Two hundred sixty yards. I was hoping for a challenge. The east half is caved in, but there are lights in the west."

Waddy interrupts, "I have one atop the wall. A lookout I'd guess. But he can't see your position from where he is."

"Okay. Maybe we can damn near even the odds before they know they're in a fight. Don't wait for my order if you hear an explosion. Fire at will. Taj says the women are confined to the Mosque and he thinks no more than a dozen bogies."

Pax comes with, "I can reduce that to ten in short order?"

"And I got one," Waddy says. "Three hundred forty-seven yards. If this thing's on and the wind stays down, I can clean out his earwax...put it from ear to ear through his *shemagh*."

"Stand down until we're inside the walls. If we find the tunnel, we'll try that way and will likely be out of range for a while. Stay cool."

Skip is eager, moves on ahead, finds the described four-foot boulder just yards from the escarpment, pulls away brush above it and finds planks. By the time Bo and I catch up, he's already loosening a plank, and with Bo's help soon, has three planks aside.

Before I enter, I speak softly into the radio and hope all are paying attention. "Going inside, dead space for a while."

I'm surprised by a very clean tunnel, beginning with a half-dozen stairs leading down to a flat five-feet-wide tunnel with nearly flat walls and wooden ricking and supports on the side.

We each turn on headlamps when well inside. Every twenty-five feet, torches are in rusty iron holders alternating on the side walls. They are the length of baseball bats and each wrapped in cloth on the end, soaked in what smells and feels like crude oil. The place would be well lit were they afire. We move a hundred paces through the tunnel before we come to a long stairway, cut in stone. In another fifty yards, we have a surprise no one mentioned. A heavy barred gate, and beyond it another steeper stairway of only ten steps dying into the bottom of a plank floor. Not only a lock inhibits entry, but it's chained.

I give it a hard jerk, mostly out of frustration, and it doesn't budge. Not only locked and chained but rusted shut.

I hate this, if we can't pry the damn thing open it means we'll have to set a charge, retreat damn near all the way back, blow it, run like hell back and up to the planks where we have no idea how long to broach. FUCK!

57

TIME FOR A CONSULT.

"Okay, let's try and pull the damn thing down. But if not possible, I say we retreat and try to either scale the wall or breach the pass-through door? What say?"

Bo scratches his head. "If we blow it, we don't know what we've got beyond those planks. And, hell, we could bring this whole tunnel down on us. No choice. Let's give it a jerk."

I can press four hundred on a good day and think Bo can probably do more. Skip is a freak, bull strong. So, if we can't budge the gate with pure muscle, it likely can't be done by humans.

"Lean in, then jerk," I suggest, and we do.

It flies open and I go on my butt. The damn thing wasn't locked, and the chain was only looped.

Both my compadres laugh, and I shush them. "We've made enough damn noise," I mumble as I brush the sand off my butt.

When we get up the stairs, we see the plank floor is hinged. We switch off headlamps. I stay with M4 ready, while they push it open. Hay and horse, camel, or donkey crap falls into the tunnel. But light does not.

I lead as I'm locked, loaded and ready and step into an ancient rock-walled stable. There are a dozen stalls and an equal number of mangers, but no babe or wisemen. In fact, no animals. And I'm glad, as the King of Kings would likely not want to be party to what I hope is about to happen.

We switch our headlamps to the lowest beam and move forward to a pair of double heavy plank doors, wide enough to accommodate a Land Rover, if both swung aside.

There's an inch gap between the doors, so I stay quiet with an eye glued, but nothing. So, it's recon time. I try the handheld. "We're in. Don't shoot anyone coming out of the stable. Sit rep?"

Pax comes right back. "My two must have hit the sack."

Then Waddy. "Mine is still in position. He's on his butt with chin on chest. I'd guess this fine guard is sawing logs. I've seen no one at the Mosque."

"Stay cool until you hear shots or see trouble coming our way."

The stable doors are barred from the outside, but the gap is wide enough that I can get the barrel of the M4 through and pitch the bar aside. It clatters on the cobblestones below, so I wait thirty seconds to pull the door aside.

All quiet.

The palace itself is two stories with more window openings, without glass, in the upper floor than the lower. The lower floor is slightly larger than the upper and, on this side, at least, there's a covered walkway all around the upper until it's collapsed at the east end.

I double key the handheld and whisper, "Going into the arched doors."

Getting double clicks back, we move forward.

We recon the lower floor, taking at least an hour to clear what must be twenty-five rooms including a two-story great room, collapsed at one end, an ancient kitchen, and storerooms.

A stairway leads to an upper floor from both the kitchen and the great room, some fifty paces apart.

"One of us should take the rear stairway," I whisper. "Loser goes," I say, and make a flat palm, scissor fingers, and fist for a rock. We all put a hand behind our back and I whisper, "one, two," and we come out on three. All have fists for rocks. So, we do it again, and Bo has a rock and Skip and I paper. Paper covers rock. I give him sign language for starting up on a double click and he's off. Bo makes his way to the rear stairway and Skip and I give him time. Then I give him the go sign, a double click. We switch off our headlamps and begin moving up as quietly as possible. But the stairs are covered with loose sand and grit, and it's tough not to scrape.

Just as we top the stairs, a voice rings out. "Ahmed?"

I'm madly trying to remember how to say 'yes' in Arabic when Skip, to my great surprise, answers, *"La, Mohammed."*

Then I remember, *la* is 'no'. And he was brilliant, as the man may have recognized his friend Ahmed's voice.

The man is yawning wide with arms outstretched as Skip closes the ten feet and throttles him with a big hand, squeezing his windpipe shut and shoving him against the wall.

The man flails with both hands trying to beat Skip away, but my big buddy pulls him to the ground and bangs his head on the slate floor so hard I fear he'll wake whoever else is in the room he stood outside of.

With M4 at the ready, I enter the room which must be forty feet long by fifteen wide. The only light is from what seems a metal or clay fire pit, and it's only glowing embers. They've either cooked there or fired it up for heat.

As I step inside, another voice rings out. "Ahmed?" This Ahmed must have been popular. As my eyes focus, I get at least eight, maybe ten, lumps on the floor. Men sleeping.

"No, motherfucker," I say, and I can see the standing man scramble for a weapon as the others are rising. I spray the room, emptying a thirty-shot magazine, drop to a knee and insert another, while shots and muzzle flashes come from the far end of the room, mostly from a doorway. Only three or four shots seem to have originated from inside the room, and they quickly were stilled. Then I make out Bo who's at another entrance. His headlamp, unlit but obvious on his head, gives him away.

As I go down to a knee, Skip opens up. As he reloads, I scan the room. There's more than one bogie flopping around and moaning. A couple are on hands and knees trying to crawl to God only knows where. I move quickly and step on the butt of an AK one of them is trying to drag along, but he goes to his belly and quiets. I take the chance of clicking on my high beam and begin collecting weapons, then realize Skip has slid down the wall and is on his butt with legs extended.

I hurry over. "Need your quick clot," he says, as if he's asking for a piece of gum.

"Where?" I ask. "Side, don't think it got bone."

"Cover us," I yell to Bo. "Skip took one."

"Lie down so I can expose it," I command, then drop my weapon and my pack and dig in for my kit.

He's trying to free his battle rattle belt, loosen his belt, and pull his shirt free, when another shot rings out—a distant shot. A man stumbles into the room, trying to keep his footing, then falls to his back. Seems our snipers are at work.

The wound is small in the entry but must have been a hollow point of some kind as the exit has blown out a chunk just smaller than a tennis ball. I sprinkle a liberal amount of quick clot, slap a compress front and back, then jerk a headdress off a nearby hostile and bind it tightly.

"Thanks, fuckhead," Skip snarls, "If I get fleas, I'm gonna kick your skinny ass."

I ignore him. "I'll call for Ji Su and an evac, while I'm heading to get the women. Stay put. Shoot any of these fuckers who twitch," I command. He gives me a nod and frees his Glock.

"Let's go," I yell to Bo. We head for the stairway.

I can only pray some jihadi son of a bitch is not spraying the room full of women with his AK, now that he's heard shots and knows a rescue must be launched.

I radio Tobias as Bo and I take up positions on the outside, either side, of the wide palm lined walkway to the mosque. "Get Ji Su moving. By the time she gets here, she should be able to set down in the courtyard."

"What's up?" Toby asks.

"Skip took one in the side."

"Getting evac," Toby says, and I go back to work.

I'm truly surprised we're not taking fire as we approach the Mosque, but all's quiet.

Two Muslim women in black burkas are at the door, standing with hands on their heads. Smart girls, I think, as I blow by them and Bo wisely stops to do a quick shake down. I only take three steps inside, when an American woman stops me.

"American?" she asks.

"Yes, ma'am, here to take you home."

"Thank God." She points at a line of women with their heads hung. "Only six Muslim women here to attend to us. We were told if we stepped outside, we'd be shot."

I count seven. "Six?"

"Yes, six. This is the first time I've seen the big one."

One of the black burka clad women glances up. I'm studying her and notice something odd about the line of her dress. Maybe a weapon. I start her way and she sweeps the burka back off her head. I raise my M4 as the bearded 'woman' tries to bring an AK47 out from under the clumsy garment.

He's yelling as he struggles to free his weapon, "Paradise is under the shades of swords," he screams. He's firing through the burka, unable to free his weapon, and kicking up dirt in front of me but is not quick enough as a half magazine stitches him from crotch to just under the left eye.

He cartwheels back and hits hard, puffing dust in a cloud as he lands in a former flower bed off the slate entry to the Mosque.

I stride over to recover the AK when one of the women moves between us and begins beating my chest with her fists. "You have killed Colonel Musa, you infidel dog."

I shove her aside into the arms of her compadres and recover the AK. As I do so, I hear the rattle of a SAT phone and pat him down until I find it. I answer in English and get excellent, but accented, English back.

"Who is answering my Colonel's phone?" the voice demands.

"Who the fuck wants to know?"

"Where is Colonel Musa?"

"He's in hell and if he's 'your colonel,' you'll soon be there as well."

And he disconnects.

The burka clad women begin that tongue rattle thing Arab women do. I ignore them and return to the lady who's stepped up to talk for the captives.

"Any one need medical?" I ask.

"No emergency. A few without their heart and other daily meds so they should be first."

I study the group of women but don't see what I seek, so turn back to the spokeswoman. "I need to speak with Simone and Connie?"

"They are not with us. They—a couple of dozen of the young pretty girls—boarded a plane right after we left the ship."

"What?" I snap, then my chin hits my chest. Then I mutter, under my breath so as not to offend the lady, "Mother, mother, motherfucker."

58

BEFORE I HEAD FOR THE GATES I FIRST CALL WADDY AND PAX, "Try and get your butts down here without breaking anything. We ain't through..."

"What?" Pax comes back.

"Explain on the way. Got more calls to make."

Then I dial Taj. "Hey, did you guys see a plane leaving Melilla right after the ladies disembarked the *Bit Tawfig*?"

"We did. Is it of interest?"

"Two dozen of the ladies, the young beautiful ones, were on that plane."

"We ignored it after it left local airspace, flying southeast, by the way."

"Any way to step back in time?" I ask.

"There is a webpage, flightaware dot com, that tracks all airplane flights. I will get on trying to backtrack it."

"Please. I've got some tail to twist and will call you if I come up with anything. You do same."

"Will do."

I ring off then call my new CIA buddy, Frazier Mendleson. Who answers on the first ring.

"Where are you?" he asks without a howdy.

"Ma'an Helu, a rundown palace and Mosque a hundred clicks southeast of Ouargla. I have the women, at least most of them, but am not waiting for the cavalry to come. I'll leave two associates, locals, who'll stand guard until the SEALs or Marines or who the fuck ever arrives to pick up the ladies..."

"Why aren't you standing by?"

"Two dozen of them, the young beautiful ones, and my charges, were separated from the rest. I'm going after them."

"Where?"

"Fuck off and stay out of the way. If you call me and have a SEAL team or a platoon of Marines ready to land, I'll read you in."

"Stand down, Reardon. We'll take it from here."

"You're saying the US has permission to interdict?"

"Not yet, but..."

"No fucking buts. I'm going. Tell the President my next call is to the NYT, BBC, FOX and maybe even the lying CNN, as much as I hate the lying press. I'm going public that I've located and freed the women and our chickenshit government is doing another Benghazi, if no one shows. So, take it for what it's worth. I'm blowing the road all to hell so it's chopper time. It's a cap rock mountain with no other way up. There are over one hundred innocent American women who want to go home."

"Reardon..."

"Stand by your phone," and I disconnect.

I hustle back to Skip and find him leaning on the wall with eight or nine dead bogies on the floor in front of him. Bo and I carry him down to the clearing between buildings, and I wave some of the American women hostages over.

"If there's a nurse among you, have them help this guy who's risked all to free y'all."

"We have three nurses and a retired doctor with us," a gray-haired buxom woman offers.

"A chopper is on the way. Find a way to light a landing area at least a hundred feet across."

"We will. Thank you, young man..."

"Take care of my buddy."

Then as I slip and slide down the cliff to the escarpment, I call Toby. "Where's Ji Su?"

"Three minutes out."

"Tell her they are lighting a landing zone on the top of the mountain. She's to take Skip to the nearest good hospital and any women she can haul with health issues, then return to a spot I'll advise. We're heading into Libya."

"You got it."

"If Waddy beats me down, tell him he and Abby are to come up and guard the ladies. And I want you to stay."

"Bullshit, I want to go with you guys."

"Need you here, pardner. No time to argue. Can't leave the ladies with mercenaries I don't know."

"All right, but know I hate it."

"I'm blowing the road, so it's shank's mare. I don't want bogies driving up. Leave the rocket launcher and one mortar with Waddy and Abby."

"Shank's mare?"

"Climbing...afoot...walking."

"Got it."

I cross the top of the escarpment to the road, then search for a deep crack and insert the five pounds of C4 and a timed detonator set for three minutes, then hustle away down the road. If the good guys are coming for the women, they'll come in choppers. Only bad guys will arrive in wheeled vehicles.

I'm halfway back to the Land Rovers when the mountain behind me explodes, raining rocks over a hundred-foot circumference.

When I reach the Rovers, I go straight to my new buddy, Sa'id, who's still bound to the steering wheel.

"How you doing, bro?" I ask.

"I am fine, considering I've had nothing to drink while you were killing people at the palace."

"I found the women. They are free."

"So, you have won this one. You will lose the next."

"I find it interesting you have not asked about your lady friend, Alia. About whom you've been so worried."

"Was she there?" he asks, looking a little surprised.

"You know fucking well she wasn't. She's with the two dozen women who were flown away just after they landed in Morocco."

He shrugs but says nothing.

So, I pull my k-bar and run a finger over the sharp blade. "Do you know what a capon is, Sa'id?"

"Capon?"

"It's a rooster that has had its nuts cut off. You're about to become one if you don't tell me where they've taken those two dozen women and who had Alia's cell phone?"

He eyes me for a moment until I slip the blade between his thighs that he's holding so tight together I have to force the blade down. "Who has her phone?"

He blanches, then speaks rapidly, "All cell phones were to be collected and given to the driver of one of the vans. It is here somewhere."

"And where is Alia?"

"She was to accompany and care for the young women."

"Where?"

"The sheik...the sheik will kill us both."

"He won't have a chance because I'm going to cut your nuts off and let you bleed out right here. Where are the young women?"

I force the blade closer to his crotch.

"Stop, stop. The sheik is at his palace near Wadi Al Hayaa in Libya, Five hundred kilometers from here. The young women have been taken to his harem. I know the place well."

Just as he finishes, my SAT phone rattles, "Reardon."

"It's Harry," the voice announces.

"Did you get permission to come in country?" I ask.

"No, but the President has ordered the Marine Corps and a team of SEALS to rescue the women, and has informed Algeria if they interfere, they will no longer have an air force and the 6th Fleet will likely drop a few shells the size of Volkswagens into the palace."

"Good, but two dozen of the young ladies are not here. I will leave one SAT phone with my two associates, locals who can be trusted, who will guard the women until the cavalry arrives."

"Have them call me on this number and we'll coordinate the pickup. Two CH-53E Super Stallions will be on their way in an hour. They'll carry fifty-five each without crowding. Along with four AH-1W Super Cobras flying close cover backed by a half-dozen F-16s, two Wart Hog A10s, and a SEAL team. The President and the 6th fleet are serious. Algeria has been advised to ground all aircraft or lose them. Where the hell are you going?"

"Libya, a place called Wadi Al Hayaa, five hundred clicks southwest, where this asshole Sheik Ali Hassan has added two dozen young unwilling American girls to his harem."

"Oh, that's just fucking great. Now you're gonna get our tit in a crack with Libya?"

"Gotta do what you gotta do. I'll expect some help shortly after I beat you there."

"Hell, you can't beat us there driving."

"Jet Ranger will beat you there. I have a hell of a head start. Speaking of that, we're a blue and white Jet Ranger heading southwest from here. We'd appreciate not getting shot down, should those F16s stumble on us."

Harry sighs deeply. "I'll advise. This President still gets red in the face when you even mention Benghazi, so I'm sure he'll have no problem pushing this mission into Libya."

"Gotta go," I say, as Abby and Pax jog up.

"All good?" Pax asks.

"Nope, we're two dozen short, including Connie and my client."

"So, where?"

"Libya."

"Good," Pax says. "I got a bone to pick with those pricks, called Benghazi."

Sheik Ali Hassan is incensed. He had decided to begin again killing the women, at least until he discovered he was in possession of the gold, but his Colonel did not answer the phone. He had no idea who it was who answered but was sure it was an infidel.

He wonders, now that he has two dozen of the women under his control, maybe he should begin killing them himself. However, he knows better than to call again from his palace. If they can trace a SAT phone, and he is sure they can, then it is too dangerous.

Instead he will enjoy the infidel women, then send one of his minions two hundred miles away, or more, to make the call—unless, of course Al-Wakim recovers the gold.

59

Ji Su arrives and sets it down perfectly in the center clearing between the palace and the Mosque, her rotors only a couple of feet from palm fronds. She loads Skip, who's bitching so much I know he'll be okay. Three women shy of heart medicine pile into the back seat of the Jet Ranger, and Ji Su is off to an Interco Petroleum camp—and back in forty-five minutes. We load up. Even leaving Abby and Waddy some defensive weapons, we still have a .338 Lapua and one Mortar with six rounds, plus our carry weapons. We crowd into the Ranger, Pax, Bo, Sa'id—who knows the target—me, all our gear, and head out.

Ji Su does some calculations, then turns to me. "Two hours and ten minutes to Wadi Al Hayaa, if I keep the pedal to the metal, but they better have fuel at the airport twenty clicks from there, or we'll be counterrotating before we get back."

"Task one, get there. Task two, get the ladies. Then we'll worry about catching a few camels back if we have to."

"Easy for you to say. My credit card's on the bird rental, and I don't know if it'll stretch for nearly the mil to replace this one if this sheik decides to keep her."

"Pax will back you up," I say, and catch an elbow in the ribs from my buddy.

"Okay. I like you better than he does, so I'll back you up."

And I get another elbow.

While in the air I call Taj. "Sir, new mission. Seems two dozen of the younger women have been taken to the palace of the guy you made via the SAT phone call. Sheik Ali Hassan in place near Wadi Al Hayaa in Libya, I'm told five hundred clicks from this Sweet Water. We're headed there now and any intel you can give us might keep us alive."

"Do you have a laptop?" he asks.

"Ji Su, our pilot has one."

"Do you have a hot spot on that SAT phone?"

"I do."

"Then get hooked up to her laptop and advise me of her e-mail. I'm sending you the last Google flyby on the place, some SAT pics if I can snake them, and anything else I can conjure up."

"You da man. I'll shoot you an e-mail as soon as I'm hooked in."

CONNIE TRIED to sleep in the hard, twin-size bed provided. She had wormed her way around until she was in a room with Simone, much to Patty and Gretchen's objection. They wanted to all stay together as if hugging each other would solve all their problems. She lay awake until she heard some commotion outside her room, fished her .380 out from inside the thin down mattress she'd been provided, strapped it to her thigh, put on the wrap she'd been given and peeked outside.

A young girl, one of the chosen ones, probably no more than nineteen or twenty, was being escorted to her room. Two women in burkas had her between them. She was bleeding from a nostril and her eyes were reddened. Then Connie's vision sunk to the girl's thighs, which she caught a glance of and could see were covered with blood.

One of the women saw her watching and snapped at her in broken English. "She will be fine…good…get well. You not worry. You are older. Young first."

It was all she could do not to pull the .380 and put both burka bitches out of their misery. She watched until they deposited the young girl in her room, then closed the door as they returned to their stations near the rose-colored entry door.

She wondered how many were younger than Simone, and if the Sheik was only 'entertaining' one per night. Maybe his well-stocked clinic provided him with Viagra?

If she knew Simone, the girl would not go softly into the night. She'd likely cause the fat Sheik and his minions to, at the least, beat her into submission, or at the worst, bury her in the desert.

Where the hell was Mike? Where the hell is the American military? How long would it be before she'd have to protect one of the girls and kill a couple of these desert slime-balls before they killed her?

Then she had the worst thought. Maybe Mike was killed back on the boat? That brought a tightness to her throat and moisture to her eyes.

She took some solace knowing that if they did get him, he got a few of them first.

Then the door opened, before she'd had a chance to disrobe, and the two burka clad women stood there.

"Who Simone?" one asked.

Simone was stirring awake, but Connie bent over her and said in a low tone that was unmistakable. "Keep your mouth shut. I'm going."

The younger woman rubbed her eyes, not fully awake, but said nothing as Connie followed the women out and closed the door behind her.

Ji Su kept a close eye on the GPS coordinates, only flipping on the landing lights for a second or two when she spotted a flat spot that looked clear. And it was. She sat us down two clicks from the five-hundred-foot-high hill that was crowned by the Sheik's palace and compound. The place was almost totally dark, at least if any windows were lighted you could not see inside as a result of the twelve-foot walls surrounding. Looking at the aerials, I figured ten acres were walled in.

Taj had emailed every piece of intel he could dig up on Hassan's lair. By the time we arrived, we knew all the aerials could tell us, and all Sa'id remembered about the interior. Taj had tapped into an e-mail account and found an invoice for an extensive alarm system. And one for five thousand rounds of .50 cal ammunition, among many other things. Of course, Sa'id had not been allowed into the harem, but he knew where the door was located.

Nor had he been in the Sheik's private area, only in the guard's quarters which were located on the far east end with the compound wall being the east wall of the dormitory style building.

He had been in an entertaining area, where a hot tub was located next to a lap pool, and, next to it, a dance floor where the sheik enjoyed belly dancers. Beyond it was a platform for musicians.

It is well past the witching hour when we touch down. It will take us twenty minutes to reach the compound. There are three entrances. Double doors that will accommodate vehicles, faced both the north and south, the north road being paved and lined with cypress, the south only a two-track. Inset in those doors are pedestrian doors to allow ingress and egress without opening the much larger ones. There is a third door, this one only a passthrough to accommodate foot traffic. It faces west, the direction from which we'll approach.

If we have any chance of surprise, we have to get in well before light.

The hill is basically barren of growth, with the exception of a few planted cypress, and only a pathway leads to the west-facing pedestrian door.

There are no lights burning that we can see, save for a small light on top of the wall at each corner, and one flanking the main gates facing north.

I catch movement in only one of the towers—the one near the gate.

We leave Sa'id, cable ties binding wrists and ankles and, in turn, binding him to a chopper skid strut, with Ji Su watching over him. We also leave her with a half-dozen grenades just in case we need her to make a bombing run, but it will be a last resort, since I saw the invoice for .50 cal. It can make short work of the Jet Ranger, and Ji Su, if the shooter has skills.

We position Pax two hundred yards from the walls in a steep walled wadi that will offer him protection in case anyone sees the muzzle flash from the mortar he is entrusted with. He has a half-dozen rounds, hardly enough to hone-in on a specific target. But the harem, where we presume the women are held, is, supposedly, on the west end, and there are five acres and a big chunk of palace on the east end. A couple of rounds from a mortar, even if poorly placed, will be a hell of a diversion. We also leave Pax with a Lapua, and at this range, he can shoot the nuts off anyone on the walls or who pursues us—if they aren't already eunuchs.

Glancing at my watch as we reach the pass-through door, it's 0136. I decide we have lots of time, if we use it wisely.

The door is not chained but is locked from the inside. I try to peek through the keyhole but have no luck, then realize the key may be left inserted into the ancient lock. There is a two-inch void at the bottom of the door, and the slate from the inside protrudes out. Now if the door isn't barred as well as locked?

"We couldn't be that lucky," I say to Bo, and he shrugs, not knowing what I'm talking about. "I saw this in a Bogart movie."

I have a folding knife in my pocket, a good one made by Leatherman with lots of tools. I pop open a corkscrew and shove it into the keyhole from my side. Damned if the key doesn't clatter to the slate on the far side.

Two swipes with the barrel of my M4 and I have the key on my side, into the lock, and she opens with a squeak loud enough to wake the proverbial dead. We stand stark-still for a moment, waiting for guards to come at a run, but nothing.

If Sa'id hasn't led me astray, it is about one hundred yards to the north-facing door to the courtyard and, inside it, a courtyard and another door to the harem. He remembers it as a beautiful rose color, flanked by red and yellow bougainvillea. It is fifty paces to the building, and we're able to keep our backs to the wall as we move along. Two doors are passed by, but neither of them painted rose, rather both the same whitewash as the walls. In the distance, another fifty yards or so, lights emanate from some large windows, striping the courtyard with the shadows of their mullions, but they are dim.

I am a little surprised that the rose-colored door is unlocked.

So, we walk right in. No one is in the outer courtyard, then a scream rattles our backbones and puts us back-to-back, panning the shadows with our M4's, hunting a target.

The scream will shame a banshee, then a bird the size of a turkey, only with a much longer tail, beats wings over the harem courtyard wall. I realize we'd been peacocked. The damn birds are among the best watchdogs in any land, but again, no one comes running. If you live around peacocks, you grow used to those piercing cries.

Still, it takes a moment for both of us to settle down, then we move to the second rose door, this one, we hope, leading into the harem itself.

As we reach it, it opens as if we're being welcomed. However, it's a very surprised Alia. I recognize her from the ship, snake a hand out and have her by the throat before she can run. She has an AK slung over her shoulder but has no time to bring it into play. I don't enjoy hitting women but give her a straight jab between the eyes and she's out. I put her on her belly in the courtyard and cable tie her hands and ankles in a hog tie, then use her scarf to muzzle and blindfold her. Sa'id will be pleased, if any of us live to ever be pleased again.

We enter, and realize we're in some kind of dormitory housing, not a harem. We begin to clear all six rooms, if the doors off the hallway are any indication. And they are, living quarters, probably for guards.

So, where are the guards?

60

"You are not the singer Simone," the Sheik snaps as Connie is led before him. She studies him, and thinks he's not only unsteady, but slightly demented. His eyes seem to have trouble focusing. His speech is slightly slurred. He turns, raises a small plate and does a reasonable job of balancing it on one knee, closes one nostril and, through a straw, snorts a line of what Connie presumes is cocaine. No wonder the fat fuck can stay awake and play into the morning hours. Of course, he can sleep all day if he wishes. The burka-clad women who led her from the harem have been replaced by two burly guards. Then the sheik turns his wrath on the guards.

"You are stupid and ugly," he says in Arabic, having no idea Connie understands his every word.

"Sorry, sir. So sorry. This one was brought by worthless women who said it was at your command."

"Leave us and bring the singer to me," the Sheik commands. And the two guards spin on their heels and escape quickly.

Connie stands before him. He's reclined in a pile of pillows of various colors—some half the size of the twin mattress she'd been assigned, many much smaller. He wears a silk robe, partially open to the belly button—not that you can see his as it's buried in rolls of fat. The man has a wattle that would make a turkey jealous, but only visible when he turns his head as a straggly salt and pepper beard hangs to his chest. Beyond the beard, the vee of a heavy gold chain supports a ruby the size of a robin's egg. Fat begins below his ears and continues to his ankles. A platter of grapes, dates, nuts, and cheeses lays on the slate before him. A hot tub steams a few feet away, and beyond it a lap pool wafts chlorine odor.

At least, Connie thinks, *they have some sense of cleanliness.*

Working hard not to show her revolt at the man's appearance, Connie gives him a tight smile.

"You must be the sheik," she says, as if interested.

He puffs up, vainglorious, "I am Sheik Ali Hassan, son of rulers of the desert, Bedouins who have ridden this country for many centuries, subjects of the great Prophet Mohammad, peace be upon him, all faithful to Islam and the Holy Quran. Black gold, which you infidels are so dependent upon, flows from my sands like water from your rivers. We will rule the world soon."

"I am impressed. I presume you have many wives?"

"Only three, however as you know, many concubines. You are now one of them. You risk punishment looking me in the eye."

"I know you are all powerful, Sheik."

Not for long are you all powerful, you motherfucker, she thinks, but smiles and as she slips off the slippers she's been provided says, "What can I do to please you, my sheik?"

He gives her a tight smile in return, and eyes her up and down.

"You can begin by disrobing?"

"Is that a restroom?" she asks, pointing to a nearby door.

"It is a dressing area with a toilet."

"May I have permission to use the toilet and disrobe in the dressing room?"

He eyes her a little suspiciously, then nods hard enough his wattle vibrates. “You may, but do not tarry.”

“Yes, my sheik,” she says, and moves to the room and enters. Simone is on her way, Connie presumes. If it is going to begin now, she wants Simone under her wing. She closes the door, giving the sheik a brilliant smile as she does.

Then she pulls the door shut, reaches into her robe, slips the .380 out of the soft holster on her thigh and checks the load. She slips the robe off one shoulder, exposing a nicely tanned breast, then opens the door and leans out just far enough to tease him with a nipple.

“My Sheik, please, I need help with a hook. Would you please?”

He eyes the breast, and she ducks back, giving him only a glance.

Sounding irritated, he snaps, “I am not your house maid, woman.”

“Then would you please call one to attend me. I need assistance before I can please you.”

He mumbles a ‘humph,’ but lumbers to his feet and moves forward as she ducks back inside.

Shoving the door aside, he enters and she, coyly, gives him her tanned, smooth, bare back as she holds the .380 pressed into the soft flesh of her stomach.

“What?” he commands.

She spins, pushes the door shut with one hand while shoving the muzzle of the .380 into a fold in his belly with the other, and pulls the trigger. His rolls of fat are almost as good as a suppressor, and the shot blows through his prodigious belly, taking out his aorta and shattering his backbone. He reaches for her throat with both hands, but without clamping down sinks to his knees with an "oof," then flops to his side as she shoves him away, wallowing like a walrus for a moment. She thinks about putting another one in his ear but doesn't want to risk the noise or waste another cartridge. It isn't necessary as he moans and groans, saliva rolling over his bulbous lips, then quiets. Eyes bulge, but do not close. She is already down to five shots and a guard, or more, will soon be back with Simone.

She shuts the dressing room door tightly behind her as she returns to the pile of pillows, removes her robe and the holster and hides holster and .380 under a pillow. Then she reclines, naked, in a Marilyn Monroe pose, but with a hand on the pistol under the pillow and waits.

ABBY AND WADDY have put the women to good use, stacking wood in a dozen piles in a circle one hundred feet across. When they hear the approach, the wop, wop, wop of more than one helicopter, they light the fires.

Then all are rocked by the low pass of a Wart Hog A10. The women begin to shout and applaud.

In less than a half minute, a Chinook chopper hovers above, then settles, and a dozen SEALs pour out and spread out. The chopper lifts off leaving the SEAL team.

Both Abby and Waddy approach, wisely with their long-arms slung and their hands on their heads.

"Where's Reardon?" a SEAL who seems to be in command demands, lifting his NVD, his night vision device.

"In Libya, chasing more of your women," Abby says. Then adds, "Things are secure here. We have neutralized all militants we've found. We have not secured every structure so be advised."

The SEAL speaks into a mike mouthpiece extending from his helmet, and other SEALs in teams of three disappear into the darkness. He speaks again into his mouthpiece and a CH-53E Super Stallion takes the place of the first bird.

Then the commander snaps, “Load up the ladies. Half in this bird.”

Abby and Waddy help the commander and one remaining SEAL begin loading the captives, who are smiling and laughing. A master loader and two Marines help the women aboard. The chopper takes over fifty women, lifts off. Another replaces it, and another loader and two crew members load the remaining women.

As the two Stallions depart, the Chinook lands again and the SEALs regroup. The commander walks over and shakes hands with both Waddy and Abby. “You two staying or do you need a lift?”

“We have got gear and two Rovers down the hill a ways. Tell Reardon he needs to repay Taj for our services.”

“Who’s Taj?” the commander asks.

“Reardon will know. Is your team going to back him up? There are only three of them, if you don’t count their captive.”

“Don’t know about a captive and have no orders to continue on. Thanks for the help,” the commander says, and follows his men into the Chinook.

And they lift off.

61

WITH HER FREE HAND, CONNIE, LYING IN A VOLUPTUOUS POSE, holds a date to her mouth, her lips pursed around it, as two guards enter. Their AK47s are slung over their shoulders, each with a hand on one of Simone's arms. Simone has her jaw set and looks adamant rather than fearful.

As they approach, they realize Connie is naked. By the way they stop and stare, you know they've never seen a beautiful, tan, well endowed, naked infidel.

"Where...where...Sheik?" one of them manages, still staring.

Connie points to the toilet. "He's indisposed."

One guard starts that way, his back to her. Connie rises with the .380 held slightly behind and, with an enticing smile, takes a step toward the remaining guard still holding Simone. With the smoothness and accuracy of one who's spent many hours on the range and on combat courses, she raises the .380, and the shot takes the guard in the throat. Without hesitating she spins, and her second shot takes the guard in the side just below the armpit, as he has one hand on the dressing room door handle. He bounces off the door jamb and tries to unsling his AK. She calmly steps forward, and her next is through his eye. He crashes through the doorway and joins the Sheik on the dressing room floor.

Then she walks back to where the first guard is on his back on the floor, both hands over the wound in his throat, blood seeping between his fingers. She considers double tapping him but doesn't want to waste another cartridge, then realizes she now has two AK47s, each with a thirty-shot banana clip. So, she pulls Simone behind her, bends and puts one in his forehead.

Then she orders Simone, "Run back to the entry door and lock it."

Simone is wide eyed but complies.

Then she returns while Connie dresses. "What now?" Simone asks.

"Check for other ways in and make sure doors are locked. We pile all we can in front of the doorways. Then we wait, hold down the fort, and pray."

JUST AS WE exit the courtyard outside the dormitory rooms, shots ring out from somewhere ahead. Both of us drop to a knee and scan the area, wondering what the hell is happening, when a half-dozen soldiers, pulling on shirts, but carrying weapons, pour from a doorway ahead. They are not headed our way, but rather toward where it seems the shots rang out.

Two of them remain behind, hooking up their trousers. I tap Bo on the shoulder, pull my Glock, recover the suppressor that's in a thigh pocket on my battle trousers and screw it on. He gets it and does the same. Before the pair still dressing can follow their comrades, we are on them. One sees us coming, so from twenty feet, I put one in his upper body mass and he wheels back, arms flailing, while the other tries to raise his weapon. Before I can even re-target, his head explodes from Bo's well-placed shot. The other four are fifty yards ahead of us, and we begin to pursue, when a tower on the far end of the complex lights the night with machine gun fire and the earth begins to explode all around us. Both of us scramble back to the courtyard door and dive inside. But the courtyard walls must be mud, and they begin dissolving as .50 cal machine-gun fire makes hash of them. Crabbing, we head for the doorway to the dorm and scramble inside. These walls are at least eighteen inches thick, so they withstand the fire much better.

But for how long?

The courtyard walls are beginning to crumble to pea gravel with the hammering fire of the fifty.

I get on the handheld. "Paxman, a machine gun tower twenty feet beyond the main gates, built into the wall. Drop a couple on them, please."

"Do my best," comes back.

The machine gunner has slowed down and is trying to place his shots with three-shot bursts. He gets another dozen rounds off before the courtyard, forty yards from the tower, explodes in a shower of slate projectiles.

"Plus forty yards, and ten degrees north," I yell into the radio.

"Say again," he comes back. And I do. In thirty seconds, another explosion, but this one I cannot see as it's outside the walls.

"You've bracketed him. But I can't help as I couldn't see how far over you were."

"Ten four. Another."

"Fucking A," I shout, and this one explodes at the base of the wall, but fifty or sixty feet this way.

"Let's try to put one down his throat," I yell at Bo and load a grenade to the M4's M203 launcher, Bo does the same and we elevate and fire. Mine is twenty yards short and Bo's bounces off the wall and explodes in mid-air.

We haven't done more than shake them up, but the firing stops. In moments, I see two men run from a door at the base of the tower. I guess they don't have the stomach for a mortar and grenades. Unless they're military types, they have no idea what's blowing up the terrain around them.

So, we head out again. Just as we step through the minced courtyard wall, small arms fire spits up chunks of slate and pieces of mud wall, and we clamor back inside, and use the fallen courtyard for cover.

"What the fuck, over," Bo says as we both go prone behind the fallen wall.

"Well, they abandoned the big boy and are no sharpshooter medals with the AKs, but I guess we got their attention. You clean?" I ask as I pick some rock chards out of my cheeks and neck.

"Got a crease on the hip, but no bone. I'm still a player."

"You need a compress?" I ask.

"Let's roll a while. I don't want them sneaking up on us."

"Let's change positions," I suggest. "No sense letting them know exactly our twenty."

"I wonder if there's a back door out of the dorm?"

"I didn't notice one," I offer.

"But the uniform building code would insist," he says, and we both manage a laugh.

I suggest, "You keep the sand slime from closing on us, and I'll recon the back door."

"Ten four," he says, and rises up to a firing position on the chunks of wall.

Just as I reach the doorway, he yells, "Hold on." And I scramble back.

"We're fucked," he says, and is pointing toward the gates, which are open. One military half-track has already entered and is quickly followed by another. Then, a third, a Toyota truck with a .50 cal mounted in the bed.

They brake and uniforms begin piling out the backs. We fire the last four rifle grenades and have them scrambling. At least two are laid out, but there are many more of them finding cover.

"Time for a new plan," I say. "Let's both find that back door or make one."

"Move it," he says, and I do.

62

There is no back door, not even a window.

Too bad they haven't adopted the uniform building code. But then again, we decide to make this building comply. But I understand why no door or window, as the back wall is also the compound wall. If we're out through it, we're out of the compound. That's the good news. The bad is, we'll be on the open slope of the mountain. Hardly a rock to give cover.

I've used my five pounds of C4, but Bo has not and now has what Skip had carried. We find a likely spot in a storeroom where the explosion will be fairly-well contained, peel off a pound of C4 and place it at the base of the wall. Then I suggest, "Let's cause them a little worry and gain us a little diversion."

Bo shrugs.

So, I call Ji Su and Pax on the radio. "Paxman, in five mikes put your remaining at the far end of the compound. Keep them in the courtyard so we don't take out the ladies. Ji Su, after he drops his last one, do a fly by and bomb them with three grenades. Both of you keep a couple in reserve in case we get our tits in a crack.

Lady, don't mess around, put pedal to the metal. There was an active .50 cal in that tower by the gate."

Pax comes right back. "What do you mean, in case? Sounds like you stepped in it?"

I laugh. "Close, but we're about to exit via a hole in the south wall. But I ain't leaving without Connie and my charges."

"Hey, there must be two dozen more bogies in there. I suggest we recon, regroup, and re-evaluate."

"I have a bad feeling these military guys might want to get rid of the evidence. My lady is evidence and so are my charges. Libyans are not renowned for their mercy. I gotta keep pushing."

"Reardon, we're four. Limited resources. They are two or three dozen, probably the latter. Let's move back and call for reinforcements. Taj can probably..."

"Got to go, throw up a diversion, please."

"You got it."

In moments, mortars began to drop into the far end of the compound. We set the C4 for one minute, trying to time it to coincide with one of Pax's mortars, but it's late.

The wall blows damn near the whole end of the storeroom away, and Bo and I scramble through as the Jet Ranger passes overhead only fifty or sixty feet off the deck. The rotor wash will confuse them, and I hope they run out to see who the chopper is and step on a couple of the grenades.

She barely clears the end of the compound when the grenades begin to explode. Bo and I haul ass down the hillside. Luckily, it's still dark. We get to a small olive grove at the bottom of the hill and turn back to make sure we're not being pursued. When my handheld vibrates.

"What's up?" I answer.

"I don't know what's up," Ji Su reports, "but those boys in the trucks must not like the sound of the chopper or the grenades or mortars. They are loading up and hauling ass. A half-dozen a-holes in white robes are running behind them as if they want to go but are being left."

"We're going back in," I say and glance over at Bo, who shrugs again.

So, I lead out, jogging back to the new doorway we've made in the wall.

Just as we reach it, I hear the sound of a chopper again, but this one is different. In fact, I see two incoming.

Chinooks. I'm praying for them being ours. Then both slide to a hover over the roof of the palace, and SEALs begin to rappel onto the roofs.

Former SEAL Bo flashes me a smile. "I'll bet I know some of those assholes."

You couldn't wipe the grin off my puss with a Claymore. "Can you raise them on the radio?"

"Not these chickenshit little things, but I can get Ji Su to get through to them."

"Advise the ladies are likely behind the rose-colored door damn near compound center. That's about all the intel I can offer, other than take out that tower just in case some ambitious local wants to get a quick trip to virginville."

He laughs and radios Ji Su.

We hold in the dorm area after advising where we're located. There are no more than two dozen rounds fired in the next few minutes. Then we get an all clear radio message and walk out, weapons slung over shoulders, over the destroyed dorm compound wall into the main compound. While we await tying up with the SEALs, I remove Alia's blindfold and muzzle.

"Alia?" I make sure she's who I think she is. And she nods. "I'm going to leave you here. I'm going to send Sa'id," her eyes widen, then she begins to tear up, "to get you. I've made him a promise you two can go free as he has helped us find you. If you return to Al-Shabaab, I will know, and I will put you on the list to join your family. Do you understand?"

She nods enthusiastically.

A uniformed SEAL walks over and extends a hand. "Commander Elliot Steel. Howdy Bo."

"Commander," Bo replies.

"You boys made a bit of a mess."

"Yes, sir. You get the bogies and the women?"

"All but two." He laughs. "They are barricaded in part of the palace and want a familiar voice before they open up."

"If it's who I think it is, they will recognize mine," I say. "They may not welcome it, but they'll recognize it."

"Commander, this woman," and I point to Alia, "is a non-combatant," a small lie, "and I have her man down below. Request you ignore her and leave her here, unharmed?"

"No sweat," he says. "However, my orders are to level this place. Suggest you take her out of harm's way."

I follow the commander another fifty yards to the east, to a door, and he raps on it and shouts, "Ladies, got someone here you may know."

"Connie, open up. You'll miss the bus home."

I can hear furniture being pulled aside then the door flies open, and Connie leaps into my arms. "You beautiful son-of-a-bitch," she says, "I was afraid you were dead."

"Dead friggin' tired, if that counts."

"Reardon," Simone says, and I back away from Connie to receive an equally enthusiastic hug from my charge, who I'm happy to say seems in one piece.

She backs away and holds both hands on my shoulders and gives me those wide-eyed gray-greens. "You're a total prick and a piss-poor bodyguard, but I like you anyway. In fact, right now I love you."

"Hold on, I got someone for you to speak to." I pull out my SAT phone and call Mort Meyer. Who answers on the first ring.

"Mort, hold on."

I hand the phone to Simone...Sally. "Papa," she says, then begins to sob. She hands the phone back to me.

"Mort, she's fine. Happy to be in the hands of American military."

"Thank God," he says.

"Later. We've got to get on the trail."

"Make sure. Tell her to call the instant she can. I want her home."

I disconnect and put an arm around her shoulder. "He wants you home, Miss Sally."

"Bullshit, we're going to Cannes to the film festival."

I stare at her a moment. Then suggest, "I'll see if I can find you a good bodyguard."

"Bullshit, you signed on. You want a bad review on Yelp, or what?"

"God forbid I get a bad review on Yelp," I say, as Connie throws her arms around me again.

"Walk me inside," Connie says, and I follow her. She crosses the room beyond the hot tub and pile of pillows and goes into a small room where two more bodies lay. One of them a very fat man.

"This your work?" I ask.

"Yeah, they kinda pissed me off."

"Kinda? I'd hate to see you really angry."

She reaches down and unhooks the gold chain from his neck, one with a stone the size of half my thumb and puts it on.

"Nice, eh?" she says, then tucks it inside the robe.

"Very nice," I say.

"Reparations. Price of seeing my boobs," she says, stuffs it inside her robe, then laughs and leads me out.

Bo and I lead the ladies down the hill to join up with Pax, then back to where Ji Su has returned with the Jet Ranger. Sa'id is tied to a nearby greasewood-like shrub. I go over and cut him free and he removes his blindfold and muzzle.

"Alia?" is the first word out of his mouth.

"She is tied and waiting up the wadi a couple of hundred yards. Do not, I repeat, do not return to the palace. It is now a target."

He nods, then adds, "But we are deep in the desert."

"I saw lights a few clicks to the north..."

"Clicks?" he asks.

"Kilometers. I suggest you hoof it there. If I return you two, I may not be able to keep you safe."

"We will...hoof it...as you say."

"Good luck. I hope I don't have to sic a drone on you?"

"You will not."

63

WE GET THE HELL OUT OF LIBYA AS QUICKLY AS POSSIBLE. JI SU ferries us to Ouargla, Algeria, then returns to the Interco compound where Skip has been treated and hauls him back. In less than a half-day from leaving the now-leveled palace, thanks to those F16s, Charley Glascock loads us in the G5.

Harry Weinstein has called me a half-dozen times, insisting I return to Spain to be debriefed and I promise to do so. A bald-faced lie.

We fuel in the Azores, fly to Miami, then to Vegas.

I'm having supper with Pax, Connie, Ji Su, and another old friend at the Golden Steer, when three uptight guys in suits stride in and FBI Special Agent Harold Stroeger flips open his ID. His first sentence is not a request. "You four are wanted in Washington, DC. Fold your napkins."

"I guess you're picking up the tab here?" Pax says, and winks at me.

"Come easy, or the hard way. Your choice," he snaps.

Isaac, our waiter, is standing nearby so I give him a heads up. "Hey, Isaac, viral video chance here. These assholes are screwing up the supper of a bunch of folks who just saved the lives of all those American women you read about in the Sun."

"That's screwed up," Isaac says, and a half-dozen nearby diners join Isaac in taking videos.

I point at my friend who's joined us for supper. "Speaking of the Sun, Agent, do you know Forrest Knowlton, reporter at the Sun?"

"I heard you were a smartass," Special Agent Stroeger says, his jaw set tightly.

"We'll finish our supper then..."

He reaches for my collar to drag me out of the booth. I come far enough to kick the struts out from under him, and he goes down hard as the other two pull their weapons.

I extend my hands. "Happy to come along, fellas, but I'm a little tired of being pushed and pulled." I turn to Forrest, "Take it easy on them. The FBI has had enough bad press for a while."

As Stroeger, red-faced, gets to his feet, we all climb out, leaving Forrest.

"Reaching for my wallet," I say, so I don't get shot, "Since Uncle Sam can't afford to pay, and hand Isaac five Benjamins.

Isaac smiles. "YouTube, here it comes."

"Give me that phone," Stroeger snaps and reaches for Isaac's iPhone.

"You gonna arrest the whole restaurant?" I ask.

Stroeger looks around and at least ten cell phones are recording videos.

"F...f...fudge," he says.

I can't help but laugh. "I only wish the Bureau had more boy scouts." We follow him toward the door, with the other two agents close behind.

I'M NOT much of a fan of Washington, D.C., particularly when it's hot and muggy, but the interrogation rooms of both the FBI and then the Company's in Langley are nicely air conditioned. Even so, I'm pissed that services for Bull Toliver—without a body--are held at nearby Arlington while I'm being interviewed, and the pricks won't break long enough for me to attend. I do send a wreath and hope Mrs. Toliver takes notice. No matter as I'll visit when out from under the thumb of the acronyms.

By the time a number of the crew, passengers, and we four are wrung through the wringer, and a number of national publications including the NYT and Washington Post have spun the tale of the *Blue Pearl,* I'm a little surprised Pax and I don't get a Presidential medal. It seems obvious weapons charges are ignored. As usual, the press reports are about half accurate, but half is enough.

Simone was convinced, or threatened by her father enough, to not go on to Cannes. She, Patti, and the boys are among those interrogated.

As soon as the government is through with us, the papers and networks are on us again. And I'm happy to have it so, as a gaggle of attorneys representing Crimson Cruise Line want a deposition. I refuse, and refer them to the press, indicating they can come out as heroes or bums depending upon me relating my story. They stand down.

We return to Vegas, refusing any interviews with anyone other than my buddy at the Vegas Sun, whom I can rely upon to be discreet.

Still, after all the press coverage I may have to get plastic surgery if I'm to find more sub-rosa work. As I've said, in my line, one doesn't want to be easily recognized.

When the final tally comes in, it seems four hostiles remain alive, other than Sa'id and Alia, who we don't mention. A deal's a deal. So over thirty are dead, if one doesn't consider those in Sweet Water and at Hassan's palace who weren't among those on board the ship. Those in the Algerian military—the Algerian, other North African, and half the world's press gave all credit for the rescue to Armée Nationale Populaire, the Algerian army. There was no mention of the U.S. making an incursion into Algeria or Libya. After all, shitholes have to save face.

Ji Su and Pax are still a thing. She's back flying tourists over the Grand Canyon.

I have never been to Australia but am boarding a flight in the morning. It seems they are having a service and hell of a wing ding for Alistair Nelson, and I won't miss it. Old warriors should not be forgotten.

I'm saddened by the fact my new squeeze, Connie, decided that Mike Reardon and Vegas were both a little exciting for her. She decided not to accompany me to Melbourne. It seems shooting an old boy in his fat belly was a little more traumatic than she let on. 'Needing a little time', is how she put it. She has a new job for some computer outfit in Austin, Texas.

I hope, for their sake, none of her new bosses are from the old school and put the heavy hand on her for a little nookie. They'll likely find their voices an octave higher for the rest of their careers.

And, of course, Mort Meyer refused to pay the second installment of fifty grand as he says letting his darling daughter get captured by terrorists is not what he considers proper body-guarding. Even so, neither he nor Simone gave me a bad review on Yelp —like I give a rat's ass. The good news is the fifty he did pay was enough to cover Taj and other out of pocket dough it cost my buddies.

I'd squeeze Mort's chicken neck; except I must agree.

I'll try and do better next time.

And there's gotta be a next time as I owe some buddies who dropped all and came running.

OTHER WORKS BY L. J. MARTIN

Other Fine Action Adventure from L. J. Martin

West of the War

Young Bradon McTavish watches the bluecoats brutally hang his father and destroy everything he's known, and he escapes their wrath into the gunsmoke and blood of war. Captured and paroled, only if he'll head west of the war, he rides the river into the wilds of the new territory of Montana where savages and grizzlies await. He discovers new friends and old enemies...and a woman formerly forbidden to him.

The Repairman. No. 1 on Amazon's crime list! Got a problem? Need it fixed? Call Mike Reardon, the repairman, just don't ask him how he'll get it done. Trained as a Recon Marine to search and destroy, he brings those skills to the tough streets of America's cities. If you like your stories spiced with fists, guns, and beautiful women, this is the fast paced novel for you.

The Bakken No. 1 on Amazon's crime list! The stand alone sequel to The Repairman. Mike Reardon gets a call from his old CO in

Iraq, who's now a VP at an oil well service company in North America's hottest boomtown, and dope and prostitution is running wild and costing the company millions, and the cops are overwhelmed. If you have a problem, and want it fixed, call the repairman...just don't ask him what he's gonna do.

G5, Gee Whiz When a fifty million dollar G5 is stolen and flown out of the country, who you gonna call? If you have a problem, and want it fixed, call the repairman...just don't ask him what he's gonna do.

Who's On Top Mike Reardon thinks his new gig, finding an errant daughter of a NY billionaire will be a laydown...how wrong can one guy be? She's tied up with an eco-terrorist group, who proves to be much more than that. And this time, the group he's up against may be bad guys, or kids with their heart in the right place. Who gets lead and who gets a kick in the backside. And if things go wrong, the whole country may be at risk! Another kick-ass Repairman Mike Reardon thriller from acclaimed author L. J. Martin.

Target Shy & Sexy What's easier for a search and destroy guy than a simple bodyguard gig, particularly when the body being guarded is on of America's premiere country singers and the body is knock-down beautiful...until she's abducted while he's on his way to report for his new assignment. Who'd have guessed that the hunt for his employer would lead him into a nest of hard ass Albanians and he'd find himself between them and some bent nose boys from Vegas! Another in the highly acclaimed The Repairman Series...Mike Reardon is at it again.

Judge, Jury, Desert Fury. Back in the fray, only this time it's as a private contractor. Mike Reardon and his buddies are hired to free a couple of American's held captive by a Taliban mullah, and, as usual, it's duck, dodge and kick ass when everyone in the country wants a piece of you. Don't miss this high action adventure by renowned author L. J. Martin. No. 6 in The Repairman series, each book stands alone.

No Good Deed. Going after some ruthless kidnappers, who want NATO,s secrets, is one thing...going into Russia is another altogether. But when one of Reardon's crew is being held, he says to hell with it, no matter if he's risking starting World War 3! Why not add the CIA and the State Department to your list of enemies when your most important job is staying alive hour by hour, minute by minute.

Overflow. Mike Reardon, the Repairman, hates to mess his own nest—to work anywhere near where he lives. If you can call a mini-storage and a camper living. But when terrorists bomb Vegas, and a casino owner's granddaughter is killed...the money is too good and the prey is among his most hated. Then again nothing is ever quite like it seems. Now all he has to do is stay alive, tough when friends become enemies and enemies far worse, and when you're on top the FBI and LVPD's list.

The K Factor. When Mike Reardon, known as the repairman for taking jobs outside the law, is invited to a meeting with the CIA, NSA, and DOD, he knows he's about to be downrange of ka ka hitting the fan.

All they want is for him to go into North Korea and extract three women; a daughter and granddaughters of NK's ambassador to China, who wants to defect. Since he's the former head of NK's nuclear program, the U.S. is more than merely interested in him.

Quiet Ops. "...knows crime and how to write about it...you won't put this one down." Elmore Leonard

L. J. Martin with America's No. 1 bounty hunter, Bob Burton, brings action-adventure in double doses. From Malibu to West Palm Beach, Brad Benedick hooks 'em up and haul 'em in...in chains.

Crimson Hit. Dev Shannon loves his job, travels, makes good money, meets interesting

people…then hauls them in cuffs and chains to justice. Only this time it's personal.

Bullet Blues. Shannon normally doesn't work in his hometown, but this time it's a friend who's gone missing, and he's got to help…if he can stay alive long enough. Tracking down a stolen yacht, which takes him all the way to Jamaica, he finds himself deep in the dirty underbelly of the drug trade.

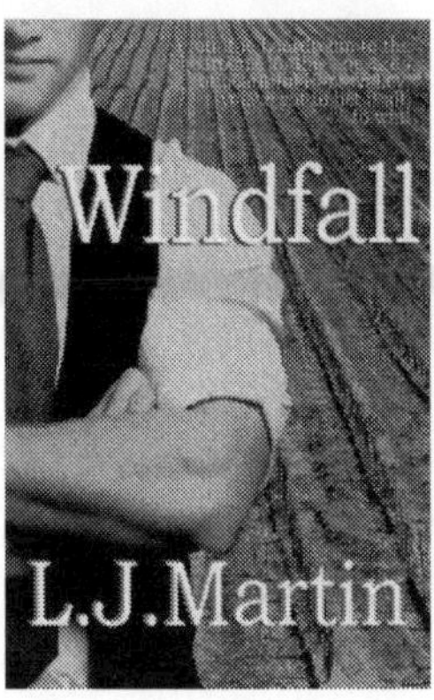

Windfall. From the boardroom to the bedroom, David Drake has fought his way...nearly...to the top. From the jungles of Vietnam, to the vineyards of Napa, to the grit and grime of the California oil fields, he's clawed his way up. The only thing missing is the woman he's loved most of his life. Now, he's going to risk it all to win it all, or end up on the very bottom where he started. This business adventure-thriller will leave you breathless.

Bloodlines. When an ancient document is found deep under the streets of Manhattan, no one can anticipate the wild results. A businessman is forced to search deep into his past and reach back to those who once were wronged, and redeem for them what is right and just. There's a woman he's yearned for, and must have, but all is against them...and someone wants him dead.

The Clint Ryan Series:

El Lazo. John Clinton Ryan, young, fresh to the sea from Mystic, Connecticut, is shipwrecked on the California coast...and blamed for the catastrophe. Hunted by the hide, horn and tallow captains, he escapes into the world of the vaquero, and soon gains the name El Lazo, for his skill with the lasso. A classic western tale of action and adventure, and the start of the John Clinton Ryan, the Clint Ryan series.

Against the 7th Flag. Clint Ryan, now skilled with horse and reata, finds himself caught up in the war of California revolution, Manifest Destiny is on the march, and he's in the middle of the fray, with friends on one side and countrymen on the other...it's fight or be killed, but for whom?

The Devil's Bounty. On a trip to buy horses for his new ranch in the wilds of swampy Central California, Clint finds himself compelled to help a rich Californio don who's beautiful daughter has been kidnapped and hauled to the barracoons of the Barbary Coast. Thrown in among the Chinese tongs, Australian Sidney Ducks, and the dredges of the gold rush failures, he soon finds an ally in a slave, now a newly freedman, and it's gunsmoke and flashing blades to fight his way to free the senorita.

The Benicia Belle. Clint signs on as master-at-arms on a paddle wheeler plying the Sacramento from San Francisco to the gold fields. He's soon blackmailed by the boats owner and drawn to a woman as dangerous and beautiful as the sea he left behind. Framed for a crime he didn't commit, he has only one chance to exact a measure of justice and...revenge.

Shadow of the Grizzly. "Martin has produced a landlocked, Old West version of Peter Benchley's Jaws," Publisher's Weekly. When the Stokes brothers, the worst kind of meat hunters, stumble on Clint's horse ranch, they are looking to take what he has. A wounded griz is only trying to stay alive, but he's a horrible danger to man and beast. And it's Clint, and his crew, including a young boy, who face hell together.

Condor Canyon. On his way to Los Angeles, a pueblo of only one thousand, Clint is ambushed by a posse after the abductor of a young woman. Soon he finds himself trading his Colt and his skill for the horses he seeks...now if he can only stay alive to claim them.

The Montana Series – The Clan:

Stranahan. "A good solid fish-slinging gunslinging read," William W. Johnstone. Sam Stranahan's an honest man who finds himself on the wrong side of the law, and the law has their own version of right and wrong. He's on his way to find his brother, and walks into an explosive case of murder. He has to make sure justice is done...with or without the law.

McCreed's Law. Gone...a shipment of gold and a handful of passengers from the Transcontinental Railroad. Found...a man who knows the owlhoots and the Indians who are holding the passengers for ransom. When you want to catch outlaws, hire an outlaw...and get the hell out of the way.

Wolf Mountain. The McQuades are running cattle, while running from the tribes who are fresh from killing Custer, and they know no fear. They have a rare opportunity, to get a herd to Mile's and his troops at the mouth of the Tongue…or to die trying. And a beautiful woman and her father, of questionable background, who wander into camp look like a blessing, but trouble is close on their trail…as if the McQuades don't have trouble enough.

O'Rourke's Revenge. Surviving the notorious Yuma Prison should be enough trouble for any man…but Ryan O'Rourke is not just any man. He wants blood, the blood of those who framed him for a crime he didn't commit. He plans to extract revenge, if it costs him all he has left, which is less than nothing…except his very life.

McKeag's Mountain. Old Bertoldus Prager has long wanted McKeag's Mountain, the Lucky Seven Ranch his father had built, and seven hired guns tried to take it the hard way, leaving Dan McKeag for dead...but he's a McKeag, and clings to life. They should have made sure...for now it will cost them all, or he'll die trying, and Prager's in his sights as well.

The Nemesis Series:

Nemesis. The fools killed his family...then made him a lawman! There are times when it pays not to be known, for if they had, they'd have killed him on the spot. He hadn't seen his sister since before the war, and never met her husband and two young daughters...but when he heard they'd been murdered, it was time to come down out of the high country and scatter the country with blood and guts.

Mr. Pettigrew. Beau Boone, starving, half a left leg, at the end of his rope, falls off the train in the hell-on-wheels town of Nemesis. But Mr. Pettigrew intervenes. Beau owes him, but does he owe him his very life? Can a one-legged man sit shotgun in one of the toughest saloons on the Transcontinental. He can, if he doesn't have anything to lose.

The Ned Cody Series:

Buckshot. Young Ned Cody takes the job as City Marshal…after all, he's from a long line of lawmen. But they didn't face a corrupt sheriff and his half-dozen hard deputies, a half-Mexican half-Indian killer, and a town who thinks he could never do the job.

Mojave Showdown. Ned Cody goes far out of his jurisdiction when one of his deputies is hauled into the hell's fire of the Mojave Desert by a tattooed Indian who could track a deer fly and live on his leavings. He's the toughest of the tough, and the Mojave has produced the worst. It's ride into the jaws of hell, and don't worry about coming back.

ABOUT THE AUTHOR

L. J. Martin is the author of over three dozen works of both fiction and non-fiction from Bantam, Avon, Pinnacle and his own Wolfpack Publishing. He lives in, and loves, Montana with his wife, NYT bestselling romantic suspense author Kat Martin. He's been a horse wrangler, cook as both avocation and vocation, volunteer firefighter, real estate broker, general contractor, appraiser, disaster evaluator for FEMA, and traveled a good part of the world, some in his own ketch. A hunter, fisherman, photographer, cook, father and grandfather, he's been car and plane wrecked, visited a number of jusgados and a road camp, and survived cancer twice. He carries a bail-enforcement, bounty hunter, shield. He knows about what he writes about, and tries to write about what he knows.

Made in United States
Troutdale, OR
02/19/2024

17797797R10251